Praise for The Runelords Saga

"[Farland] explores the very nature of virtue and finds disturbing contradictions at the heart of every moral question.... When I reached the end of *The Runelords*, and saw grace arise from a devastating battlefield where too many great hearts lay dead, Farland had earned the tears that came to my eyes. It was not sentiment but epiphany."

—Orson Scott Card, author of *Empire*, on *The Runelords*

"The suspense is real, the action is nonstop, and the characterizations continue to convince.... [This is] a series that has put Farland on high-fantasy readers' maps."

—*Booklist* on *The Lair of Bones*

"Sometimes truly terrifying, sometimes impossibly sweet, *The Lair of Bones* is a tale sure to entrance any reader. This is a superb story with deeply empathetic characters."

—Sara Douglass, author of *The Serpent Bride*

"Sure, *Brotherhood* has incredible edge-of-your-seat, nail-biting battle scenes—the finale being an exceptional example—but Gaborn's struggle to make a decision, and then his facing the consequences, is equally thrilling. *Brotherhood of the Wolf* is a welcome sequel."

—*Starlog*

"The author's imaginative approach to magic, coupled with a richly detailed fantasy world and a cast of memorable heroes and villains, adds depth and variety to this epic tale of war and valor."

—*Library Journal* on *Wizardborn*

"*Worldbinder* is more character driven and less action intense than the previous books in the Runelords saga.... [It] can stand alone appealing to apocalyptic fantasy fans, but series fans will definitely enjoy Farland's newest tale."

—*Alternative Worlds*

Worldbinder

David Farland

TOR® fantasy

A TOM DOHERTY ASSOCIATES BOOK
NEW YORK

This is a work of fiction. All the characters, organizations, and events portrayed in this novel are either products of the author's imagination or are used fictitiously.

WORLDBINDER

Copyright © 2007 by David Farland

All rights reserved.

A Tor Book
Published by Tom Doherty Associates, LLC
175 Fifth Avenue
New York, NY 10010

www.tor-forge.com

Tor® is a registered trademark of Tom Doherty Associates, LLC.

ISBN-13: 978-0-7653-5584-3
ISBN-10: 0-7653-5584-1

First Edition: September 2007
First Mass Market Edition: August 2008

Printed in the United States of America

0 9 8 7 6 5 4 3 2 1

For Mary, as always.

With special appreciation to Matt Harrill
for his copious help.

WORLDBINDER

> *Though your heart may burn with righteous desires,*
> *your noblest hopes will become fuel to fire despair*
> *among mankind.*
> *That which you seek to build will crumble to ash.*
> *War shall follow you all of your days, and though*
> *the world may applaud your slaughter, you will come*
> *to know that each of your victories is mine.*
> *And thus I seal you, till the end of time. . . .*
> *—Asgaroth's curse upon Fallion*

The tree riveted Shadoath as she stalked into Castle Coorm. It was no more than a sapling, perhaps eight feet tall, with a dozen branches spreading wide in a perfect umbrella. But the sight of it smote her at even a hundred yards, urging her heart to melt. Every winding branch was perfect. Every crook of every twig seemed to have been preconceived by an artistic genius before being executed. The leaves were darkest green above, a mellow honey beneath, and looked something like an oak. The bark was the rich golden color of ripe wheat, warm and soothing, inviting to the eye.

Shadoath had seen such a tree once before, countless ages ago, on another world.

No, she thought. It can't be.

But she knew that it was. It wasn't just how the tree looked. It was how it made her feel. Her eyes wanted to drink it in from the distance. Her arms wanted to embrace it. Her head and shoulders yearned to shelter beneath it. Her lungs ached to breathe the perfumed air that exuded from its leaves. Her eyes longed to lie beneath it and stare up, and dimly she recalled the ancient days, when those leaves emitted a soft golden light during the nights, and those who took pleasure beneath it would peer up through layers of foliage and try to make out the light of distant stars. The sight of its limbs made her yearn for perfection, to be better than she had ever been, to do more than she had ever done, to *change* for the better.

The tree was dangerous, she knew. Left alive, it would grow and develop, rising up like a mountain, insinuating its branches for miles in every direction. It would silently tug at the minds of men, urge them to become its servants. Left alone, it would do even more. It would silently nurture the souls of men, urging them to become virtuous and perfect.

Every instinct in her shouted, Kill it now! Burn it down!

Only the shock of seeing it stayed her hand.

There were mighty changes going on in Rofehavan. The children born in the past generation were more like Bright Ones from the netherworld than children of the past.

And now the One True Tree had risen again.

She wanted to be sure. She studied the knotty roots coming up from the grass. The tree had been planted in the green at Castle Coorm, in the center of a roundabout. A small rock wall, perhaps four feet tall, surrounded the tree. A fountain rose at the back, water splashing down gray stones from the mouth of a gargoyle. At one time there had been a pleasant rock garden here, rife with flowering vines. A few of them still remained, trumpet flowers of red.

But Shadoath could not look for long. The tree drew her eye, the golden bark rising from the grass, where the small roots were already beginning to splay wide, questing for purchase; the bole of the tree twisting as if in torment; the branches rising up to embrace heaven.

Shadoath stood peering at it, and all weariness seemed to leave her, all of her aches and worries. It was as if she laid aside every care, and an upwelling of hope rose inside her, strange longings.

The tree is my master, and I am its servant, her body told her.

But a voice whispered inside her, the voice of the tree. "You are *my* master; how may *I* serve you?"

An image of their true relationship formed in her mind. Neither was whole without the other, the tree told her. Neither of us should live alone.

Damn, she realized, the young tree has already gained consciousness. Left alone, it would become wise and venerable and forbidding.

There was a rustling sound behind her, one of the guards on the castle wall. Across the courtyard, Warlord Hale was stumping down from the tower, lugging his great weight along as fast as he could. She had almost forgotten that he existed, even though he was the one who had sent the urgent message asking what to do about the damned tree.

"So," a girl asked, "do you like my tree?"

Shadoath shook her head, let her vision clear, and suddenly spotted the young woman there beneath the tree, squatting cross-legged upon a rock. Shadoath had been so captivated that she hadn't seen the girl, even though she sat in plain sight, as quiet and motionless as a mushroom.

She was some indeterminate age between twelve and sixteen, Shadoath imagined, with hair so pale yellow it was almost white, and eyes as pale as sea foam. Her skin had the greenish cast of one who was Wizardborn, and she wore a robe that looked not to have been woven, but to· simply have grown around her as roots that interlocked. It was the pale green of new leaves. She bore a staff of golden wood, hewn from the tree itself.

"I love your tree," Shadoath said.

The girl smiled broadly, stood, and raised a hand, beckoning Shadoath to come forward, to rest beneath its limbs.

Shadoath could hear Warlord Hale pounding down the

wooden stairs, his huge bulk an assault upon them. He was nearly to the door of his keep.

Now that her mind had cleared, Shadoath realized *why* the young wizardess had chosen to plant the tree here in the courtyard of Castle Coorm. It was to honor the last Earth King, Gaborn Val Orden, of course. This had been his residence before he wandered off into the wilderness to die.

So the wizardess had brought the tree here in his honor. She wanted to restore him to the people's memory even as she and her damned tree created a new world order.

Shadoath reached the rock wall, and the young woman stretched down to give her a hand.

That's when Shadoath struck, as quick as the thought touched her.

Shadoath had taken the body of a warrior this time, a pale assassin from Inkarra, with skin whiter than bone, hair the color of spun silver, and pale blue tattoos that covered her arms and legs. Shadoath's speed was blinding, and her curved dagger bit into the wizardess's armpit with great force.

Shadoath grabbed the proffered hand, for Earth Wardens, as this young wizardess surely was, had great skill at both hiding and healing. Shadoath held on while the young wizardess tried to leap back and buck, like a young deer. She saw the girl's pleading eyes as warm blood pumped over Shadoath's hand.

Shadoath twisted the blade, and she saw strange visions. Suddenly she seemed to be standing in deep rushes at the edge of a pond while a huge grouse thundered up from the ground. Obviously the vision was meant to startle her, get her to loosen her grip, but Shadoath held on.

Suddenly she seemed to be holding a great bear whose vicious fangs were mere inches from her throat. Shadoath drew out her blade, plunged it beneath the young wizardess's sternum, and let it quest for her heart.

The bear disappeared, and for a moment she saw the

wizardess's true face, her pupils constricted to pinpricks, and she saw an image of the One True Tree as it might be someday, with tens of thousands of people living beneath it, giving it water and food, giving it life, even as it sheltered them from the elements and from the eyes of all enemies.

And then the young wizardess was dead, nothing but a piece of bloody meat gurgling and jerking at Shadoath's feet.

Shadoath pulled her away from the tree, for she knew that the tree itself had healing powers, and might even be able to raise the newly dead if her body remained beneath its boughs for long.

"Why?" the tree begged.

Shadoath merely smiled secretively as she dragged the bloody girl far across the green.

The bloated form of Warlord Hale appeared at the door of the keep, his head towering above those of his guards: he trundled across the cobbled pavement to meet Shadoath.

"Killed 'er, I see?" he said. "Glad you were up to it. I tried it myself a dozen times, but couldn't seem to get near her, even though she never went more than a dozen yards from that tree. What do ya want me to do with the damned tree now, chop 'er down, burn it?"

Shadoath considered as Warlord Hale babbled on inanely.

"It's one of *those* trees, ain't it? I told the boys it was, a World Tree, just like the old tales. Didn't know what to do with it. Didn't want to just let it stand—bad for morale. That's why I sent for you."

Hale obviously yearned for approval, so Shadoath said, "You did well, sending for me."

"So, do I chop it down?"

The human spirit would revolt at such a task. It might even break. She doubted that many of Hale's men could do it. But Hale was far enough gone in the ways of evil that he could hardly be called human anymore.

Shadoath considered. She wanted the tree dead. But there was one thing that she wanted more—Fallion Orden. For nearly a year now, since she had lost the battle at the Ends of the Earth, she had been considering ways to subvert him—or barring that, to destroy him. She had been taking deep counsel with others of her kind, and they had begun to devise a trap. All that they lacked was the right bait.

Could this be it? Fallion Orden craved to restore the Earth, make it whole, as it had been before the cataclysm. And the very fact that the One True Tree had been reborn was a sign that the restoration—somehow, beyond Shadoath's understanding—was moving forward rapidly.

Fallion did not know it yet, but he would need the wisdom of a World Tree in order to advance his plans.

Given that, would not the spirit of this tree call to his? And would not his spirit call to the tree?

And when the two met, would it not be a good time to thwart both of their plans?

"There is good news in the Netherworld," Shadoath told Warlord Hale as she considered what to do. "The Queen of the Loci has escaped. The Glories sought to bind her in a Cage of Brilliance, but their powers failed them. They are not as strong as they were in ages past, and we have managed to free her. She is gathering armies more powerful than ever before. Remain true, and your reward shall be great and endless."

"Glad to hear it," Warlord Hale said. "I—I am true to you, you know."

There was malice in his eyes, she saw, and desire. He wanted to give his soul to her, let his spirit become the home of a locus. Because her kind had trained him from youth, he believed that in doing so he would gain a type of immortality, that his soul would be bound into the black soul of the locus, and carried down through time.

He was fit for it, she knew. His soul was a black pit. There was true and monstrous evil in him, and he would be a comfortable abode for a locus. But he yearned to be possessed so badly that she could not resist the urge to deny him this reward.

"Soon," she promised. "Your time is coming."

She turned to the tree, regarded it coolly. "Leave it alive for now. I want Fallion Orden to see it."

1

THE HOMECOMING

I do not know when I first began to dream of healing the Earth. There was so much pain in the world, so much suffering and heartache. It could have been when I was among the Gwardeen. One of our fliers, a small boy of six named Zel, was feeding a hatchling graak, and the great reptile took the boy's arm. It was an accident, I am sure. But try as I might, we could not staunch the flow of blood, and Zel died in my arms. I remembered thinking, In a better world, I could have saved him. In a better world, children would not have to die this way.

It was only three years later that I began to be haunted by a dream of a wheel of fire, a vast rune, and I began to suspect that there was a way to heal our broken world.

—from the journal of Fallion Orden

They came creeping through the woods just before dawn, four of them, weary but resolute, like hunters on the trail of a wounded stag. They halted at the edge of the trees, silently regarding summer fields thick with oats and the brooding castle beyond.

"Castle Coorm," the leader, Fallion, whispered. "As promised." The sight of it filled him with nostalgia and soothed his frayed nerves like mulled wine.

The pre-dawn sky still had one bright star in it, and the castle mostly lay in shadows, the limned walls looking soft blue instead of white. There were pinpricks of yellow in the tower windows, and watch-fires burned outside the city gates like blistering gems. The dancing fires, the smell of the smoke, beckoned him. But Fallion merely stood silently regarding the scene. The castle was falling into ruins, but was obviously still inhabited.

He had seen too much devastation, too many ruined cities since his return to Mystarria. The Courts of Tide had been laid waste. Its once-fair streets were now dark lanes, blockaded by gangs that fought like wild dogs to protect their few scraps of food and clothing. The women and children there had a haunted look. They had suffered too much rape, too much plunder.

The sight of it had left Fallion reeling. In a more perfect world, he told himself, the women would wear flowers in their hair, and children would not learn to fear strangers.

Upon the death of Fallion's father, Gaborn Val Orden, assassins from a dozen lands had descended upon Mystarria, hoping to strike down Fallion and his brother. These weren't ordinary assassins. These were powerful runelords that had taken brawn, stamina, speed, and grace from their subjects, making them warriors that no commoner could hope to withstand. And though Mystarria had been a wealthy country then, with many strong runelords of its own, it could not withstand the sustained onslaughts of such men.

Only by strengthening its forces could it hope to survive, but that required forcibles—magical branding irons that could draw out an attribute from a vassal and then imbue it upon the lord.

But there was a dearth of forcibles. The rare blood metal from which they were made was running out. Rumors said that the lords of Kartish, far to the west, were hoarding what little they found, intent on protecting their own realms in the dark times to come.

Chancellor Westhaven, who had been left in charge of Mystarria, had even taken a journey to Kartish, hoping to sway those who had once been allies.

He had never returned. Some said that his mournful spirit could be seen at night in the towers at the Courts of Tide, wandering the hallways, rummaging through the empty lock-boxes in the treasure room.

And so Mystarria had been attacked on a dozen fronts, like a great bull taken down by jackals that ripped it apart and gorged themselves while leaving their prey still only half alive. Its treasuries had been looted, its towers knocked down, its farms and cities burned, its lands divided. The Warlords of Internook held the coast, while Beldinook took the east, and Crowthen to the north split the rest.

Frankly, after the rapes, the looting, and the murder, Fallion did not see that there was much of a country left worth fighting over.

He eyed the remains of Castle Coorm, dully surprised to see it still intact.

The towers of the castle stood, but dark stands of ivy grew up them, looking like rents in the darkness. The eastern-most walls were a decrepit gray, most of the lime having washed away after years of winter storms. A lone bullfrog bellowed amid the placid reeds of the moat.

Fallion held to the shadows. He wore a gray half-cape, fastened with a silver cape pin in the form of an owl, long black hair sweeping back over his shoulders, brown eyes so full of light that they seemed a perfect mirror for the distant fires. A naked blade gleamed silver in his hand.

He studied the fires, and for an instant an image came to mind of a vast rune made of flames, encircled by flames—The Seal of the Inferno. It had been almost three years ago that he had first seen it in a dream while staring into the hearth after a midwinter's dinner. Since then he had begun practicing his skills as a flameweaver, listening to the many tongues of fire, seeking inspiration in sunlight. He knew which direction the seal lay, deep in the Underworld. The wheel of fire haunted him, came to mind a hundred times a day. He could not so much as glance at the sun or even a silver moon without seeing the afterimage of the rune imprinted on his retina.

He had crossed the oceans to find it. Just a couple hundred more miles now, and he would descend into the Mouth of the World, hoping to locate the Seal of the

Inferno and repair the damage to it. By mending its defects and binding it to the Seal of Heaven and the Seal of Earth, he hoped to restore balance to the world, to remake it in the perfect image of the One True World of legend.

Behind him came Rhianna, following so close at Fallion's back that she touched him. Her fierce blue eyes looked troubled, and she clung to her quarterstaff as if she was lost at sea and it was the only thing that might save her from drowning.

"I remember this place," she said, her voice shaky. "I remember . . ."

She placed a hand on Fallion's shoulder and just stood. Her flawless face was white with shock, a grimace of pain formed by the slash of her lips.

For nearly a decade, Rhianna had blocked out her memories of this place. But now, Fallion could see, they threatened to overwhelm her.

At her back stood Fallion's younger brother, Jaz, followed by their foster sister, Talon. Jaz carried a war bow carved from ruddy red reaver's horn. Talon bore a light saber that some dainty gentleman might have worn for a night on the town, but in her practiced hands, the blade would never be confused for a mere adornment.

"What do you remember?" Fallion asked Rhianna.

Rhianna's brows drew together in concentration; she recalled racing down a mountain on a force horse that had been richly endowed with runes of brawn and metabolism. Fallion sat in the saddle ahead of her, and she clung to him for dear life. Even then she realized that she was falling in love with him. She remembered thinking him strong and handsome, and she prayed that he would be able to save her. They must have been traveling at eighty miles per hour, for the pines at the margin of the road seemed to fly past. Her heart pounded as if trying to beat its way out of her chest, and in her young mind, she could not imagine that she would live until she reached the castle. Her stomach had ached, and she worried that something was eating her. A strengi-saat had placed its eggs in her womb to hatch, and the young were eating their way out. She remembered it all.

"We were being chased by monsters," Rhianna said, suddenly planting her staff firmly in the ground. She had been a child back then, with a child's fears. But for years she had been practicing with weapons, and she was growing dangerous. The staff that she bore now was bejeweled and covered in runes. It had once belonged to the Earth King himself. She grimaced. "Now we're back, and *we're* the monsters."

Jaz laughed. He always seemed to be light of heart lately. Rhianna had come on this journey because she loved Fallion, because she would throw herself in death's path to protect him. But Jaz had come because, as he'd said, "I've been following him around since I could crawl. I don't see why I should stop now."

Jaz said, "I was sure we'd blundered past this place ten leagues back. And look, there are *people* inside. You think if we beg nicely, they'd part with a mug of ale?"

Jaz sat down and tried pulling off a boot. It had mud inside and came free with a sucking sound.

"People will do astonishing things for money," Fallion said, "even part with perfectly good ale."

He turned back to the castle. The long war had taken its toll. A village had once thrived on the hill below, a place named Weeds. A few dozen cozy mud-and-wattle cottages had grown up here with roofs thatched from wheat straw. As a child, Fallion had imagined that they were living things, lounging among the herb and flower gardens, partitioned with rock walls. The homes had been shaded in the long summer by fruit trees.

He regarded the ruins of a cottage on a knoll, and suddenly had a memory from when he was a child of three. In it, his father had come home from his wanderings, and had taken him out into the village among the crowds. Fallion had ridden on his father's shoulder, until his father stopped beneath a cherry tree on the knoll. There,

Fallion pulled the red cherries from the tree, and they were so ripe that they burst at his touch, and juice ran thick down his fingers. He licked it off and picked his fill, all the while begriming his father, he was sure now.

But his father had only laughed with delight.

Fallion remembered riding upon the shoulders of a king, being taller than everyone, looking down upon men that had dwarfed him, wishing that he could be that tall forever.

He smiled. It was a good memory, and one of only a handful that he recalled of his father. The journey across the ocean had been worth making just for that.

But no cottages graced the fields anymore. Nothing was left but burned-out remains: their rocky husks down in the distance looked like dead beetles.

The folk in the castle had probably burned the houses so that the monsters would not be able to hide in them. *Strengi-saats,* the enemy was called in the old tongue, the "strong ones."

And it was rumored that worse things had begun to haunt the woods. It was rumored that one of them might even haunt Castle Coorm.

"Castle Coorm has become an island, a refuge of stone besieged by a wilderness of trees," Fallion mused. "Now there's not a hamlet within thirty leagues."

"We should know," Talon groused. "We just floundered through every bog between here and the Courts of Tide." She crouched, resting on her heels.

Fallion was more leg-sore and hungry than he had ever been. Worse, he had a bad cut on his calf. It wasn't much, but the smell of congealed blood drew strengi-saats.

He wasn't sure if he should try to rest here. He had heard a strange rumor of this place, the strangest that he'd heard in his life. It was said that several years past, a woman of Coorm had given birth not to a child, but to a tree—a short, stunted tree with a handful of roots and two gnarled limbs. The tree, it was said, had bark that was a ruddy gold. Fallion wondered at the tale. It was said that the woman's flesh was green, like one of the Wizardborn filled with Earth Powers, and some speculated that her offspring was a "World Tree," like the One True Oak of legend that had spread its branches wide, giving shelter to all of mankind at the beginning of creation.

Among the peasants, the idea of a woman giving birth to a World Tree somehow did not seem beyond the realm of possibility. After all, since the coming of the Earth King, Fallion's father, the world had changed. The children born after his coming were stronger than men in times past, wiser and more purposeful, even as the world around them grew stranger and more treacherous. Men were becoming more perfect.

So was evil.

The tree, so the tale went, had been planted in the castle green, where it could be protected and admired, but then a bandit came from the woods, Lord Hale, a man of great power.

It was said that he slaughtered the wizardess.

Many had fled from Coorm then, and for years now, there had been no news from the castle.

Suddenly, a woman screamed down below.

"What's that?" Jaz asked. He pulled on his boot, leapt up. It was not the drawn-out wail of someone grieving past loss. It was announced first by grunts and short yelps of pain, shrieks of terror.

"Someone is fighting," Fallion said.

"Someone is dying!" Rhianna corrected.

From across the fields, at the eastern verge of the woods, a deep snarl erupted, like the sound of thunder on the horizon, followed by the strange bell-like cry of a strengi-saat.

In the woods just up the hill, a pair of crows suddenly cried out, "Claw, claw, claw."

Fallion glanced up. The woods here had been burned back, blackening the great oaks, searing away the brush, leaving the strengi-saats fewer places to hide, Fallion speculated. Up in the nearby trees, he spotted the crows.

The birds were half asleep, but they watched the castle as if it were the sprawling carcass of a dying giant.

The woman screamed again, her voice echoing from the castle walls. Fallion, willed his heart to slow, and listened.

The sounds of the scuffle at Coorm came to him with unnatural clarity, as often happened in the mountains on a clear morning.

He wished for more, half-wished that he had taken endowments of hearing or sight from others. Some had offered when he left—the children that had served under him in the Gwardeen, there in the outposts at the Ends of the Earth. But he had declined. It was an evil thing to take an endowment from a man, for if a man gave you his strength, his heart might fail thereafter. Fallion could not bear the thought of using another person that way. Still, he had nearly three hundred forcibles in his pack as part of his inheritance, and if the need was great enough, he knew that someday he might yet have to take endowments.

There was a gruff cry, a man shouting, "Damn the wench," followed by a smack, the sound of a fist pummeling a face. "She bit me."

The woman's wail went silent, though she grunted and struggled still.

"Open the gates!" the attacker cried in his deep voice. "Open the damned gates, will you?"

In the hills, strengi-saats roared.

"They're going to give a woman to the strengi-saats," Rhianna whispered.

The thought horrified her. She found her heart pounding so hard that she was afraid it would burst.

The strengi-saats wouldn't simply eat the woman. Though they were fierce carnivores, with claws like reaping hooks and teeth like scythes, they didn't simply rend one's flesh. No, one of the females would rape the woman, inserting a long ovipositor into the woman's womb so that it could incubate half a dozen leathery eggs.

Then the strengi-saat would drag the woman into the woods, hide her high among the limbs of a tree, and keep her, terrified but alive, until the eggs hatched, and the young ate their way from the woman's body.

"Fools," Fallion growled. "What are they thinking? In killing her this way, they only reinforce the numbers of their enemies."

"Something more heinous is going on here," Talon concluded. "Perhaps that is what they want—to increase the numbers of the strengi-saats."

The castle's gate began to creak open. Talon clutched her blade, which was as long as her arm and two fingers in width.

Fallion studied the sentries along the wall. He could see their shadowed forms, pacing. There were no more than half a dozen. Two were peering down inside the gates, watching whatever struggle was occurring, but the others showed better judgment, and kept their watch still.

The castle gate swung out, and a pair of burly guards in chain mail and helms dragged the woman outside, hurled her to the ground. The guards turned, trudged back into the castle, and slammed the gate.

Fallion could see a tangle of blond hair on the woman, a white night dress ripped and dirty. She cried in terror and tried to pull her torn dress up, covering her breasts.

She looked forlornly at the gate, went and pounded on it.

"Better run, lass," one guard shouted from the wall. "In ten seconds, our archers open fire."

She peered across the darkened fields. There was no shelter out there, only the ruins of a few cottages.

An arrow bounced off the ground at her bare feet, and then another. She leapt away from them, gathered her courage, picked up her skirt, and took off running.

West. She was heading west, toward a tall hill where a lip of woods protruded closest to the castle.

"Not that way, silly wench," Rhianna hissed.

From the western hill, a strengi-saat raised a barking call, one that Rhianna recognized as a hunting cry.

The woman stopped in her tracks, spun, and headed east, closer to Rhianna's direction, racing along a muddy track that looked black among the fields.

Rhianna saw where it would reach the woods, just two hundred yards to the north. With any luck, Rhianna thought, I could meet her there.

But it would be a race, with the strengi-saats hot on the woman's trail.

Rhianna leapt forward, racing through the dark woods.

We'll have to fight them, Fallion realized, chasing after Rhianna, leaping over a fallen tree, running through a patch of ashes. The morning air was wet and full of dew, thick in his nostrils, muting the biting tang of old ash.

Fallion pumped his legs, driving hard.

In a more perfect world, he thought, a rescuer could run with infinite swiftness.

As he raced, crows came awake, squawking and taking flight in the night air, black wings raking the sky.

"The strengi-saats are coming!" Jaz warned, as he and Talon raced up behind Fallion.

Out across the field, several large, nebulous shadows moved in from the east. Fallion could not see what lay within them. The strengi-saats drew in the light, deepening the darkness all about them. In the night, in the woods or upon a lonely street, so long as they remained still they would stay hidden, camouflaged among their shadows. But running across the fields, their strange ability did them little good. True, their forms remained indistinct, but their presence was easily detected.

The woman reached the woods just ahead of Rhianna, then halted and dropped to her hands and knees, gasping for breath, looking up to peer about in wide-eyed terror. She glanced in Fallion's direction but seemed not to see him. It was not until Rhianna's boot snapped a twig that the woman leapt in terror, rising up with a small branch as her only weapon.

"Don't be afraid," Rhianna whispered. "We're friends."

Rhianna turned and took a guard position, peering among the trees, her staff at the ready.

The young woman stood staring at them all, holding her stick out like a rapier. Apparently she could not believe that anyone would be out here in the forest by night, among the strengi-saats. "Who are you?"

Fallion peered hard. The woman looked to be eighteen or nineteen, a little younger than he. Her face was familiar.

"Ten years is a long time," Jaz offered. "But not long enough so that I would forget your name, Farion. Your father was a good teacher."

Farion stood rooted to the ground, shaking. "Jaz?" she said, incredulous, then looked to Fallion. "Milord?" she cried, dropping to one knee. Tears began to flow freely down her face. "I—we thought you dead. I thought you had died ages ago."

"We're sorry to have left," Fallion said. "Our enemies were too numerous to fight. It had to look as if we were dead."

"Have you come to take back Castle Coorm? Where's your army?" she looked back into the woods, as if hoping that thousands of runelords marched at his back.

"There is no army but the four of us," Fallion admitted.

The words seemed to break Farion's heart. She sagged to the ground, as if all hope were lost, and just began to sob. Nearby, Fallion heard the rumbling growl of a strengi-saat.

Dawn was still minutes away, but it was dark here in the woods. He knew that a fire would keep the monsters at bay. It would also alert the soldiers at Castle Coorm to his presence.

"All is lost then," Farion muttered. "All is lost."

"Not all," Fallion said. "I'll gather an army soon."

Farion shook her head. "Lord Hale tried to force me to

his bed. I fought him, and he threw me out, as an example to the others. I'm afraid . . . he'll make an example of my sister. She is only thirteen." She looked forlornly to each side of the woods. Then she peered up into Fallion's eyes. "Please, she's all that I have left."

"Damn," Jaz swore, looking to Fallion, urging Fallion to fight. He added hopefully, "The men on the walls have ashen bows. Mine has a farther reach."

"So," Fallion said, "you'll fire on the guards while I batter down the gate? I think your jokes are getting better."

The group had not planned to stop at Coorm. They had more urgent business farther on.

Now they had to stop, Rhianna realized. They couldn't leave these women to suffer. A woman alone might live a night or two here in the woods, but the strengi-saats would get her in time. Rhianna knew by the look on Jaz's face that live or die, he would not leave Castle Coorm without a fight.

But Fallion seemed reticent.

What's wrong with you? Rhianna wondered. We both know what it's like to be children, to be held in the clutches of an enemy. Don't you dare walk away from this, Fallion. If you do, I will stop loving you.

But Fallion looked to the west longingly, unsure.

He wants to mend the earth, Rhianna thought. The need presses him, and it breaks his heart to hold back, even for a worthy cause. He must weigh the risk that many might die during the time that is lost against the certainty that this one *will* die.

"All right," Fallion said at last. "I'll free your city. But afterward, we will have to redouble our speed."

Relief flooded through Rhianna. I'm right to love him, she thought.

Fallion kicked some leaves into a pile, knelt over it, and sparked some flint against the hilt of his sword. The leaves were dry in midsummer and caught fire instantly. If Farion thought it strange that they took fire so fast, it did not show in her face. Only relief was revealed there.

In moments a fierce little blaze was going.

"Is your father well?" Fallion asked. "I have often missed his counsel."

"His Dedicates were killed years back," Farion said. "He lost his wit, his stamina, his metabolism. All of the lore that he once knew, it's all gone. For a while, Lord Hale made him his fool, but now he is little more than a simpleton for me to care for. He fetches wood and can feed the cats, but he's no use for aught else."

Fallion grieved silently. In all of the realm there had not been a man who loved learning half as much as her father, Hearthmaster Waggit. Among the many ruins that Fallion had encountered in the week since his return to Mystarria, this one seemed to sadden him the most.

He peered into the flames for a long moment, and the Seal of the Inferno appeared, like a burning wheel, imprinted upon his retina. He pulled a log onto the fire. The dancing flames seemed to beckon him.

Off to his left a shadow moved, perhaps thirty paces from the fire. A strengi-saat. He peered in its direction, and the shadows thickened.

"Jaz," Fallion warned. He picked up a stick from the fire and hurled it toward the shadow. The twig flipped end over end, hit something and blazed bright, revealing the strengi-saat.

It was a large one, perhaps eighteen feet from nose to tail, but had looked smaller as it bellied low to the ground. Its jaws were wide enough to carry a man whole, and its head was leathery and seemed to have scales instead of fur like that found on its back and belly. Ugly black hide stretched over a face as naked as a buzzard's. It had no ears, only tympanums, round membranes the size of plates, just behind its enormous eyes. It whirled to race away.

Jaz fired. The arrow *plocked* into the monster's chest, skewering a lung. Black blood gushed out in a fountain as the strengi-saat roared and began rolling among the pine needles. Rhianna shouted and rushed toward it, her staff at the ready, and the monster leapt away, hoping to escape. It lunged off into the shadows, leaving Rhianna far behind. Fallion knew that it would only find a quiet place to die.

The sun had not yet risen, but the sky was growing light. In a moment, the bright disk would rise and hang like a shield upon the shoulder of the world. Fallion warmed his hands by the fire, let its energy seep into him for a few moments longer.

For the past year, he had been seeking to master the flameweavers' arts in earnest. He could feel the energy building inside him, a hidden inferno. When he judged that he could hold no more, he abruptly stood and announced, "Let's go deal with this Lord Hale."

Far above Fallion a star shone so dimly that it could not be seen, a light so distant that even upon the darkest of nights it was only a hazy malformed speck in the vastness of space, unremarkable, unknown. Fallion had never seen the star, for only those with many endowments of sight could discern it. He had never gazed up from a meadow at night and wondered whether worlds spun in lazy circles about it. He had never dreamt that it might harbor people similar to his.

Yet upon that world a young man, not entirely human in form, faced challenges of his own. . . .

2

UPON A FAR WORLD

When the great Rune of Creation was shattered, the One True World shattered with it into a million million Shadow Worlds, each a distortion of the perfect whole, each diminished.

Do men even exist on such worlds? I used to ask. I believed that they must, at least on some of those worlds, for the Bright Ones dwelt upon the One True World, and we are but shadows of them.

How many times had I wondered if upon one of those shadow worlds there was another me, a twisted mockery of what I am, or a shining example of what I might yet become.

If I were to walk upon such a world, I wondered, and happen upon my shadow self, would I even recognize myself?

But never did I guess that it would happen in my lifetime. I do not blame Fallion for what he did. None of us could ever have guessed the terrible consequences of what would come.

—the Wizard Binnesman

The Great War was finally near an end, and mankind had lost.

The castle at Caer Luciare was now a last and lonely refuge perched on the sides of a mount. The forbidding wastes below were a rocky tumult. To the north, west and east, the ruins of ancient cities climbed above the scree. The vast oaks that had once refreshed this land were gone, tree and acorn, razed during battles with the wyrmlings, and now the fields boasted little but boulders, weeds, and thistles. Only in a few distant fens could green still be seen.

Refugees had swelled Caer Luciare's numbers to more than thirty-eight thousand. The High King himself had come after the fall of Gonart, and the Light of Dalharristan had resorted here with his family now for six years. And this past month alone, four hundred good Kartoche warriors with skin whiter than bone had journeyed north to take refuge among Caer Luciare's ranks.

Everyone said that the warlords were preparing for some fierce assault against the evil that dwelt in the north, at Rugassa.

Had you been walking the tower at Caer Luciare that morning, you might have seen Alun, a young man of nineteen who still seemed far more a boy than a man, down on the green outside the gates amid a swarm of dogs. The hounds around him bayed excitedly at the promise of the hunt, while mastiffs woofed.

Alun knelt with his neck and back bent like a willow frond as he groomed an old hound. Alun was a gangrel, he was, with a crooked nose, stick-like arms, and a head and hands that were too meaty for his body. His leather trousers and red wool tunic were matted with hair and smelled of dog.

The dogs looked fierce in their masks and cuirasses of boiled leather, their wicked collars bristling with spikes. Yet the nubs of their tails wagged furiously, belying their fierce appearance. Their tails wagged despite the fact that some of the dogs knew that they would die this day as the warriors scoured the forest, hunting for wyrmling "harvesters."

There weren't enough dogs for the hunt, Alun knew, not enough healthy ones. He had others in the kennels, limping on mangled paws or with bellies ripped open; right now he was preparing to send Wanderlust into the fray.

"What do you say, love?" Alun asked the hound as he combed. He wanted her to look nice, in case she died today.

Wanderlust was old. The black hair on her snout had gone gray. Her joints were swollen, and as Alun held her muzzle, peered into her loving brown eyes, and strapped on a fighting collar, she barely managed a slow wag of her tail, as if to say, "Another battle? I'm so weary, but I will go."

At first glance, she didn't look like much of a dog. But Wanderlust was more than a common hound. Her mother was a sand hound, a breed so named for its sandy color, renowned for its good nose. But her father was a brute, descended from three strains of war dog. Wanderlust was almost as large as a mastiff, and she had a warrior's heart. Even in old age, if she smelled a wyrmling, she would be first to the fray.

Alun put on Wanderlust's mask, as red as a bloodied skull. He had fashioned it himself, and it reminded him that all too soon there be nothing left of her but a skull. If the wyrmlings didn't get her, age would.

A hound named Thunder rushed up and bayed in Alun's face. Alun gave Thunder a stern look, warned him to go sit, then Alun twisted over to dig in his big rucksack for Wanderlust's cuirass.

A shadow fell over Alun; he looked up. Warlord Madoc stood above him, a tall man in his forties, astonishingly big-boned and broad at the chest. He was a powerful man, as relentlessly bred for war as any of the dogs in Alun's care. His bald head was painted in a red war mask, though he had not yet donned his armor. At his back were his twin sons, Connor and Drewish, both eighteen, in masks of blue. Alun drew back reflexively, for Drewish had often kicked him.

"G'day, milord," Alun said. "Nice day for a hunt." He nodded toward the wastes. The rising sun sprang above the fog-shrouded vales, staining the mist in shades of rose.

"Fagh! I grow weary of hunts," Madoc groused, his tone equally full of fatigue and disgust. He nodded at Wanderlust. "Sending the old bitch out?"

"Aye, milord."

Warlord Madoc grew thoughtful. "You're grooming her for her burial. She deserves such honor. But I have a more vital task for her today—and for you, I think."

"Milord?"

"Master Finnes tells me that your dog has a nose so strong that she can track the trail of a quail a day after it has taken to air—even if it flies over open water."

"True enough," Alun said, his heart suddenly pumping, excited to hear that Wanderlust might get a reprieve.

"Then, I need you to track . . . *someone.*"

Alun wondered whom. He had not heard of any criminals that had escaped the dungeons or highwaymen hiding in the wastes. No one dared stray outside the castle these days. "Who, milord?"

"Swear on your eyes and your hands that you won't tell?"

That was a serious oath. If Alun broke it, Warlord Madoc would require his eyes and hands as payment. "I'll nay tell nobody."

"I want you to track Daylan Hammer."

"Milord?" Alun asked, surprised. Daylan Hammer was a hero. No, he was more than a hero, he was a legend, not some common criminal to be hunted and spied upon. Tales of his exploits stretched back for centuries. It was said that he was immortal, that in his youth he had traveled to another world, where he had drunk a potion that somehow let him cheat death. Some thought that he might even be from another world. He could not be killed, yet he had a habit of disappearing for decades on end, then showing up again. He had come to Caer Luciare last summer, at the end of the month of Wheat, and had been wintering all season.

"You heard aright," Madoc said. "Daylan Hammer has a habit of abandoning the hunt, taking off into the wastes alone. There is a pattern to it. If I'm right, he'll leave the hunt today. I suspect him of foul deeds. I need to know where he goes."

Alun must have looked worried. At the very least, he did not know how to answer.

"Are you up to the task?" Madoc demanded. "Would you risk the wastes alone, with nothing but that dog?"

"I'm—not afraid," Alun said. "Wanderlust will warn me if there is any danger about."

"Do this for me," Madoc said, "and I'll make you Master of the Hounds. . . ." He fell silent, letting this sink in. "With the title comes your freedom and a grant of all of the rights owed to a warrior of the clan. . . ."

Alun's jaw dropped in astonishment. He and his ancestors had lived as serfs for generations. They were the most ill-bred of mankind—the servant caste—made slaves by nature. As a child, Alun had often been told that warlord Madoc would geld him when he got older so that he wouldn't pollute the blood lines. Alun had never dared to dream of rising above his fate.

But as a warrior of the clan, he would gain the right to own property. He would someday be able to buy himself a fine house instead of sleeping in the kennels among the dogs. He would eat at the warlord's table and drink the warlord's wine, instead of eating scraps. He would be eligible to marry a fine woman, a warlord's daughter. "Master Finnes is growing old," Madoc explained. "He tells me that you know dogs as well as any man alive, and you will be a great service to the clan. You are ready to move up in this world."

Alun listened, but worried. Compliments, he found, were like grease on an axle. When applied liberally, they will speed one along on a journey—but soon wear out.

Madoc was offering too much for this one small act of service. There was more going on here than Madoc let on. At his back, Drewish only leered.

Madoc is afraid to his send his own sons to spy on Daylan Hammer, Alun realized. This game is more dangerous than it appears. It's not just the wyrmlings I have to fear—it's Daylan himself. If he's involved in some plot, he might kill to cover it up. That's what Madoc fears. That's what he suspects.

Indeed, Sir Croft had died under suspicious circumstances on the hunt some four weeks past, off on the trail alone. Now that Alun thought of it, hadn't someone said that Croft had gone out to search for Daylan Hammer?

But at the time, Alun hadn't given that a second thought. He'd imagined that Croft was slain by a wyrmling before he found the immortal.

Daylan Hammer seemed to be a virtuous man, wise and brave. He was as handy with a joke or a song as he was with a bow—and after centuries of practice, no one was handier with a bow. Everyone admired him. He was ... the kind of lord that Madoc could never hope to be.

Is Madoc's jealousy clouding his judgment? Alun wondered.

"You suspect him of Croft's death," Alun said.

Wanderlust inched forward, pressing her muzzle into Alun's chest, reminding him that she needed her cuirass. Up at the castle gate, hooves thundered on the drawbridge as a pair of warriors issued forth, and in the fields below the castle, a murder of crows began to caw and fly up out of a field of oats.

Madoc grinned. "Smart lad," he said. "There's more to you than meets the eye. I suspect him of murder, and more. If he is the traitor that I think he is, I'll tie his hands behind his back and let the headsman take a few swings at him."

Drewish laughed, "Then we'll find out just how immortal he really is."

If I follow Daylan Hammer and find something to accuse him of, what then? Alun wondered. If Madoc succeeds in taking vengeance, for the rest of time people will remember me as the man who betrayed Daylan Hammer.

Madoc seemed almost to read his mind. "It is possible," he said, "that Daylan Hammer is as fair as he seems. But I have found that it is a rare man who can really be trusted. Every man's hand seeks his brother's purse, especially in days like these. And if Daylan Hammer sees some advantage in betraying us . . .

"I'd send a warrior again, or Connor or Drewish, but you have a chance to succeed where they would fail. If Daylan catches you, you can tell him that you were out hunting for a lost dog. That is, after all, your lot in life, and it would sound feasible that you would go out and hunt for an animal that you love."

"I think . . ." Alun said, "that Daylan Hammer is a good man."

"Good to who?" Madoc asked. "Is he loyal to this kingdom? Of course not. He was born before it was, and it will fade and die long before he does. We are like dreams to him that come vividly in the night and just as soon vanish. I make plans for my lands. My serfs know that we will plant barley in the field for three years, and let it lie fallow for two. But think how Daylan Hammer must scheme. What does he plan for these lands in a hundred years, or a thousand, or in ten thousand?

"More to the point, what will he do to bring those plans to bear? Will you and I suffer for it?"

Alun grunted thoughtfully, stroked Wanderlust on the back. Most likely, he would find that Daylan was guilty of nothing, and by humoring Warlord Madoc, Alun would earn his gratitude. But if Alun discovered anything of import . . . he'd be well rewarded.

"I'll do it, milord," Alun said.

As Warlord Madoc and his sons strode across the greens well out of earshot, Drewish asked his father, "You wouldn't really grant Alun clan rights, would you? Mother thinks he should be gelded. He's more of a cur than any of the dogs that he sleeps with."

"I'll keep my end of the bargain," Madoc said. "I must prove to my people that my word is good. Let him marry a warrior's daughter, if he can find one who will sleep with him. We'll send him and his offspring to the head of every battle."

"What if Daylan discovers what we're up to?" Drewish asked. "He is a persuasive man. Alun would gladly follow him, I think, right into a kezziard's maw, if the old man asked it of him."

"We can trust Alun," Warlord Madoc said. "Daylan Hammer has no coin to buy the lad, and we're offering him . . . more than he could ever dream. He'll betray Daylan Hammer."

"How can you be sure?" Drewish asked.

"His dogs," Madoc replied. "Every day, Alun sends them to their deaths, betraying those that love him best. He's grown adept at betrayal."

❧ 3 ❧

A WARM RECEPTION

In my dreams, it was always the same. I stood in the Underworld, and a great wheel of fire was emblazoned before my eyes, the Seal of the Inferno.

There were other Seals, the Seal of Heaven, the Seal of Earth—but those were already mended, or at least, were far along the path.

I stared into the rune. To a commoner it would have looked only like a bowl of fire, tongues of flame in greens and reds and blues, sputtering aimlessly. But to my eyes, I read purpose and meaning in those flames. They whispered to me, telling me their secrets. And I watched how they subsided and reappeared in patterns that could not have been random, and I began to understand. The pain of the world, its despair and torment, was written in those flames. They were bent and tainted, cruel and deformed. I knew that with only the

*smallest changes, the slightest of twists, I could fix
them. And in mending them, I would mend the world.*
                            —from the journal of Fallion Orden

Fallion strode purposefully down the rutted road toward
the gates of Castle Coorm.

The sun was rising now, a brilliant gold rim of light on
the horizon and not a cloud in the sky. Behind him, the
others followed.

Each of them bore a torch, though Fallion made sure
that his burned the brightest.

"Torch-bearer." That was Fallion's name among the
flameweavers. Somehow, as he bore the torch toward the
castle, he wondered if it was only descriptive, or if it was
prophetic.

The castle gate was closed, the drawbridge had been
raised again. Fallion could see a pair of mallards grabbling
in the serene waters of the moat, splashing and preening,
while their chicks bobbed about in their wake. But whenever he looked to the drawbridge, he suddenly had a flash
of light that pierced his eye, and he saw the Seal of the
Inferno, burning inside a ring of fire.

"Look," Jaz muttered. "There's the old rock where I
used to hunt for that bullfrog. Do you think it's still there?"

Fallion glanced at the rock, there at the side of the
moat, with rushes growing up around it. He smiled at the
memory. "Go and see, if you want."

Jaz laughed. "Hey, can rocks shrink? This whole castle
seems much smaller than it used to be."

The guards atop the castle wall had taken notice of
them, raising their bows and nocking arrows, crouching
between the merlons atop the castle wall. There were
eight archers. One guard raced down into the depths of
the castle.

Fallion marched right up to the edge of the moat,
where he and his brother had fished as children.

"That will be far enough!" a guard shouted dangerously from the wall. "State your name and business."

"My name is my own affair," Fallion said. "I have
come to challenge Lord Hale to personal combat, to
avenge the honor of this girl, the Lady Farion—and to
avenge the honor of the land of Mystarria."

Fallion heard a gruff laugh and the sound of heavy
boots pounding up wooden stairs in the gate tower, just to
his left. Lord Hale did not come swiftly. He came in a
measured pace, ponderously, thump, thud, thump. By the
creaking of wooden steps, Fallion could tell that he must
be a hill of a man.

But when Lord Hale appeared, leering down over the
battlements, Fallion was not sure that he was a man at all.

Lord Hale was huge, nearly seven feet tall and four
feet wide at the shoulder. There was no beauty or grace
in him. His flaccid jowls were so pale that he might never
have spent a day in the sun, and his silver eyes were lifeless and hollow, like pits gouged in ice. He was bald on
top, with a circlet of long greasy hair that covered his
ears. It seemed to be silver on the ends, but looked
almost as if it were rotting at the roots, like a tuft of cotton that has festered in its boll through the winter.

But it wasn't just the man's hair that seemed to be rotting. There were blotches on his forehead, yellow fungal
growths layered over a patch of dirty warts.

He was a toad of a man, a festering toad, dying from
cankers.

And then there was his expression, his manner. He
leaned his fat elbows upon a merlon and peered down
upon Fallion with a superior air, and there was such
malevolent intent lined upon every inch of his face, that
Fallion had seldom seen the like.

It isn't just his hair that is rotting, Fallion thought. It is all
of him. The evil in him is so strong, it's rotting him away.

Fallion peered at him, through him. He could detect no
locus in the man's soul, no festering evil from the netherworld. But Fallion had learned that not all evil men har-

bored the parasites. Greed and stupidity alone accounted for much evil in the world.

"I know you," Hale leered. "I knew you'd come back. I told her, I did. I says to Shadoath, 'Let me watch the castle here. They always come back.'"

So, Fallion realized, the man worked for Fallion's old enemy. Hale had manned his outpost for years, and even now perhaps was unaware that the war was over and that Shadoath had lost. The very fact that Hale had come with Shadoath, though, gave Fallion pause. And briefly Fallion wondered if Shadoath had returned—if the locus had taken a new body.

Perhaps Hale is not human, Fallion thought. Shadoath had brought fallen Bright Ones and golaths with her from the netherworld, along with her strengi-saats. It was possible that Hale was something other than human, some breed of giant.

Hale studied Jaz, Rhianna, and Talon, gave an approving nod. "So, I knew you'd come back," he said smugly. "But I didn't know you'd come back like salmon—to spawn."

He burst into a round of crude laughter, and some of the archers on the wall followed suit.

He plans to kill us, Fallion knew, but he won't try it yet. He wants to savor the moment, draw it out.

"So, I remember you," Hale said. "Do you remember me?"

Fallion shook his head. "No."

"We've met before," Hale said. "I'll give you a hint. It was on that day you run off."

Fallion remembered. Lord Asgaroth had brought troops to the castle, surrounded it, and then demanded that Fallion's mother offer up her sons as hostages.

Fallion himself had stood on the wall and given his answer, commanding the archers to open fire.

"I remember," Fallion said, not completely sure. "A fat man on a pony, a giant of a target, rushing off. I remember a fleeting thought, 'How could they miss that one!'"

Lord Hale roared in glee. Oh how he was savoring the

moment. Fallion calculated that in an instant, he would command his troops to fire.

So Fallion took the initiative.

"I did not command my men to fire lightly," Fallion said. "It is a grave thing to take another's life, even if it must be done to satisfy justice."

Hale mocked his choice of words. "Oh, it is indeed a *grave* thing to take a life. Ain't it lads?"

"I'm sorry now that I must take yours," Fallion said. "I offer you one last chance. Surrender yourself, and I will be lenient."

It was a sincere offer, but Hale merely grinned patiently and said, "Come and take my life, if you think you can."

Fallion raised his hand, as he had upon that fateful day, and called out to Lord Hale's troops. These were no men that he recognized from the old days when his family held this castle. These were rogues and bandits that had crawled out of the hills.

"You men upon the walls," Fallion shouted. "I am Fallion Sylvarresta Orden, heir to Gaborn Val Orden, and rightful lord of this realm. I bid you to join in helping restore peace and prosperity to the land."

He looked toward Lord Hale, and shouted "Fire!" as he made a pulling motion with his fist.

None of the archers fired upon Warlord Hale. But then Fallion hadn't expected that they would.

Hale laughed in derision, looked right and left toward his archers. At his glance, the men stiffened, drew their bows to the full. His patience was at an end, Fallion could see. He was tired of playing.

In apparent resignation, Fallion said, "If your men won't obey my command, perhaps the heavens will." He raised his hand a second time and shouted "Fire!"

He let go of some of the energy that had been stored in him, sent it questing behind him, used it to heat the torches so that they all flared up in an instant.

He gathered that heat and sent it racing through the air. The torches sputtered out as a dozen ashen war bows suddenly superheated and burst into flames. The well-oiled strings and the lacquer made perfect fuel.

At that instant, Fallion's friends scattered, and Fallion drew a wreath of smoke about him, just in case any of the archers had the presence of mind to try to fire one last shot with the flaming bows.

A couple did, muttering curses as the arrows flew. But the sudden flames had spoiled their aim, and the worst that happened was that a fiery arrow blurred past Fallion's shoulder.

Lord Hale barely had time to register his surprise. Perhaps he had not seen the unnatural gleam in Fallion's eye, or perhaps he had not recognized it as the mark of a flameweaver. Too late he saw his mistake.

Fallion reached into the sky, sent his energy out and used it to gather motes of light from the heavens, as if trapping flies within a web.

From horizon to horizon the skies went black. Then he drew the light toward him in a fiery funnel, an infernal tornado that dropped white hot into his palm.

For half an instant, he let the fire build, and then hurled it toward Warlord Hale.

The fireball struck, hitting the warlord's oily skin, his clothes, and Hale shrieked and tried to bat the flames away. But Fallion only intensified them, sent energy streaming into him so that as an outer layer of hair or skin or fat burned, steam rose from the inner layers, drying them until they caught flame too, then the layer below took fire.

It happened quickly, a few seconds at most, but Fallion burned the man, turning him into a fiery pillar of blackened ash and pain.

Only his eyes Fallion left untouched, so that Hale's men might see the horror in them.

Lord Hale flailed about, shrieking, and then just staggered over the wall and dropped into the moat like a meteor, where his carcass sputtered and fumed in the water.

The guards all dove for cover, lest Fallion target one of them next.

Cheers arose from the commoners that Lord Hale had kept as his slaves in the castle, and suddenly there was the pounding of feet on stairs as some of them began rushing the guards, intent on taking vengeance for years of abuse.

Fallion and those outside the castle could do little now except wait for the drawbridge to open.

He peered at the bridge, and a Seal of the Inferno blossomed in his mind, a fiery wheel, striking him like a blow.

It seems so near, he thought. The seal must be nearer than I imagined.

He wiped his eyes with the back of his hand, trying to clear his vision.

There were screams and the clash of arms coming from the castle. He worried for the peasants who were giving their lives in this battle.

He did not like the brutality, but he could not deny the people their well-deserved vengeance.

They hunger for it, Fallion thought, and by the Powers, after the horrors that I've seen, I'd like my fill of it myself.

❧ 4 ❧

TAKING COUNCIL AT TWILIGHT

Better to die a fair death than to live as a wyrmling.
                    —*a saying in Caer Luciare*

Dogs can talk, Alun knew, and right now, Wanderlust was telling him that she smelled a wyrmling.

Oh, a hound doesn't speak in words, but their bodies can tell you volumes.

Wanderlust stood with her muzzle pointed down a dank trail in the deepest shadows of a swamp, growling far back in her throat. Her tail did not wag, as it would if she only smelled a stag or a bear. Instead, her flanks quivered nervously, and the nub of her tail was as steady as a stone.

She turned and looked back at him, imploring with her eyes, asking what to do. If the wyrmling had been near, she'd have taken small leaps backward while peering in its direction. No, the trail was hours old.

"Leave it," Alun whispered, gripping his short spear. "We've got better things to do." He pointed to Daylan Hammer's prints in the mud.

After accepting the honor of the hunt, Alun had gone to his room and retrieved his leather boots and a light spear. He took no armor, no heavy steel, sacrificing safety for speed. Daylan Hammer was small, but it was said that he could run with the speed of three men.

Catching the immortal's scent had not been hard. Alun had simply gone to the barracks where Daylan slept and stuck Wanderlust's muzzle into his bed. From there, the hound easily tracked him through the woods, even though Daylan rode on horseback.

Alun had to race to keep up all morning, but at no time had Daylan Hammer ever gotten more than two or three hours ahead of him.

As Madoc had predicted, Daylan Hammer had broken off from the hunt early. He'd ridden south of the castle for nearly ten miles, through the rocky Hallow Hills and down into the swamps beneath. Then he'd left his horse when the muck got too thick, and set off on foot.

He was traveling fast. Even in a mire he could outrace a commoner, it seemed, especially one who had to worry about making any noise that might alert his quarry. Alders and willows raised their leafy branches all around, and Alun had to make sure not to step on fallen twigs.

Fortunately, Alun had figured out where Daylan Hammer was going. There was a hill not a mile ahead, a small rise where, in some distant past, the ancients had raised a sand-stone tower. Large images had been carved into the inner walls of the stone—likenesses of six beautiful women; thus it was called the Tower of the Fair Ones. Though the wind and rain had ravaged the outer ramparts, the women were still there today, safe and protected. Legend said that it once had been the home to a wealthy merchant who kept his daughters under strong guard, safe from the attentions of ill-bred suitors

In fairer times, it had been a popular retreat for lovers.

Alun hurried along through the brush, with Wanderlust silently urging him on. She had never been one for barking much, and Alun had taught her not to bark at all when on the trail of an outlaw.

Because the ground was soft and he did not want Daylan Hammer to know that he was being followed, Alun took his path parallel to the hero's track. As the ground rose, cover became dense. Blackberry bushes tangled among a few evergreens and fern thickets. The water in the nearby swamps was warm, for much of it came from hot springs and geysers high on Mount Luciare, and was diverted through the castle to heat it, even in winter. Because of this, the plants here had an easy winter, and were larger and lusher than in the valleys nearby.

When Alun finally spotted the old tower rising above the woods, he halted. He was only a hundred yards off, and he could see Daylan Hammer there with his back to Alun. The immortal had leaned a log against the tower, which was only about forty feet high, and now was climbing the log, using it to scale the tower wall.

Alun retreated beneath the low branches of an evergreen for cover and lay in the shadows with one arm resting around Wanderlust to keep her quiet.

Daylan Hammer reached the top. The roof had caved in ages ago, and so the immortal merely balanced upon the narrow rock wall. After a moment, he took off his cape and threw it to the ground, then unsheathed his war hammer and let it fall, too.

He relaxed for a long moment, shook out his auburn hair, and just stood, gazing up toward the sun, as if taking his rest, daydreaming.

Daylan Hammer looked like a young man, perhaps in his mid-twenties. He was short of stature, even among the poorly bred, but of course was dwarfed by those of the warrior caste. He had a weathered face, his beard cut short. But there was agelessness to his blue eyes, as if he had seen far too many horrors and had loved far too often and had grown weary of life.

Alun wondered what the immortal dreamed about. Perhaps, he imagined, Daylan Hammer had been in love with one of the beauties whose image was housed inside. Perhaps he comes here only to mourn her.

As minutes stretched into hours, Wanderlust grew bored of the watch, and soon lay in the shadows of the evergreen, snoring. As the sun began to drop toward the horizon, Alun fell to dreaming himself. There was a chance that he could be freed. And he began to think about what that would mean.

Wanderlust whimpered in her sleep. Her paws were in the air, and she waved them just a little. Dreaming of the hunt, of rabbits or harts, Alun figured from her smile.

He could understand dogs. Their body language spoke volumes. Not like women. You can look at a pretty lass and never have an idea what she is thinking, if she is thinking at all.

Alun didn't have a lover, had never even kissed a girl. He had once approached Gil the fishmonger and asked for his daughter's hand in marriage, but the man had laughed in his face. "What? An oaf who stinks of dogs wants to marry my daughter what stinks of fish? What malodorous little tadpoles you would spawn!"

The fishmonger's daughter was nice to look at. She had long brown hair and eyes as solemn as an old hound's. And she didn't talk much. That was a fine trait, in Alun's estimation. He had been teased rudely as a child, and couldn't bear the presence of gossips or scolds.

Once I become a clansman, he imagined, Gil will bring his daughter by the hand and beg me to marry her.

And what will I say?

"What, you want me to marry your daughter what stinks of fish?"

He'd laugh and turn the man out.

And then I'll be alone again, he thought.

So if not the fishmonger's daughter, who will I marry?

There were plenty to choose from—daughters of old warlords who were penniless, daughters of wealthy merchants who would hope to add a title to their fortunes.

Why not marry the best? he wondered.

And suddenly he dared imagine the impossible.

The best. The best would be well bred and wealthy. She would be beautiful to look upon, but she would also be generous and good of heart. She would love him, and not disrespect him for coming from a low breed.

A young woman came to mind. He had never thought of her before, not in that way. Her exalted station had been too far above his. Her name was Siyaddah, and her father was the Emir of Dalharristan.

She had spoken to Alun often, for as a young woman she had loved to come to the kennels and play with the new pups, petting them and bringing scraps from the kitchens and bones for the pups to wrestle over.

Siyaddah had the brownest eyes, almost as black as her hair. They sparkled when she laughed, and her skin was dark and silky.

She had always treated Alun as more than a slave. She had laughed with him as if he were a friend, and once she even laid her hand upon his arm; highborn women almost never did that. He had wondered if she had feelings for him.

Once my rank is secure, Alun thought, I could ask her father for her hand in marriage. He won't go for it. But if he said no, what would I have lost?

He strongly doubted that the Emir would say yes. There were rumors that he was saving his daughter, that he hoped to marry her to High King Urstone's son.

Alun thought, But that will never hap—

A huge shadow fell over him, followed by the pounding of heavy wings. Alun's heart leapt in his chest. He suddenly felt as a mouse must feel when touched by the shadow of the hawk.

He peered up in terror and saw some beast. It wasn't a drake. This thing had vast translucent wings of palest gold that rippled in the air like sheets moved by the wind.

A wyrmling Seccath! Alun thought, fear rising in his throat. Alun had seen a Seccath only once, nine years ago, when he was but a boy. The High King himself had captured it and brought it to Castle Luciare, where it was stripped of its wings and held prisoner deep in the dungeons, even to this day.

The Seccath winged its way straight toward Daylan Hammer, and Alun had the forethought to realize that the immortal had no weapon to protect him.

Just as Alun was about to shout a warning, the Seccath folded its wings and dropped to the tower wall, opposite from Daylan Hammer.

"Well met," Daylan Hammer said.

The wyrmling settled onto the wall. She was a pale-eyed woman with blond hair shaved short and with huge bones. Her neck and forehead were tattooed with cruel glyphs, prayers to Lady Despair. There was no beauty in her that Daylan could see, unless one thought that brutality could be considered comely.

Not for the first time, Daylan considered how decency and innocence were inextricably mingled with a human's concept of beauty. On almost every world he had visited, in any nation, a person whose face was smooth, childlike—innocent, and compassionate—was considered more beautiful than one who was not. Not so among the wyrmlings.

Indeed, it was believed that the wyrmlings' ancestors had been human, but they had been bred for war over so many generations that they had evolved into something else. So there was an inbred cruelty and wariness to the woman—a rough and hawkish face, a scowl to the mouth, blazing eyes, and a wary stance, as if she only hoped for a chance to gut him.

Her artificial wings folded around her now, making her look as if she were draped in translucent yellow robes. Behind her, the dying sun hung just above the horizon like a bloody eye.

The wyrmling peered at Daylan, cold and mocking in her rage. The wyrmlings could not abide light. It pained their eyes and burned their skin.

Humans feared the darkness, and so they had agreed to meet here now, in the half-light.

The sight of her sent a shudder through Daylan. Thoughts of compassion, honor, decency—all were alien to her, incomprehensible. The maggot that infected her soul saw to that.

"Well met?" she asked, as if trying to make sense of the greeting. "Why would it be well to meet me? Your body trembles. It knows the gaze of a predator when it sees it. Yet you think it well to meet me?"

Daylan chuckled. "It is only a common greeting among my people."

"Is it?" the wyrmling demanded, as if he lied.

"So," Daylan said, "you asked for proof that your princess is still alive."

"Can you name the day she drew her first blood?"

It was a difficult question, Daylan knew. The wyrmlings kept great beasts to use in times of war—the world wyrms. Among wyrmlings, time was measured in "rounds" which lasted for three years—the length of time that it took between breeding cycles for a female wyrm. Each day in a round had its own name. Thus, there were over a thousand days in a round, and if Daylan had to lie, he would have had a slim chance of guessing the right day.

"Princess Kan-hazur says that she drew first blood upon the day of Bitter Moon." That was all that he needed to say, but he wanted to offer ample proof. "It was in the two hundred and third year of the reign of the Dread Emperor Zul-torac. She fought in the Vale of Pearls against the he-beast Nezyallah, and broke his neck with his club."

Daylan knew a bit about politics among wyrmlings. As he understood it, the "he-beast" was in fact the Princess's own older brother. He would have been larger and stronger than her, but the princess claimed that her brother was also less violent, and therefore less "able to lead," by wyrmling standards.

"Aaaaah," the wyrmling sighed. "A fine battle it was. Kan-hazur won scars both of flesh and of the heart that day."

"Yes," Daylan said. "And now, do we have a bargain?"

❧ 5 ❧

A LIGHT IN THE HEAVENS

Death never comes at a timely hour.
—a saying of the netherworld

Alun waited for the two to leave—the wyrmling flying back north, while Daylan Hammer climbed gingerly from the wall.

He let Daylan Hammer have a five minute lead, and then hurried for the castle.

I'm in a real fix now, Alun decided. It was eleven miles back to the castle, and he'd never be able to make it before dark. The wyrmling harvesters would come out by then. Indeed, the last sliver of sun dipped below the horizon as he began his race, and he knew that he had perhaps a half an hour of light, and there would be only the faintest waning moon tonight.

Maybe I'll get lucky, he thought. The lords have been hunting the harvesters hard. There can't be many around the castle.

But he had little hope. Wyrmling harvesters butchered humans, taking certain glands that the wyrmlings used for elixirs. Thus, the castle attracted the wyrmlings like wolves to a carcass.

So Alun ran, heart pounding, sweat streaming down his forehead, his back, his neck and face. He came up out of the bogs into the wastes and kept to a rocky ravine, the dry bed of creek.

The shadows grew long and deep, and he struggled to keep up with Wanderlust.

The dog will warn me of danger, he thought—until he rounded a boulder; something large lurched in front of him.

He heard the sound of steel clearing a scabbard, and Daylan Hammer's boot knife pressed up against Alun's nose.

"What are you doing?" Daylan demanded. "Why are you following me?" Daylan studied him with a cold eye.

"I, I, I uh, was looking for a lost dog," Alun explained, coming up with the lie. "Wanderlust here is my favorite."

The dog growled at Daylan Hammer but didn't dare attack. Oh, she'd try to take him if Alun so commanded, but Alun knew that if he ordered her to kill, Daylan's knife could plunge through his eye before the hound ever got a bite of the immortal.

Daylan smiled, sheathed his knife. Apparently he decided the Alun didn't represent much of a threat. "You've followed me for hours."

"I didn't see nothin'!"

"You didn't see me meet with a wyrmling Seccath?" Daylan smiled at the lie, as if it were nothing.

"No!" Alun insisted.

"Then you're a terrible spy, and not worth the half of what they're paying you."

Daylan sat down on a large rock and patted a spot next to him, inviting Alun to rest. Alun was gasping from fear and exhaustion. Daylan suggested, "Lean your head between your knees. Catch your breath."

Alun did as he was told, unnerved at the realization that there was nothing he could do to protect himself from a man like Daylan Hammer. "What are you going to do with me?"

"You mean do to you?" Daylan laughed. "Nothing. If I wanted to kill you, I'd leave you here in the waste for the wyrmlings. They'd take a meager harvest from you. But I won't leave you alone, and I won't harm you. I just want to know one thing: who sent you?" His tone was mild, affable, as if he were asking what Alun thought of the weather.

Alun sat gasping for a moment. It was no use lying. If he lied, Daylan might leave him for the wyrmlings, and that would be that.

But there was something more to it.

He liked the way that Daylan had asked. When Madoc had come, he'd stood over Alun with his brutish sons at his back, and had taken an intimidating stance. There were subtle threats implied, Alun suddenly realized.

But even when he made the mildest of threats, Daylan didn't sound serious. Indeed, he was smiling, as if sharing a joke.

"Warlord Madoc," Alun said at last. "Warlord Madoc sent me."

"What did he say about me? What does he suspect?"

"He thinks that you're a traitor, that you killed Sir Croft."

"Sir Croft got *himself* killed," Daylan said. "He followed me, as you did, but he didn't keep to his cover as well. I didn't see him, but the wyrmling did. She caught him. By the time I heard Croft's cries, the harvest had been taken."

Alun said nothing.

"Did you hear our conversation?" Daylan asked, "Mine and the Seccath's?"

Alun shook his head. "I was too far away to hear anything. I didn't dare try to get close."

"Ah," Daylan said. "I am trying to make a bargain with the wyrmlings. They have High King Urstone's son. They've held him hostage now for more than a decade. And as you know, we have Zul-torac's daughter. Zul-torac has forsaken his flesh, and lives only as a shadow now. He cannot spawn any more offspring, and so his daughter is precious to him. I hope to make an exchange of hostages."

"Prince Urstone is still alive, after all these years?"

"Barely, from what I understand."

"And is he even human?" Alun asked. "Surely by now they've put him in a crystal cage and fit him with a wyrm."

"He's resisted the cage, and the wyrm," Daylan said. "He is still human." Alun doubted that anyone could resist the cage for so long. It was said that the pains one endured there made a person long for death, long for release. Better to let a wyrm infest your soul, lose your humanity, than to resist. "Through a messenger, I have put questions to him," Daylan explained, "moral questions that no person infected by a wyrm could have answered correctly. The crystal cage destroys most men, but others it only purifies, filling them with compassion and the wisdom that can only come from having endured great pain and perfect despair."

Alun peered up, hope in his eyes. If Daylan was right, then the prince was the kind of hero that men only hear of in legends.

Daylan Hammer grasped Alun by the wrist. "Old King Urstone is failing. He won't last much longer than that dog of yours.

"In three days, a thousand of the strongest warriors in Caer Luciare will ride north to attack the wyrmlings, to take back the fortress at Cantular. In seventeen years, no attack so bold has been attempted, for word of such an attack might well drive Emperor Zul-torac mad with bloodlust, and the life of Prince Urstone would be forfeit.

"And so I am trying to negotiate an exchange of hostages—before the attack takes place."

"But, once we give up their princess," Alun asked, "won't the wyrmlings attack Caer Luciare in force?"

"Of course they will," Daylan said.

Alun didn't understand. The immortal was giving up their hostage, the only thing that had protected the Caer for more than a decade. If Alun understood him aright, with the hostage lost, the wyrmlings would attack, and by the end of this week, everyone that he knew could be dead.

"This is madness!" Alun shouted. "You've gone daft! King Urstone would never agree to such a plan. What do we gain? You are just hurrying our end!"

"The end is coming, whether we like it or not," the immortal said. "Warlord Madoc has convinced the others to make this assault in an effort to secure the borders. Madoc is a fool who dreams of rebuilding the kingdom. Others are tired of hiding, of watching our numbers dwindle away day by day, and so they hope to die fighting, as warriors will.

"But once Madoc takes Cantular, the prince's life is forfeit, and Emperor Zul-torac will retaliate. The wyrmling code demands vengeance. They have a saying, 'Every insult must be paid for in blood.' Zul-torac's honor will demand that he hit us hard, even if he must cut his way through his own daughter to do so."

Alun still didn't understand. There was no justification for giving up their hostage. Daylan Hammer was making a token gesture, trying to save two lives for what . . . a week?

"I don't see any value in trying to save the prince," Alun said. "If we are all to die, why not just hit them, and let the prince be damned?"

"That's how Madoc would have it, isn't it?" Daylan said. Alun realized that he was right. "It sounds courageous, daring. Many lords applaud his courage. But think: what if mankind is not wiped out? What if a few hundred or even thousands of you were able to run off into the wilderness, or hide in the caves beneath Caer Luciare? What then? If the prince dies and Madoc manages to win the battle, who will the kingdom fall to when the High King dies?"

"Warlord Madoc," Alun said, for the High King had no other heir.

"Madoc himself might not be a bad High King," Daylan Hammer said. "But what of his sons? To put them on a throne would be a disaster. If Madoc or his sons were to learn of my plan, you know that they would oppose it. They could easily sabotage it. No one would blame them if they put the wyrmling princess to the sword.

"I'm not hoping just to save just our prince, Alun, I'm hoping to save our kingdom, our people."

A chill wind suddenly swept over the rocks, down from the mountain.

There were too many ifs in Daylan's argument.

"Let's say you're right," Alun said. "Let's say that the lords take Cantular, and the wyrmlings in a fit of rage come and wipe us all out, as seems most likely. Then . . . what will all of this have accomplished? The sum of all your acts is what, to save one wyrmling princess?" The thought was absurd. "Is there something you're not telling me?"

Daylan smiled, and suddenly he looked old and weary and bent. "There is indeed," he admitted. "I believe that it is time to free the princess. I believe that we should stop using her as a shield, even if there is no hope for our people."

"How so?" Alun asked, a sudden fear rising in him. Would Daylan Hammer throw away their hostage for nothing?

"No one should be put to such indignity. No life should be so abused. You've stolen her freedom, terrorized her, and victimized her. She was but a child when she was captured. Does your weakness as a nation, your cowardice, justify such behavior?"

"They did it to us first," Alun pointed out.

"They took a warrior captive. Your people took a child. It's not the same. But even if the acts were equal, does that mean that because the wyrmlings are cruel and craven, you would fall to their estate? Don't you realize that that is precisely what they want? The maggots that infect their souls cannot possess your body so long as you remain pure enough, innocent enough. As a people, you cannot let yourselves sink to their level. There is great power in doing what is right, and letting the consequences be damned. It is the safest course, even when the peril appears great, for it is better to lose your life than to throw away your soul.

"Alun, I'm not trying to just free a pair of hostages. I'm hoping to lift this pall of shame that covers Caer Luciare. I'm hoping, in some small way, to redeem this people."

The drawbridge fell open, and all that Fallion saw within the courtyard was the tree, seemingly tall now, nearly thirty feet. Every branch, every twig, seemed to be a wonder, the product of some superhuman artistry.

The villagers, bloody and bedraggled, were crowded around it, shouting in joy, cheering for Fallion, for freedom, their voices seeming to come from a great distance, like a wind rushing above a vast forest.

"Milord," one old woman shouted, "remember me?" Fallion smiled. He did indeed. She had been a scullery maid in the castle; she had taught him how to cook a pudding.

"And me, milord?" a man cried. It was the cobbler who had given Fallion his pet ferrin as a child.

And as the bridge lowered, all of the weight of his

journey washed out of Fallion, and he felt renewed—not just rested in mind, but refreshed in spirit.

It was more than the homecoming. It was the tree that influenced him.

Now was the time to do things. Now was the time to become a better person, to seek perfection.

The urge came to him so clearly it was almost a command.

But as the bridge dropped farther, Fallion began to realize that something was horribly wrong. There was darkness among the branches, a lingering shadow, and the tree had almost no leaves, and those were only on the top-most branches, though it was high summer.

And as he saw the bole of the tree, scarred and blackened by flames, he began to understand why.

The bridge dropped, and he saw it now. The tree was surrounded by a circular wall of stone. And within that wall of stones, worms of green flame sputtered and burned, while white-hot sparks shot out from time to time amid a rune of fire. It was the Seal of the Inferno.

The image smote him, went whirling before his eyes, filling his vision. He blinked and turned away, sought to clear his sight, but the image could not be pushed aside. He stood before the Seal of the Inferno, and it forced itself upon him.

Serve me, a voice demanded in the whispering tongue of flames. Give your all to me.

Fallion dropped to one knee and held his forearm against his eyes.

It wasn't supposed to be here. The Seal was supposed to be in the Underworld, linking the Seal of Heaven to the Seal of Earth. By smoothing out its flaws, Fallion hoped to bind the shattered remains of the One True World back into a single whole.

But this thing before him, it was lying naked in the open, like a festering wound.

Even with his eyes clenched, the rune thrust itself on his consciousness.

You cannot escape, it whispered.

"Fallion?" he heard Rhianna calling desperately. "Fallion, what's wrong?"

"The Seal," Fallion shouted. "It's breached! It—has been *sullied, warped.*" He could think of no other way to describe the damage. The rune had been twisted, subverted by some malicious power. It was raging, wanton. It should have been controlled, a shining thing of golden light. All that he saw now was dangerous wreckage.

The same power that had broken the Seals in the beginning did this, he realized—the Queen of the Loci.

"Can you fix it?" Rhianna asked, her voice seeming to come from far away.

A tremendous fear welled up in Fallion. The Seal shouldn't have been here. He knew of no human-born flameweaver who was powerful enough to have re-created the Seal. Only the Queen of all Loci could do that. He worried that she might be near.

In his dreams, fixing it had been so easy. But now, confronted by the abomination itself, he wasn't sure.

Seeking fuel, Fallion reached up into heaven and grasped the light, pulling it down in fiery cords, letting it build.

He opened his eyes, staring into the wheel of fire, searching for its flaws.

Shapes began to emerge. To a commoner, it would have only looked like a bowl of flames, endlessly burning without a source, but to Fallion, there was meaning within those shapes.

One had to watch, to study the patterns, see where new flames appeared, where old ones died, how they twisted and flickered, how tall they rose. He could read the meanings of their movements if he had enough time to study them. But how much time would it take? Weeks, he suspected. Months. Years. There were runes hidden within runes here, a maze of them. He would have to pace himself, work in short sessions.

Fix the biggest problems first, he told himself.

Blue tongues of flame erupted and spouted seemingly

at random, and white phosphorous airs rose and sputtered. He could hear tongues of flame muttering and cursing in torment at how they had been twisted. But those were mere distractions.

A serpentine incandescence burrowed through the rune, emitting sparks.

It represents the worm at the world's heart, he realized. But why is it so large?

He followed its shape backward, saw its tail wrapped around the bole of the golden tree, searing it, even as the worm drew away the light from its branches.

What an abomination! he thought.

Fallion hurled a ball of flame, used its energy to sever the tail that bound the world wyrm to the One True Tree. There was a crackling sound, a roar of fire, and the shadows fled from around the tree.

The flames cursed Fallion, and struck back, like some living thing. A blast of heat surged into him, filling him.

Almost, Fallion burst into flames. The inferno begged Fallion to let go, to leave his flesh behind and become one with Fire, as his master had years ago at the battle for Shadoath's Castle.

"No!" Fallion shouted, knowing that he had no choice but to fight. The Seal of the Inferno was a deadly puzzle. Either he had to heal it, or it would destroy him.

In his dreams, he had always repaired the rune. The dream came every night, and it had always been the same. The flames spoke with a million tongues. In his dream he tamed them, taught them to speak with only one.

He looked to the field where a bowl of flames should be, and saw the flames. But almost instantly they snuffed out, leaving only two.

For a moment, he knelt with mouth agape, unsure how to proceed. This is where he was to bind the worlds, bring all of them into one. But only two flames remained in this bowl. Each flame flickered and swayed in its own dance.

For long seconds Fallion held still, waiting for the other flames to reappear.

The heat continued to build in him, threatening to overwhelm him. He could feel it in the back of his throat. Steam began to rise from his cloak.

Desperate, Fallion lashed out, hurling back the heat that threatened to overwhelm him, and bound the two flames into one.

The fires of the Seal lashed out, roaring toward Fallion, and then died in an instant.

Suddenly all that remained was a ring of smoke rising around the golden tree.

In the ensuing silence, Fallion found his heart pounding and sweat rolling down his face. There was no voice coming from the remains of the fire. There was no voice in the tree.

"Is it over?" Jaz asked.

All around them, the world seemed to return to normal. Fallion could hear the morning bird song as robins and larks worked the nearby meadows. The rising sun stood golden in the sky. A faint breeze stealing down from the mountains cooled his skin.

And overhead, a great light began to fill the sky.

Daylan Hammer fell silent for a long moment, leaving Alun time to ponder his words.

"Can't, can't you help us in some other way?" Alun asked. "You visit the netherworld it is said. Surely . . . there is some weapon that you could lend us?"

"You think that better weapons can save you?" Daylan mused. "You ask for a dangerous thing. I've heard tales of entire worlds that have been leveled—all because one like me handed out such weapons to those in need.

"It is forbidden.

"Even if I gave them to you, they could not save you. In time, your enemies would capture them and turn them against you.

"Besides, you have all of the weapons that you need to destroy this world."

Alun tried to imagine what he could be talking about. Swords? War clubs? "What weapons?"

"Hate," Daylan answered. "Your people don't just live under the shadow of the wyrmlings. You have fallen far beneath it. In a generation, there will no longer be any difference between them and you."

Daylan fell silent, then at last asked, "So, what will you tell Warlord Madoc?"

Alun thought hard. If he told the truth, he might gain his freedom, untold riches. He could marry well and live happily.

And if he lied. . . .

Then Daylan would free Princess Kan-hazur, leaving his people to withstand the full onslaught of the wyrm-lings. Prince Urstone would come to rule, hopefully to help any who escaped.

Even if my people survive, Alun wondered, will House Urstone ever reward me?

He had never caught the eye of the High King. It seemed too fanciful a notion to entertain.

Suddenly there was a bright light in the sky, as if a star had been born.

Alun did not become aware of it all at once. Instead, it seemed that for several seconds it became brighter and brighter.

He looked up, and saw a pale disk, as big as a moon. A star is falling, Alun thought. It's coming right at us.

The light grew brilliant, and suddenly Alun recalled hearing a tale of a meteorite that had crashed into the mountains years ago, filled with iron from the stars. But he realized that anything as big as this would surely smash him when it hit.

Fallion peered up at the growing orb. He could see blue—vast seas, and the actinic white of clouds whirling above them. He saw the blush of the morning sun striking clouds at the terminus. He spotted a continent, with a great red desert and snow-topped mountains. He could make out silver veins of rivers, the emerald green of forests, a lake shaped like a kidney.

People around Fallion began to cry out in astonishment and fear, and some threw up their hands to brace for the impact.

"What's that!" Alun shouted, still peering at the coming world. He could not believe that his life was over. He wanted Daylan Hammer to explain the sight away, offer some comfort.

He looked at Daylan Hammer, whose eyes were wide with wonder. "It's the end of the world," he said as the huge disk suddenly filled the whole sky.

"This is the end!" Talon cried.

Fallion stared at the coming world, fear coursing through him like a bolt of lightning, and whispered, "No, my friends, it is only beginning."

The ground trembled and groaned, and a mighty blast raked Alun's face. There was a fire in the heavens.

Wind roared all around him, and tornados of light touched down.

Alun threw up his hands to protect his eyes, and gritted his teeth.

Two worlds collided, folding into one. There were no crushing rocks falling from the sky, no vast craters formed, no plasma spewing from the far side of a ruined world.

Instead a rain of atoms fell, sizzling past one another through the vast empty spaces that exist between the nucleus of one atom and another.

To Fallion, the impact felt as if a great wind roared through him. He could feel it pelting him on the head and shoulders, driving through him, and leaving through the soles of his feet. Bolts of static electricity raced every-where, across the surface of the castle, and there was a rushing sound so loud, accompanied by screams, that it felt like the end of the world.

And suddenly the ground whirled and began to lurch beneath his feet. He could feel a hill rising beneath him, the ground shooting up so fast that his knees buckled.

The walls of Castle Coorm trembled and rolled as if during an earthquake. The east wall bucked, spilling into the moat, and the queen's tower canted to one side and collapsed. Huge stones surged up through the ground, their faces seeming weathered by centuries of erosion.

Suddenly the atoms sliding through empty space halted, joining together as tightly as a key in the lock of a manacle, according to some pattern laid out in the master rune an eternity in the past.

The ground lurched to a halt, and Fallion felt an impact. No blow by a human hand could have been so devastating. It was as if a giant slapped him, sending him into oblivion.

❧ 6 ❧

A NEW WORLD

When we plow a field to ready it for planting, much is lost. The holes and homes of mice and snakes are torn apart, the struggling roots of last year's herbs are bro-ken. To me, the mouse and the herb are wondrous things, to be enjoyed and treasured. But we lay them waste—all in the hope of some distant harvest. Thus in making one marvelous thing, regretfully we put an end to another. —the Wizard Sisel

Fallion woke with a groan, only becoming conscious in slow increments. His eyes fluttered open, but the dust in the air was so thick that he soon had to close them.

Everywhere, the townspeople were screaming for help, and Jaz was shouting, "Fallion, there's something wrong with Talon!"

Lying still for a second, Fallion tried to collect his strength. He felt half-dead. He was so feeble that he could hardly lift a hand. It was as if he had suffered an endless illness, and only now might be on the way to recovery though he felt as he might just as easily die.

"Fallion? Can you hear me?"

"Coming," Fallion managed to say.

Fallion looked toward Jaz, could see his dim outline through a haze of dust as thick as any fog, crouching above Talon. Rocks had risen all around, a jumble of them.

Fallion felt so weak, he didn't know if he could stand, so he summoned all of his strength and tried to crawl toward Talon on his hands and knees, but as he lifted his left hand, he found that a thick vine was latched to the meaty part of his palm.

He tried to pull away, but it hurt too much. Upon closer inspection, he saw that the vine wasn't latched to his palm—it was growing through it. The trunk of the vine, about a quarter inch in diameter, ran cleanly through the meat of his palm and continued out the other side.

He peered at his palm for half an instant, trying to understand.

Two worlds combined, he realized. And upon those worlds, two living things had occupied the same space.

So a vine grew through him. But what was wrong with Talon?

Dread surged through him as he drew his dagger, hacked through the vine, pulled it out as if it were an arrow, and then clasped his hand and tried to staunch a raging flow of blood.

Talon was hurt, Jaz had said. What if she has a bush growing through her, or a tree?

Why did I even bring her? he wondered. He hadn't needed her. She could have stayed home, found some boy to love. But she'd wanted an adventure.

He peered up, but the dust was too thick to make out Talon. His energy was coming a little better now. He climbed to his feet. The gritty dust got in his eyes, and he had to stagger, half-blind, toward Jaz.

By the time that he got there, Rhianna and Farion were circled around, both of them having crawled too, both swearing and uttering curses.

She's dead, Fallion thought. Our little Talon is dead. He'd always thought of her as a sister, a fierce little sister, and he tried to imagine how he would break the news to Myrrima, their foster mother. Their foster father, Borenson, was a warrior, and he would take it stoutly, though it would break his heart. But Myrrima . . . she was too tender to bear such news.

As he got close, he rejoiced to see that she was breathing, her chest rising and falling.

"She's out cold," Jaz was telling the others.

Jaz looked up, moved back for Fallion to get a better view, and Fallion gasped.

Their Talon had changed. At first, he thought that it was only a matter of growth. Talon had always been a diminutive girl, combining her mother's lithe body and her father's strength. But she was diminutive no more.

"What do you think?" Jaz asked. "Seven feet tall? Maybe more?"

That looks about right, Fallion thought. And three across the shoulder. She looked as if she weighed a good three hundred pounds, all of it muscle.

Her face remained much the same, or, at least Fallion could still see Talon's resemblance in it. But it stretched in an odd way. There were two strange humps above her brow, like those on a calf that is about to sprout horns, and her forehead seemed thickened, as if a bony plate had grown there. Her cheekbones were similarly armored. She groaned, opening her mouth as if to curse at some bad dream, revealing canines that had become over-large.

"What happened?" Jaz asked.

Fallion suspected that he knew. Some other creature must have been standing where Talon was, on that shadow world, and the two of them had become one.

❧ 7 ❧

THE HUNTER AWAKES

There was a time when the Knights Eternal were Lady Despair's most fearsome weapon. But as her powers grew, so did the powers of her minions, and the walking shadows, the Death Lords, began to haunt our dreams. With the merging of the two worlds, though, we should have guessed that it was only a matter of time before the Knights Eternal reestablished their dominion.   —*the Wizard Sisel*

Gongs were tolling in Rugassa, their deep tones reverberating among the rocks in the fortress, seeming to come from everywhere and nowhere, thundering up from the center of the earth.

Upon the toll, Vulgnash awoke in the tower crypt, and with a powerful kick threw off the lid of his coffin.

Gripping its sides, he inspected his rotting flesh. His skin had dried, becoming gray and leathery, and his flesh had cracked and wrinkled. Maggots had burrowed trails through his arms.

How long, he wondered, since last I walked the earth? He had hoped to remain dead for eternity this time.

But Lady Despair summoned him, and he rose at her

bidding. He had promised his service to the Great Wyrm, whether it be in life, or in death, and now he had to answer the call.

Besides, he would rather be summoned into the presence of Lady Despair than into that of the Emperor.

From the condition of his hands, he imagined that it had not been long. Three years since last he woke, perhaps five, no more.

Yet Vulgnash felt as if he had been pummeled. Every muscle in his body ached; he had seldom felt so weak.

He climbed from the coffin, and stood for a moment, stretching his red wings wide to get the blood flowing and staring down through a tower window. People rushed everywhere a thousand feet below him, like beetles in a dung hill.

The fortress was in ruins. Walls of black basalt looked as if they had split during an earthquake.

He peered out beyond the city gate, to see if the fortress was under attack, and stared in awe. There was a strange and wondrous change in the land: a forest stood out on the plains before the castle. The plains should have been barren. Last he knew, they were burned twice yearly so that no army could draw near without being seen.

But here was a forest of hoary pine trees that looked to be a thousand years old. And strange birds flew up out of it, like none that he had ever seen before.

How long? he wondered. A thousand years? It can't be. My flesh would have turned to dust, and I would be beyond the power even of Lady Despair to call.

And now the gongs were sounding, announcing that the Great Wyrm demanded his presence.

Vulgnash swore, strode to his closet, and drew on a crimson robe to hide the ruin of his face, then went striding down the stairs, into the great hall.

He felt so weak, he needed sustenance; and so as he entered the great hall, where servants went scurrying about in terror, their eyes wide in fright to see him, he grabbed a small girl of eight or nine.

"Your life is mine," he whispered, then placed five fingers upon her skull—one between her eyes, two upon each of her eyes, and his thumb and pinky finger upon her mandibles.

At this touch, the girl's blood turned to ice water in her veins, and she wet herself.

The girl tried to withdraw in terror, but his fingers held to her flesh as if it were his own. Some of the servants that saw groaned or looked away in horror; one cried out the girl's name in mourning, "Ah, little Wenya!"

With a whispered incantation, the girl's passions—her longing for life, her hopes and ambitions—and the fire in her soul that drove them were drawn away.

The spell went to work, and the girl's flesh, rife with water, began to sag and putrefy, even as Vulgnash's own flesh gained heft and a less unwholesome color.

When he was done, he let the girl fall away, a dry and rotting husk. He felt refreshed, but not refreshed enough. He would need to feed on others before he regained his full strength.

But the gongs were tolling, and he had no time for it.

He grabbed a torch from a sconce, then went striding down to the lower levels. Powerful guards cringed in terror as he passed, for they knew what Vulgnash was.

The black basalt tunnels were cracked and broken, and often the passageway was littered with rubble and boulders. Vulgnash waded through or climbed over as the need took him.

Is this why she summoned me? he wondered. A mere earthquake? But no, he knew that there must be some greater threat to the realm.

In his weakened state, the race left him drained.

The great fortress of Rugassa was built upon the crown of a volcano, and his spiraling journey downward felt like a plummet. All the while, the gongs grew louder, more insistent, until at last he had gone far enough, and the corridor opened into the audience chamber.

Two others had arrived before him and stood at each

side of the chamber like an honor guard, robed all in crimson. Thul and Kryssidia were their names.

She has summoned three of the Knights Eternal, Vulgnash realized, a full quorum. Great need must be upon her.

A platform jutted out above a lake of boiling magma, which heated the room like a blast furnace. Tunnels high up allowed the hot air to escape, while lower vents, one of which sat directly behind the platform, allowed cold air to rush in.

Thus as Vulgnash reached the end of the platform, he found himself at the mouth of the vent, a chill wind whirling all about him, making his blood-red cape flutter like a caged bird. Without the refreshing wind, no mere mortal could have withstood the heat of this place. Even Vulgnash would have succumbed in time. He peered down, hundreds of feet below, into the pool of magma.

"Lady Despair," Vulgnash cried. "I hear your summons, and obey."

The lake of magma below him was red hot. Suddenly it boiled madly and the lake began to rise. Molten stone churned, and the level kept rising, until it seemed that the platform itself would be swallowed by magma.

Then the mouth of the great wyrm appeared, rising from the molten flow.

She was a hundred yards in diameter, and her mouth, which had five hinges, each jaw shaped like a spade, could have swallowed a small fortress.

She rose up, and magma streamed off of her.

Vulgnash dropped to one knee and bowed until the bony plate on his forehead touched the hot floor.

A great rushing voice filled the room. "Speak, Vulgnash. I feel that your mind is clouded by questions."

Vulgnash dared hardly admit it to himself. He was not used to questioning his master. But he could not hide his thoughts from the Great Mother.

"How long?" he asked.

"Four years, since last I summoned you."

"But . . . there is a forest growing outside the gates," Vulgnash objected. He knew that he had to have slept for centuries.

"A great and strange thing has happened," the wyrm said. "The world is changed, made anew by a powerful wizard, named Fallion Orden. He has combined two worlds into one, his and ours. He is our enemy. He must be dealt with."

That any one wizard could have such power seemed unimaginable. "You have but to command me, my master, and I will throw myself into battle no matter how fearsome the foe. But . . . how do we fight such a creature?"

"Have no fear," the Great Mother said. "I brought Fallion here by design. In his world, his power was great. But in this new world . . . he cannot withstand you. He is a flameweaver, talented in some ways, but he is only a child in his understanding. . . ."

Vulgnash smiled, his lips pulling back to reveal his overlarge canines. If there was one thing that he understood, it was the weaving of flames. He had been mastering his skills for millennia.

The Great Mother continued. "Take the three into the woods south of the ruins at Caer Golgeata. You will find a golden tree there. Destroy it, root and limb.

"You will also find humans, small in stature, led by the wizard Fallion. Bring him, and prepare his spirit to receive a wyrm."

Vulgnash knew that powerful enemies sometimes required wyrms of great power to subdue them. Knowing which wyrm was to take him might make a subtle difference as to the type of tortures Vulgnash would use to prepare the victim. "Is there a particular wyrm that I should prepare him for?"

The answer struck Vulgnash with awe.

Lady Despair answered, "I may choose to possess him myself."

TALON

Life is an endless awakening.

 As a child, we awaken to the wonders and horrors of the universe.

 As young adults we awaken to our own growing powers, even as young love enslaves us.

 As adults, we awaken to the worry and responsibility of caring for others.

 Last of all, we awaken to death,
And the light beyond.   —High King Urstone

In the tallest tower of Castle Coorm, Fallion kicked open the door to a small room and stood for a moment, letting his eyes adjust as motes of dust floated in his view.

The room had served as his bedroom as a child, a room for both him and Jaz. But as Jaz said, it had grown smaller over the years.

The room was filled with trash—broken chairs from the king's hall, a broken wheel from a wagon, various tools with broken shafts—all things that had some worth but needed the tender care of a good wood-wright.

Beneath the litter, Jaz's bed still remained, but Fallion's was gone. Gone also were their treasures—the princely daggers that had hung on the wall, the fine curtains that had once hung over the window, the carved and painted animals that Jaz had played with as a child.

Fallion had hoped to find something to remind him of his childhood, but there was nothing. Nor had he found much of worth in Warlord Hale's chamber. It seemed that everything of worth had long ago been destroyed, sold off, or stolen.

He closed the door, then climbed the stairs to the

uppermost tower, where his mother's far-seers had once kept vigil.

There, upon a mossy roof that was growing weak from rot, he peered out across the altered landscape. Rocks rose up in a tumult, twisted and eerie. It was not as if they had just thrust up from the ground, broken and new. Instead, they looked to have been sculpted by wind and rain over millennia. Their forms were graceful, strange, and utterly out of place.

In the past hours, the dust had begun to settle, and though a yellow haze obscured the heavens, in the distance the ruins of ancient cities could be seen in half-a-dozen directions, their stonework marvelous and otherworldly, and their broken towers soaring high.

Yellow moths of a type that Fallion had never seen fluttered everywhere, clouds of them rising above the forest, apparently unnerved at the vast change.

Fallion felt unnerved, too. The sun was too bright, and rested in the wrong place in the sky. The plants seemed to have a strange metallic tang. A great weariness was on him, sapping his strength. He felt on the verge of collapse, and feared that if he slowed down, if he stopped for even a minute, he would just lie down and never regain the strength to rise again.

Rhianna climbed the stairs behind him, came up to him wordlessly, then just stood stroking his back.

"Has Talon stirred?" Fallion asked.

"Not yet," Rhianna answered. Talon was still unconscious, resting in the hovel where Hearthmaster Waggit lived. Fallion had come here to search for richer quarters, but Warlord Hale's room had been a pigsty, full of rotting food and foul odors.

"This is a trap," Fallion said as he peered out above the woods. "This whole place is a trap. We should leave."

"Not without Talon," Rhianna said. "I couldn't leave her, and neither could you. We'll have to wait until she's ready to travel."

She had been unconscious for hours. Fallion worried

that she would die. Certainly, there had been others in the village that had died. One had been crushed under rocks when a wall buckled; others had perished from wounds received in taking the keep. Two elderly men apparently died for no reason at all, except, perhaps, from the shock of the change.

And there were other oddities. Another young man had grown large and distorted, like Talon. He too was unconscious.

Four people had apparently vanished altogether; Fallion suspected that they lay crushed somewhere beneath the rubble. Fallion could hear their sons and daughters even now, down among the castle grounds, calling out their parents' names in vain.

Another young girl had a large gorse bush grow through a lung during the change and would not make it through the night.

Talon might not make it, either, Fallion knew. Whatever she had become, it might not survive.

"You should go down among the people," Rhianna said. "There is talk of throwing a celebration tonight."

"I'm not in the mood to dance or sing," Fallion said. "They shouldn't be, either."

"You saved them," Rhianna said. "They want to honor you."

"I didn't save all of them."

"Perhaps not," Rhianna said, "but I heard a woman talking down there. She said that 'Under Warlord Hale's rule, we were all dead. But good Fallion has brought us back to life.' That seemed reason enough to honor you."

Rhianna took his hand, squeezed it. She wanted to infuse him with the love that she felt, but she knew that it was incomprehensible to him, for the love that she felt was not something that she had learned in her mother's arms. Her love was deeper, and more profound. She had once given an endowment of wit to a sea ape, and had learned to see the world through its eyes. It had been as devoted to its master as a dog would be. It had adored its master. There were no words to describe the depth of its affection. And now, Rhianna felt that way about Fallion. Only long years of practice allowed her to keep from constantly following him with her eyes, or from stroking his cheek, or kissing his lips. She dared not let him know, for she knew that it was a burden for one to have to bear unrequited love.

"If the villagers want to honor me," Fallion said after a moment, "tell them to post a heavy guard. And tell them not to wait until tonight. There may be worse things in those woods than strengi-saats now." He sighed, stood resting with his palms upon the head of a gargoyle for a moment, as if bestowing a blessing, and then when he had regained his strength, said, "I'll go check on Talon."

He stalked down the stairway in a foul mood. As he descended, he found himself in darkness, until he came out upon the green. Three women were tending the tree, tenderly wrapping the scars on its bark in tan linen.

A few hours ago, Fallion remembered hearing them cheer as he freed them from Warlord Hale.

Unbidden, words came to mind, a cruel voice speaking in a hiss. "Though the world may applaud your slaughter, you will come to know that each of your victories is mine." In his mind's eye, he saw his old enemy Asgaroth upon his fine blood mare, a tall man in black, wrapped in shadows. And once again Fallion felt his shirt tear open, felt the words scrawled upon his chest formed from runes of air, like insects marching over his skin.

Fallion bit his lip. A cold certainty was upon him. The crowds had applauded his slaughter not hours ago, when he'd killed Warlord Hale, but the taste of victory was sour.

Fallion gazed at the tree for a long moment. He felt strange in its presence. It made him want to be a better man, and he recalled hearing its voice earlier, its cry for help. But now there was only a deep silence in his thoughts. It was as if the tree were fast asleep.

He hurried down a back street where cobbles had come out of the road, leaving it pitted and muddy. He ducked into Waggit's hovel, saw Waggit puttering about the hearth, looking here and there, as if trying to decide whether it was time to build a dinner fire. Waggit's endowments had aged him. His hair had gone silver, and it was long and unkempt. He still had the height of a warrior, but the muscles in his chest and shoulders had grown thin and wasted.

He looked up from the hearth, "Fallion!" he said in glee. "You've come home!"

So much had changed over the years, Fallion felt surprised that Waggit even recognized him.

Waggit shouted in glee and danced a step. "It's good to see you, boy!" He leapt across the room, gave Fallion a hug, and burst into tears.

"Good to see you, too, old friend," Fallion said, taking the proffered hug. And it was.

Waggit's summer jacket was worn and old. To Fallion he felt too thin in the ribs.

"Where have you been—" Waggit asked, "off fighting reavers?"

It was ground they had covered only hours ago, but Waggit had already forgotten. "Nothing so grand, I'm afraid," Fallion said. "I went sailing to the Ends of the Earth, to Landesfallen."

"Ah!" Waggit said. "I hope they fed you good." It was the best reply he could come up with. He stood with head cocked to one side, as if hoping to be of some help.

"I ate well enough," Fallion said. "Any word of advice today, old friend?"

Waggit peered hard at Fallion with rheumy eyes, his face growing desperate as he tried to recall some tidbit of forgotten lore. His lower lip began to tremble, and he cast his eyes about the room as if searching for something. At last, he merely shrugged, then burst into tears.

Fallion put his arms around the old man. "There now,"

he said. "You've given me enough wise counsel to last me a lifetime."

"I . . . can't remember," Waggit said.

"I'll remember for the both of us," Fallion said. He hugged Waggit once more, wondering at the cruelty of forcibles.

Waggit had not been born a fool, he once told Fallion. But he had slipped into an icy creek as a child, while fetching water for his mother, and had nearly drowned. After that, his ability to remember was stolen, and he ended up working the silver mines.

But when the reavers attacked Carris, he had fought them with his pick, actually killing a few. For his courage and strength, he had been granted a few forcibles, and with a few endowments of wit and stamina, had made himself a scholar, one of the wisest in the land.

Now the folk who had granted the endowments, his Dedicates, were all dead, and with their deaths, Waggit's ability to remember had died too, along with the lore that he'd once mastered.

Did my father do well or ill, granting him endowments? Fallion wondered. *Would Waggit not have been happier to remain a fool than to gain great wisdom and lose it all?*

Fallion fought back his sadness and ducked through a curtain into the cozy room where Talon lay upon a low cot. She had grown too large to fit on it.

Jaz had covered her with a coarse blanket, and now he knelt beside her, his shoulders slumped from weariness, so still that he looked as if drawing a breath was almost too great a chore.

"How is she doing?" Fallion asked. "Any change?"

Jaz shook his head slightly.

"There is a chair here in the corner, if you would like it," Fallion offered.

Jaz shrugged. "I know. I was too tired to get up and sit."

Fallion slumped in the chair.

Jaz did not turn. As he gazed at Talon, his face was lined with grief.

"I thought for sure," he said softly, "that when you healed the worlds, we'd get cloudbursts of beer, and the meadows would sprout dancing girls as pretty as any flower. . . ."

"Sorry to disappoint you," Fallion said.

"What's wrong with us? I feel like a burrow bear that's been pulled out of its hole in mid-winter. I just want to sleep for a few more months."

"Jaz, we have to go away," Fallion said. "We have to get out of here, now."

"What do you mean?" Jaz did not move. He looked as if he was too tired to care.

"That rune, it was a trap. The tree was the bait. Once my mind touched the rune, I knew that I had to mend it or die. But it couldn't be mended, not really. It was meant to do only one thing, to bind two shadow worlds into one. I didn't bind all of the worlds into one. I didn't heal anything. I fear I've made things worse."

Jaz nodded almost imperceptibly, as if he couldn't muster the energy to care.

"Jaz, no human sorcerer made that rune. It was beyond the power of any mortal to form. I know who made it: our father's ancient enemy, the Queen of the Loci."

Now Jaz looked at him, cocking his head just a bit, peering at him from the corner of his eye.

"She's here, Jaz, somewhere. She knows what I've done. She tricked me into doing it."

"Maybe, maybe she was just testing you," Jaz suggested. "Maybe she wanted to see if you really could bind the worlds. If the wizards are right, she was never able to do that. If she'd been able to, she'd have bound all of the worlds together into one, under her control."

"It was a test," Fallion agreed. "But in passing it, I failed us all."

Jaz finally drew a deep breath, as if trying to muster the energy to rise. "Go then, if you must," he said. "I can't leave Talon behind. And we can't let the Queen of the Loci catch you. If she does, we both know what she will try to force you to do—bind the worlds into one, all under her control."

Fallion hesitated. He couldn't bear the thought of leaving Talon, not like this. He wasn't certain what was wrong with her. Perhaps in the melding, her organs had become jumbled up. Perhaps the creature that lay before him had two hearts and only half a lung. He couldn't be certain.

He only knew that in binding the two worlds together, he had not done it perfectly. There had been mistakes, dangerous errors. The vine that had grown through his hand was just one of them, and the stinging pain and the bloody bandage that he now wore were constant reminders.

What if I'd tried binding all of the worlds into one? Fallion wondered. What if those little errors had been multiplied a million million times over?

It would have been a catastrophe. I would have destroyed the world.

Maybe that is why the Locus Queen set this trap—to see what would happen if I succeeded.

There was a pitcher of water on the bed stand. Fallion felt thirsty but too tired to take a drink. Still, he knew that his body would need it.

Talon suddenly groaned in her sleep. "Ishna! Ishna! Bolanda ka!" She thrashed from side to side. Her voice was deep and husky.

"What did she say?" Jaz asked.

Fallion shook his head. It was no language that he had ever heard, and he was familiar with several.

He wondered if it were just aimless babbling, the ranting that came with a fevered dream.

Fallion got up, found a towel on the bed stand, and poured some of the cool water from the pitcher onto the towel.

He knelt beside Talon and dabbed her forehead, held

the rag there with one hand and touched her cheek with the other, checking for a fever.

She was definitely warm.

He had been holding the rag on her head for all of thirty seconds when her eyes sprang open wide, filled with terror, and she backhanded him.

Fallion went flying as if he'd been kicked by a war horse.

In an instant, Talon sprang to her feet, as if to do battle, knocking Jaz aside. "Wyrmlings!" she shouted, her eyes darting about the room, trying to take everything in.

"Talon, it's okay!" Jaz said. "You're all right! You're with friends."

Talon stood, gasping for breath. At seven feet tall, she dwarfed all of those around her, dwarfed the tiny room. Every muscle in her arms and neck seemed strained, and she took a battle stance. In that moment, she seemed a fearsome warrior, more terrifying than any man that Fallion had ever seen. Her eyes darted about, as if she was trapped in some nightmare. Slowly her vision cleared. She recognized Fallion and Jaz, but merely stood in shock, trying to make sense of the situation.

"It's all right," Jaz assured her. "You were only dreaming. You were just dreaming. Do you know where you are?"

Talon peered down at the floor, so far below her, and then peered at her hands, huge and powerful, as if trying to make sense of them. "Am I still dreaming?"

She studied Fallion, who lay on the floor, holding his arm where she had hit him.

Fallion remembered being trampled by a bull and taking far less hurt. He tried moving his arm experimentally. He didn't think that it was broken, but it would be black and blue for weeks.

"No," Jaz said. "The world has changed. Two worlds are combined, and I guess . . . you changed with them. We're not sure what happened. . . ."

Fallion waited for a reaction. He had thought that she would weep for her lost humanity or sit and sulk. Instead, shock and acceptance seemed to come almost at the same moment.

"I see," she said, peering at her hands as if considering the implications of his words. Then with a sigh she said, "Let's go see this new world."

More than anything, this showed Fallion the depth of the change in Talon. Gone was the young woman Fallion had known.

Talon reached down to take Fallion's hand. He proffered his good hand, but when she grasped it, Fallion cried out in pain. "Not so tight!"

She looked at him in disbelief. "Sorry. I, uh, barely touched you."

He felt sure that she was telling the truth. He also felt sure that if she wanted, she could tear his arm off as easily as she could rip the wing off of a roasted chicken.

She pulled Fallion to his feet, then stalked out of the room on unsteady legs, as if trying to become accustomed to her new size.

She strode out into the street, went to the gate tower, and by the time she reached it she leapt up, taking the stairs four at a stride. Then she just stood for a long moment until Fallion caught up.

"Damn," she whispered when he drew near. "You've made a mess of things."

"What do you mean?" Fallion asked. "Are you ill?"

"Fallion," Talon said, "I feel great. I feel . . . better than I've ever felt before." She turned and peered at him. "You've done me no harm. In fact, it is the opposite. I feel more . . . whole, than I ever felt before."

Fallion understood what she meant, partly. It was said that all of the worlds were but shadows of the One True World, and some wizards suspected that a man might have shadows of himself on each of those worlds.

Somehow, Fallion suspected, he had bound Talon to her shadow self.

"Nightfall is coming," she said. "The . . . wyrmlings will come with it. We have to get away, get to safety."

Fallion couldn't imagine any place safer than the castle, even in its poor repair. Nor did he know what a wyrmling was. But this world was in ruins. And the wyrmlings were the cause.

There is a rule to war. The first rule, Fallion had been taught, was to know your enemy.

"What are wyrmlings?" he asked.

"Giants."

"Like you?"

"Larger than me," Talon laughed. "I am human, bred to be one of the warrior clan, large and fierce. My ancestors were bred to be this way, much as you breed dogs of war to increase their size, their viciousness. And though I am larger than a human of feral stock, the wyrmlings are more than a head taller than me, and outweigh me by hundreds of pounds. We are but feeble imitations of the wyrmlings. And we true humans are almost all gone. There are fewer than forty thousand of us left.

"The wyrmlings hunt by night," Talon explained, "for they cannot tolerate light. They eat only meat, and they worship the Lady Despair."

"I see," Fallion said.

"No, not really," Talon answered. "There's more to tell, and it will take hours to do so. But first, we must get away from here."

"Where do we go?"

Talon peered into the distance, closed her eyes in consternation. "I can't remember. . . . It's like a dream. I see the place, but I can't put a name to it."

"Then give yourself a moment to wake," Fallion said.

Talon peered into the distance for a long minute. "Luciare. The fortress is called Luciare."

"Where is it?" Fallion asked.

Talon closed her eyes, concentrated. She could see her mother and father there. Borenson was much the same in both worlds she decided, but Talon's mothers were not the same woman at all. How would that work? she wondered. Where is my father—in Luciare, or back in Landesfallen? And what of my sisters and brothers?

She wanted to find them, make sure that all of them were well, that they had survived this transformation. But the world had shifted, and she was on strange ground.

Talon shook her head. "I'm not sure. Everything's . . . wrong. I'm not sure I've even been here before. She nodded to a distant peak to the south, one with a distinctive hump upon the eastern flank. "That could be Mount Shuneya. That means that Luciare would be west, west by southwest, maybe—a hundred miles, or a hundred and twenty. We can't make it tonight, or even tomorrow. . . ."

They wouldn't be able to make it even in four days, Fallion suspected, not with him in his current condition. But he could hear the urgency in Talon's voice.

He looked up at her and wondered, Why don't I have a body like hers? Why didn't I combine with my shadow self?

Instead he felt frail, worn.

This whole place is a snare, Fallion realized. The one who set it couldn't know for sure when I would come, or even if I would come. But now that the wire has been sprung, the hunter will be upon us. Fallion suspected it, and Talon seemed to feel it in her bones.

"How long before the wyrmlings get here?" Fallion asked.

"They have fortresses nearby, within thirty miles," she said. "And there might be hidden outposts even closer than that. If the local commanders know to watch this place, they'll come tonight. Even if Lady Despair has to send assassins from Rugassa, they could be on our trail by dawn."

So, Fallion thought, a race is on.

"We'll have to keep under the cover of trees, lie low in the woods during the night, and run through the days. . . ."

"How do you know all of this?" Fallion asked. "How can you be sure?"

A look of confusion washed over Talon's face, and she shook her head. "My father, the man you know as Sir Borenson, is . . . Aaath Ulber—High Guard. I . . . we are Warrior Clan."

So Fallion felt even more convinced. Talon hadn't merged with some beast. She had merged with her shadow self, with the woman she had been on this world.

Are all of them so large? Fallion wondered. It would explain the strange ruins, so high and soaring. But no, Talon had been but a girl, and had been diminutive at that. The humans of this world wouldn't all be so large. He suspected that most would be larger.

I've brought us to a land of giants, he realized, giants that have almost been destroyed by the wyrmlings.

A sudden fear took him. Whatever was coming, he didn't think that he could fight it. He'd fallen into a trap. He had been forced to join these two worlds together, and he saw the ruin that had followed.

He could not fix what he had done. He had no idea how to un-bind the two worlds.

And he suspected that his Queen of the Loci was rejoicing in what he had done.

Perhaps the best way to thwart her plan, he considered, is to continue my journey to the Mouth of the World and finish binding all of the shadow worlds all into one.

But he considered the damage he had done, and wondered now at the wisdom of that.

If he bungled this further, he could destroy the world, not heal it.

And there was a second worry. Perhaps that proposed course of action was exactly what the enemy wanted.

Talon turned to Fallion, gave him a calculating gaze. Then her eyes snapped to Jaz who was still feebly making his way across the courtyard below, too weak to keep pace.

Fallion marveled at the change in Talon. She looked vibrant, energized.

"How soon can we be ready to go?" she demanded.

"I'm ready now," Fallion lied, feeling too fragile for a forced march. "But you've been asleep for hours. We thought that you would die. The question is how do you feel?"

She smiled, showing her overlarge canines. "Never better," she said, a tone of wonder creeping into her voice. She peered down at her hand again, clenched it and unclenched, as if realizing it was true. "I feel like I could crush rocks in these hands."

"I think you're right," Fallion said. "You nearly crushed me."

❧ 9 ❧

THE COUNCIL

A king who is weak and ineffective is a kind of traitor, and bringing such a man down can be an act of patriotism.
                                                    —*Warlord Madoc*

Alun struggled up toward Caer Luciare, his mouth agape.

There were trees everywhere, huge firs on the skirts of the mountain, white aspens along its top. They had grown in an instant, appearing as if in a vision, their shimmering forms gaining substance.

He had seen them as he fainted, and when he woke, aching and weary, everything had changed. The sun was still up, marvelously drawn back in the sky, and the hills were full of dust clouds and birds.

Daylan Hammer was nowhere to be seen.

Wanderlust had stayed at Alun's side, and once he got

to his feet, the dog set out on Daylan Hammer's trail again. The dog was able to track him through the thick sod, heading straight for Caer Luciare.

But as Alun neared, he peered in stunned silence at the devastation. The fortress was in ruins. The mountain it had rested upon had dropped hundreds of feet in elevation, and with the drop, the whole structure of the mountain had changed. A stone cliff had broken away, exposing tunnels hidden beneath it like the burrows of wood worms in a rotten log.

Steam from the hot pools beneath the castle hissed out of a dozen rents, and the streams above the castle had been diverted. Waterfalls now emptied down the cliffs from three separate tunnels.

Everywhere, people were rushing to and fro like ants in a broken nest, and Alun staggered up to the castle in a daze, feeling wearier than he'd ever been.

He worried what would happen if the wyrmlings should attack. With the rents in the fortress, they'd have easy access. It might well be indefensible.

He put Wanderlust in the kennel, made sure that the dogs all had food and water, then went looking for Warlord Madoc.

He found him in the battle room, with the High King and his lords, having a shouting match. Daylan Hammer was there, too, and the Wizard Sisel. High King Urstone looked haggard upon his dais, as much shocked by the devastation as Alun. The Warlords standing in the audience hall appeared angry, as if seeking a target for their frustrations.

"I say we strike now, and strike hard!" Madoc roared.

"And leave ourselves defenseless?" the Emir asked. "There are breaches in our defenses. We need men to repair them, strong men like our warriors, and we need time." The Emir was a tall man for one of his kind. He was shorter than Madoc, and much narrower of shoulder. But he held himself like a king, and thus seemed to cast a long shadow.

"And if the wyrmlings have such breaches in their defenses," Warlord Barrest asked, "would it not be the chance of a lifetime? We might break into their prison with ease, and release the prince, and send out assassins against Zul-torac."

"What weapon would you use to pierce his shadow?" the Emir asked. "Can it even be slain?"

"It can," Madoc said, "with cold iron and sunlight."

"That is but a presumption," King Urstone said. "No one has ever killed a Death Lord."

The Wizard Sisel said, "I think it is more than a presumption, it is a calculated chance. Sunlight would loosen the monstrous spells that bind his spirit to this world. It should weaken him to the point that he could be slain."

King Urstone was a bit taller than Warlord Madoc, but narrower at the shoulder. He wore no badge of office. Instead, he wore a shirt of plain chain mail, covered by a brown cape, as if he were but another soldier in the castle. His face was wise and lined with wrinkles, and his beard, which was light brown going gray, made him look wiser still. He said reasonably "Attacking Zul-torac is foolhardy. You can't reach him. He never leaves the warrens beneath Mount Rugassa. He hides among the shadows with the other Death Lords. You'll never expose him to light. And if you were to attack, his reprisals would tear our realm apart. Let there be no talk of antagonizing Zul-torac. It is only because we hold his daughter hostage that we have enjoyed what little peace we could find these last few years. So long as Zul-torac lives, we can hope to live."

The Emir had always been wise in counsel. Now he bent his head in thought. "Even if we tried to strike at the north, we might well find that this devastation—this spell—is but a local affair. It may have no effect upon Rugassa."

He looked to the Wizard Sisel. "What think you, wizard? Is it a local affair?"

The Wizard Sisel leaned upon his staff and bent his head in thought. His face was burned by sun and wind, with cheeks the color of a ripe apple. His hands and fingernails were dirty from his garden, and his robes looked bedraggled. But he carried himself with dignity despite his ragged attire.

He was a powerful wizard, and it was his wards and enchantments that had long helped protect Caer Luciare. All ears bent as he voiced his opinion.

"It is no local affair," the wizard said. Of them all, only his voice sounded calm and reasonable. "We saw a world fall from the sky, and now the whole world has changed. Grave changes have occurred. I feel it. The earth groans in pain. I can feel it in the soil, and hear it among the rocks. What the cause is, I do not yet know. But this I can say: it is time to prepare for war, not go to war. Did a wyrmling cast this spell—perhaps even Zul-torac himself? If so, he may have known the destruction it would bring. Leaving the castle now, leaving it undefended, would mean that we are playing into the enemy's hands. And even if it was not a wyrmling who caused this destruction, this spell will rile them. Casting it is like beating a hornets' nest with a stick. My feeling is that the wyrmlings will strike at us, no matter what."

"Then it is even more imperative that we take Cantular now," Madoc said. "By taking the bridge and holding it, we can forestall any attempt at a more serious attack."

"Your argument is persuasive," King Urstone said. "Almost, I would ride to war now. If Sisel is right, the wyrmlings will soon be on their way, and my son's life is forfeit, for I cannot put my love for him above the needs of my people—

"However," King Urstone continued, "I would have the counsel of Daylan Hammer on this, for he has wisdom gained over countless ages. This spell that is upon us, Daylan—this new world that fell from the heavens—have you heard of the like?" Urstone was an aging man, much worn by his office, and looked as drained as Alun felt. But he was of the warrior caste, and he was a powerful man. Indeed, Alun had never seen the king show a hint of weariness, until now.

Daylan Hammer strode to the center of the audience hall and pulled himself to his full height. Among the warriors, he was a small man, for none of them were less than a foot taller.

"There has never been the like," Daylan said, "in all of the lore that I know. But upon the netherworld there has been the hope that such a thing would be."

"A hope?" King Urstone asked in dismay.

"There has been the hope that someone would someday gain the power to bind worlds together.

"Long ago, there was but one world, and one moon, and all men lived in perfect contentment, in perfect peace. There was no death or pain, no deformity, no poverty or war or vice.

"But one went out from among our forefathers who sought power. She sought to wrest control of the world from the others. The control of the world was bound into a great rune, the Seal of Creation. She sought to twist it, to bind it to her, so that she would become the lord of the earth.

"But in the process of twisting it, the Seal of Creation was broken, and the One World shattered into many, into thousands and tens of thousands and into millions—each a world orbiting its own sun, each a flawed replica of that One True World.

"The world that you live upon," Daylan said, "is but a flawed shadow of that world, like a piece of broken crystal that can only hint at what it once was."

Daylan Hammer paused, and High King Urstone demanded. "Why have I never heard this lore?"

"It has been lost here upon your world," Daylan said. "But it is remembered elsewhere, on other worlds.

"There has been a hope, a prophecy, that one among

us would gain the power to bind the shadow worlds into one. If so, then I know who has done this. It may be that he has gained that power at last—"

"Or?" King Urstone demanded.

"Or it may be that the enemy has gained such control. Long has she endeavored, hoping to learn how to bind worlds into one. But that skill has eluded her."

"This is madness," Warlord Heddick cried. "What proof do we have that any of this is true?"

"If it is proof that you want," Daylan said, "look inside yourselves. Some of you must feel the change. In the past two hours alone I have heard a dozen people talking of strange dreams, of other lives that they remember. If I am right, many of you have combined with your other self, a shadow self. And our captains tell us that thousands of our people have just vanished. I suspect that they are scattered across the earth, having also combined with their shadow selves. Those 'dreams' that you are having are not dreams, they are memories. They are the proof that you seek, and if you question those who have them, you will find that their stories, their memories, corroborate one another. Do any of you have them?"

Several warlords looked dumbfounded. Of them all, Warlord Madoc seemed most affected by Daylan's words. His face went pale with shock, and he stood, trembling.

The Wizard Sisel bent his head in profound thought and muttered, "This matter . . . demands attention."

It was at this moment that Warlord Madoc happened to glance toward the doorway and saw Alun standing there. He smiled secretively, nodded toward Daylan.

Immediately the blood drained from Alun's face and his heart pounded. He feared that he would be called upon to betray Daylan Hammer, to speak against him here in public, and he was almost as afraid of speaking before the king as he was of dying. He swallowed hard, looked around.

Daylan had asked Alun to lie in his behalf. Daylan

claimed that his own plans were superior to those of Warlord Madoc.

But were they?

Did Alun dare let the immortal steal off with the Princess Kan-hazur? Did they dare throw aside their shield now, when the castle had burst apart at every seam?

"What do you advise?" King Urstone asked Daylan Hammer.

"I think," Daylan said, "that the Wizard Sisel speaks wisely. I think that you should look to your defenses, mend the walls of your fortress. It has served you well for many years, and you will need all of your strength to hold it now."

The king nodded his head in thought, and Alun knew that he was persuaded to keep his troops home. It was the safest course, and to provoke the wyrmlings would be to condemn his son to death. Even after these many years, the king was loath to do so.

"Wait!" Warlord Madoc said, stamping his foot to gain attention. "Your Highness, before we give heed to the counsel of Daylan Hammer, there is something that you should know. Thrice in the past six weeks, he has left the hunt and gone off on his own. Four weeks past, I sent Sir Croft to follow him, and Sir Croft was found dead. Today, I sent young Alun here."

He turned abruptly. "So, what did you learn?" Warlord Madoc demanded.

Alun caught his breath. If he told the truth, the warlords would test to see if Daylan Hammer truly was immortal.

If he lied, it could mean death for everyone else.

And then there was the matter of his reward . . .

"Daylan Hammer went to the Tower of the Fair Ones. There . . . he met with a wyrmling—" Alun said.

There were howls of outrage from the lords, "Traitor! Death to him!" Instantly the room flew into a commotion.

There was no time for questioning Daylan Hammer.

He reached for his saber in a blinding flash, even as he tried to dodge toward the door. The angry lords took this as a sign of guilt.

Among commoners, he would have escaped easily.

But he was among warriors, men bred for battle for five thousand years. War clubs were thrown, and he dodged one, took another in the back. It sent Daylan sprawling, and he flashed his saber and neatly sliced the hamstring of Warlord Cowan. Madoc's son Connor took that moment to lash out with a vicious kick to the head that knocked Daylan Hammer halfway across the room, right into the arms of Madoc himself, who grabbed the immortal and pinned him to the floor with his bulk.

There were shouts of "Hold him!" "Grab him!" "Ow, damn!" "Throw him in the oubliette; maybe a swim in the piss will settle him down!"

Soon, half a dozen of the younger warlords each had a piece of Daylan—an arm here, a leg there—and though Daylan thrashed and kicked at them, they went lugging him past Alun, taking him to the oubliette.

Alun saw Daylan's face red with rage and exertion as he passed.

"Alun?" Daylan said in dismay, astonished that the lad had betrayed him.

And then the young warlords were gone, dragging their prisoner to the oubliette.

The king hunched upon his dais, looking old and bewildered, while the warlords waited upon his word.

Alun found himself staggering forward. He wanted to explain what Daylan had done, his reasoning, for he was sure that that would earn Daylan some leniency.

But the very notion that Daylan was conspiring with the wyrmlings proved his treachery as far as the warlords were concerned.

"Uh," Alun began to say, but a huge hand slapped him on a shoulder, startling him. It was Drewish, leering down at him threateningly.

"Well done," Drewish whispered. "You will dine at

our family's table tonight. And tomorrow, you will come with us into battle, as one of the warrior clan."

At the promise of reward, Alun fell silent.

The old king nodded at his men, his face filled with endless sadness.

"Madoc is right. There may never be a better time to attack," the king said. "For long I've hoped to win my son's freedom, and I've listened to Daylan's counsel. But I can hesitate no longer. The good of my people must outweigh my own selfish desires. Prepare for battle."

❧ 10 ❧

A MAN OUT OF FAVOR

Peace can be found in any clime, and any circumstance. He who has learned how to face death and dishonor without fear cannot have his peace taken from him.
                                    —*Daylan Hammer*

Daylan Hammer struggled against his captors as they bore him to the dungeons. He thrashed and kicked, but even with four endowments of brawn, he couldn't match the combined strength of the warrior clan. These men had been bred to battle over too many generations and were too large. In fighting them, he only risked breaking his bones.

So he battled them, but at a measured pace. He didn't want them to guess his true strength.

They dragged him to the dungeons.

There were fine cells at the top, places where nobles had been held captive in ages past. Now, only a few scraggly paupers filled the cells. Justice in Caer Luciare didn't lend itself to long prison stays. A few lashes with a whip for disturbing the peace, a lopped-off hand for stealing, a day in the stocks for questioning a lord's character—those were the kinds of punishment that were dealt out. The prison was used mainly to hold criminals for a few hours before sentencing.

So Daylan hoped for a nobleman's cell. But they bore him below, past the torture chamber where tongs and forges and bloodied knives gave mute testimony to past retributions.

The Princess Kan-hazur was in a cell near the door. He saw her sitting, dressed in gray rags, her pale hair a ragged mat. She was larger than most of the warriors, topping eight feet, and though she was but eighteen, her long, powerful arms looked as if they could snap a man in half.

She growled as the warriors passed, and lunged, grabbing one by the collar and ramming his head into the bars.

Daylan kicked hard then, using the diversion to nearly break free.

But years of confinement had left the princess weak, and within a moment the warrior had her by the hair, twisting her head around until he could get her in a stranglehold.

The warriors carried Daylan past her cell, to a small grate, and Daylan fought fiercely at that point, managing to kick one warrior in the face and loosen a few teeth, just before they shoved him into a foul hole.

He slid down a rough incline perhaps forty feet, before he landed in a pool of feces and urine that was chest-deep.

There was little light in this place. He peered up above, perhaps a hundred feet. Light shone through a few privies. He was below the soldiers' barracks.

The walls were slick with excrement, the slope far too steep for a man to climb.

The dark waters were hot and smelled of sulfur. Obviously, they had trickled in through some crack in the rock from the hot springs that were used to warm the city in the winter. The water was too hot for comfort.

There was a jangle of keys up above as his captors locked the iron grate. Someone laughed and shouted down at him, "Dinner!"

A loaf of bread came bouncing down the slimy slope, to land with a wet plop. Daylan picked it up. It had been old and crusty.

For a long moment he stood, assessing the situation.

The smell was atrocious, but he knew that you could get used to any smell. He had been in some dire places in his life, but nowhere as foul as this.

There was nowhere to sit, nowhere to rest. The cesspool left him only a small space to stand in, perhaps only ten feet across. And he imagined that when he got tired enough, he could try to float.

But the excrement in the cesspool had the consistency of quicksand. A layer of water and urine covered the top, perhaps to a depth of four inches, and all beneath that was a sordid stew.

To try to rest would be to drown.

Of course, that was what he was here for. That was his torment. He could stand in the muck while soldiers rained their urine down on him, or dropped a foul hail upon him, waiting for days without food or drink, until the High King decided that it was time to fish him out, bring him to his trial, and, hopefully, condemn him to a speedy death.

Or he could choose to rest, and thus to drown.

He tried wading a bit, and found objects that were sharp and hard rolled and shifted beneath his feet—the bones of those who had chosen to drown.

After a few minutes, the sound of the captor's harsh laughter died away, and he was left to himself.

I am supposed to deliver the princess to the rendezvous point tomorrow, he realized.

That will take some doing, he thought, emitting a bark of painful laughter.

So much had changed in just a few hours. He wondered if the wyrmlings could keep to the bargain now, even if he did manage to deliver her.

He thrashed about, trying to find a comfortable place to stand.

Perhaps if I can climb up to the grate, he thought, I could squeeze through the bars.

But the climb looked impossible. Without a rope it was hopeless.

Even endowments of brawn and grace would not let him negotiate that slick slope.

I'll have to dig my fingernails into the rock, he thought, to get any purchase. Maybe then, I could climb out.

But even to try would attract attention. Once news of a captive broke out in the barracks, many a curious eye would be aimed down the privy holes.

That is, until tomorrow, Daylan realized.

The troops were to leave at dawn.

As if to confirm his worries, someone called out from above, "Look, there's a rat in the pisser."

"Well then, you know what to do," a gruff voice laughed.

A steady yellow rain began to fall.

"You men sat at my table," Daylan shouted up. "Which of my songs or jokes offended you so?"

There was no answer from above.

With no other recourse, Daylan Hammer merely folded his arms, closed his eyes, and tried to remember fairer days.

UPON A BED OF STARS

Not even a village idiot will honor a lord of poor character, and any man who builds a noble character—whether he be low-born or high—will find himself honored by all. —Hearthmaster Waggit

It was with a heavy heart that Fallion left Castle Coorm. There were over a hundred and eighty people left in the castle, mostly impoverished families with grubby children, too little food, and no way to protect themselves.

If Talon was right, they would be in grave danger so long as they stayed in Coorm.

"Leave here," Fallion warned them. "Stay in the caves beneath the castle tonight. There are boats that can take you out through the underground river in the morning, so that the little ones will not have to walk so far. They'll carry your food, too. Whatever you do, don't show your faces above ground tonight. Stay hidden till morning, then make your way north to Ravenspell, or east to the Courts of Tide. There should be people there, greater safety. Travel only by day, and hide yourselves at night."

He looked at a young boy, no more than three, terrified and vulnerable. His right cheek was bruised, and his eye swollen shut.

Fallion patted his head, whispered some words of encouragement.

In a more perfect world, he thought, children would never know such fear.

He wished that he could do more for them. He was tempted to stay behind, lead them to safety himself, but Talon had objected. "If we're right, you're the one that the enemy is searching for. Staying with the refugees would only slow you down—and place them in greater danger."

So Fallion left amid sad farewells, hugging Hearth-master Waggit and Farion, departing the castle an hour before sunset, taking only his three friends and some food. At the castle gate, Fallion and the others raised their swords in salute, crying out, "Sworn to defend."

The people cheered, not realizing that the salute carried sad memories for the four. For it was on just such a journey from this castle that they had first sworn their oaths to one another.

Fallion took one last longing look at the golden tree, tried to let its form become etched in his memory. For a long moment, he listened, hoping to hear its voice in his mind once again. But there was nothing.

Regretfully, he struck out through the meadows, heading toward the mountains to the west. The air was full of the smell of pines, clean and refreshing, and the warm sun beat down on the fields.

With every step, Fallion found himself threshing wheat and oats, knocking the full kernels from the stalks. Grasshoppers and honeybees rose up in small clouds as they passed.

Soon his party reached the coolness beneath the woods. Sunshine slanted through the trees, casting shadows, while light played upon motes of dust and pollen in the air.

The woods filled with the chatter of jays, the thumping of woodpeckers, the peeps of nuthatches and occasional coo of a mourning dove.

It would have been a perfect walk, if Fallion hadn't felt so drained. The weariness lingered with him, left him so sapped that he could hardly walk, much less keep up with Talon's grueling pace. Still, she urged him on.

Jaz often complained, for he was as weary as any, but Rhianna merely kept silent, following at Fallion's back like a shadow, sometimes whispering encouragement.

The old road to Hay was a road no longer. In this new

world, it was filled with rocks and scree, gouged by canyons and blocked by hills. Sometimes along the path, Fallion saw further evidence of the damage done by his spell—trees growing up insanely through boulders, a nuthatch impaled by a tuft of grass, speared through by a dozen small blades, struggling vainly to break free.

And he wondered at the damage done to himself. Why am I so weary? He found sweat rolling off of him, a steady sheen, even though the day was cool.

But not all of the "accidents" were bad. As they walked along near sundown, they came upon a vine growing in the shadows of some rocks. It looked like some kind of pea, with a few brilliant white blossoms and it had berries on it—perfectly white berries, like wild pearls, that glowed brightly among the shadows.

Rhianna stopped and peered at them in wonder. "What are these called?" she asked Talon.

Talon merely shrugged. "I don't know," she said. "I've never seen them before, never heard of them—not in either world."

Fallion could only imagine that two plants had combined, creating something that was better than on either world. Whether the light-berries, as he decided to call them, had ever existed on the One True World, he did not know, but he liked to think that they had.

Rhianna picked a dozen berries, carried them in her palm for a ways.

It wasn't until they stopped that night in a rocky grotto, shielded on three sides by rocks and from above by a huge pine tree, that Fallion came up with a theory for his fatigue.

They plunged into the blackness of the grotto, a place that would be decidedly easy to defend from strengisaats. Jaz threw down his pack, dropped onto a bed of pine needles, and said dramatically, "I'm dead."

Fallion brushed some twigs off of a mossy bed. A firefly flew up out of a nearby bush, then others began to shine, turning into lights that danced and weaved among the trees.

Rhianna laid her light-berries down, but Fallion saw that they were fading.

That's when the realization struck. "Of course you're dead," Fallion told Jaz. "And so am I, and Rhianna."

Rhianna halted, peered at him in the shadows, as did Talon. "All three of us are dead—at least we were on this world."

"What do you mean?" Talon asked, standing above him like a hulk.

"Talon, you said that humans were almost gone from this shadow world. How many are left?" Fallion asked.

"Thirty-eight thousand."

"Yet on our world, there were millions," Fallion said. "Talon I've been wondering why *you* joined with your shadow self, but we didn't. Now I understand. We have no shadow selves here."

The others peered at him, and Fallion talked in a rush, thinking aloud. "We were hunted as children, Jaz and I, from before our birth. Rhianna was, too. On this world, our other selves failed to survive. That's why we feel so . . . dead."

There was a long silence. "You're scaring me," Rhianna said. She sat down on unsteady legs, nearly collapsing from exhaustion.

"If we died on this world, wouldn't we remember at least some of our lives?" Jaz asked. "Shouldn't we remember being children?"

"Does dust remember?" Talon asked.

There was a drawn-out silence as Fallion considered the implications. He wondered if he even had a history on this world. Had he died, or had it been one of his ancestors? Perhaps he'd never been born here.

"Fallion," Rhianna asked with rising concern. "You came on this quest because you want to heal the world, bind the shadow worlds into one perfect world. But have you considered the possibility that in that world, perhaps none of us would exist?"

"We feel half-dead now," Jaz said. "Would we die if all the worlds were bound?"

Fallion had no idea.

If I bind the worlds, heal them, Fallion wondered, is it possible that I would be doing it for others, and not for myself?

And what about those unfortunate souls like me? Would I doom them to oblivion? Or would we all live, filling a single world to the breaking point?

He had no answers. But suddenly he realized that he had to stop his quest to mend the worlds. For years now he had felt driven. But now he needed some answers before he could proceed.

"Talon," he asked. "In the city of Luciare, is there an Earth Warden, a wizard that we can talk to?"

Talon thought for a moment, then nodded. "Sisel is his name. Our warriors are strong, but I think that it is by his powers more than any other that the city has been preserved."

"Then I must talk to him when we reach the city," Fallion said.

The party laid down then, Rhianna cuddling up at Fallion's side. Talon took the first watch. Everyone seemed to be lost in their own private thoughts for a long time, and soon Fallion heard Jaz begin to snore while Rhianna fell into a fitful sleep.

Fallion laid abed that night, under the gloom of the trees, the brief flashing of fireflies nearly the only source of light.

A few stars shone between the branches of the trees. His mother had taught him that stars were only distant suns, and that worlds like his drifted around them. He wondered what the worlds that circled these suns were like, and he wondered if somewhere up there one of his shadow selves might be looking down upon his own world.

Fallion kept an eye on Talon, who merely rested with her back to the rock. There was little chance of them being discovered by wyrmlings, but Fallion had to worry about strengi-saats, and perhaps beasts that he'd never even imagined.

"Tell me stories," Fallion asked Talon when the others were all asleep, "about your life in the castle, about your father." He wanted to keep her awake as much as he wanted to hear stories.

"I . . . don't remember much," Talon said softly. "It's all like a dream, one that you've forgotten and then struggle to recall in the morning. I remember things, but they're so . . . disjointed."

"Then tell me what you remember the best."

And she did.

On this world, Borenson had married a woman, but not Myrrima. She was a woman of the warrior clans, a fit mate, and Borenson had dutifully sired seven children upon her.

Talon had been raised in a crèche with the other warrior children, trained to fight. She had been taught her duties as a warrior, and saw breeding as one of those duties. Her father's rank was so high that she was greatly desired by other men, but few were considered suitable mates. Her father had been consulting the genealogies, trying to decide which man would win her as the prize.

Hers had been a grim life, and narrow, Fallion thought. There were no happy childhood memories, unless one counted a score of victories in mock combat—or the slaughter of her first wyrmling at the age of fourteen—as happy memories.

The news saddened Fallion. He had hoped that life on other shadow worlds might be happier than life on his own. At the worst, he thought it would be a distorted reflection, but a reflection nonetheless.

He had to look hard to see any similarities between the worlds. The land wasn't the same. The low hills of Coorm were mountains here, and much else had changed.

The warrior clans of Shadow, as he decided to call the other world, hardly looked human.

But the more he considered, the more that he saw that the worlds were alike. There were pine trees and bears on both of the worlds, harts and hares.

He asked about reavers in the underworld, and Talon assured him that they existed. "But the wyrmlings went to war with them a century ago. They don't pose a threat. Not like they did on our world."

Perhaps, Fallion thought, but he could not be sure.

"And yet . . ." Fallion mused. "In both worlds, the plight of mankind is great. My father used his Earth Powers to save millions. If not for him, our world would have been destroyed, as this one has been destroyed."

Fallion fell silent for a long time.

"So the worlds really are reflections of each other," Talon mused.

"No," Fallion said. "I think that they are not reflections so much as distortions, distortions of the One True World. I think a great war is going on there, and few are left among mankind."

The thought had never occurred to him before, but it felt right. It was said that the Queen of the Loci had tried to seize control of the Great Seals in ages past, and during a battle she had rent them, breaking them.

Fallion had always imagined that the story ended there. But the battle for control still goes on, he thought, upon countless shadow worlds.

Rhianna called out softly in her sleep, "Fallion?"

He glanced back at her, lying beneath the shadows of the pine. She rolled over in her sleep, using her arms as a pillow.

"Fallion," Talon whispered, "what happened to all of the people on our world? Are they all still alive? Did you bring them all with us?"

Fallion had been worrying about this very thought through much of the evening.

"I believe so," Fallion said. "Jaz, Rhianna, and I are all

half-alive. The folk in Coorm too, though some of the older ones, it seems, could not endure the shock."

"You don't sound certain."

"The problem is," Fallion said, "in both worlds, this area was a wilderness. There might be millions of people living in Indhopal, but that is a thousand miles away, and until I see them, I can't be sure."

"I'll bet they're a little confused!" Talon smiled, showing her oversized canines. "Millions of humans on this world again—that will be good news to the folk of Luciare. Father will dance when he learns of it."

"But will they be worth much, fighting your giants?" Fallion wondered. He knew that they wouldn't, not if they had only their own strength. "Are forcibles used among the clans?"

Talon shook her head. "Such magic has not been heard of. The three hundred forcibles we brought with us will be a great prize for the clans."

Fallion started to speak, but Talon reached over and threw a hand over his mouth.

"Shhhh . . ." she whispered, "Wyrmlings."

Jaz seemed to be snoring loudly in the sudden silence. A few crickets filled the night with song. Fallion listened for the tell-tale pad of running feet through the forest, the crack of twigs.

But what he heard was a flapping, like the leathery wings of a graak.

Talon looked up. Fallion could see patches of night sky through the tree branches, the burning fires of distant stars. He could hear flapping nearby, and another pair of wings just downhill.

He dared not speak. Jaz kept snoring, and Fallion leaned down and covered his mouth lightly.

The flapping was not close—perhaps two hundred feet in the air and another three hundred feet to the south. The creature would never be able to hear over the sound of its wing noise.

Fallion craned his head, trying to get a look at it, but rocks and the tree barred it from his sight.

"You didn't tell me they had wings," Fallion whispered when the creature had flown on.

"They don't," Talon said. "Not all of them—only the highest in rank, the Seccath. The wings are very rare and magical. Those wyrmlings are hunting for us, I suspect."

Fallion wished that he had seen them. He wanted to know how the wings worked, but Talon could not tell him.

Talon went to bed a while later, and Fallion stayed up long enough to make sure that she fell asleep, and then woke Rhianna for her turn at guard duty.

He briefly told her of the wyrmlings, and asked her to listen for the sound of wings.

He lay down. He was so tired, he was half afraid that if he fell asleep, he might never wake.

But all of the worries of this day kept him awake. He worried for Waggit, for Farion, for some nameless boy with a swollen face. He wondered how many had died this day and how many more might suffer because of his mistake.

In a more perfect world, I would be a better man, he told himself.

As he lay there filled with such gloomy thoughts, Rhianna lay down beside him, stroked his face once, and then kissed him passionately.

She leaned back afterward and peered into his eyes.

There, she thought. Now I've shown him.

The last time she had kissed him thus was when his mother died. To Rhianna's knowledge, he hadn't been kissed by another girl since, save once, when a young lady of the Gwardeen had shown her affection.

He stared up at her in wonder. The light-berries lay upon the moss around him, and it seemed to Rhianna that he was lying in a field of stars.

He had never hinted that he might love her. But I am

born of the royal houses in both Crowthen and Fleeds, she told herself, and I am as worthy of his love as any.

"I know what you're thinking," Rhianna whispered.

She straddled him, as if to hold him, then leaned down and kissed him again.

For two years she had hidden her desires. She could hide them no more.

Fallion stroked her cheek, and she could see the want in his eyes. But tenderly, he pushed her back.

"What is this?" he asked. "I know how you feel. I've seen your love growing in the way that you look at me, at the way you linger in my presence. You are one of the most beautiful women that I know. But you and I are too much like brother and sister."

She loved him. Fallion knew it. But he had always kept himself aloof. He had done so in part because he knew that someday he might have to marry another in order to seal a political alliance.

But Fallion had remained aloof for a more important reason: he knew in his heart that he did not love her in the way that she loved him.

She smiled secretively. "I know that you want me." He did not deny it. "And every day, I want you more."

Fallion knew that Rhianna's mother was from Fleeds, a land where women ruled, and where they chose their mates much as they chose their stallions. In hindsight he should have known that she would try to claim him in this way. "So why do you choose to profess your love today?"

"It's just," she said hesitantly, "today, more than any other, I wanted you to know that you are loved."

"I see," Fallion said, a forlorn chuckle rising from his throat.

"You saved my life," she said. "And you saved my soul. And you'll save this world, too. The time will come when the people of this world will thank you."

He felt grateful for the gesture, even if it had caught him by surprise.

He rolled his hips, dislodging her, and threw her down into the pine needles. Then he leaned over her, and returned her kiss gently.

He looked into her eyes for a long moment, until she asked in hope and wonder, "What is this?"

"It's a token of my gratitude."

❧ 12 ❧

STRANGERS IN ONE ANOTHER'S ARMS

Even the greatest of heroes and men
Are less than what they might have been.
                              —a saying of Mystarria

Warlord Madoc lay in bed that night, unable to sleep. The great changes that had taken place worried him—the breaks in the castle wall, the rise of forests where only stones and thistles should have been.

There was a new power in the world for him to contend with—a power greater than his sword, a power even greater, perhaps, than the wyrmlings.

That power had devastated him. Like so many others in the city, he had been struck down when the worlds collided. That did not bother him much. He had been knocked unconscious before.

What bothered him was the waking dreams.

In his dream, he had been a farmer, a free man with but one cow to give milk and a brood of thirteen children to drink it all. In his dream, he worked from sunrise to sunset every day, just to feed his family. In his dream, he loved his wife more fiercely than he knew a man could love, and even though there were no wyrmlings in the world, he still fretted about the future, for a hail storm in the spring could ruin a crop or grasshoppers in the summer might eat him out, and that might be as disastrous as any wyrmling, and if his cow dried up because the howling of some distant wolf frightened her, it would be as bad as a famine.

No one of import knew his name in this dream. No king feared him; no warriors vied for the honor of eating at his table. He had no rank or title. He had no future.

And yet, most disturbing of all, in the dream he was a happy, happy man.

Upon awaking, Madoc had thought it only a strange dream, vivid and disturbing. He recalled so many details—the way that the lilac bush outside his house perfumed the night air, the games of horse he played with his children, the profound joy that he took each night, sometimes three times a night, in making love to his wife, Deralynne.

Could that all have been real?

His wife lay beside him, and he could tell that she, too, was troubled. He had told her of the war council, of Daylan Hammer's words.

More troubling still, the woman he slept beside was not the wife he'd loved on that shadow world. She was a warrior woman with bones as big as an ox and an unkind temperament. She had borne him sons, but took no pleasure in the making of them.

At last she reached out and squeezed his hand, as if to comfort him. It was an odd gesture, one that she had never performed before.

"I dreamed," she said, "that I was a cobbler's wife, and that I was childless. We . . . were wealthy, I suppose. We had everything that we could want, except for the one thing that I wanted most—a daughter. And then the raiders came, the damned warlords of Internook, and they plundered our house, took all that they wanted, and burned the rest."

Madoc considered this. He wondered if she might go searching for the cobbler of her dreams. He wondered if he should go searching for Deralynne. His home with Deralynne had been in a peaceful land called Toom, where stories of raids and looting in faraway places were just that . . . stories.

Were the loves that they had forged in another life any less meaningful than the ones that they had forged here?

At last, he asked the question that burned in him.

"If you could have that life, would you?" Madoc asked.

"I would kill anyone, risk anything, not to," she said. She turned to him then, the moonlight shining through the window just barely revealing the curve of her face, the glint of an eye.

"We are a wealthy family," she said, "held in esteem. You could be High King someday. You *should* be High King. What has Urstone done for this people? For years his son has languished in prison while the wyrmlings consolidate their hold. To do nothing in a time of war, that is treason. Urstone should be . . . replaced."

Madoc had never considered murdering the king before. It was a repugnant idea.

Yet he knew that she was right. The kingdom needed a strong leader now more than ever, and Urstone had become too enfeebled over the years.

To kill him would be to serve the people.

13

THE WAYFINDER

Death is the perfect huntress, and she will find us all.
Lady Despair, make me worthy prey this night, swift
and elusive.   —*a prayer for wyrmling children*

Less than an hour before dawn, just as the first birds
began to peep querulously at the coming light, the
Knights Eternal found the human fortress south of Caer
Golgeata, as Lady Despair had promised.

They circled the small castle twice from above, studying its curious workmanship, then dived into the courtyard. As Vulgnash landed, his wings folded neatly
around him like a bloody robe.

Vulgnash studied the tree in the courtyard while his
companions began the hunt. The undersides of its leaves
gleamed softly in the starlight, creating a numinous
glow. The sound of its leaves whispering in the night
breeze soothed his jangled nerves, aroused feelings of
hope and longings for decency that had long since abandoned him.

As Thul hunched with his cowl around his face and
crept from door to door sensing for living things, Kryssidia merely crouched upon a wall, watching for guards.

"They're hiding," Thul hissed at last, his voice as dry
as a crypt. "But they are here."

"Of course they are here," Vulgnash said. There was
tall grass and vines outside the castle gate, and only a few
pairs of feet had trampled them. If the inhabitants of the
castle had fled, they'd have left a larger trail.

With any luck, the wizard Fallion Orden would still be
here.

Vulgnash leapt up a stone wall, strode to the tree. He

caressed its golden bark, found it soothing and pleasant to the touch. It had an exotic scent to it, like cumin, only sweeter.

With his finger he drew a rune upon the tree, then stepped back a few paces and uttered a single curse word.

The bark squealed and shattered, as if lightning took the tree, and suddenly it was blasted with rot. Fungi the color of butter and snow covered it like a scab, and burst up from beneath the rents in the bark. Leaves shriveled and turned the gray of dirty rags.

Vulgnash stood back as the heavy scent of decay filled the courtyard.

In death most of all, Vulgnash thought, the tree was beautiful.

There was a hiss from across the courtyard, at the mouth of the keep. "Here," Thul whispered.

Kryssidia swooped down from the wall on crimson wings, like a giant bloodied crow, while Vulgnash strode to the door in question.

Thul pushed upon it, and the heavy door swung inward.

Interesting, Vulgnash thought. I had imagined that they would bar it. But of course, by doing so, they would have signaled where they were hid.

Thul stood by the open door, and his long dark tongue flickered like a snake's. Vulgnash tasted the air, too. His senses were acutely attuned to the smell of death, and every creature, no matter how much alive, also had a taste of death to it—an odor of decaying skin, putrefying fat. Yes, there was more than a hint of death in the air. There was the smell of those who were wounded and dying.

Moving almost as one, the three drew their blades and crept into the keep, walking as softly as shades. Some small starlight came in shafts through the windows. Vulgnash bent his will upon it, scattered it backward, so that the three became one with the shadows.

They followed the familiar scent of death through the

halls, found a stairwell going down. The scent was stronger there.

They crept down the stone steps, halted just in front of the door.

The smell of decay was strong. Someone stood just on the other side, guarding the door, a human, an older man. There was no fear in his scent. He did not know that he was being stalked.

Kryssidia pushed on the door, this time using only the power of his shade.

This door was barred.

The Knights Eternal looked at one another, and then as one bent their wills upon the door.

It shattered inward as if a rampaging bull had charged into it. Shards of wood and splinters flew everywhere.

A frightened old man cried out, "What? What? Who goes there? I, I, I have a sword."

Vulgnash had learned many languages in his long life, but he did not recognize this one. The old man's words were meaningless.

The man shouted, "Help! Someone! Everyone!" He drew a sword and began swinging wildly in the darkness. Obviously, he was not a wyrmling. He did not even have the poor night vision of one of the warrior clan. He was blind and helpless in the dark.

"Shawve zek Fallion Orden?" Vulgnash hissed. Where is Fallion Orden?

The old man cried out, lunged forward, aiming only at the sound of Vulgnash's voice. Thul grabbed the man by the wrist as he passed, and squeezed so tightly upon the ganglia of his wrist that the fellow's swords clattered to floor, even as the bones of his wrist shattered with a crackling sound.

The old man let out a groan of pain, falling to his knees, and Thul grabbed his face, preparing to drain the life from him.

There were shouts down the hallway, the sound of more guards coming, and Vulgnash's heart leapt in joy.

There would be enough lives to feed all three here to-night! Indeed, Kryssidia was already leaping ahead, eager to sate his appetite.

"Wait!" Vulgnash commanded before Thul could take the old man's life. "I will have an answer to my question first."

He reached down as Thul held the old man's weapon hand, and grabbed the man's finger. The old man shrieked and fought as Vulgnash knelt down and cleanly bit it off.

Men began racing into the hallway now, five men with torches that threw dancing shadows. They were shouting as they sought to engage Kryssidia.

The fools did not know that you cannot kill the dead.

He batted them aside as if they were pups, smashing skulls and breaking bones with every blow.

Meanwhile, in the weak torchlight, Vulgnash spat the bloody finger onto the floor, where it lay twitching.

"Azgan ka u-zek Fallion Orden." Show me the way to Fallion Orden.

Suddenly the finger spun, as if moved by an invisible hand, and then drew to a stop, pointing due west.

So, Fallion was gone, and the old man knew which way he had gone. Vulgnash saw the terror in the old man's eyes, revulsion at the bloody finger, a palpable sense of betrayal at what it had done. Vulgnash smiled, gladdened by this small act of torture.

The sun was coming. It was probably too late to go hunt for the wizard now. But there was time to eat, time to grow fat from the life force of others, and all three of the Knights Eternal were famished.

"Thul," Vulgnash said, "you may eat him now."

14

THE WASTELAND

To the eyes of the true men of Luciare, every object holds within it various levels of life or death, and so in formal speech, all nouns end in the appropriate suffix.

A living woman might be named Norak-na, Cloud Alive. But when she dies, her name becomes Norak-bas, Cloud Departed.

All living trees and animals hold life in them, and thus end with -na. Warmth and water also hold na, as does fertile soil, the wind, and the clouds.

Things that hold death within them include all weapons, sterile soil, bitter cold, and fire.

Given this emphasis on life and death, it is no surprise that the wizards of our world place so much emphasis on "Life Magic," magic which draws energy from one living thing to another, in an effort to sustain them both.

And while some might think that death magic is the antithesis of life magic, it is not. There is no power in death. Death Lords kill by draining energy from living things into themselves. Thus, their power is not the antithesis of life magic, merely a perversion of it.

—*the Wizard Sisel*

Bird song filled the woods as Fallion woke—nuthatches and wrens proclaiming their territories. Rhianna lay beside him, her cheek pressed against his chest, and he took his waking slow. The morning sun slanted through the forest, and as he watched the nightjars and ricks winging through the dim light, it seemed as fine a dawn as Fallion could remember.

Sunrise was still half an hour away.

He felt rested, and though his normal vigor had not returned, he could tell that healing was coming. A day or two more, he thought, and I will be better.

As the foursome ate a hasty meal, Talon bore the news. "We have to make good time today, get as far away from here as possible. Are you up to running?"

None of them were, but each nodded yes.

And so, without further ceremony, they ran.

They raced over mountain trails in the half-light and plunged down a steep slope into an oak forest that was as pretty as any that Fallion had ever seen. The graceful limbs of oaks, thick with moss, twisted high in the air, with nothing but leaf-mold and a few fallen limbs beneath them. The group scared up herds of deer as they ran, and hares and foxes, and once Jaz pointed out a rare gray lynx as it leapt up into a tree.

There was no sign of wyrmlings, no sound of hunting horns behind them, no footprints in the dirt.

By the crack of sunrise they left the forest and ran into the open sun, through fields much like those that Fallion remembered from his youth, endless fields of grass and black-eyed Susans, with only a few trees in the distance, winding along the banks of some creek bed.

On his own world, this land had been devastated by reavers, left devoid of settlements, and even now Fallion worried as he ran.

Some primal sense warned him that nothing was quite as it seemed. There were wyrmlings here, yes, and reavers, and strengi-saats. It was as if enemies that he'd never imagined and never fully understood were all preparing to combine against him.

Heightening his fears now was the fact that it was late summer, and the grass had died off. Only a few golden strands of straw still stood. There was no cover, no place to hide, and Fallion remembered the sounds of heaving wings.

There could be wyrmlings in the trees ahead, or in the trees behind, just watching the fields, marking them as they ran. Talon had assured him that wyrmlings would not attack in the daylight. The full sun burned their eyes, burned their pale skin too easily.

But they could still see. They could be watching from a line of trees.

And so he ached for cover.

As they ran, he noted that certain tender flowers and vines had begun to die off in the night. They were wilted, as if they had been plucked up by the roots.

Once, when they rested beside a brook, Talon squatted to inspect some watercress that looked sickly; her face grew sad. "It's the blight," she said, her voice thick with regret. "I fear it will take all of these plants before long—the green meadows and fields of flowers, the willows and oaks. Such things will only be a memory, a dream. And once again, this world will become a wasteland."

"A blight?" Jaz asked.

"The Death Lords' blight," Talon said. "The wyrmlings put a curse upon the land, years ago. Most of the plants died off. Only the cruelest of weeds and thorns eke out a living now."

"What is a Death Lord?" Fallion asked.

"They are leaders among the wyrmlings. They are . . . like wights," she said. "They're more spirit than flesh and bone. Indeed, they have no bones at all, and one would be hard pressed to discern their flesh, for they are no more substantial than smoke or a morning fog. But unlike the spirits that haunted our world, the Death Lords are powerful sorcerers who choose their fate. They choose to remain suspended between life and death, between our world and the fields of nothingness. Thus, they become masters of both worlds."

Fallion became chill at the thought, and throughout the day as they ran, he noticed more and more that the plants were indeed failing.

He worried for farmers in faraway places—the orchards and vineyards of Mystarria, the wheat fields of

Heredon. How would his people survive if this blight took hold of the land in those places?

And as the day drew out, he saw more and more tokens that Talon was right. In two days, maybe three, the forests and meadows they had passed through would become a wasteland.

Once, in the distance, they saw smoke to the north, hanging lazily over a stand of trees.

Talon cursed, and they struck south at a full run, until they passed another line of trees.

They skirted in its shadows, following the winding course of a stream, careful to be quiet. In the shade of the woods, the tall grass held the morning dew, and they marched along soundlessly.

Talon took the lead for the morning, but at one point she stopped them all, her body going taut, her hands out-stretched, pointing, and peered into the deep shadows just at the edge of the woods.

In the tall grass about fifty yards away, a young man stood. His chest was naked and matted with fur. His tawny hair fell down over his shoulders like a lion's mane. His eyes were strange and wild.

He stood perfectly still for a long moment, and Fallion could not help but notice that there was something wrong with him. His eyes looked terrified, like those of an ani-mal, and he had no arms.

Talon did not speak, but the young man suddenly turned his head as if looking for an escape.

That's when Fallion noticed the antlers. At first he had just thought them to be limbs from an alder, but now he saw them clearly, three tines to the side, as the young man turned and bounded away like a hart, on four strong legs, each of them slamming into the ground simultane-ously, and then thrusting him upward in mighty bounds. He looked like a hart, sailing through the air and then falling to the earth with each bound, as he raced away across an open field.

"What is that?" Jaz asked in amazement.

"A legend," Talon said, "and not one from your world."

"A legend?" Fallion asked.

"A galladem," Talon said. "Legends say that in ages past, the galladems were friends of the true men. Those that hunted wolves and bears would often have them come to their campfires, where the galladems would tell tales of the forests. They would tell what the trees dreamed of as they slumbered through the long winter, and would translate the songs of birds into the human tongue. They helped guide the men on their hunts, for the wolves and bears and rock lions were enemies to the galladems."

"Can you talk to him?" Jaz asked.

Talon shouted across the fields in a strange tongue, and the galladem halted for a moment, stared back at her quizzically, and then began walking away slowly.

In defeat, Talon said, "It has been hundreds of years since last a galladem was seen. I fear that we no longer speak the same tongue."

"What did you say?" Gaborn asked.

"I spoke the words of a blessing in the old tongue," Talon said. "May the fruits of the forest and the field be yours. May you bask in sunshine in the meadow, and find shelter in the hills. May you refresh yourself with cool water, and never know want."

Suddenly the creature stopped; it turned its head at a seemingly unnatural angle and shouted back.

When it fell silent, it bounded away.

"What did it say?" Rhianna begged. Talon had to think a bit.

"It spoke in the old tongue," Talon said. "I think . . . it said that 'the earth is in pain. The stones cry out in torment, and jays bicker and the wrens wonder why.' It warned us to watch for wolves upon our trail, wolves that cannot die, and it wished us well."

Fallion wondered for a long time. When I melded these two worlds, did I heal them just a little bit? Did I help restore a creature to life that was only a legend—or had the galladem been there upon the shadow world all along? Perhaps it was just a rare specimen, the last of his kind.

Fallion had no way of knowing. Nor could he be sure what its warnings meant.

But soon they were back to running. With each step their feet brushed the full heads of wheat and oats, sent the seeds scattering. Fallion imagined that it was music, a rattle formed by nature, and the sweat streaming from him watered the earth like a rare rain in the dry season.

He lost consciousness as he basked in the full sunlight, and all that was in him was motion, the sound of his lungs working like a bellows, the jarring of footfalls, and sigh of the wind, the droning of bees and flies in the meadows.

At noon they found an abandoned "inn," and Jaz begged for a halt. Talon's pace was brutal, and none of them had their full strength yet. Fallion had been loath to mention it in front of the others, but his legs felt weak and rubbery, and his head had begun to spin. During the run, he concentrated on keeping one foot in front of the other, and hoped that soon he would get his second wind.

But he suspected that he would never get a second wind. So he was glad when Talon called a halt, determined to have a brief rest and a quick meal.

"It looks as if there is a brook down beyond those trees," Jaz said. "I'll go fill some flasks for us."

Fallion was glad for that. He wanted some water, but it looked too far to go.

"Eat," Fallion told the others. "But keep your portions small. Better to take little and often than to eat much."

He got into his pack, pulled out his food. The good people of Castle Coorm had provided well. He suspected that Farion herself had packed the food. There was fresh bread and well-aged cheese, roast beef, and a small savory pie that smelled of chicken and onions. There were even a few fat strawberries.

Fallion ate those first, for their juice was staining his

pack. By then, Jaz had returned with the water. Fallion decided to save the beef and the savory for later, so he took some bread in his mouth and strode about, studying the inn.

It was like no building that Fallion had ever seen. It was laid out in a circle, and huge stone slabs formed the walls. There were three levels, one atop another, with a watchtower built at the very pinnacle. Each stone slab in the wall was thirty feet tall, rectangular in shape, and six feet wide. The slabs were fitted together so perfectly that a mouse could not have squeezed between them, and once there had been fair carvings embedded in the stone— images of a hunting party riding with hounds, chasing an enormous elk. But the images had been chiseled down by vandals, and now there were foul markings laid over the fair, glyphs painted in black, white, and red.

Talon went inside, and Fallion ducked his head in. The building had been gutted by fire, but the vestiges of campfires showed that it was still used as a shelter sometimes.

Fallion stepped back out into the sun, for it smelled unhealthy inside, and he studied the glyphs with mounting curiosity. He had never seen writing that in itself seemed evil. But here it was—glyphs portraying a giant spider with a child beneath it, images of warriors decapitating women, a man eating an enemy's liver.

"What do these glyphs say?" he asked Talon when she came back outside.

Talon glanced away, as if she feared to look upon them. "Wyrmlings have camped here," she said. "It is their writing. They paint in only three colors—black, white, and red, for those are the only colors that the wyrmling eye can see."

"Can you read the glyphs?"

"Some."

Talon pointed up at a black circle with a red squiggly line coming out of it. "This is the symbol of Lady Despair, the great wyrm that infests the world. Like the worm in an apple, her influence continues to spread, until the whole will be diseased. She is the one that the wyrmlings venerate, and obey. The rest of the writing is a prayer to her."

She pointed to the white spider above a black child. "This is a prayer that the Stealer of Souls will leave our human children stillborn. The rest of the glyphs . . . you can imagine."

"The Stealer of Souls?" Fallion asked.

"He is a wrym, what we would call a *locus* on our world, a wyrm of great power."

Fallion's heart skipped. He'd known that wyrmlings were giants of some kind, like the frowth giants on his own world. But they were more than just giants, they were giants infected by loci, by creatures of pure evil that fed upon their spirits and led them into deeper perversion.

Fallion had faced loci before and sent them into retreat. But somehow, he wasn't eager to face them now.

Too much had changed. Too much was still unknown.

"Tell me more about the wyrmlings," Fallion said.

"They are tall," Talon said, "half-a-head taller than even our largest warriors, and strong. It is said that they were human once, but you could not tell by looking at them. For eons they have served the wyrms, thinking it an honor to be possessed by one of the mighty. There is no kindness in them, no decency or truth. They respect only power. They are motivated only by fear and greed. The best of them have no wyrms in them, but even they are dangerous beyond all measure. They would gladly tear you from limb to limb, hoping only that by doing so they might be found worthy to be taken by a wyrm. The worst of them . . ." Talon shuddered, turned away.

"What?" Fallion asked.

"The worst of them are possessed by powerful loci, sorcerers who remember lore that should have best been forgotten when the world was young. These are the Death Lords. You do not want to meet them . . ." her voice trailed into a whisper, "but I fear we have no choice. We heard the sound of wings last night. They are coming."

Fallion shuddered. He peered at the image of Lady Despair, at the world beneath her, and suddenly he saw a wheel of fire again, the Seal of the Inferno, burning like a forge. He blinked the image away, rubbed his eyes.

Was it only in my dreams that I could heal the Earth? he wondered.

"You said that the wyrmlings were once human—" Fallion said, and a thought struck him so sharply that he leapt to his feet.

"What?" Talon asked.

Could it be? Fallion wondered. Everything on this world, he suspected, had its shadow on his own. What were the wyrmlings a shadow of? Certainly not the reavers. Talon had said that the wyrmlings fought reavers.

Could they have had human counterparts on his world?

Skin of white. Eyes that cannot abide the day. They worshipped Lady Despair. Wasn't it the Inkarrans who so often worshipped the Dark Lady death? There had been wars between the royalty and the death cults for ages.

"Where did the wyrmlings originate?" Fallion asked.

"That knowledge is lost," Talon said. "They destroyed the southern lands millennia ago, and then moved to the west, to what we call Indhopal. Only in the past few decades have they come to the north and east. They move like a plague of locusts, destroying everything in their path."

"Inkarra," Fallion said with some certainty. "They are Inkarrans."

Surprise washed over Talon's face. "Of course, I should have seen it."

"But knowing that doesn't help us," Fallion admitted. "We weren't facing an Inkarran invasion in our own world, at least not like this. It's as if our histories diverged so far in the past, that the two worlds are hardly the same."

Talon grunted her agreement.

This world is a snare, Fallion reminded himself. The loci brought me here for a reason. They brought me here because they have an advantage here.

And then he had a new fear. The dreams had begun shortly after he had slain the locus Asgaroth. It was said that beings in the netherworld could send dreams across space. Had an enemy sent him these dreams?

If so, healing the Earth might be far beyond his grasp. The enemy might have sent him a false hope. He had not really healed this world so much as simply bound two corrupt worlds together.

Is that all that the enemy wants? Fallion wondered.

He had no way of knowing, but the very question left him deeply troubled. And as they took off again that afternoon, he could not shake the apprehension that he had become the unwitting tool of the enemy.

They ran for nearly an hour, across a broad expanse of plains. Fallion glanced back, could see the trail they'd left, the bent stubble pointing the way like an arrow, and it filled him with worry.

At the end of an hour, they saw a line of trees and imagined that it foretold another brook, but when they reached it the ground dropped suddenly, and there was a broad canyon more than two miles across.

Within it ran a raging torrent, brown water churning and foaming, while huge trees torn and uprooted swirled in the flood. It was as if a dam had broken, and the whole world seemed to be washing away. In Fallion's own world, no river like this had existed. But here, the mountains were taller, and the range that had been called the Alcairs bulged into a different formation. Now it seemed that with the changes in the land, the river was washing away trees that had stood for centuries. Most disconcerting of all to Fallion was that the water was flowing west, when it should have been going east. He could only imagine that the river snaked back in the proper direction at some point.

"Damn," Talon swore. "This is the River Dyll-Tandor. I had hoped that it was farther north."

"Is it always this treacherous?" Rhianna asked.

Talon shook her head. "Not in the summer. There were some vast lakes in the mountains. With the change, it looks as if they are emptying."

"Can we swim it?" Rhianna asked.

Everyone turned and looked at Rhianna as if she were daft. Fallion's legs were already shaking from weariness.

"I'm not up to it," Jaz said. "But how about if you swim it, and we'll all climb on top and ride you, like you was a boat?"

Fallion could not escape the feeling that this flood was his fault. "There has to be another way across."

At that, Talon bit her lip uncertainly. "There is—a bridge, downstream, at the city of Cantular. But it will be guarded."

"How many guards?" Fallion asked, wondering at the odds. There were four of them, and though he had never seen a wyrmling, he was up to the challenge of fighting a few, if he had to. Fallion was good with a sword. And in the full light of day, he still had his flameweaving skills to draw upon.

"Dozens, maybe hundreds," Talon said. "There was a vast fortress there at one time, and the bridge has always been a strategic point. The wyrmlings will have it well garrisoned." She eyed Fallion critically. "Wyrmling archers are good," she said. "They use bows made of bone."

He understood what she was saying. Fallion had skill as a wizard, but a flameweaver could die from an arrow wound as easily as any other man.

"Then we will have to take great care," he warned.

15

THE CHASE

*It is said that the Knights Eternal never die. But some
would argue that they never have lived, for the Knights
Eternal are recruited from stillborn babes.*
                                        —the Wizard Sisel

In the cool morning air, Vulgnash and the Knights Eternal raced through a glen, their long legs carrying them swiftly. They had fed well during the night. Fourteen strong men they killed, draining the life from them. They were sweet, these small humans of the otherworld, filled to bursting with hopes and desires that humans on this world seemed to have forgotten.

Vulgnash could not recall when he had last tasted souls so sweet, like fat woodworms. Other humans that he had taken lately were empty, like the husks of dead beetles.

There had been other small humans at the fortress besides the men—women and children. Vulgnash and his cohorts had left them. Perhaps the Knights Eternal would go back to feed upon them at another time.

Now, he was sated, full of hope himself. He hoped to catch the wizard soon.

Already, the morning sun was coming, slanting in from the trees to the south-east. Kryssidia looked toward it mournfully, as if begging that they stop and find a cave in which to hole up for the day.

"Patience," Vulgnash growled. "We may catch them yet."

The humans had left a trail that was easy to follow. Even without Thul's infallible sense of smell, Vulgnash could have followed the scuff marks among the pine needles, the broken twigs and bent grass.

Vulgnash used his powers to draw shadows around them, so that they traveled through a lingering haze. Had anyone spotted them there, they would have only seen an indistinguishable mass of black, loping through the gloom.

Finally, they reached a grotto, a place where the rocky crown of a hill thrust up, with a cliff face that rose some eighty feet on three sides. A few gnarled old pines cast a deep shadow in the cavern.

"The scent of humans is strong here," Thul growled. "The scent of death is strong on them. They bedded here for the night."

It was a good place to bed down, Vulgnash saw. It had hidden the humans from prying eyes during the night, from *his* prying eyes, and its shadows would hide him from the burning sunlight.

"They can't have gotten far," Vulgnash said. The sun had hardly cracked the horizon. "They might only be a few hundred yards on their way."

Kryssidia hissed in protest, but Vulgnash went racing down the hill, heading west, using all of his skill to run silently over the forest floor, sometimes leaping into the air and taking wing when the brush grew thick or rocks covered the ground.

Thul raced ahead, loping along, stooping every dozen feet to test the ground for a scent. They glided down a long slope, into a forest of oaks that opened up, inviting more light.

Slanting rays of morning sunlight beat through the trees, cutting Vulgnash's flesh like a lash. He drew his cowl tightly over his face and bent the light to his will, surrounding himself in shadows.

All too soon, they stopped at the edge of a wood. Before them lay a broad expanse of golden field, the morning sun shining full upon it in the distance, so that a line of light cut hard across his vision.

Kryssidia hissed and turned away, but Vulgnash squinted, even though the light pierced his eyes like nails.

There in the distance, perhaps only a quarter of a mile away, he could see four figures racing through the endless open fields of summer straw. Bright yellow flowers grew tall in the field, with dark centers. They bobbed in the soft morning breeze.

So close, he thought. So close.

The humans could not have known that he was on their trail. Vulgnash and his men had moved as softly as shadows. And though the humans were running, they were not running in their speed. Instead they jogged, conserving their strength as if for a longer race.

Vulgnash peered at the bent grass they left in their wake. In the starlight, the trail would look as dark as a road.

"Tonight," he said, "we will take our hunt on the wing. Though they run all day, we will be upon them within an hour."

❧ 16 ❧

CANTULAR

See to it that no enemy ever crosses the River Dyll-Tandor without paying a toll in blood.
— *the Emperor Zul-torac*

The sun was riding low in the sky, drifting down into a yellow haze by the time that Fallion's group reached the ruins of Cantular.

They had followed the river for miles, keeping to the edge of the woods, where deer trails and rabbit trails would hide their track, and suddenly they rounded a bend, and saw the city sprawling there in its ruin. A vast stone fortress made up the bulk of it, hundreds of feet long and a full forty feet tall.

Whether it had been deserted for five years or five thousand, Fallion thought that it would look much the same. The massive sandstone slabs that made up the walls of the city were monolithic, and looked as if they might stand for eternity. Here, holes had been dug, and the slabs had been made to stand up like pillars. Then enormous stone slabs were laid atop them, forming massive roofs.

A thousand wyrmling troops could be hidden inside, and they'd have taken up only a corner of the fortress.

There were no fields for crops or pens for animals. Those had been razed long ago. But even from a distance he could see the remains of orchards, the larger trees standing in even rows, their fruit having gone wild, while saplings grew in their shadows.

"It looks deserted," Jaz said hopefully.

"Looks are often deceiving," Talon said.

A great bridge still spanned the river. Colossal stones served as bastions against the raging flow, and though trees and wreckage battered them, the foundations of the bridge still held. The waterline was high, though. If it rose even another two feet, it would swamp the bridge. Beyond the bridge, out in the lowlands, the waters had flooded an area that was miles wide. Fallion suspected that he might be witnessing the birth of a new sea.

At each end of the mile-long bridge squatted another massive stone fortress with a drawbridge, guard houses, and crenellated towers.

"The majority of the garrison will be on the far side of the river," Talon hazarded. "In fact, I'm not sure how well-guarded it will be here on the north. There might be only a few. There might be no guards at all."

"So we might be able to fight our way through the north tower," Fallion said, "but even if we do, we have to deal with the fact that there is another drawbridge at the far end."

"True," Talon said, "but say that we fight our way through the tower on this side. We can run a mile before we hit the far side. From there, we can jump into the water and swim. It might be a distance of only thirty yards, rather than a swim of a mile."

Fallion didn't care for the plan. Even if they did swim to shore on the far side, they could find themselves trying to swim though a hail of arrows.

And then what? If they made it to shore, the wyrmlings would be on their trail at nightfall.

"Right, then," Rhianna said. "Let's get to it."

"In the morning," Fallion said. He wasn't the kind to hesitate, but the more he studied the situation, the less he liked it.

"In the morning?" Jaz asked. "Why not now?"

"It's too close to nightfall," Fallion said. "The wyrmling troops are waking. If we attack now, we'll attack them in their strength. And even if we break through to the far side of the river, we'll have to worry about them dogging our trail for the rest of the night. We should wait until morning, hit them in the light of day."

Talon nodded her assent.

"Where will we stay then?" Jaz asked.

Fallion didn't like the idea of camping in the open. The trees along the river had been fairly thick, but in the flood, many had washed away. The scrub that was left could hardly hide a pair of rabbits.

"We'll sleep in there," Fallion said, nodding toward the ruins.

"Among the wyrmlings?" Jaz asked.

Fallion liked the idea. He was certain that the wyrmlings were hunting him, as Talon feared, and tonight they would be scouring the fields and forests. But the last place they would look would be here, in the heart of a wyrmling fortress.

"Like I said," Rhianna said, "let's get to it."

And so in the failing sun, they crept along the riverbank, keeping low.

There in the shadows, they found a vine thick with light-berries and picked a few. The vine had begun to wilt, and Fallion guessed that in a day it would be dead.

So they made their way to the edge of the ruined city. A great wall had once surrounded it, but the wyrmlings had knocked it down in a dozen places. Enormous battering rams, huge logs with iron heads shaped like foul beasts, still lay abandoned outside the gates. Evil symbols had been scrawled on the broken walls. Fallion could see the glyph of Lady Despair.

It was in the final approach, when they ran across an open field and leapt through a gap in the broken wall that they were most exposed.

But at the most, they were only visible for a few seconds.

They ran up to the side of a building and hunched, waiting to see if an alarm sounded. If they were attacked, Fallion wanted it to be there in the open, in the failing light, rather than in the corner of some dark building.

When no alarm sounded, they crept down an empty street, keeping close to the walls.

Fresh tracks in the dirt showed that wyrmlings walked down the street often.

They were in an old merchant quarter. Stalls lined both sides of the streets, and in some places the merchandise still moldered. Bolts of cotton and flax sat rotting in one stall, broken chairs and a baby crib in another, clay pots in a third.

Down the street, a gruff laugh sounded, almost a snarl. The wyrmlings were awake.

Fallion did not dare venture farther into the city. Fallion spotted a likely place and dove into an abandoned smithy with a circular forge, a bellows, and an overturned anvil.

In the back, a leather curtain formed a door, separating the smithy from the living quarters.

They raced inside.

"Up or down?" Talon asked while Fallion's eyes were

still adjusting to the gloom. He realized that in the change, she must have improved her night vision. When he could finally see, he made out a wooden ladder leading up to a loft. Another went down to a pantry.

A partial skeleton lay sprawled upon the floor, a few scattered bones wrapped in a rotten dress. The skull had been taken.

The ladder was rotting, too. Fallion imagined that a giant would have to worry about breaking a rung as he climbed. So Fallion decided to go up it. Besides, if the group was attacked, Fallion would rather defend from above than beneath.

"Up," he said, racing quietly up the ladder.

He reached the top, found a bedroom. A child's bed, with a mattress made of straw over some wooden slats, rested near the chimney, and a wooden horse lay on the floor. Otherwise the room was bare. A window stood closed, the last of the sunlight gleaming yellow through a pane made of scraped hide.

The dust on the floor had not been disturbed in years.

"This will do," Fallion said.

He peered about the room. The walls were formed from sandstone and looked to be a good two feet thick. The roof itself was a great slab of stone.

He felt safe here, protected, like a mouse in its burrow.

Everyone climbed into the room, and Fallion considered pulling up the ladder. But he suspected that if anyone was familiar with this place, they would notice what he'd done. Better to leave everything undisturbed.

A TURN ON THE DANCE FLOOR

An undeserved reward cankers the soul.
—*Daylan Hammer*

At the feast in the great hall in Caer Luciare that night, Alun threw the remains of a greasy swan's leg over his back, food for the dogs. The king's mastiffs were quick to lunge from their beds by the fire to scuffle for it, and as the growls died down, Alun could not help but turn just a bit, to see which dog had won.

It was a pup of nine months, young enough to be fast and hungry, big enough to hold his own.

Much like me, Alun thought with a satisfied grin. He was half drunk on the king's wine, though the meal had hardly begun.

It would be a feast tonight. The warriors would need their strength tomorrow as they ran north for the attack. The big men would keep a grueling pace. A warrior was expected to run ten miles in an hour, a hundred miles in a day, and the run would last from first light to full night.

Only by covering the ground in a single day could the warriors hope to gain the element of surprise in their attack.

Horses could not be used, for they would not be able to withstand the grueling pace.

Alun could only hang his head in despair. He could never make such a run. It would soon be apparent to all that though he might be named a warrior, he was in fact only a fraud.

Indeed, now that the lords were finishing the main course, the festivities would begin. There would be jugglers and dancing, a fool who aped the lords.

But first—

Madoc stood, and his men began banging the table with the butts of their knives, with mugs or bones— whatever they had at hand.

"Good sirrahs," he roared for quiet, for the room was huge and hundreds of people sat at the tables. There had not been a feast so well attended since last summer's eve. "Good sirrahs and ladies," Madoc roared. "I have an announcement. Today let it be known to all—to lord, to lady, to warrior and commoner alike, that Caer Luciare has a new Master of the Hounds, our very own Alun."

There were shouts and cheers from the many nobles gathered about as Madoc brought out a large gold cape pin that bore the image of three racing hounds upon it. It was a lovely thing. More importantly, it was the badge of his office, and with great ceremony, Madoc pinned Alun's cape with it, inserting the prong and then twisting until the spiral pin was locked in place. Then he took Alun's simple old brass cape pin and set it upon the table.

The applause died down quickly as the guests prepared to return to conversations, but Madoc roared, "And, let it be known that Alun has proven himself this day to be a man of great courage, a man of decisive wit, of firm resolve, and a man of uncommon character. Indeed, he is no longer a common man at all in the view of House Madoc. Not a vassal. It is with heartfelt appreciation, that I name him a warrior of Clan Madoc, and a defender of the free."

At that there was far less clapping. Many of the nobles just stared in confused silence for a moment. Alun was not a warrior born, after all. He was an ill-bred gangrel. Everyone could see it.

Yet, sometimes, the honor was won, every generation or so.

There were excited whispers as women went asking their men what Alun had done.

What will they think? Alun wondered.

He did not care, or at least he told himself that he

didn't. He peered across the room, to the royal table off to his left, where the High King ate. There, to his right, in a place of honor, sat the king's long-time ally and best friend, the Emir of Dalharristan, resplendent in a coat of gold silks, his white turban adorned with a fiery black opal.

And four seats down sat his daughter Siyaddah, her dark eyes glistening in the candlelight. She looked at Alun and smiled gently, as if welcoming him to the nobility.

She remembers me, Alun realized. And she thinks fondly of me.

His heart hammered and his mouth grew dry.

She is not so far above my station. I am a warrior now.

He took a drink from the goblet of wine, but a single swallow did not satisfy his thirst, so he downed it all, a rich red wine in a silver goblet.

He had never taken a drink from a goblet before. He picked it up, looked at it. It was a beautiful thing, with two feet like a swan on tall legs, and feathers on the outside, and a swan's long neck bent and forming a handle.

Such a mug, he realized, was worth more than his life had been worth as a slave. With it, he could have bought his freedom twice over.

Now?

He nodded to one of the serving children that waited against the wall. A boy of six ambled forward, struggled to fill the mug from a heavy cask of wine.

Alun sat and waited. He waited while the fool went strutting around the room, aping the lords and ladies. He waited as minstrels sang while the dessert pastries were passed around.

He waited until the king called for a dance.

Then he downed another mug of wine and went to ask Siyaddah to join him upon the dance floor.

His feet were unsteady and his aim went afoul as he veered across the room, avoiding collision with those on the dance floor only by swerving wide.

He was greeted with astonished looks as he got to Siyaddah's table, bowed, and asked, "Your Highness, may I ask you to dance?"

Alun looked to her father, the legendary Light of Dalharristan, whose face remained expressionless, but who merely gave a slight nod.

"I think you just did," Siyaddah said.

Alun had to stand there thinking for a long moment before he figured out the logic to her words.

She joined him on the dance floor. Alun had never danced like this before. It was a stately court dance, with lots of strutting about together while the men occasionally stopped and raised the ladies' hands while they twirled.

Alun had no knack for it. His overlarge feet kept getting tangled, and he didn't know when to let a lady twirl, and twice he imagined that he was supposed to twirl, too. He heard some fellow laugh, and Alun's face grew red as he realized that a great deal of the problem had to do with the fact that he was falling-down drunk.

He stopped dancing then, and Siyaddah gave him a warm smile. "Don't be so hard on yourself. It's only your first dance. You'll catch on."

And then the tense moment was over and she was moving again, and he was content to prance and watch her twirl. There was light in her eyes, and laughter, and light in her hair. It seemed to sparkle, until he realized that she had a powder in her hair, a powder made from diamonds, he imagined.

"Congratulations," she said at last, "this is a great day for you. You should be proud—Master of the Hounds."

He liked the sound of that, coming from her lips. But it reminded him. He had not gone to the kennels yet tonight. He had several bitches ready to whelp, and he really thought that he should go check on them. It was a good time of year to be Master of the Hounds, with the puppies coming.

"We're expecting new litters soon. Hart's Breath, she should have her first litter tonight or tomorrow. Do you remember her?" Siyaddah had played with her as a pup, not more than two years ago.

Siyaddah shook her head no.

Of course she doesn't remember, Alun thought. She played with so many pups. She didn't know their names. You are such a fool, he told himself.

Embarrassed, he quit talking. It was time for Siyaddah to twirl again.

She looked lovely, so dainty. Her dark skin, almost chocolate in color, contrasted sharply with her white silks. And beneath the silks, he could see the shapely contours of her body.

That is the whole reason for the dance, he realized, to allow young bachelors like himself to ogle the maidens.

"Tell me," Siyaddah asked, "what great deed did you do to deserve such an honor, being raised to the warrior clan?"

Cold fear ran through his veins, and Alun found that his tongue would not work. He did not want to tell her what he had done. "Oh, nothing," Alun said.

He hoped that she had not heard the truth yet. He hoped that she would never hear.

"Was it for spying upon Daylan Hammer?" she asked.

"I . . . yes," he admitted. He stuttered to a stop for a moment and then continued prancing.

"And tell me," Siyaddah said, "how was that brave?"

She thinks I'm a fake, Alun thought. She knows I'm a fake.

"It is thought . . . that he killed Sir Croft."

"And did he?" Siyaddah asked playfully, but Alun discerned more than playfulness in her voice. There was a bit of a challenge to her tone. There was a smile on her face and light in her eyes. She was not trying to show disrespect toward Alun. But it was obvious that she thought well of Daylan Hammer, that she doubted his guilt.

"I don't believe so," Alun whispered, lest anyone overhear.

She flashed him a brief smile. "Your view conflicts

with countless others," she said. "There are some who are calling for Daylan's head, claiming that there can be no good reason that he would be meeting with the enemy. They say that questioning would do no good, for he would surely lie. Others think that he should be allowed to defend himself. I . . . find it hard to believe that he is in league with the enemy."

"My thoughts exactly," Alun said.

"Still, it required no less bravery on your part to follow him, to take the risk," Siyaddah said.

Was it bravery, Alun wondered, or greed?

"And he did meet with a wyrmling?" she asked.

"Most assuredly."

"That must have been frightening," she said.

Not very. I was hiding, Alun thought.

"To what end did they meet? I wonder," she said.

Alun stopped dancing. His heart was hammering and he suddenly felt over-warm. All of the rich food felt as if it was turning to a ball of grease in his stomach. He feared he would retch.

"Sometimes," Siyaddah said gently, without condemnation, "it takes great courage to do what is right."

Alun turned and fled, bumping into dancers, hurrying from the great hall. He raced outside, stood gasping for air as he leaned against a pillar.

Does she know? he wondered. Does she know why Daylan Hammer met with the enemy—risked his own life, his own honor to meet with them? Or does she only guess?

She only guesses, Alun decided. If she knew, she would have told me. But she believes him to be a man of virtue.

It was said that Daylan Hammer ate at the High King's table. Siyaddah would have been in range to hear his jokes, or his songs when he took the lute. She would know his heart better than Alun did. She was a sensitive woman, and perhaps had come to know Daylan better than others around him.

Perhaps she's even in love with him.

No, that can't be, Alun thought. He is too small and strange, too different from us.

Alun went staggering to the kennels.

Back to the dogs, where I belong, he thought.

There, he found things much as he had suspected. Hart's Breath had gone into labor and given birth to a pup, and had that frightened look that bitches get when they deliver their first. What is wrong with me? Hart's Breath's body language asked as she puttered about, her hips quivering, eyes wide as she sniffed at the pup. What is that black thing squirming on the floor?

Alun stayed with her, stroking her forehead and whispering words of comfort, while she continued to deliver. He held up each newborn for her to sniff, introduced the pups by complimenting her. "Ah, you're such a good dog," he would say as she licked each pup, "such a good mother. And look how pretty your babies are."

Soon, she wagged her tail at the sight of each new birth, proud of her offspring, and when Alun left her there late at night, she was happiest hound in the world.

He was weary and nearly sober when he made his way back to the King's Keep. The feast was long over, the tables cleared, the servants gone to bed. Two guards stood outside the door and barred his way.

"I need to speak with King Urstone," Alun said at their challenge.

"At this hour?" one asked. "Regarding what?"

Distantly, from up above, Alun heard a man sobbing, the sound faint and distant as it came through an open window. The king sobbing in his chambers as he mourned.

"It concerns a plan to save his son," Alun said.

They did not send a messenger to ask the king if he wanted to be disturbed. The guards looked at each other, and one of them grabbed Alun by the bicep and pulled him into the keep as if he'd just apprehended a thief.

Alun found himself shivering in terror. He was about

to tell the king of Daylan Hammer's mad plot to save his son.

Warlord Madoc will have me stripped of my office when he finds out what I've done, Alun thought.

❧ 18 ❧

IN THE COLDEST HOUR

There are those who criticized High King Urstone for his weak mind, but it was never his mind that failed him. Rather, it was his great love that brought him down. —the Wizard Sisel

An hour before dawn, the coldest hour of the night, the Wizard Sisel went to the High King's door with Shaun the baker in tow. A single knock, and they were in.

King Urstone was sitting at a desk, writing out orders for work to be done during his absence. He had commanded that no other work be done until the castle was set in order. No housewife was to wash the family's clothes. No merchant was to be found selling in the streets.

Instead, there were slabs of rock that needed to be hauled up and set in place. There were buckled walls that needed mending. And every man, woman, and child would be required to work at it the next day.

He was fully dressed in the same maroon robe and gray tunic that he had been wearing at dinner. But he looked to be in better spirits than Sisel had imagined he would.

"Sisel," he asked. "What may I do for you—and Goodman Shaun, is it?" The king had an excellent memory for names but he always asked timidly, afraid that he might offend someone by making a mistake. Thus he gratified and honored them even though his voice held a tone of apology.

"I have something to show you, Your Highness," Sisel said. He turned to Shaun. "What is your name?"

The baker looked back and forth between the king and the wizard, and at last he said, "I'm not rightly sure anymore."

King Urstone wondered if the man had taken a blow to the head.

"It used to be Shaun," the baker said. "But it was Hugheart on that other world, Captain Hugheart."

Ah, the king thought, this again.

"And what was your calling on this other world?"

"I was a lord, a runelord," Shaun said. "I . . . was a royal guard at Castle Corneth, in the land of Aven."

"You claim to be a runelord," Sisel asked. "Can you explain to the king what that is?"

"I was given attributes by vassals—strength, speed, stamina, wit. They gave it to me in a ceremony. We used branding irons, called forcibles, to make the transfer. The brands left scars on me."

Shaun rolled up his sleeve, displaying his bicep. On it were a dozen small scars, burned into his flesh, each a circle with its own design within. King Urstone had never seen the like. But still, the story sounded like madness.

"Show the king what you can do," the wizard said.

Shaun the baker, a man that King Urstone had once played with as a child, suddenly leapt eight feet in the air, somersaulted with the agility of a cat, and dropped to a crouch. As he landed, he slammed a fist into a table that was made of slate. The table shattered as if it had been hammered with a maul.

The king stared in awe. No man in the kingdom, no matter whether he was warrior-born or not, had such strength.

The wizard reached into a pocket, pulled out a small red stone. "Your Highness, behold the most deadly weapon in the world!"

The king peered at the stone. He was an educated man. "Corpuscite?" he asked. It was a metal, softer than lead, and when put to the tongue tasted salty, like blood.

"It is called blood metal, upon that world where the runelords dwelled. And it is exceedingly rare there."

"But . . . there's a whole hill of it—" the king began to say.

"South of the city," Sisel finished. "We will need it, if we are to defend ourselves. And I have begun a search of the city. We will need to find someone who has worked as a facilitator on this other world, a wizard who can make the branding irons we need and transfer attributes from one person to another. If we hurry, we could have warriors like Shaun here in place before the wyrmlings next attack."

"Where are the vassals who gave you these powers?" the king asked.

"In the land of Aven, far to the north and east of here," Shaun said. "I must surmise that they are still alive, for if they had died, their powers would have been stripped from me."

Sisel licked his lips. He had obviously been thinking much. He continued, "My lord, I have a confession. Daylan Hammer mentioned that there are some among us, like Shaun, who lived other lives, who had shadow selves upon that other world. Such people are now two halves, bound into one. I am one of those. I served as an Earth Wizard in this other world, and I have begun to remember things . . . strange things. But the memories come hard. Sometimes, it is like pulling teeth to recall a single detail. My name was Binnesman, and I was a counselor to a wondrous king, a hero like none that our world has ever known."

"Why then," King Urstone asked, "don't I remember anything?"

The wizard glanced away, as if unsure what to say. "Because you did not exist on that world. You had no

shadow self there. You died there before the worlds were
sealed as one."

"I see," King Urstone said. He somehow felt sad,
cheated, as if he had lost something.

"Not everyone had a shadow self. There were great
wars and turmoil upon that world, as there are here. People were being slain by the thousands, by the hundreds of
thousands. So some of our lives . . . did not overlap."

King Urstone turned away, went to the balcony and
opened the door. Rich flowers and shrubs grew in pots
outside, and their scent perfumed the night. Somewhere
among the shrubs, a nightingale responded to the light
with a heart-breaking song.

He tried to consider the repercussions of this new
intelligence.

"Will the wyrmlings know?" he wondered aloud,
"about the powers inherent in the corpuscite, I mean?"

"Even if they don't, we must prepare for the worst,"
Sisel said. "Others have begun to remember. I went to
the hill to get this corpuscite, and as I approached, I
found men digging in the night. They ran away."

"Who?" King Urstone demanded.

"I saw no faces, but they will be back. If I were you, I
would send some of my own men there, now, and have
them begin to dig in earnest."

"Of course," the king said. He looked to Shaun, "Sir
Hugheart, will you see to it?"

"As you wish, milord," Shaun said. He did not ask for
further direction, nor did he hesitate to carry out the
order. Shaun merely spun on his heels and strode from
the room, as a trained soldier would.

I am but half a man, King Urstone thought. Men like
Shaun, they are complete in a way that I never can be.
They will have twice the knowledge, twice the wisdom
of men their age.

Such men would be of great benefit to the world, the
king mused.

When Shaun was gone, the Wizard Sisel peered hard

into the king's eyes, and whispered, "There is another matter, Your Highness. This wondrous king that I served, this great hero of the shadow world—is your son, Areth Sul Urstone. Upon the shadow world where he was born, he was known as Gaborn Val Orden. I know this as certainly as I know my own name. He had great powers, greater than you can imagine. We must see to his rescue immediately. If Zul-torac gets even a hint of what he can become, his life . . . will be worth nothing."

King Urstone began to tremble. Everything seemed to be happening so fast. The men were set to march on Cantular within the hour, and King Urstone dared not call a halt. The Dyll-Tandor was flooding, creating a barrier around his lands, and he needed to take the bridge at Cantular, seal his borders. But so much else needed to be done, too.

"Tell me this," King Urstone asked. "On this other world, this shadow world, did I die well?"

Sisel smiled warmly. "You died in a great battle, in defense of your family and your people. None ever died better."

"Well then," King Urstone said after a thought, "let's see that it doesn't happen again." He smiled weakly. "I have learned that a plan is already underway to free my son. That is why Daylan Hammer was meeting with the wyrmling. He was trying to arrange an exchange of hostages, my son for the wyrmling princess. And I can see to it that the plan moves forward. If all goes well, by dawn tomorrow, Areth will be free."

"Do you trust the wyrmlings to keep such a bargain?" Sisel asked after some thought.

"No. But do I have any other choice? What army will I batter down the gates of Rugassa with? How else will I free my son?"

But the king began to think—I could batter their gates with an army of runelords.

The wizard frowned in consternation. "I don't like this plan. I don't trust the wyrmlings. And there are some in our ranks I trust even less. Warlord Madoc has campaigned long and hard to lead an attack. For years he has waited. You and I both know what he seeks."

"I'm afraid," King Urstone said, "that I can see no good reason to deny him, and every reason to move his plan forward. This great change that has been wrought upon the earth will alarm the wyrmlings, and they are most dangerous when so alarmed. If the wyrmlings *are* coming, we need to take the bridge at Cantular—as much as we need to save my son."

The wizard shook his head. "Your son is worth more than a bridge, believe me."

"Would you still counsel me then to halt the attack?"

Sisel shook his head sadly. "No. I fear, milord, that the enemy is wiser than we would hope. They may already know about the lore of the forcibles, and who they now hold captive. And if they know, there will be no trade for your son, and no saving him. Go forward with your plan, and let us hope for the best."

❦ 19 ❦

DARK WATERS

I find that the best way to endure ugliness and pain is to remember beauty. Always in my memory, it is the face of a woman that gives me strength. Her name was Yaleen.
                                                    —Daylan Hammer

Daylight came to the privy, the softest blush of light shining through the holes up above. With the dawn came an unwholesome rain as hundreds of soldiers relieved themselves of the waste from last night's feast.

Daylan Hammer stood stoically, head bowed, mouth tightly shut, and endured.

He had been standing so long that once in the night, all of the blood had rushed to his feet, and he had staggered and fallen in the mire.

So he had learned, and now he raised his feet every now and then, stamping them in the filth, so that he made sure to keep blood pumping to his head.

It will end soon, he thought. The warriors will be leaving at dawn.

And after an hour, they seemed to be gone. No more foul rains hurtled down, no crude jests or harsh laughter assailed him.

He waded to the far end, then reached up and began trying to climb out of the privy.

There was little to hold onto. The walls were wet and slimy. Mold and unhealthy funguses grew upon them, making them slick. There was no brickwork or mortar here, with crevices that he might slip his fingers into, just solid rock worn smooth over the ages.

Still, he had to try.

He pressed his fingernails into a sheet of mold, hoping that it might give him some purchase.

He was wet, soggy, and that added extra pounds.

He pulled himself up slowly, and let the urine drip off of him a little, hoping to reduce his weight. But the sheet of mold broke free, and he slid back.

I would weigh less if I were naked, he decided.

He did not want to suffer that indignity. He didn't want to risk having someone see him squirming as he struggled up out of the privy.

On the other hand, I doubt whether I ever want to wear these clothes again, he told himself.

With grim determination, he shucked off his pants, ripped off his tunic, and began the climb.

It took him nearly an hour to get ten feet up the wall. But from there, the slope suddenly got steeper. By then, his fingernails and toenails bled, and he was straining every muscle.

He dared not rest. He was too wet and slimy. Each time he laid against the wall, he merely slid back into the cesspool.

If I were dry, he thought, perhaps I could get more friction, perhaps I could make it.

And so he clung in one spot, sweat streaming down his forehead and from his armpits and chest, hoping to get dry enough so that he might find some purchase.

All of his endowments of strength and grace could not suffice to get him one foot farther up the wall. Only superhuman effort had gotten him this far at all.

Suddenly, he heard a soft thud, and a coil of rope came twisting down out of the darkness.

Who? he wondered. Daylan had seen the grief-stricken look on Alun's face when he'd been arrested. He wondered, Is he trying to make amends?

But it wasn't Alun who spoke. It was the High King himself, his mournful voice echoing in the small chamber.

"Daylan Hammer, the troops are assembled at the gate, and soon they will be gone. The guard will be light. There are those who would thwart you, if they knew of your purpose. But I wish you well. By the Powers that preserve us I beg you, save my son."

❧ 20 ❧

TROPHIES OF THE HUNT

There is a special bond that develops between the hunter and the hunted. They share a similar thrill, a visceral excitement that is only aroused when a life is placed in jeopardy. It is Lady Despair's will that

*everyone should learn the joy of the hunt. And in the
proper time, everyone should share the thrill of being
hunted.*   *—Zul-torac*

As the shadows deepened and grew long upon the land,
Fallion and his friends huddled in silence. Fear and
anticipation were thick in the air, and none dared stir in
the small loft. Every tiny noise, every little breath, every
scuff of a foot as it was rearranged on the wooden floor,
seemed amplified, as if striving to give them away.

The heartbeats of Fallion and his friends sounded as
loud as drums.

There was little light. A handful of dying light-berries
lay sprawled upon the floor.

This is not natural, Fallion thought, as his pounding
heart drummed faster, filling the small room with its
deep, echoing beat. He peered around the room at the
others. This is a spell of some sort, perhaps cast by a sorcerer of the air.

He tried to still his breathing, remain quiet. He could
not really see the others in the room. The light-berries
had gone too dim. He could only sense their presence by
virtue of sound, by body heat, by scent. Only the slightest bit of starlight shone through the hide window pane.
Yet he could tell that they were struggling to remain
silent, too.

"By the Powers," Talon swore softly, "the hunters are
on our trail." She spoke in a whisper, but the sound
seemed to echo through the room like a shout.

What kinds of hunters have such power, Fallion wondered, that they can magnify the heartbeats of their prey?

Almost, Fallion feared that his very thoughts would
echo from the stone walls like a song.

Outside the room, down on the street, he heard marching feet, a hundred or more wyrmling troops. There was
the usual clanking of armor, the swearing in some
strange tongue, and the gruff shouts of a commander.

But there was something more. There was an itching across the bridge of Fallion's nose, a crawling sensation that Fallion had learned to recognize long ago. Loci. There were loci in the soldiers outside, beings of pure evil.

They're coming for us, he thought as sweat dribbled down his brow. He gripped his long sword firmly, wishing now that he had taken those endowments of brawn proffered by his friends among the Gwardeen.

No, I do not wish that, he told himself. They will need their own strength in the days to come. And his heart went out to them, there across the sea, as he silently wished them well.

He strained to hear if the marching feet would stop at the small shop, to hear if the soldiers would turn.

Perhaps, he thought, someone saw us enter the building. They could come right to us.

But no, after several long minutes, the soldiers marched down the road, heading back east, toward Castle Coorm.

Perhaps that is where they are going. Perhaps they have orders to hunt for me.

At long last, the sound of marching feet faded into the distance, and everyone let out a sigh.

But the sounds of the room were still amplified. The heavy breathing still resounded from the walls, even louder than before.

They're coming for me, Fallion knew, the winged hunters. They're coming, and they're getting closer. Any minute now, and they will be here.

He almost wanted to risk a little light. He had used his flameweaving powers during the heat of the day to store energy, and right now it was leaking from every pore. To those nearby, his skin would feel fevered.

But he dared not risk it.

So he waited for a long half hour. The sounds of their breathing, of hearts pounding, grew ever louder.

Something whisked past the window, blocking out the

starlight for an instant—an owl perhaps. Fallion hoped that it was only an owl.

A moment later, the sounds faded. The room went quiet. Fallion could still hear the blood pounding in his ears, but it was greatly diminished.

Rhianna gave a relieved sigh, and Jaz whispered, "They've left."

Suddenly the massive stone roof went blasting into the air, as if tossed aside by the hand of an angry god. The huge slab walls shattered, seemingly hit by battering rams, and Fallion found himself sitting exposed upon a platform.

Overhead, blotting out the stars, were three beings, floating in the air. Their great wings spread out wide as they hung in a soft breeze, every so often flapping almost silently.

All three of them were clothed in red.

Fallion had never sensed such evil, not in Asgaroth, not in Shadoath. It was palpable, like a stink.

"We're found!" Jaz shouted, drawing his bow. Rhianna shrieked and leapt to her feet, battle staff at the ready.

Talon cried out, "Ah, the Knights Eternal. We're undone!"

Fallion knew of only one way to fight a locus. He did something now that he had tried only once before.

He blazed, sending out a bright light, as blinding as the sun. Light bled from every pore, spreading from him like a beacon. One of the Knights Eternal threw up a hand to shield his eyes. At that moment, Jaz loosed an arrow.

It blurred like a bolt, striking one of the creatures in the chest.

The Knight Eternal let out a resounding wail, a freakish cry as if from a wounded wolf, and then crumpled, bits of decayed flesh raining down, even as its wings collapsed like a sheet in the wind.

Vulgnash whirled, looked to where Kryssidia had been. The Knight's flesh had come unbound.

No weapon forged by mere mortals should have been able to do that. Only weapons enchanted by a powerful undine could do that, and Vulgnash had rid the earth of such wizards long ago.

The light intensified, striking Vulgnash like the sun, lashing at him. The human wizard was powerful, more powerful than any that he had met in five thousand years.

I know this one, Vulgnash realized. The Torch-bearer walks the earth again.

This disconcerted him, but did not strike fear into Vulgnash's heart.

The Torch-bearer had great powers. But he had greater weaknesses.

Fallion blazed like the sun, wielding the light as if it were a sword. He could see the loci now in his enemies, as he used the light to pierce their spirits. The spirits of his enemies were like balls of soft blue light, with tentacles of energy worming through them.

In a healthy person, the light would be brilliant, effervescent.

But Fallion spotted black parasites feeding upon the husks of the creature's shriveled souls—dark forms that looked like enormous water fleas. They were the loci.

"By the Powers," Fallion commanded, "depart!"

He lashed out, sending his brilliance to burn the loci, hoping to sear them into oblivion.

And as quickly as he did, the light faded.

One of the Knights Eternal stretched out a hand, and all of the light Fallion radiated snuffed out.

Fallion sent a surge of energy, hoping to break the spell, and a fiery rope of heat went twisting into the enemy's palm.

The Knight Eternal hurled the fireball back toward Talon, and it took all of Fallion's skill to shunt it aside before it washed over her.

"Flameweavers!" Rhianna shouted.

I'm defenseless, Fallion thought.

Jaz tried to nock another arrow, but as he did, one of the creatures dove and pointed a finger.

A blast of icy wind washed over the group, hit them like a blow. Jaz and the others cried out and went sprawling across the floor. The wind was colder than the tomb, and it sucked the air from Fallion's lungs.

Fallion fell backward, found himself dangling over the edge of the wall. Suddenly he was cold, so deadly cold that he could not feel his hands, his feet, his face. His heart beat frantically, but Fallion could not move. His muscles would not respond.

He tried to lift his hand, to cry out or run, but every nerve seemed frozen.

I'm dead, he thought. I'm dead.

The enemy dropped from the sky, landing on the wooden floor with a thud, and came striding over to him.

Fallion could not so much as blink.

A tall figure all in robes and a cowl loomed above him, revealed by the light of a crescent moon. The evil of its presence smote Fallion, washed over him like filth; Fallion tried to crawl away.

The wyrmling peered at him, then reached down and stroked Fallion's cheek. Like a lover, Fallion thought. He stroked me like a lover. But, No, he realized. He strokes me like a hunter who admires a prized kill.

The cowled figure spoke in a strange tongue, yet there must have been a spell upon Fallion, for he also heard words ringing in his mind.

"Welcome, little wizard," the wyrmling said, "to *my* world."

SMALL FOLK

As a young man, I was taught that to be a warrior is the epitome of virtue, and that warriors should be held in greater esteem than other men. We are the protectors, after all.

But what does a warrior create? Should not the farmer pruning his orchard be granted equal esteem? Should not the mother nursing her child be deserving of greater praise?

All of my life, I have felt like a fraud. I have been humbled by humble men.

Never was it more so than when I first saw the small folk of the shadow world. —High King Urstone

Alun came staggering into camp on rubbery legs that night, well after dark. He was supposed to have run a hundred miles, but of course his energy gave out.

The other warriors drove him anyway, hurling curses and encouragement at him in equal measure. "You're a warrior now!" "Move those damned spindly legs!" "Does a wolf tire when it runs to battle?"

They laughed, and the tone seemed kindly enough.

But they were going to kill him, Alun knew.

He realized it as soon as his legs gave out, and he went sprawling in the dirt.

Drewish had urged him on with a swift kick to the ribs and a derisive laugh, and had rushed on. But Connor had only halted long enough to yell, "Get off your lazy ass. We'll have no laggards."

Alun had fumbled about, gasping for air, and Connor just rolled his eyes. At last, he picked Alun up by the scruff of the neck, half carrying him, and ran, holding him upright, forcing him to move his tired legs.

After a few miles of this, Alun fainted, and woke to find that some burly soldier was carrying him on his back as if he were a corpse. When Alun groaned, the fellow laughed and dropped him to the ground. "Come now, no bellyaching. We're off to battle. Let's hear a war song out of you."

And that was when Alun knew they were going to kill him. Madoc had given him the honor of joining the clan, and now he'd send him to the front of the line to be slaughtered by wyrmlings.

They weren't about to let a mongrel like Alun breed with their precious daughters.

That was it, he imagined. Or else they want to kill me because they know what I did. Had someone told Madoc about his meeting with the high king?

The king had assured Alun, "This meeting must be kept private. Tell no one. I want to see my son take the throne someday. Not just for me, but as Daylan Hammer has said, for you, too, and for your posterity."

No, Madoc and his men don't know what I did, Alun decided. They only know what I am.

And so he ran as well as he could, and he was dragged and carried and kicked the rest of the way.

He didn't make it a hundred miles. But he had run forty, he felt certain.

It was a good account for one of the serf-born caste. There were rumors that one of his great grandmothers had been bedded by a warrior, and thus he claimed some decent blood. But the same could be said of every serf in the kingdom.

Every bone in his body ached, and when he tried to pee that afternoon, there was blood in his urine from the pummeling his kidneys had taken during the run. He felt too tired to care.

The last few miles were the hardest. They had reached

a strange canyon called the Vale of Anguish. Here, odd rock formations stood, piles of rubble that often looked more like men than rocks should, almost as if monstrous deformed beings had been turned to stone.

There were caves in the hills here where the warriors could hide for the night, and get some sleep—or fight, if they were backed into a corner.

But when he got to camp, lit only by starlight and a scythe of a moon, it was abuzz with excitement.

"They found little people—" someone was saying, "tiny folk that don't know how to talk. They live in huts made out of stones, with roofs made from sticks and straw. There's a whole village of them, just beyond the hill."

Alun would never have believed such nonsense under normal circumstances, but in the last day, the world had turned upside down. Forests had sprung up where there should be none. Mountains had collapsed and rivers changed their courses. Anything seemed possible.

"Little people," a soldier laughed, "what good are they? Can't eat 'em, can you?"

For effect, he tore off a huge piece of bread with his teeth, as if he were rending a little person.

"Maybe we'll find some use for their women," another jested, and he was joined by gruff laughter.

Alun wondered. He wanted to see these little folk, but his legs were so sore that he didn't think that he could walk up the hill. Still, he grabbed a loaf of dry bread from a basket, along with a flagon of ale, and slowly crept up the steep hill, past soldiers who were feeding and laughing.

He caught bits of conversation as he went. "River's flooded up ahead, they say. We'll have a rough swim of it."

"I can't swim," a heavy warrior said.

"Don't worry," the first said. "You just float, and I'll drag you along."

"That's the problem," the heavy one said. "I can't float. Bones are too heavy. I sink like an anvil. Always have. I just hope the king lets us take the bridge."

Atop the hill, High King Urstone, Warlord Madoc, the Emir of Dalharristan, the Wizard Sisel, and other notables all stood beneath a stand of sprawling oaks, peering down at a strange little village.

As the soldiers had said, there were houses made of small stones, and other houses made of mud-and-wattle, all with roofs formed from thick layers of grass, tied in bundles and woven together. There were small gardens around the houses, all separated from one another with rock walls.

There were folks outside of the houses, worried little folk, men with spears and torches, women with clubs. They weren't as small as Alun had hoped they would be. He wouldn't be able to pick one up in his hand. But they were short, more like children than adults, that was certain.

King Urstone was admiring their village. "They're tidy things, aren't they," he said. "Clever little houses, lush little gardens. Perhaps we could learn from them."

"I suppose," one of the warlords said. "Though I don't see much good that will come of it."

"What will we do?" King Urstone asked the lords around him. "They're obviously frightened of us, but we can't just leave them here, unprotected, with the wyrmlings about. The harvesters would have them in a week. For their own sake, we have to get them back to Caer Luciare, even if we must drag them."

"We could try leading them," the Emir said in his thick accent. "Perhaps if we offer them bread and ale, they will think well of us?"

"I think . . . I can talk to them," Warlord Madoc said, his voice sounding dreamy, lost in thought. Then he took off, striding downhill.

The small folk began shouting, waving their weapons, and Madoc unstrapped the great ax from his back, gently set it on the ground, and called out something in a strange tongue.

Alun had never heard such words before, and he wondered where Madoc could have learned them.

Suddenly, on the northern horizon, a white light blazed so brightly that it looked as if a shard of the sun had fallen to earth.

Everyone turned to see what was going on. Several people gasped in wonder.

"It's coming from Cantular," the Emir said.

Indeed, even with the naked eye, Alun could see that the bright light issued from Cantular. The sandstone buildings glowed gold in its brilliance, and long shadows were cast everywhere. The city itself was still a good four miles distant, though, and Alun could see little else.

The Emir pulled out an ocular—a pair of lenses made from ground crystal, held together by a long tube. He aimed the ocular toward the city, touched a glyph on the side of the tube, and spoke the name of the glyph.

Suddenly, an image appeared shimmering in the air, a dozen feet behind the rod.

It was an enlarged replica of the city, far away.

Alun could see clearly that a man stood atop a building, a man so white-hot that he glowed like the sun. He waved a sword, while above him three wyrmling Seccaths in crimson robes hovered in the air like hawks.

"Sweet mercy," the Wizard Sisel cried, "the Knights Eternal have been loosed!"

But Alun's fear quickly turned to wonder. There were people fighting the Knights Eternal, four small humans like those in the village below. A bowman loosed an arrow, and one of the Fell Three plummeted from the sky.

The bright one blazed even brighter, and light flooded the sky across the horizon.

Then the horizon abruptly went dim.

The ocular showed the scene, ropes of fire twirling between the bright one and a Knight Eternal, and then the lights went out, the humans dropped in a faint, and a pair of wyrmlings plummeted from the sky, like falcons stooping for the kill.

What happened next all took place in shadows. The ocular could not reveal much in so little light.

The warlords stood staring in dumb amazement.

"You saw that?" one of them cried. "Their archer slew a Knight Eternal! He killed one of the Three!"

Another warlord asked, "Are all of these small folk such warriors? If so, they would be grand allies! We had better make them allies, before they slaughter us all."

High King Urstone glanced down the hill at the poor farmers with their torches and clubs. The whole village together didn't look as if it could fend off a single wyrmling beggar. The king said thoughtfully, "I think that those four were folks of some import. They would have to be for the wyrmlings to send the Three after them." There were grunts of agreement.

The Emir said thoughtfully, "Daylan Hammer said that it was a wizard who bound our worlds together. One of those small folk is obviously a wizard. Could it be that he is the one who bound our worlds?"

"Look," one of the lords said, "the Knights Eternal are dragging them away. I think they've taken your wizard captive."

Madoc, who had been down in the valley, came huffing up the hill, his breathing ragged with excitement. He was looking to the north, where the lights had been.

"Then we will have to free the hostages," King Urstone said. "Perhaps that is why we are here. The Powers conspired to draw us here, lest some greater doom fall upon us."

"You would fight the Knights Eternal," Madoc grumbled, "in the dark, in a fortified position? That's madness. You'll foil our mission!"

The High King bit his lower lip. "Those small folk slew one of the Three. If we learn how they did it, we may be able to win this war once and for all." He gave Warlord Madoc a stern look. "The world has changed. We have more than just our own people, our own vain

ambitions to think about. We will attack an hour after
dawn, in the full light of day, and hunt the wyrmlings
down. If any of the Knights Eternal are still abroad, we'll
take off their heads. If done by the light of day, it might
take weeks before they can rise again. No word of what
happens here must reach Rugassa."

❧ 22 ❧

HIDDEN TREASURE

*One cannot be perfect in all things, but one can
become perfect in some things.*   —*Vulgnash*

Thul ransacked the prisoners' packs, pulling out spare
garments, studying trinkets and mementos, then casting
everything aside as if it was excrement. The Knight Eternal's cowl and robes hid his face, but his disgust showed
in every angry move.

The prisoners lay frozen upon what was left of the
floor of the house, scorched as it was from the battle. The
touch of the grave was upon them, and they lay para-
lyzed, like mice that have been filled with scorpion's
venom.

The spell would wear off by dawn.

"I see only three packs here," Vulgnash said. "Where
is the fourth?"

Thul glanced around, looking for sign of a fourth pack.
"Perhaps it fell when we pulled the walls off," Thul
answered.

"Find it," Vulgnash said.

Thul growled in resentment, and then walked around,
carefully studying the ground. "I don't see one. I think . . .

the wizard is their leader. He would not carry a pack. He would make the others carry."

Vulgnash could not argue with that. No wyrmling lord would stoop to such menial chores. He climbed down to the ground level and grabbed some withered vines, long tendrils of morning glory that had been burned by the sun. When he had several feet of them, he leapt in the air, flapped up to the prisoners, and threw the vines upon Fallion in a twisted heap.

"Bind them firmly," he commanded.

The vines began to slither, twisting around the hands and feet of each prisoner, clamping legs together, cinching the arms tight against the chest.

When the prisoners were firmly bound, Vulgnash knelt and studied their weapons. He touched the fine reaverbone bow that Jaz had held, and recoiled in horror. There was *life* in that bow, the blessing of a powerful undine.

He kicked it over the edge of the house with his boot, studied the other weapons. They were similarly accursed. He kicked them all into the bushes behind the little shop. "Rust upon you, and rot," he hissed, casting a spell. In a month the fine steel would be nothing but mounds of corrosion, the bow turned to dust, and the wooden staff would be food for worms.

Thul turned away from the packs, went and hunched over one of the small humans, the smallest of the women. Vulgnash glanced at him, saw Thul reaching down to place a finger over each eye.

"Do not feed on her!" Vulgnash hissed.

"But she is sweet!" Thul said. "Besides, we only need the wizard."

"We need them all," Vulgnash countered. "We must get the wizard to accept a wyrm. Sometimes, a man cannot be tortured into it, but he will break if another is tortured in his place."

Thul growled deep in his throat, whirled, and went back to the packs, began hurling things around in his rage.

There was a clanking, the sound of some bits of metal,

copper perhaps, banging against one another. Thul dumped a bag of rods upon the floor, sniffing at them. "What are these?" he asked. "I smell wizardry."

Vulgnash strode to him, knelt and peered at the rods, thinking that perhaps they had stumbled upon a human harvester, and that these were his harvesting spikes. But the rods were not made of iron. They were made of corpuscite. Each rod was about the length of a child's hand, from the bottom of the palm to the tip of the middle finger. Each was about the diameter of a small willow frond.

And at the tip of each was a rune, one of the primal shapes that had formed the world from the beginning.

Vulgnash picked one up, studied the rune. It was easy to decipher for those who were wise enough to see: *swiftness*. Attached to the rune were others—*seize, confer,* and *bind*.

He had never seen such a device, but instinctively Vulgnash knew what it was. The rod had been created to transfer attributes from one being to another.

"This is a weapon," he told Thul in rising exhilaration, "a marvelous weapon."

With mounting excitement he poured out the other branding irons, studied each one in turn: resilience, memory, strength, beauty, sight, hearing, smell, song. A dozen types of runes were represented, and Vulgnash immediately recognized that he could make others that the creators had not anticipated—greed, cruelty, stubbornness—the list was endless.

"But can you make them work?" Thul demanded.

Vulgnash could not wait to try. But first he had to get the prisoners back to Rugassa. His wings could not carry so much weight. He'd have to take the prisoners overland.

"Take these rods to Zul-torac," Vulgnash commanded. "He'll know what to do. I'll bring the prisoners to Rugassa in three days."

"Yes, Master," Thul said. He grabbed up the small branding irons, raced to the edge of the platform, and his crimson wings unfolded and caught the air. In a moment he was gone, rising up into the starlight.

Fallion lay petrified, a bone-numbing cold coursing through his body, his legs and arms unable to move, bound tightly. He was so cold, he could hardly think. He could do little in the way of making plans. He acted only on instinct.

He sent his senses out, questing for a source of heat. The sun had gone down long ago. There was no heat left in the stones around him, nor in the Knight Eternal.

Even his friends were perilously cold. He could not draw from them, not without killing them.

Wyrmlings came from the fort then, filling his field of vision. They were like men in some ways, monstrous men as pale white as bone, with misshapen skulls, huge and powerful.

One of them heaved Fallion over his back like a carcass, then carried him down the ladder and out along the stone street until they reached a wagon. Upon it lay a huge stone box. There were no horses or oxen to draw the thing. Instead it had handles on the front. The cruel contraption was a handcart, powered by the sweat of brutish wyrmlings.

The wyrmling shoved the stone lid off the box with one hand, a feat that should have required several strong men, then tossed Fallion in without ceremony. Moments later, Talon, Jaz, and Rhianna each tumbled in beside him, and the lid scraped closed.

Fallion could feel the cold begin to wear off. The numbness in his hands was fading; he clenched and unclenched his hands, trying to get the blood to flow.

He reached out with his mind. He could feel heat from the wyrmlings. A dozen of them surrounded the little carriage. He tried to use his flameweaving skills to siphon off their body heat.

He did not need much, just enough to burn the cords that bound his hands.

Instantly it felt as if a wall crashed down between him and the wyrmlings. The little heat that he had in his body drained off, and Fallion was left reeling in pain from the cold.

For only an instant, Fallion tasted blinding agony, and then passed out.

It seemed like long hours before his thoughts returned. He had to fight his way through a seeming tunnel of pain. His teeth chattered and he shivered all over.

He didn't have the strength to fight his captor. He didn't even dare try.

Next time, he feared, the Knight Eternal would drain him of heat completely.

The wagon tilted as one of the wyrmlings lifted the front end, and then the wheels began to creak as it jolted down the uneven road.

North, Fallion realized dully as he felt the wagon turn. They are taking us north. But what lay that direction, he did not know.

He thought he'd try his tongue, even though it felt swollen and foreign in his mouth, as if some slab of meat were caught in his throat. "Talon? Talon? Where are they taking us?"

There was a long silence.

At last Jaz answered, "I think . . . our sister is dead. I can't feel her breathing."

It was blackest night in the box. Fallion turned and peered toward Talon.

In his memory, they were all back in their little home on the Sweetgrass. It was the night before they set out, and all of the neighbors had come. Lanterns hung from the peach trees in the front yard, shedding light upon the bounteous feast that had been set before them—piles of strawberries and fresh peas from the garden, succulent greens and wild mushrooms, mounds of spiced chicken, steaming muffins.

There had been music and celebration with a band that had come all of the way from Rye.

And there had been worry. Fallion had seen it in Myrrima's eyes, and in Borenson's, for Fallion was setting sail to the far side of the earth and heading into the underworld, where the reavers dwelt.

Fallion had felt so cocksure of himself.

"Take good care of my baby," Myrrima had begged. She loved Fallion as if he were her own son, he knew. She had never treated him with any less kindness or devotion, even though he was only hers by adoption. But Talon was her first-born, and a girl, and Myrrima had always doted on her when she was young.

"I'll take care of her," Fallion had promised.

"Bring her back alive, and whole," Myrrima begged, fighting back tears. Fallion could see that she wanted to run into the house, to hide herself and cry.

"When we come back," Fallion had said, "it will be in a more perfect world, and Talon will be whole and beautiful, more beautiful than you can imagine."

Myrrima had smiled faintly then, wanting to believe.

Fallion reached out with his senses, could find almost no warmth in Talon's body. The Knights Eternal had drained it all from her.

What have I done? Fallion wondered. He'd brought a change upon the world, but Talon had become a monster, huge and grotesque, nearly as bad as the wyrmlings.

And now she lay at the verge of death.

Rhianna began to weep. Fallion could hear her sniffling.

"Are you all right?" she asked.

"So cold," Fallion said through chattering teeth. He'd never felt anything like it, not even in the coldest arctic storm.

Rhianna rolled over to him, showing more strength than he possessed. She leaned against him, draping her body over him like a blanket. "Here," she whispered. "Take the heat of my body."

He continued to tremble, hoping that her warmth might keep him alive. No words of gratitude seemed sufficient. "Thank you," he managed weakly. And then he realized that he felt so close to death, he might never get a chance to speak to her again. "I love you."

All through the long night, the wyrmlings toiled down the road, the wagon shuddering as if it would burst each time it slammed into a rut, the wheels of the wagon creaking.

It was wearisome, trudging behind that wagon, when Vulgnash could so easily take to the sky. But the wizard inside the stone box was subtle, and Vulgnash could not leave him unguarded.

Several times throughout the night, Vulgnash drained the heat from the boy, drawing him into a state near death, then keeping him there for long periods, letting him wake just enough to regain some strength before drawing him back down again.

Vulgnash wearied of the job.

By dawn I could be in Rugassa, he thought, studying the branding irons, uncovering their secrets, unlocking their powers.

But no. I am condemned to walk, to guard the little wizard.

Vulgnash would do his mistress's bidding. He was flawless in the performance of his duties. He always had been.

But how he hated it.

So they marched through the night, through a fair land where the stubble of wild grasses shone white beneath the silver moon, through the night where forbidding woods cast long shadows as they marched over the hills.

There was little risk of attack. These lands had been taken by the wyrmlings years ago, and the warrior clans had long since lost the will to fight for their return.

Vulgnash saw nothing in the night but a pair of wild oxen; some stags drinking beside a pool; and a young wolf prowling in a meadow, jumping about as it hunted for mice.

It was only when they spotted a village in the distance that Vulgnash took pause. It was a village full of new humans, of runts. Their cottages looked restful, lying in the fold of a vale. Smoke curled up from last night's cooking fires, and he could see goats and cattle in their little stick pens.

Vulgnash had not given much thought to the runts. The wizard he had caught was one of them, and he wondered now if perhaps some of the wizard's kin might not come looking for him.

As a precaution, he stopped the wagon. "Go down to that village," he told his warriors, "and kill everyone."

He stood guard as the wyrmlings loped off across fields that glowed golden in the moonlight. A couple of dogs began wagging their tails and barking as the wyrmlings approached, but their barking grew frantic as they realized that some new terror was approaching.

A human man came to a door to investigate, just as the wyrmling warriors approached; a wyrmling hurled a spear through him.

Then the warriors were on the houses. They did not go in through the doors. They kicked down walls and threw off the roofs. They screamed and roared like wild beasts, striking terror into the hearts of the little ones.

And then they ran down anyone who tried to escape.

They made sport of the slaughter, ripping off the legs of living men, pummeling mothers into the dirt, searching through the rubble of broken houses to find the babes, then squeezing them as if they were small birds.

In all, it took less than fifteen minutes, but it was time well spent.

Vulgnash felt as if he had accomplished something.

They ran afterward, for more than an hour through the night, the warriors' hearts pumping hard from bloodlust, until they reached an old abandoned hill fort. It had a single watchtower that looked out over the rolling hills, and a great room and a kitchen that had once garrisoned troops. Beyond that, there was nothing more but some moldering sheds, their wooden roofs weighed down by moss and blackberry vines.

The birds had begun to sing and the stars were dying in the heavens. The fort looked like a good place to camp for the day. In fact, there was no other place on the trail behind and no likely spot ahead for many hours. The old fort was Vulgnash's only choice.

❧ 23 ❧

BENEATH THE UGLY STONES

A scholar once told me that he could prove that men of renown lived longer than others. The wise woman of the village, the hero of battles, the acknowledged master of his craft—whether it be a baker or smith or only a chandler. Each lived an average of seven years longer than others of their kind.

"The secret," he said, "is praise. We all need it. It is a tonic that restores both the body and soul. Children need it to grow up to be healthy.

"Unfortunately, the stupid and the wicked need it too, and so often are undeserving. Look to the motives of those who commit crimes, and all too often they do it hoping to raise themselves in the esteem of others.

"And it is also for the praise of others that good men do well. Thus our need for praise can prod us down the path of goodness, or onto the avenues of evil."
                                          —*the Wizard Sisel*

"King Urstone is groping for eels," Warlord Madoc told his sons that night. "This plan of his—rescuing this otherworld wizard—it's a vain hope. He is only fore-stalling the inevitable."

"The death of his son?" Drewish asked.

"Aye, the death of his son," Madoc said. The army had bedded down in the caves, but Madoc and his lads were in a small vale beneath the shadows of three huge sandstone rocks, each looking like some monstrous face, twisted and grotesque.

"You would think that Urstone would have forgotten him by now," Connor said. "You would think that he'd have given him up for dead."

"Mmmmm," Madoc grunted in agreement. "It's a point of honor with him. He wants to be seen as a man of compassion. He can't let it be said of him that the wyrmlings love their children more than he does. It would make him somehow . . . callous, tainted."

"Do you think the wyrmlings *do* love their children more than we do?" Connor asked.

Madoc scratched his painted chin thoughtfully. "A mother bear will do anything to protect her cubs. A wyrmling is no different. They have the instinct, and they've got it strong. Zul-torac is as bloody-handed a wyrmling that has ever led a war, but still he loves his daughter, and she is made all the more precious by the fact that he can bear no more."

"Can a wyrmling really love?" Connor asked.

"Not in the way that humans do," Madoc said. "But they have feelings—greed, fear. But wyrmlings do not love, they merely rut. They give their children as servants to Lady Despair in an unending succession, and so long as their lines continue, they believe that she will not punish them in the afterlife."

Madoc didn't know much about such things. He had never really studied wyrmling philosophy. He was only repeating snatches of lore that were repeated around the campfire. He had never quite understood why the wyrmlings failed to wipe out Caer Luciare. Kan-hazur was just a worthless wyrmling child in his estimation. It only made sense that Zul-torac would hunt down the last of mankind, even if he had to hack his way through his own daughter to do so.

Yet for a dozen years now, the wyrmlings had let the city go. Never had it been attacked in force. The only incursions came from wyrmling harvesters that haunted the wood and fields outside the castle, taking only the unwary.

Yet Madoc had developed a theory as to why the wyrmlings didn't attack, a theory so monstrous, he had never dared to speak of it openly, a theory that had been borne out—in part. Only now did he voice his concerns.

"My sons," he said. "There is a good reason that the wyrmlings have spared us. They need mankind. Their harvesters need our glands to make their foul elixirs. King Urstone has never thought this through, but the wyrmlings would not dare to kill us all. Instead, they let us live, like pigs fattening in a pen, waiting for the slaughter. It isn't our hostage that has saved us for so long. It is . . . necessity."

Drewish smiled and gazed up into the air. Obviously, the idea amused him. "If we are but animals waiting to be harvested, why not cage us?"

Connor laughed. "Because it takes work to feed a pig, to keep him caged. Why not let the pigs feed themselves?"

"The caged animal is easier to kill."

"There's no sport to hunting a pig in its pen," Madoc said with a smile. "And the wyrmlings are nothing, if not lovers of blood sport."

It was true. The wyrmlings were bred for blood-lust. Without men to hunt, they would quickly begin slaughtering themselves. Madoc knew that the wyrmlings could indeed harvest glands from their own kind—but that would soon lead to bloody war.

Connor seemed uncertain. "Are you sure this is true?"

"Certain," Madoc said. "My men captured a harvester

last winter. It was only with fire and the tongs that I could pull the truth from him.

"And five weeks ago, we took another, and did him until he told the precise same tale."

Madoc took a deep breath, gave the boys a moment while he let the information settle in. "Now, there are these little folk abroad. A village here, a village there. How many of them could there be?"

"Thousands," Drewish guessed.

But Madoc gave him a knowing look and shook his head. "Millions, tens of millions. On the other world, there was a great kingdom in the north, the land of Internook, that was filled to overflowing. To the east, there were hordes of millions in Indhopal. In this world, there was a rare metal, used to make magic branding irons called forcibles, and with these, the lords of the land would take attributes—strength, speed, intelligence, and beauty from their vassals. Such lords became men of unimaginable power."

Madoc held up a bit of red stone, showed it the boys in the starlight.

"What is that?" Drewish asked.

"Corpuscite," Madoc said, "what the little folk called blood metal in their own tongue. It is used to make forcibles. It was rare in their world. But it is not so rare in ours. There is a hill of it near Caer Luciare. Already I have miners digging it up."

He let the implication sink in. From Drewish's unappreciative look, it was obvious that the boy didn't understand the full implications of the discovery, but soon enough, he would.

Madoc was quickly learning that there were others like himself, hundreds who had lived separate lives on both worlds. Soon enough, he would find someone among the clan who had been a facilitator on otherworld, a mage trained to transfer endowments, and then Madoc would be in business.

"It is only a matter of time before the wyrmlings

discover this, too," Madoc said. "It is only a matter of time before they realize what our warriors might do if we unite these small folk under a single banner and lead them to war. It is only a matter of time, before they realize the threat that we pose, and try to smash Caer Luciare into oblivion!"

"What shall we do?" Connor asked.

Now was the moment for Madoc to speak his mind openly. "King Urstone is a fool, too weak to lead this people. So long as his son is held captive, he won't risk attacking Rugassa. We must . . . eliminate the king."

"How?" Drewish asked with a tone of relish in his voice.

"In the heat of the battle, tomorrow, when no one is looking," Madoc said, "it would be a good time for a spear-thrust to go astray."

Connor seemed shocked by the idea. He had always been a good lad, in Madoc's opinion. Sometimes, such decency can be a fault.

"Stick with me," Madoc said, "and someday soon, you shall rule a nation."

"Which one of us?" Drewish asked.

Connor turned to him in obvious confusion. "Me, of course. I'm the oldest."

"And I'm better able to lead," Drewish countered, leaping to his feet, a dirk ringing from the scabbard at his knee.

Connor yelped, leapt back, and drew his own dagger. His jaw tightened and his muscles flexed as he prepared for battle.

Madoc stood up, placing himself between the two, and glared at Drewish dangerously, as if begging him to attack.

"Two kingdoms," Madoc promised. "One for each of you."

THE ESCAPE

I often tell myself that I should never underestimate the goodness of the human spirit. Time after time, I have found that I can count on the mercies and tenderness of others. Perhaps it is because I constantly look for and nourish the good in others that I am too often dismayed to find abundant evil in them, too.
                                    —Daylan Hammer

Daylan climbed the rope up to the grate and clung for a long moment as he listened for guards. There was only the sound of the wyrmling princess pacing in her cell.

There were no other prisoners so far down in the dungeon. Daylan had watched for them as he was borne through the hallway. So it was with little concern of being discovered that he felt around at the lock.

The good king had left him a key. It turned easily, and Daylan Hammer was free of the oubliette.

He climbed out, and stepped on a bundle on the floor. In it, he found his war hammer, a dagger, a flask and some food. The king hadn't had the foresight to leave Daylan any clothing. He was still naked, covered with filth.

He carried his few goods past some cells, squinting as he peered in, somehow hoping that there might be food or clothing in one. Straw in the corners served as the only mattress that a prisoner down here might get, and with no other recourse, he finally went into an open cell and used some straw to scrape off the muck.

It didn't help much.

I didn't escape the oubliette, he decided. I brought half of it with me.

He imagined trying to break free of the city, a naked man covered in dung.

That will cause no small stir, he thought, fighting back a grim smile.

When he finished, he went to the cell of Princess Kan-hazur. A guttering torch revealed her. She was hunched in a corner, in a fetal position, with her elbows on her knees and her hands wrapped over her face. She peered at him distastefully from the corner of an eye. "You here to rape me?"

"No," Daylan said as he tried his key in the lock. He felt a sense of relief as it clicked open. As he had hoped, the king had provided a master key to the prison.

"Too bad," Kan-hazur said, "I could use a little sport. And from the looks of you, that's all you could offer."

Daylan did not smile at her dry wit. He was so befouled, she could not possibly have wanted him. She was only making jest of him.

"Where did you learn to talk so filthily?" Daylan asked.

"At my mother's breast," Kan-hazur said, "but nine years in this stink-hole has perfected my skills."

Daylan searched her room. There was a bucket of water on the floor.

"I've come to rescue you," Daylan said. He picked up the pail, let the water stream over him slowly, and washed off the filth as well as he could.

Kan-hazur stared at him for a long moment. "I'm not a fool. I don't believe you."

"It's true," Daylan said. "I've set up an exchange of hostages—you for Prince Urstone."

He had expected her to smile at this point, to weep or show some gratitude. But she merely glared at him and refused to move.

"Lady Despair teaches that the sole purpose of life is to teach you humility," Kan-hazur said after a long moment. "And true humility only comes when you reach the realization that no one—mother, father, lover, ally, the Powers, or any force of nature—gives a shit whether you live or die.

"I have mastered humility."

Daylan considered the implications of those words. The princess didn't believe that her father valued her life, not enough to give up his own hostage, certainly. Was she right? The tone of her words was forthright. She was convinced.

"Believe it or not," Daylan said, "I care if you live or die. I wish you well."

"You don't even know me," Kan-hazur countered. "I am a wyrmling, and I am your enemy."

"On some worlds," Daylan said softly, "it is taught that the sole purpose of life is to master love, and the epitome of love is to love one's enemies, to wish well those that hate you, to serve those who would do you harm. It is only through such love that we can turn enemies into allies, and at last into friends. I have spent millennia mastering love."

Kan-hazur laughed him to scorn.

"Come," Daylan said, reaching for her hand.

She refused to give it to him.

"Please?"

"You're taking me to my death," she said, "whether you know it or not. My father would lop my head off in front of you, just to prove how little he cares for me."

"That's a lie, whether you know it or not. Even a wyrmling cares for his child. It is in your blood. Your presence here has kept this citadel safe for nine years. If your father cared so little for you, he could have proved it a thousand times over, by attacking."

Kan-hazur shook her head.

"Even if he does not love you," Daylan said, "he has forsaken his flesh, becoming as the Death Lords. He cannot sire another heir." The princess showed surprise, and hope flickered in her eyes. "Come, what have you got to lose?" Daylan asked. "We can stop in the market, get you some good meat before we go, let you feel the wind in your face and see the stars tonight. Even if your father comes to kill you, as you believe, wouldn't it be worth the trip, just for one last pleasure?"

"Don't trade me," Kan-hazur said, suddenly fearful. "Take me outside the city, and let me go in the wild. I can find my way back to civilization."

Daylan understood. By running away, escaping back to her own kind, she could start a new life. She might even be heralded as a hero for having escaped. But if she stayed, if he tried to trade her, she was truly afraid that her father would make an example of her punishing her for her weakness.

"I won't lie to you," Daylan said. "If I let you go, I would lose any hope of winning back Prince Urstone."

"Why?"

"Because, as I said, I have negotiated an exchange of hostages."

"No," she said. "Why won't you lie to me? People always lie. Even humans. Lies are . . . necessary."

He understood what she meant. Most people lied, trying to hide what they felt or believed about others. Such dishonesty was the foundation of civility, and Daylan agreed that such lies were necessary.

But some people lied only to manipulate. A merchant who hated a client might greet him as if he were an old friend, feigning camaraderie while hiding his own personal distaste.

And to gain greater advantage, he might even deceive the client, lying about the value of merchandise, or when delivery dates could be met.

Among the wyrmlings, such lies were a way of life.

And if Daylan had wanted to manipulate her, he could easily have promised to take her out of the city and let her go, and then reneged at an opportune moment.

"I will not lie to you," Daylan said, "because in part I value you. A human is not a tool to be manipulated. To try to make you my tool would be to demean you. And I will not lie to you, in part, because to do so would make me a lesser man than I want to be. My word needs to be trust-worthy always. If it is not, then I can never be trusted.

"That said, Princess, I ask that you come with me on my terms. Or, if you like, you may stay where you are, and the deal I have negotiated with your father will be forfeit."

Kan-hazur crouched in the corner, pondering his words. Daylan had never expected to have to try to convince her to leave. But the wyrm that fed upon her soul was a con-trary thing. It shunned reason, trust, and compassion.

He suddenly realized that perhaps he needed to manipulate her in ways that she understood—fear, greed, shame. But to do so would violate every principle of the order that he lived by. Gentleness, loving kindness, gen-tle persuasion—those were the means that he was allowed to use in such circumstances.

He chose gentle persuasion. "I have a question, princess. You say that the purpose of life is to master humility. But once that is done, what have you gained?"

She glared at him. "Once you realize that the universe is a cold, uncaring bitch, it means that you have only one choice in life—to fight for what you want. It forces you to live by self-determination, and that is the mother of all virtues."

Daylan nodded. "I, too, value self-determination, and see it as a fertile ground from which virtues may grow. So, I have to wonder: If you are resolved to lead a self-determined life, how is that to be done here in this cell? Are you going to sit here and die where King Urstone's men have placed you? That doesn't sound like self-determination to me. It sounds as if you are their pawn. Or would you choose instead to go back and claim your empire, even if it means that you must fight your own father for it?"

She glared at him. At last she climbed to her feet. Day-lan offered her his hand, but she rejected it.

"I will not take my empire because you give it to me," she growled. "I will take it because I *can*. You have arranged my release for your own reasons, and I will owe you nothing."

Daylan shrugged. "It doesn't matter to me which evil wyrmling rules the earth. You're all much the same."

Still, she followed him out of the cell.

In the torture chamber, Daylan found a ragged tunic beside a rack. Someone had torn it off a prisoner before flogging him. The tunic was overlarge, but it would have to do.

They climbed the stairs stealthily and found a single guard on duty. He was sitting at a table, snoring loudly. In one hand he clutched a finely gilded wine bottle as if it were a lover. Obviously, the bottle was a gift from the king.

Daylan Hammer and Princess Kan-hazur unlocked the prison door, and were unleashed upon the world.

❧ 25 ❧

THE HARVEST

A hero is not always brave and strong. More often, he is but a common man who finds the courage and strength to do what he must, while others do not.
—Fallion the Bold

They're going to kill you, Alun thought as he ran in the dawn light. Watch your back in this battle.

Alun raced along the uneven highway to Cantular, hulking warriors both ahead and behind. The road had become a ruin since the change. The once-smooth highway, paved with stones four feet thick, was now broken and uneven. The roots of great oaks had thrust up through the stone, and old streambeds cut through it.

So Alun watched his feet as he jogged. There was little else to see. A summer's fog left the vale gauzed in white. Trees came out of the mist as he passed.

There was only the heavy pad of the warrior's feet, the clink of bone armor, and the wheezing of breath.

Alun's legs still ached from yesterday's run. But he covered the uneven ground well enough. Only so often would someone shove him from behind, shouting, "Move along, maggot!" or some other such insult.

He could not hear well with his helm. It was made for a bigger man, and fit him ill. As a child, Alun had played soldier and worn wooden buckets on his head that fit him better. The armorer had passed the bone mail and weapons out at dawn. The armor had been brought here ahead of the war party, secreted in a cave. The bone armor that Alun wore was carved from a world wyrm. The older it got, the lighter it became, but it was supposed to be tougher than a bear's hide.

Alun bore an ax into battle. Once again, it was too large to feel right in his hand. But it had a big spike on one side, and another at the end, and he imagined that he could pound a spike into a wyrmling's knee if he had to.

Alun peered ahead and behind, searching for Connor or Drewish. They were the ones who would most likely put a spear in his back. But he caught no sight of them.

So he ran, grateful that he only had to run. The troops had been cut into two divisions. Three hundred men had set out upriver at the crack of dawn to swim across the flood. They would take the fortress on the far side.

Six hundred ran with him now, hearts pumping, each of the warriors seemingly lost in private thoughts.

"Don't look so down," a soldier said at Alun's left.

He glanced over, saw a large soldier, an older man, perhaps in his forties. Alun recognized him. He'd come to the kennels at times to bring the dogs in after a hunt. Alun couldn't recall his name.

"First battle?" the soldier asked.

"Yeah," Alun said. He'd wanted to nod, but he didn't want to look all out of breath.

"Just remember, they're more afraid of you than you are of them."

"Really?" Alun said. He couldn't imagine it.

"Nah," another soldier behind them laughed. "He's having you on. They're wyrmlings, damn it, and you're just the scrapings on their boots."

Greeves—that was the man's name. Greeves laughed too, and Alun found himself laughing just a bit. It felt good to laugh, knowing that you might die.

"Just remember, keep yourself hunched low," Greeves said. "Don't come at the enemy head-on. Veer to the right or the left. And when you lunge in for a stab, don't aim high. Pick a low target—a kidney or their knees. Then leap back. Got it?"

They raced on through the thick fog.

There was sudden shouting up ahead, troops jostling. Alun was in the rearmost third of the division. Suddenly he saw the High King and a dozen warlords off to the side of the road, peering ahead. Connor and Drewish stood at the king's back, and Alun peered at them fearfully, afraid that they would follow him, that they would slide a blade between his ribs in the heat of the battle.

He stumbled, tripping on the heel of one of the soldiers in front, and then he realized that a gray shadow loomed above them all. They had reached the fortress. They had seemingly reached it in an instant.

The ring of metal, the cries of dying men suddenly came loud, echoing down from the stone walls. Alun was startled to find the battlefront so close ahead. He pounded along the road, and the soldiers beside him broke into song:

> What shall they say when the day is done
> Of battles fought and glory won?
> I was first into battle,
> I struck fear in my foe,
> I was first to land a bloody blow!

Suddenly they were in a seeming canyon, walls rearing high above them on either side—the fortress. A heavy war dart came hurtling from the tower above, clanked against a man's helmet, and bounced away. Alun glanced up at the crenellated tower, tried to see the wyrmling that had thrown it, but archers along the street sent up a rain of arrows and the wyrmling dove for cover.

And then he saw his first bodies, human bodies, men of the Warrior Clan littering the roadside—spears and arrows in them. And then he was rushing beneath an arch, and there were huge doors that had been battered down, and Alun raced into a courtyard.

Everyone but him seemed to know where to go. Soldiers to the left fanned out to the left, those to the right went right. Alun couldn't see any sign of battle, but he heard cries in the mist all around him.

He hesitated.

"Out of the way!" a soldier shouted, shoving him aside.

A black arrow whizzed out of the fog, plunked into the neck of a fellow behind. Alun whirled, saw the man stagger back in shock, pull the arrow free. Blood gushed from the wound, but it wasn't much, and he looked at Alun and laughed, "I'll be all right." A second arrow plunged into the man's chest.

Alun decided that it was safer to be anywhere but here.

A huge warrior went charging past him, shouting a battle cry and bearing an ax in either hand, and Alun decided: I want to be behind that monster!

He gave chase, and soon he saw the warrior, tearing through a dark doorway ahead, his arms swinging like mad. A pair of wyrmlings blocked his way. They were larger than the human warrior, but they fell back before the onslaught, and Alun went racing into the building.

His warrior was ahead, across the room, doing battle at another doorway.

The dead littered the floor all around, both human and wyrmling. Apparently the wyrmlings had fought to secure the doorway, and the battle had gone back and forth. Alun glanced behind him, afraid that Connor or Drewish might have followed.

Someone cried, "Help!" and Alun peered into the shadows. A man was down, blood gushing from a wound to his chest. Alun moved to give aid.

He heard a growl, saw a wyrmling commander trying groggily to rise up from the heap on hands and knees, his black armor slick with blood. He was reaching for a small pouch tied to his war belt. His helm was cracked, and he had a deep wound to the scalp.

Not deep enough, Alun thought, and buried the pick end of his ax in it.

The wyrmling collapsed, still clutching his pouch.

Curious, Alun reached down, drew the pouch from the wyrmling's dead hand.

Perhaps there is some treasure here, he thought, imagining golden rings or amulets.

But when he opened the pouch, he saw only three crude iron spikes, rusty and bent, each about four inches in length.

Alun stared at them in wonder, for they were a treasure greater than gold. They were harvester's spikes—iron nails encrusted with glandular extracts drawn from those that the wyrmlings had killed. The extracts granted a man tremendous strength and threw him into a bloodlust, at least for awhile.

A warrior came rushing in behind. He must have seen Alun finish off the wyrmling, for he shouted to Alun, "That's the way lad!" then stopped and peered at the spikes. "A harvester! You killed yourself a harvester. Use 'em up, lad. Good men died to make those."

The fellow snatched one of the spikes from Alun's hand, and Alun thought that he was stealing it. He protested, "Hey!" and turned to confront the fellow, just as the man shoved the spike into Alun's neck, piercing the carotid artery.

And the dried fruit of the harvested glands surged through Alun's veins.

His first reaction was that his heart began to pump so violently that he feared it would burst. Then his mouth went dry and he felt nauseous as blood was diverted from his stomach to his extremities.

And then the rage came, a rage so hot that it drove all thoughts from his mind. Blood pounded in his ears like the surging of the sea.

He let out a blood-curdling cry, grabbed an extra ax from a fallen comrade, and suddenly found himself charging through a mist of red, leaping over fallen foes, lunging past warriors of the clan.

A wyrmling suddenly appeared before him in a doorway, a huge creature with an ax, his face covered with beastly tattoos, his oversized canines hanging out like fangs. He wore thick armor and wielded a battle-ax and a shield. Alun felt no fear.

Somehow, in the haze of war, Alun saw a flash, and for an instant it was Drewish that stood before him.

Alun went mad with blood rage.

I am immortal and invincible, Alun thought in a haze, and he leapt high in the air. The wyrmling raised its shield defensively, but the harvester's spike in Alun's neck had given him super-human strength. He swung an ax, cleaving the shield in two, striking through, and burying his ax into the wyrmling's skull.

As Alun's weight hit the falling monster, Alun saw three more wyrmlings in the shadows behind it.

Good, there are more! he thought, laughing in glee.

And so he fought in a haze of red. The battle was like a dance, him leaping and twisting in the air, swinging his ax.

Some conscious part of his mind warned: Watch your back. They still want you dead!

But that was the last conscious thought that he had.

Sometime later, an hour, two perhaps, he came out of the haze. He was in a room, a barracks, where only the tiniest crack of light shone through a single door.

He still had one ax, though the head had broken off of the other and he held its haft in his hand. He was swinging his good ax into the corpse of a wyrmling, screaming, "Die you cur! Die, you damned pig!"

There were a dozen wyrmlings sprawled on the floor, each of them hacked to pieces.

Several human soldiers were standing in a doorway, peering at him and laughing.

Alun's heart still raced as if it would explode, and his arm felt so tired that he did not think it would heal in a week. He had a bad gash on his forehead, and blood was flowing down over his eyes. And the other soldiers were laughing at him.

"Here now," a commanding voice said, "that's enough of that, lad. You killed 'em already." The soldiers guffawed.

Alun peered up in shock. It was a captain.

"I killed them?" Alun asked, not believing his ears. But the memories rushed through his mind, ghoulish apparitions.

The captain walked up, pulled the spike from Alun's neck, and gave him a bandage to staunch the wound.

"You're lucky—" the captain said, "a little fellow like you, fighting like a harvester." He held up the bloody spike. "It gives you strength and speed and murderer's instinct, but it was made for a wyrmling that stands eight feet tall and weighs five hundred pounds. You took a monster's dose. You're lucky that your heart didn't explode."

Alun suddenly felt weak. The glandular extracts were leaving his body, and it was all that he could do to stand up. He was breathing hard, gasping for breath, and cold sweat dimpled his forehead.

The captain shouted orders to the men, "Clean this place out! Leave no door unopened, no cubby-hole unchecked. Be sure of every enemy. The king wants the heads off of them. Bring them out into the light of day, and throw them in the courtyard."

So the grisly work began. Alun spent the next fifteen minutes feeling sick, staunching the flow of blood from the gouge in his forehead, wrapping his head up in a bloody bandage, and hacking the head off of a dead wyrmling and lugging it out of doors.

He tried to remember how he had gotten the wound, but could not account for it. He tried to remember where his helmet had come off, but never could find it.

He discovered that the troops had entered a barracks, had caught the wyrmlings sleeping. Many of them did not even have their armor on.

When he was finished, he was a bloody mess, and the captains came through and counted every body, then went out and counted every head.

The king and the warlords came now, admiring the heads stacked in a pile. Connor and Drewish were still there, at the king's back. Neither of them had bloodied themselves in battle.

Drewish leered at Alun, seeming to enjoy the spectacle of him wounded.

Imagine how he would laugh to see you dead, a little voice whispered in Alun's mind.

"Two hundred and fifty," the captain reported to the warlords. "That would be five squadrons, even."

"And of our own dead?" King Urstone asked.

"Fifty and four."

"Not bad," someone whispered in the line beside Alun, but he saw the king's face, saw him mourn. He had too few warriors as it was. He regretted losing even one man.

"And what of the Knights Eternal?" the king asked.

"No one saw any sign of them," the captain confirmed.

King Urstone nodded, looked worried, and then the troops headed across the bridge.

By then the fog was lifting, and Alun found that he was unaccountably hungry. The long run of the day before, a sleepless night, the hot work—all combined to build his appetite.

So they raced across the bridge, and Alun was surprised to see the water so high, the trees and wreckage floating down the muddy river.

They reached the far shore, found the drawbridge down. Their own men cheered their entry, and Alun realized, We've taken it! We've taken Cantular!

It was the first real victory for mankind in many years, and the cheers were bounteous, over-excited.

Like boys who have bloodied the nose of a bully, Alun thought, not knowing that the fight has just begun.

"Search every building!" the king shouted. "Look in every house, every market stall. I want word of the Knights Eternal, and of their prisoners."

The king and his counselors went striding down the street, heading toward the east end of town. The men began to fan out, searching in every direction. Alun just followed the king, following along in his wake. He was afraid that someone would stop him, make him go and do some real work, but no one did.

They reached the markets, found the stall where the battle had taken place. It wasn't hard to find. The walls of the home here had peeled back, and the roof had been thrown off. There were scorch marks on the wooden platform where the battle had been fought.

The king and the warlords climbed the platform, looking around. Alun didn't feel comfortable following them up there, and so he went to the side of the house. There were some rags draped over a bush, and he stood by them for a second.

Clothes, he realized. Too small for our people.

He peered into the bushes, saw a leather backpack behind the clothes and a sword on the ground.

"Your majesty," someone shouted. "I found something."

Alun grabbed the sword, saw a marvelous battle-staff lying nearby. He grabbed it and the pack, and began stuffing it with clothes. Then a couple of other soldiers were there beside him, combing the bushes for more.

Alun raced up onto the platform, and dropped the spoils there on the scorched wood. Others were doing the same. More clothes, some packs, a bow made of reaver horn, and arrows.

The men laid out the goods on the ground, and the Emir of Dalharristan bent to inspect them. "Don't draw those swords. Don't touch anything. We don't know what kind of curses might be laid upon these things."

He looked first at the bow of ruddy reaver's bone, using the toe of his boot to flip it over. "There are no glyphs upon it," he said, "at least not that I can see."

The Wizard Sisel reached down with his staff, bent so low to the floor that he almost touched it with his head. He sniffed at the bow. "But there are blessings on it," he said. "It is clean. I can smell the virtue in it."

The king looked at the wizard doubtfully. "But the power to bless has been lost. That is old magic!"

"Not on the world where these come from." Sisel peered at the sword as Alun lay it down. "Draw that blade, young man."

Alun did. The steel was lighter than steel should be, and gleamed like polished silver. "A fine blade," Sisel said. "Their steel is better than ours."

Sisel peered up at the soldiers all around him. "No one use that blade, at least not against a common foe. There is a blessing on it. Save it for the Knights Eternal, or better yet, the emperor himself."

"Who will carry this sword?" High King Urstone asked.

None of the lords dared step forward, and Alun dared not offer to keep it. But the High King smiled at him. "Sir Alun, is it not?" the High King asked as if they had never spoken. "You are our new . . . Master of the Hounds?"

"Aye, milord."

The High King looked up to the bloody rag tied around Alun's head. "You look as if you've acquitted yourself admirably in this battle. Were you able to draw any blood?"

Alun fumbled for something to say, his mouth working aimlessly. Some soldier nearby guffawed. "He did more than draw blood. He slew near a dozen."

There were gulps of astonishment from the gathered lords, and Alun saw Drewish, there at the king's back, glare at him dangerously.

"Proof once again that it is not just the size of a warrior that determines the battle," Sisel said, exchanging a look with the king.

He's talking about the small folk, Alun realized. I wonder what has been said?

"Well then," High King Urstone said gently, "it looks as if we have a new champion among us. Will you do the honor of bearing this sword until we can return it to its rightful owner?"

Alun gripped the sword experimentally. It was strong and powerful and light in his hand, not like the heavy axes that he had been forced to bear. "Aye, milord. It would be an honor."

The king smiled. He studied the marvelous staff, with its gems set near the top, and runes carved along its length. He peered up at the Wizard Sisel. "Would you take this?"

Sisel shook his head sadly. "That staff was not meant for me. It fits a man of a smaller stature." He looked to the Emir. "It would suit you well."

The Emir picked it up, swung it expertly, and it was his, at least for the time being.

The men went back sorting through the treasure. In one pack, they found a small bag, and within the bag was a golden signet ring. The ring featured an ancient symbol—the face of a man with oak leaves for his head and beard.

"This is a dangerous thing," the Emir said, shoving it aside with his toe. "One should not lightly bear it, especially among the woods."

"The glyph of the Wode King?" Urstone asked.

"Spirits are drawn to it," the Emir said. "No man should carry such a token."

"Unless—" the wizard Sisel said, his brow furrowed into a frown, "he bears it by right."

Sisel himself drew his powers from the earth, and his

powers were greatest in the forest. He seemed not to fear the strange ring.

"Do you have the right to bear it?" King Urstone asked.

"No," the Wizard Sisel said after a long moment of thought, "but I *will* take the risk, until we find the one who does." He picked it up swiftly, shoved it into a pocket of his robe.

Suddenly, Alun had a strange feeling, as if a cold wind were blowing through him, as if unseen spirits encircled him. He found himself wishing that he were anywhere but here.

The lords pawed through the packs, finding bits of food. There were trinkets scattered among them—a locket with a woman's face painted upon it, a bracelet made of shells. But nothing seemed to be of import.

A soldier came after a bit, dragging a pair of red wings with him. "We found this in their armory—the wings from a Knight Eternal."

That was a great treasure indeed, for anyone could wear those wings, and the king knew that his lords would fight over them. "By ancient law," King Urstone said, "I decree that these wings will belong to the man who slew our enemy." He nodded to the soldier, "Keep them safe until we find the rightful owner."

It was moments later that one of the soldiers on the ground shouted, "I found another pack."

This one had not been opened. Beyond the foodstuffs, a man's clothes and mementos, this one held a leather bag.

When the king dumped its contents onto the floor, the wizard Sisel whistled in admiration. It held nearly a hundred smooth rods made from some rusty looking metal.

"These are a runelord's forcibles," Sisel said, holding the rods up for the king to see. "We must get these to the castle at once."

The king did not speak openly before the men about the forcibles' use. Instead, he nodded secretively, then sent a detail of four men to carry them back to the castle.

It was moments later that a captain came and reported,

"We've searched the city. There are no signs of the prisoners that were taken here last night, or of the Knights Eternal. But there are fresh wagon marks on the road north, and many feet have trod it."

"So," Madoc said, "they've gone north."

The morning was half over. Most likely, the wyrmlings were far, far ahead.

"We must follow, then," King Urstone said. "We must reach them before nightfall."

❧ 26 ❧

THE TEMPLE OF DEATH

The fiercest battles we fight in life seldom leave visible scars. —the Wizard Sisel

Fallion came to, rising up out of dreams of ice and snow. Ice water seemed to be flowing through his veins instead of blood. His hands and feet were frozen solid. He tried to remember how he'd gotten here, when it had gotten so cold.

"Someone left the window open," he said. That was it. Jaz liked to sleep with the bedroom window open, and often times in the fall, Fallion got too cool in the night. In his distorted dreams, he imagined that Jaz had left the window open all winter, and that was the cause of his current predicament.

He moaned in pain and peered about, but there was no light.

"Fallion," Rhianna whispered urgently. "Draw heat from me."

He wondered how she had gotten here. He tried to

recall what the weather had been like when he went to sleep last night, but everything was a blank. All that he knew was bitter cold and pain.

"Draw heat from me, Fallion," Rhianna whispered urgently.

Without thought, Fallion reached out and pulled a little warmth from her. She gasped in pain, and instantly Fallion regretted what he'd done. He lay there trembling from the cold, numb and filled with pain.

Rhianna pressed herself against him. She could feel him trembling all over. She'd never known anyone to shake so badly. Even as a child, when the strengi-saats had taken her into the forest, wet and nearly naked, she had not suffered so.

Now, Rhianna began to shiver too, and she felt as if she were sinking endlessly into deep, icy water.

She dared not tell Fallion that she was afraid he was killing her. My life is his, she told herself. It always has been, and it always will be.

But something in her ached. She didn't want to die without really ever having lived. Her childhood had been spent with her mother, running and hiding endlessly from Asgaroth. Then for years, her mind and body were taken captive by Shadoath. For a couple of years she had finally been free, but every minute of her freedom had been a torment, for she had fallen in love with Fallion so deeply that her life was no longer her own.

I don't want to die without ever having learned to live, she told herself, and lay there with teeth chattering, struggling to give Fallion her warmth.

Slowly, Fallion became aware of his predicament. His legs and arms were bound tightly, cutting off the circulation. It seemed to make the cold keener. He remembered the squeak of wagon wheels, the jostling. The muggy air in the stone box.

But now they were somewhere outside the box. He could feel an open space above, and suddenly heard a wyrmling's barking growl in another room.

We're in a building, he realized. Distantly, he heard the chatter of a squirrel, and if he listened hard, he could hear nesting birds up above, cheeping to their mother.

We're in the woods, he realized. It's daylight outside.

The night came flooding back to him—the battle at Cantular, his ruthless attackers, the news that Talon was dead. Despair washed through him.

I must get free, he thought. If I don't do it, no one can. He tried to clear his mind of numbness, of fatigue, of pain.

He reached out with his mind, felt for sources of heat. He touched lightly on Rhianna, Jaz, and Talon. She was still warm, too warm.

Talon's alive! he realized, tears filling his eyes. But the spell that the Knight Eternal had cast had drained her, leaving her torpid, near death.

"Talon's alive," Fallion whispered for the benefit of Jaz and Rhianna, "barely." Rhianna began to sob in gratitude.

Fallion reached out, quested farther, and found the wyrmlings in another room, off to his right. There were several of them. Their huge bodies were warm.

He wouldn't need to drain much from them. He touched them, let their warmth flood him.

There was a shout in the other room. "Eckra, Eckra!"

Heavy feet rushed through the door, and Fallion heard the rustle of robes. He knew what was coming. The Knight Eternal would drain him of all heat.

Unless I drain him first, Fallion thought.

In a desperate surge, Fallion reached up to drain the life's warmth from the Knight Eternal. To do so would require more control than he had ever mastered.

But as he did, he discovered too late that the creature looming above him had no life's heat. It was as cold as the stone floor beneath them.

"Eckra," it cursed, and suddenly the cold washed over Fallion again, and he was lost in a vision of winter, where icy winds blew snow over a frozen lake, and somehow Fallion was trapped beneath the ice, peering up from the cold water, longing for air, longing for light, longing for warmth.

High King Urstone sprinted through the early morning, a thousand warriors at his back, as they raced along.

With the great change, dirt and grasses had sprung up over the old road in a single night. It didn't erase the road so much as leave a light layer of soil over it with clumps of stubble growing here and there. The wyrmling trail was easy to follow.

There was only one set of wagon tracks in the dust, along with the tracks of a dozen wyrmling warriors.

They stopped at a brook that burbled over the road, and several men bellied down to drink. It was the heat of the day, and sweat rolled off them. A few cottonwood trees shaded the brook, making it a welcome spot, and King Urstone shouted out, "Ten minutes. Take ten minutes here to rest."

He saw a fish leap at a gnat in the shadows, and watched for a moment. There was a pair of fat trout lying in the water.

Warlord Madoc came up at his back, and asked, "Will we catch them today, do you think?" At first the king thought that the warlord was talking about the fish. King Urstone shook his head, trying to rid it of cobwebs and weariness.

"Aye, we'll catch them," the king assured him. "We got a late start, but it should be enough. The wyrmlings are forced by their nature to travel at night. But the days are far longer than the nights, this time of year. We should be on them well before dark."

Madoc nodded and seemed to find no fault with the logic. That was odd. It seemed to the king that Madoc always sought to find fault with his logic nowadays.

"It will be a rough fight," Madoc said, "with two Knights Eternal in the battle."

"We have weapons to fight them with," the king said.

Madoc bore one of those weapons, a dainty sword that was nearly useless in his immense hand. He pulled it from its sheath, showed it to the High King. A patina of rust had formed on the fine steel blade. "Sisel said that these had been blessed, but I say they're cursed. This rust has been spreading like a fungus since dawn."

The High King smiled, not in joy, but in admiration for the enemies' resourcefulness. "I would say that they are both blessed and cursed. We will have to put that sword to good use before it rots away into nothingness."

"You gave that fool Alun one of these swords to bear," Madoc said. "Will you let him bear it into battle?"

"You call him a fool? You are the one who made him a warrior, and he acquitted himself well in battle this morning, by all accounts. Do you now regret your choice?"

"Of course not," Madoc blustered. "But . . . he has no training with the sword, and it is an enchanted weapon!"

"Your point is well taken," King Urstone said. Alun had fallen behind the war party. He didn't have a warrior's legs, couldn't hope to keep pace. The king had assigned some men to help him along, even if they had to lug him like a sack of turnips.

The king's mind turned to worries about his own son, and so he suggested, "Perhaps we should find another to bear it. Your son Connor, he is trained with the sword, is he not? It is said that he's quite good. Would he like the honor?"

"I, I, uh—" Madoc blustered. He knew his son was clumsy with the sword. He had a strong arm, more fitted to the ax. More importantly, he wasn't about to send his son charging into battle against the Knights Eternal, enchanted sword or no.

King Urstone fought back the urge to laugh.

Madoc often complains to his friends that I'm a fool, King Urstone realized, but the man has never fared well in a match of wits with me. "Have no worries," Urstone said at last. "*I* will bear that sword into battle, and cleave off the head of a Knight Eternal."

It was altogether fitting that the king do it. Urstone had been trained with the sword from childhood, and there were few men alive who could hope to match him with it. More importantly, it was said in Luciare that "the king bears upon his shoulders the hopes of the nation." In ancient times, it was believed that the combined hopes of a people could give a warrior strength in battle.

These weapons were enchanted with old magic. Perhaps, Urstone thought, *there is old magic in me, too.*

Thus, the fight that he was racing to was not just a battle between two individuals. Urstone would be pitting the hopes of Luciare against the powers of Lady Despair.

Madoc grunted, "That would be best, I think. Yes, that would be well."

Urstone peered hard at him. *He doesn't hope for my success in battle,* he realized. *He hopes to see me die.*

Yes, how convenient would that be, King Urstone slain in a glorious combat, a hero's death, leaving Madoc to rule the kingdom.

But I have a son still, a son who can spoil his plans.

Tonight at dusk the trade is supposed to be made, only a dozen hours from now.

"Wish me luck?" the king asked.

"Most assuredly," Madoc said. "My hopes rest upon you."

Nightfall was many hours away when a wyrmling guard came from the watch room, crashing down the stairs three at a time.

"Humans are coming, warrior clan!" he roared. "The road is black with them!"

Vulgnash leapt to his feet. For two hours he had been sitting with nothing to do, listening only to the occasional talk of the small folk in their room, whispering in their strange tongue, as quiet as mice. He had strained his ears. He knew that he would not be able to understand the meanings of their words. He had no context to put them in, but often, he had found, when learning a new language, it was best to begin by familiarizing himself with the sounds. He had been silently cataloguing the vowels and consonants, occasionally trying them out on his tongue.

Now, with a battle coming, there were other matters to attend to.

He raced up to the tower. The sunlight was as bright as a blade there, slanting down from the east. There was no cloud cover.

To the south he could see the human war band, sunlight glancing off their bone helms, as yellow as teeth. The men ran in single file, bloody axes in their hands. In the distance, racing down the winding road, they looked like a huge serpent, snaking toward the horizon for almost a mile.

They would reach the fortress in less than half an hour.

His captain raced up behind Vulgnash. "Master, shall we evacuate, head into the woods?"

There were trees all around. Leaves hung thick upon the oaks and alders. But they would not offer the protection that Vulgnash needed. His wyrmling troops could cope with the light much better than Vulgnash could.

"No, we'll fight them here."

The captain tried not to show fear, but he drew back. Vulgnash was condemning him to death.

"I'll deepen the shadows around the fortress," Vulgnash said, "and I will place the touch of death upon each of you, give you my blessing. And I have these—" he reached to a pouch at his throat, pulled it hard enough to snap the rawhide band that held it. The bag was heavy with harvester spikes.

"Take three to a man," Vulgnash told him, placing the bag in the captain's palm, "no more."

The wyrmling commander smiled. He and his men would die, but it would be a glorious death, fighting gleefully in a haze of bloodlust, lost to all mortal care.

"Shall I have the men kill the captives," the commander asked, "as a precaution?"

Normally, that is what Vulgnash would have done. He

would have made sure that no matter what effort the humans spent, they would lose in the end.

But his master's command was upon him, and Vulgnash always executed her commands to perfection.

"No, leave them," he said in resignation. "If the warriors win through, I may have to come back and take them again."

They're going to kill me, Alun thought, as he raced along the road. Connor and Drewish are going to kill me now. Don't let the dogs get behind me.

He worried about Connor and Drewish. The fact that wyrmling warriors might be on the road ahead, led by the immortal Knights Eternal, somehow did not seem as sinister.

Of course, he was falling-down weary.

His legs had turned to mush, and he could run no more. He was wheezing like a dying man, unable to get enough air no matter what, and chills ran through him while beads of sweat stood out cold upon his brow.

They charged up a hill through the woods, and Alun stumbled and sprawled on his face. For a moment he lay on the ground, laid out like a dead toad, and he was happy, for so long as he was on the blessed ground, he could rest.

"Up with you," a soldier chided, grabbing him by the arm and yanking. Another soldier took him by the other arm, and soon they were carrying him, each of them cruelly holding an arm. "Move those legs, damn it. There are wyrmlings ahead, and we need you to fight them all for us."

Alun knew that he would be no good in this fight. There had been three harvester spikes in the little packet that he'd found, but he had dropped that somewhere back at the fort. He'd searched the floor for it, but never found the spikes. He felt dirty and shameful for having used them at all. They were, after all, made from glands taken from folks captured at Caer Luciare. Folks like Sir Croft, or that little boy, Dake, that had disappeared last month. The harvester spikes were an affront to all decency. Yet now as he went into battle, he yearned for the thrill he'd felt before. Without them, he would be lost.

Suddenly there was shouting up ahead, "We've cornered them! We've got them!"

And the soldiers went charging up the hill, trees whisking by on either side, bearing Alun like a marionette.

Alun hoped that the battle would be over by the time that he reached the spot, but they came upon an old hill fort formed from great gray slabs of basalt. Trees grew up around it, and brush and blackberry vines, leaving it a ruin, hidden in gloom.

Indeed, the gloom grew thick around it, so dark that one could almost not see the door. The harder that Alun peered, the deeper the shadows seemed to thicken, until the door was just a yawning pit in the blackness.

Even as he watched, the darkness seemed to readjust. Shadows that should have fallen from the east now twisted, coming from the north or west.

Whatever hid in that fort, it did not want to be seen.

A handcart sat out front, one of the heavy kind that wyrmlings used to haul equipment to war, with huge wheels all bound in iron. A stone box lay spilled beside it, tossed on its side, the heavy stone lid lying upon the ground.

There was no sign of the hostages, no sign of battle. The old fort was deathly quiet. The soldiers surrounded it, and the High King and his counselors stood peering at it, considering.

"Shall we put the torch to it," Madoc asked, "smoke them out?"

"No," King Urstone said. "It might harm the hostages. Nor can we batter down the wall or risk them in any manner." He nodded toward a captain. "Take down a good stout tree. We'll need a ram to get through that door."

He turned and searched the crowd, until his eyes came upon Alun, who was bent over, panting from exertion. The king strode over to him, and there was hardly a sheen of sweat upon his forehead. He peered at Alun with deep blue eyes, and asked, "Alun, may I have use of the sword?"

Alun drew it from the scabbard and was dismayed to see that the sword, which had reflected light like a clear lake this morning, was dulled by a layer of rust.

"Milord," he apologized. "I'm sorry. I should have oiled it."

"It's not your fault, Alun," the king said gently.

He turned to the troops.

"Gentlemen, there are wyrmlings in this fortress, and I mean to have their heads. Most of you know that the Knights Eternal are most likely holed up with them, like a pair of badgers. We'll have a hard time of it, digging them out. But if all goes well this day, we shall rid ourselves of the Knights Eternal once and for all."

There was a tremendous roar as men raised their axes and cheered.

Vulgnash leaned over the bound bodies of the small ones. He stood in what had once been a kitchen. There was a chopping block in one corner, for the hacking of meat, and a pair of stone hearths to one side. At his back was a window that had been boarded up long ago. He had checked it, in order to make sure that there was no clear passage. Blackberry vines grew beyond the window to a height of twenty feet, blocking out the light.

Outside, the sound of chopping stopped. The warrior clan had their battering ram now, and soon would be at the door.

His wyrmling guard stood ready to receive them.

Outside, there was a shout. "You in there: release your prisoners and we will let you go free."

Vulgnash knew a lie when he heard it. The humans

were only seeking assurance that the small ones yet lived.

He considered taking the small wizard outside, holding him up with a knife to his throat, letting them know the danger of pressing this attack. But too many things could go wrong. The wizard could grasp the sunlight, use it as a weapon. Or the enemy might fire an arrow, killing the hostage, and leaving Vulgnash to suffer his master's wrath.

So he crouched and drew his blade. All the while, his mind was occupied, reaching out to the shadows, drawing them close, wrapping them around the old hill fort.

There was a crashing at the door, and painful light cut through the room.

"Now," Vulgnash shouted, and his warriors shoved the harvester spikes into their necks. Instantly the bloodlust was upon them, and they began to howl and shriek like creatures damned as they lunged from the shadows.

The warrior clansmen charged the breach, fear in their pale eyes. Their breath fogged in the cold air of the room, for Vulgnash had blessed this place with the touch of the tomb.

The wyrmlings grabbed the first warriors to breach the door, long pale arms snaking out of the darkness, and each used a meat hook in one hand to drag a warrior back while hacking with the other—thus clearing the path for more victims. A volley of arrows sped through the doorway, taking one of his over-eager wyrmlings in the eye. The big fellow fought bravely for several seconds before he staggered to his knees. A human lunged through the door and split his skull like kindling with a single blow from the ax.

With the first blood spilled and the first death, the ground was now blessed, and Vulgnash felt his own powers begin to gape wide, like the mouth of a pit.

The first wave of warriors burst into the room in earnest and found themselves lost in the suffocating darkness, unable to spot a target before they were slaughtered.

The dark fortress filled with screams.

Rhianna kicked Fallion's leg, and Fallion came awake slowly. They were lost in blackness as the screams of warriors and the clash of arms rang out.

For long minutes, Fallion lay, desperately trying to clear his head.

The sorcerer had his hands full for the moment, and Fallion reached out with his mind, questing for a source of heat. He could feel the bodies of creatures living and dying nearby, but dared not draw from them. To do so might alert the sorcerer. Fallion realized now that his questing touch had alerted the sorcerer in times past.

But there was a roof to this building, a stone roof, and the sun had been shining full upon it all through the morning. The warm stone held the heat.

Ever so carefully, Fallion reached out with his mind, searching, and began to draw the heat into him.

There is a saying among wyrmlings. "In a well-built fort, a single warrior should be able to hold off a thousand."

Vulgnash knew of such fortresses—the sea fort at Golgozar, the old castle upon Mount Aznunc. This was not such a fort.

Still, as the first wave of human warriors faded, he was proud of his warriors. Only one wyrmling had fallen in battle, while dozens of the war clan lay slaughtered upon the floor.

"Drag back the bodies," he shouted during the lull in battle. "Leave a clear killing field."

His wyrmlings complied as best they could, throwing the bodies back, heaping them to the roof. But they weren't able to finish the job before the second wave burst upon them.

A dozen men rushed the door, each bearing torches, war cries ringing from their throats. The light cut through the shadows, and in that instant, his wyrmlings were vulnerable. The gloom lessened, and the humans launched themselves into battle.

One of his warriors took a killing blow. An ax slashed through his armor, and guts came tumbling out. But the bloodlust was upon the wyrmling warrior, and he fought on. Another took a spear to the neck, and too much blood was flowing. A third got cut down through the knee.

Still his men fought—not with bravery, but with madness in their eyes. Vulgnash threw his energy into deepening the gloom, and men screamed and died in the smoky air. The smell of blood and gore perfumed the old fortress. Corpses littered the floor; blood pooled beneath the wyrmling's feet.

Vulgnash used his powers to feed the frenzy. Death was in the air. Death surrounded them. As one human warrior took a blow, the ax slashed through the armor and grazed his chest.

Vulgnash stretched out a hand, and the skin flayed wide. Ribs cracked and a lung was exposed. The human cried out and fell gasping to the floor before a man could touch him.

His wyrmling warriors began to roar in celebration, dancing upon the bodies of the dead.

Only three of his men had expired, and two hundred humans lay in their gore.

Death ruled here.

There was no time to rest before the third wave hit.

A hail of arrows announced the attack, came blurring through the doorway. Even in the shadows they found some marks. His men could no longer retreat far from the door, for their path was blocked by the dead.

Five good wyrmling warriors took arrows. Three of them sank slowly to their knees.

And the humans did not rush in. They gave the arrows time to do their work.

The wyrmling soldiers roared in frustration, screaming curses and insults at the humans, trying to lure them in. But the human forces were well trained, and did not respond to the taunts.

It was fifteen long minutes before the third wave came. The warriors rushed in so silently, Vulgnash did not hear them coming. They came with torches this time; every man among them had a torch.

Vulgnash used his powers quickly, snuffed the torches out, sent the smoke circling into the lungs of the human warriors.

The humans gasped and choked, struggling for breath as they fought.

And the slaughter began in earnest.

Vulgnash hardly needed warriors to fight for him now. The deaths of so many men, the fleeting life energies, only fed his powers. He felt invincible.

Warriors rushed in, and Vulgnash did not wait for his men to attack. He stretched out his hand, and rents appeared in men's flesh, long slashes that looked as if beasts had torn them.

The room was filled with warriors with torches, a mob of them, and Vulgnash pointed to one of his fallen wyrmlings and uttered a curse. The wyrmling's body exploded, and giant maggots erupted from its gut, raining down through the room.

The human warriors shouted as the maggots began to eat their flesh.

Vulgnash felt something odd. The room was colder than a tomb, colder even than it should be.

He sent his mind questing, found the little human wizard stealing heat.

Vulgnash rushed back, stepped on the wizard's neck, and reached down, sucking the heat from him. It came snaking out in a fiery cord.

But the wizard's distraction had served its purpose.

At that instant, more torch-men rushed into the room.

His wyrmlings shrieked, blinded by the light, and fought on. They had fought grandly, as harvesters will, leaping into battle, axes hacking off heads and chopping through armor. They had roared and fought when they'd taken a dozen wounds, but it was a losing battle.

Vulgnash whirled and sent the fire that he had drawn from Fallion hurling into the darkened room. The humans screamed and died in a rush of flames, as did the last of his own wyrmling warriors.

"See what your insolence has cost?" Vulgnash raged at Fallion.

The humans retreated from the fire, fleeing the fortress.

The last of his wyrmlings were left gasping, propping themselves up on their knees, struggling to stay alive. First there were three, then two, and at last one sank to the ground with a groan.

Vulgnash was left alone in this place of death.

He peered at the lengthening shadows. The warrior clan had been at the attack for an hour. He'd held them off for that long. But sundown was still many hours away.

"I saw only one of the Knights Eternal," the captain reported. "He hides at the back, in the doorway to the kitchen. I think that he has the hostages there."

High King Urstone sat on a rock, sharpening the other-worlder's long sword. Oiling and sharpening seemed to do little good. It was rusting even as he worked.

"Even one Knight Eternal is more than anyone can safely deal with," the Wizard Sisel said. "And I fear that this is Vulgnash himself."

"It's as cold as the tomb in there," the captain said. "My veins feel like they are frozen."

The captain grimaced in pain, reached down his shirt, and brought out a large maggot. It was perhaps three inches long and as thick as a woodworm. Even as he held it, the maggot swiveled its head this way and that, struggling to bite him. The captain hurled it to the ground and gave it the heel of his boot.

"Even to get close to Vulgnash brings a small death," Sisel told the king. "You must be wary."

"He's not the worst of Zul-torac's terrors," the king said.

The captain cleared his throat. "One more thing. Watch your footing in there. The floors are slick. He has turned that place into a slaughterhouse."

"Not a slaughterhouse," Sisel said, "a temple—where the high priest of death administers the ordinances of death."

King Urstone smiled weakly. This wasn't a task that he relished doing. Hundreds of his forces were gone, and he still hadn't gotten the badger out of its den.

"Do me a favor, captain. Have some of your men go out back. There should be a door to the kitchen, or a window at least. Get them open."

"The brush is thick back there," the captain said. "It will take a while to get through it."

"Make lots of noise," the king said. "I could use a distraction."

King Urstone peered up. The Emir stood over him, holding the other-worlder's staff, inspecting it. Of all the weapons, this one alone had remained untouched by the Knight Eternals' curse.

"Do you think that will do you any good?" Urstone asked.

"I hope so," the Emir said. He would bear it into battle. He was as faithful and capable a warrior as King Urstone had ever known, a true friend.

Madoc himself bore the dainty little sword, while two dozen archers had each commandeered a single arrow from the other-worlder's quiver.

"Right then," the king said. "Let's go."

He gave one final look to the Wizard Sisel and asked, "Is there a last blessing you might bestow upon me?"

The wizard got a bemused expression, stood for a long moment as if trying to recall something he'd heard in the distant past. King Urstone had expected no boon, but he could see the wizard's mind at work.

There is something, King Urstone thought, some lore that he recalls from the otherworld.

"Don't go into battle like this," Sisel said at last. "Don't go in haste, or fear, or rage." He glanced up to the trees. "Take a look around. Look at the trees, the sunlight, the grass." He fell silent, and King Urstone could hear the sound of woodpeckers in the distance, a squirrel chattering, and after a moment, the squawk of a jay. "This is a lush land, full of life. Look at this fortress. In better times, it could be put to use as an inn. It would be a pleasant place to stop and have a meal.

"But Vulgnash has turned it into a tomb.

"Light and life oppose him. In there, he hides from them. You must draw upon these, if you will defeat him."

The wizard reached into his pocket, drew out some pea pods that he might have harvested from his garden. "Take these with you. There is life in them. And after this meeting, you would do well to plant the seeds somewhere."

King Urstone noted that the wizard called this a *meeting,* not a battle.

King Urstone smiled. It sounded like madness. Taking seeds into battle?

The wizard saw his look, and gently chided him. "Don't put such faith in your arms. They will do you no good in there. How many strong men have died this day, putting their faith in such weapons? And don't go prepared to die. Nearly every warrior who confronts death prepares himself to die. Look inside yourself and find hope. Can you think of no great reason to live?"

Only last night, King Urstone had succumbed to despair and had been prepared to go into battle and lose his life. But then he had learned of the forcibles, and of a plan to save his son, and of the small folk who now inhabited the land. All of these things were renewing a hope that he had thought long dead. "Your words to me last night gave me hope," King Urstone said, "great hope indeed, and a reason to live."

Tonight my son will be free, he thought.

"Good," Sisel said, reaching up and clutching the king's arm in token of friendship. "Then go now, not as a servant of death, but as a minister of life." He looked pointedly at Madoc, "Leave these others behind. You have no need of them."

King Urstone did not charge in as the soldiers had. He was not going to run blindly into a trap. Nor would he shirk his duty, or stumble on quavering knee.

He strode resolutely to the mouth of the fortress, of the tomb, and planted himself just outside the broken door.

His breath streamed cold from his mouth, and his blood turned to ice water in his veins. He could see heaped bodies lying in a pool of black blood. The air smelled thick with death.

A shadow filled the room before him, a black mass. He could not make out a human form, but he could hear labored breathing, and he could sense a monstrous evil hidden within.

The king advanced toward the doorway, and Vulgnash caught sight of his weapon, the other-worldly steel gleaming red in a shaft of sunlight.

Even that brief image undid him. Vulgnash held back a shriek, half blinded by pain, and threw a hand in the air to shield his eyes.

He looked at the king, and heard voices. For half an instant, he had a vision of King Urstone as a young man, kneeling upon one knee, surrounded by his warlords. Each of them laid his left hand upon the young king's head, and a wizard spoke for them all. "Upon you we place the hope of all our people. Though you be king, you are a servant to us all."

There was great power in such words, whether the humans knew it or not. Vulgnash could feel the hopes of many surrounding the king, shielding him like a battle guard.

Vulgnash stretched out his hand, hoping to rend the king from a distance, but his curse could not touch the man.

And there was life all around him, white-hot life. He carried seeds upon him.

The king halted, just outside the door, and planted his long sword in the ground, then stood with his hands folded over the pommel. The blade was angled so that red sunlight cut through the blackness, causing Vulgnash great pain.

What is this? Vulgnash wondered. Where did the humans learn such lore?

"Vulgnash," King Urstone called out. "Show yourself."

Vulgnash held to his shadows.

The king hesitated for a long moment, and then shouted, "Vulgnash, I offer you your life."

Vulgnash laughed, "That is not in your power."

Suddenly, a wizard stood at the king's back, a plump man with a sun-burned face and a brown beard going gray. He too bore seeds upon him, and the life within him was like a white-hot fire. "But it is in mine," the wizard said. "Come out, and I will heal you. I can give you life, fresh and clean, unlike any that you have ever known. You will be a slave to no one. I can give you *your* own life. I cannot remove the wyrm that gnaws upon your soul. Only you can do that. A life devoted to clean thoughts and good deeds will drive it out."

Could it be? Vulgnash wondered. Could I be granted life, after more than five thousand years?

"I rejected life long ago," Vulgnash hissed. "I reject it now."

The king lowered his eyelids in sign of acceptance. "If not life, then I can give you oblivion with this sword," he intoned softly. "Eternal sleep and forgetfulness."

Vulgnash drew himself up, and for the first time in centuries, he felt disconcerted. Something was wrong. Normally, his victims were filled with fear, an emotion that worked to Vulgnash's benefit.

But this king knew better than to hope to slay a Knight Eternal in anger. Such hopes were false hopes, and would only have worked to his demise.

Yet he advanced anyway, without fear, and offered Vulgnash something more terrible than death—life. He carried seeds upon him, and the hopes of his people, and he bore an accursed sword.

It was as if Vulgnash stood before some mage king who had walked straight out of some long forgotten legend. King Urstone's calm demeanor hinted at a tremendous reserve of power.

Against such a man, I dare not stand, Vulgnash decided.

With a roar he bent his will upon the door to the kitchen, used his mind to slam it shut. The door trembled in its frame and dust rained down. He bolted it, then raced to the small ones, glared down at Fallion Orden.

Everything in him warned that he should kill the young wizard. But Lady Despair had commanded otherwise.

In that moment, Vulgnash had no choice but to flee.

In the space of a heartbeat the roof exploded off the old fortress, fifteen tons of stone hurtling four hundred feet in the air.

The watchtower was thrown aside as if it were a toy, dashed aside by an angry child.

Urstone's men screamed and raced for cover.

Fearing the worst, King Urstone charged the bolted door, hit it with his shoulder. The rotting wood gave way, and the door split cleanly down the middle.

He caught sight of his target, a hunched figure cowled in red, clutching a sword.

The Knight Eternal hunched above the prisoners, motionless.

The roof of the building crashed somewhere in the distance, shattering trees and leaving a wake of ruin.

Sunlight slanted into the building, playing upon motes of dust that danced in the air.

And the Knight Eternal merely stood there, unmoving.

King Urstone peered at him. It was no living man that

he saw, only a rotting corpse with sunken eyes, wrinkled skin like aging paper.

The king plunged his sword through, just to be sure. The sword pierced easily, as if he had struck a wasp's nest. The organs were desiccated, the bones weak with rot.

"He is not there," the Wizard Sisel said softly. "I fear that his spirit has fled, and that we shall meet again."

Sisel reached up and touched Vulgnash's cheek.

"We should burn this dry husk," one of the king's men said. "It will make it harder for him to re-corporate."

"That is just an old wife's tale," Sisel replied. "Vulgnash will just find another suitable corpse to inhabit; by sundown he will be on our trail. Still, take the heads off of the dead here in this room. We don't want to leave bodies lying handy for him to use."

"Take the wings off of him," King Urstone said. "I claim them as my own."

The wizard looked down at the four hostages, laid out on the floor. The vines that bound them suddenly loosened and fell away, as if drained of some infernal will.

The doorway behind them filled with men—warlord Madoc and the Emir and dozens of warriors.

The wizard spoke softly to the otherworlders for just a moment, then smiled and said to Fallion in his own tongue, "Fallion Orden, I'd like you to meet the grandfather that died before you were born." He nodded toward King Urstone, then spoke in the king's tongue, "And King Urstone, I would like you to meet the grandsons that—upon your world at least—were never born."

❦ 27 ❦

A PAIR OF KINGS

Hope should never come unlooked-for. It should always be held in your heart. —the Wizard Sisel

"Your Highness, this is outrageous!" Warlord Madoc burst out. "Surely you don't believe this."

Madoc was red with rage. He had waited all morning for a chance to take the king from behind, but there had been no opportunity. The king hadn't waded into battle until the very last, and then he had gone in alone. Madoc couldn't put an end to him, for there would have been too many witnesses.

Now this mad wizard was trying to foist these other-worlders off as new-found heirs.

"Outrageous?" Sisel said. "I think not. Fallion Orden here is the first-born son of Gaborn Val Orden, a king of great import upon his own world. Fallion's grandfather lost his life in battle before Fallion was born. That man was you, King Urstone, upon that shadow world. He was your shadow self. And so when the worlds combined, you had no other half to combine with.

"In the same way," the wizard continued, "on our world, their mother was lost while she still carried her firstborn in her arms."

King Urstone bowed his head in thought. Areth's wife had died while he was away, killed in a wyrmling assault. The wyrmlings had tried to take her prisoner, but she had slipped from their grasp and thrown herself from the tower wall, with her babe in arms. She gave her life rather than let her child be raised among the wyrmlings—for had she been taken, her royal child would have been raised as one of their slaves.

King Urstone had always felt guilty for this. I should have been there to protect her, he thought, instead of staying out for the night on patrol.

"It doesn't matter who they are," Drewish shouted. "They cannot be heirs to the throne. Look at them: they're not even warriors."

King Urstone looked down at the little humans. They squatted on rocks in the sunlight, shivering, away from the infernal slaughterhouse, and rubbed their wrists and knees, trying to get back some circulation.

One of the girls was large, though, like one of the Warrior Clan. Her face was familiar, but he could not put a name to her.

"It's not size that is the measure of a warrior," she said in their own tongue. "There are few among you who could best King Orden here in a fight."

Urstone laughed at her feisty tone. "And how, sweet lady, would you know?"

"Can't you tell?" she asked. "I am Tholna, daughter of Aaath Ulber. But I also lived upon a shadow world, where Aaath Ulber's shadow self spent half a lifetime training young King Orden here in battle."

The king knew Tholna. Her father was one of his two most trusted guards. But he had disappeared after the change, like so many others. King Urstone had wondered if he were even alive.

Now Tholna turned up here in the wilds, with these otherworldly humans.

He could detect no change in her. She claimed to be two people at once, but if that was so, it seemed to King Urstone that the smaller creature had been subsumed, swallowed whole.

"This is all very befuddling," King Urstone said. "I don't know what to say. You tell me that these are my grandsons, but common sense says that they are no get of my son's, and therefore cannot be heirs. And yet . . ."

"Yet what, milord?" Madoc asked, his tone a tad too demanding.

"I must think this matter through." To suddenly have two new heirs, that would certainly spoil Madoc's plans for his own sons, King Urstone knew. He liked the idea of thwarting Madoc's plans. But claiming these . . . otherworlders as heirs might put them in danger from Madoc and his men, and that would be unfair to the small humans.

So King Urstone was hesitant to even consider them as heirs. Besides, these children did not really come from his own blood. But he felt a connection between them that could not be denied.

There are small people in the land now, King Urstone thought. They will need a great leader. Perhaps this young wizard-king will be that leader.

Sisel took King Urstone by the bicep and said, "Your Highness, walk with me for a moment."

In all of his life, the wizard had never touched King Urstone that way, had never dared command him. By that alone, King Urstone recognized that the wizard felt an overpowering need.

They walked up the road a few hundred feet, well out of earshot of the troops.

"Milord, you must get Prince Fallion to safety. Zultorac has already sent the Knights Eternal to apprehend him. By sunset, Vulgnash will be making his report to the emperor, and a sea of troops will be dispatched. He will spare no resource. He will attack us in force. We have two or three days to prepare at most."

"Are you sure?" the king asked.

"Yes. Fallion Orden *is* the wizard who bound our two worlds together; he represents a far greater danger than the emperor has ever faced before."

King Urstone peered at Fallion. He was small by Warrior Clan standards. He could not have stood more than six feet, a full two feet shorter than King Urstone himself. He had a slender build, though he was well proportioned. But there was something unsettling about him, a threatening gleam to his eye, a confidence that the king associated only with the most dangerous of warlords.

"I'm beginning to like this little fellow more and more," King Urstone said.

"Don't make the mistake of naming him as an heir yet," the wizard said. "It will only infuriate warlord Madoc."

"Oh, I won't do that," the king said. "Not until I know him better. But I do value the lad. He cost me many good men today."

King Urstone looked to the south. "I want to see my son, my own flesh and blood. I want to be there tonight when Daylan Hammer makes the exchange. Will you come with me and the little ones?"

It was a long hard run, even for one of the Warrior Clan—a hundred and fifty miles in less than ten hours. King Urstone would need the handcart to carry the small folk on, and he would need guards. But he believed that he could make it. He was warrior-born, after all. He just wasn't sure if the wizard could make it. Still, Sisel seemed to have physical resources far beyond most men of his stature.

"I wouldn't want to miss it," the Wizard Sisel said.

❧ 28 ❧

FROM DUNGEONS TO DAYLIGHT

Ultimately in life, the heights that we attain depend upon two things: our ability to dream, and the self-control we exert to make those dreams come true.
                    —the Emir Tuul Ra, of Dalharristan

"Daylan, what are you doing?" Siyaddah called out in the marketplace. She was at a spice merchant's stall, where she had been studying strands of ginseng root that were splayed out in all of their glory upon a bed of white silk.

Daylan swiveled his head, afraid that the city guards would descend upon him. Most of the inhabitants of the castle were busy working at repairs, using weights and pulleys to haul massive blocks of stone up the mountain. The work was proceeding with marvelous rapidity, for most of the damage, it seemed, was cosmetic. But even with the whole city conscripted into labor, there were people to feed and sick folks that needed tending, so some of the market stalls were open.

So vendors at their stalls were calling out to every straggling customer, while women strode around in groups, inspecting vegetables and fruits, as if it were any other day. Nature seemed not to notice his distress. Golden butterflies and white moths fluttered among the hanging gardens that were a part of every house and shop. The sweet smell of mallow and mock orange flowers wafted through the byways, perfuming the cobblestone lanes sweeter than a baby's breath. Swallows that nested in the cliffs darted among the blue shadows of trees and shops, snapping up bees and moths, their green feathers glistening like emeralds when struck by the sun. The streets of Luciare were a riot of life.

In the meantime, Daylan grunted and struggled to shove a large wheelbarrow through the half-empty street. The wyrmling princess lay hidden inside, with cotton bags thrown over her while a few dozen chips of stone lay artfully displayed in the corners.

"What's going on?" Siyaddah demanded. She climbed to her feet, a broad smile of greeting on her face, all filled with the irrepressible energy of a bounding puppy.

"If you must know," Daylan hissed as she drew near, "I'm trying to escape from the dungeons."

"Oh," Siyaddah said, drawing back a pace, suddenly embarrassed and afraid. She studied the nearby vendors and shoppers with a fearful eye. But no one seemed to have noticed her outburst. No one had been within forty feet of them, no one except the ginseng vendor, a woman so old that she could no longer hear. Siyaddah's had just been another voice in the throng. Suddenly the irrepressible energy was back. "So, can I help?"

Daylan could not help but smile, "Dear girl, where were you when I was chest deep in—well, unpleasantness?"

Siyaddah drew close, as if to hug him, but then caught a whiff of him and decided better.

"I'm here now," she said. She looked down into the handcart. "Is there someone under those wraps? It looks like someone is in there!"

"Shhhh . . ." Daylan hissed in exasperation. "How did you recognize me? I spent hours on this disguise!"

He had indeed spent the better part of the morning sneaking around the city searching for clothes. The robe that he wore, with a peasant's hood, hid his form and most of his face. And he'd cut his beard and grayed it with ash. He'd then hunched over, like a bent old man, as he bore his load of refuse out of the city.

"I knew you in an instant," Siyaddah said. "You're the shortest man around."

"I was afraid of that," Daylan intoned. "That's the problem with living among giants." He shook his head in resignation, looked down the street. The guards at the city gate were talking among themselves amiably. Some peered out beyond the gate. There was no chance of a wyrmling attack on such a bright day, and the biggest problem was likely to be some street urchin who stole a cabbage. But if that happened, the vendor would raise the hue and cry. Daylan had been relying upon the relaxed atmosphere to make his escape. After all, who would look twice at a grubby old man?

Daylan eyed Siyaddah thoughtfully. She was a pretty young woman, exotic in her way. Her skin was as dark as chocolate, and she wore white silks in a flowing style that had once been common in Dalharristan among women who were eligible for marriage. And she was petite, compared to those of the warrior clan, for the folk of Dalharristan had never been large. She stood perhaps only a hair above six feet.

She will do nicely, Daylan thought.

"If you would like to be of help," Daylan said, "go down to the city guards, and flirt. Do you think you could manage that?" Flirting was not an activity that proper young women had engaged in back in Dalharristan. But then, neither were young women in the habit of aiding convicts in their escapes.

"Well, I've never done anything like that myself, but I think I can manage," Siyaddah said. She turned and strode gracefully down the street, aimed like an arrow at the guards. Daylan watched her for a moment, mesmerized by her walk. She had an engaging way of rolling her hips.

She moves like a swan, he thought, each pace bounding forward just a bit, just enough to make you want to catch your breath.

He smiled. Ever so subtly, she was already flirting. And the eyes of the guards already had riveted upon her.

Daylan hefted the handles to his wheelbarrow with a grunt, bent his head and back like an old man, tried to stand tall so that he looked more like one of the big folk, and followed her down to the gate.

Siyaddah had the guards huddled around her as he passed.

"I heard that there are strawberries down by the brook," she was saying, "and the thought of them made me so hungry, and everyone is working so hard on repairs, I thought that some others might like them, too. Do you think that wyrmlings haunt the place? They eat strawberries too, don't they?"

"No, no," the guards all agreed. "Wyrmlings only eat pretty young girls. But you shouldn't find them by the brook. It's too open. Just stay clear of the trees, and you should be safe."

A look of panic crossed Siyaddah's face, and she asked, "Are you sure? I would feel so much safer if one of you came with me."

But of course the city guards all had their posts to man. A couple of the young ones stood with chests puffed out ever so subtly, and one suggested, "I would be glad to take you down to pick strawberries this afternoon."

Siyaddah smiled fetchingly, the damsel saved, as Daylan breezed past the guards and on out the gate.

The road down the mountain was steep enough so that the wheelbarrow moved easily, but not so steep that he had to worry about it running away with him. Still, for the next two miles he plodded along quickly, eager to be away.

The changes to the landscape in the past two days were amazing. He marveled at the trees along the way, wild hazelnuts and chestnuts filled with squirrels. Mourning doves cooed among the trees, and he heard the grunt of wild pigs. A stag actually crossed his path down by the creek.

Such things had not been seen here in ages. Only two days ago this had been a wasteland.

The city of Luciare had looked especially lush, too. By law, there were planter boxes in every window and beside every door. Herbs and wildflowers grew in a riot from them, filling the streets with perfume, filling the city with life. The flowers looked healthier than ever, rejuvenated, as if by weeks and weeks of summer rain.

That was one of the secrets of the city's protection: life. Luciare was a city of life pitted against a wilderness of death. The power of the Death Lords was weakened here.

Daylan only hoped that the Wizard Sisel was strong enough to keep the land whole this time. He had been fighting a losing battle for decades.

Daylan was just rounding the bottom of the mountain, near the dump where rock was to be cast off, when Siyaddah came loping down the hill.

"Daylan," she called excitedly. "Did I do well?"

Like so many of the young, she had not yet learned that doing well was its own reward. She craved praise, which Daylan saw as a sign of her immaturity. Her brain still functioned primarily on an emotional level.

"Yes," he said softly, lest anyone come around the bend. "You did ever so well."

"Who have you got hidden under those sacks?" she asked, reaching down to snatch them off.

Her face turned to a mask of shock at the sight of the wyrmling. Her lower jaw began to tremble, and she shot Daylan a look that said, "You have five seconds to explain yourself, and then I will begin to scream."

As for her part, Kan-hazur curled up, hiding her face from the sunlight. "My eyes are bleeding," she moaned.

"Nope," Daylan corrected. "They're just streaming with tears. You'll be fine soon."

He turned his attention back to Siyaddah. He didn't relish the idea of having to fight Siyaddah, of gagging her and tying her up in the brush until this whole affair was settled. He didn't even have the ropes to do a proper job, though he imagined that if he tore his cotton bags into strips, he might manage to fashion some cords that would hold her.

But the code he lived by demanded better.

"Princess Siyaddah, I would like you to meet Kan-hazur. I am taking her out of the city, at the king's command, in the hopes of arranging an exchange of hostages—the princess for our own Prince Urstone."

Siyaddah studied his face for a moment. Comprehension didn't come dawning slowly, as it would on some dullard. It slid across her face in the blink of an eye, and then she was considering the deeper implications of all of this.

If Prince Urstone was still alive, he might soon be free. Twenty years ago, he had been wed to Siyaddah's aunt. Her father had been the prince's closest friend and ally, going out on war campaigns with him many times. Siyaddah knew that her father loved the prince like a brother, and for years had hoped that Areth Urstone would regain his freedom. Even as a child, her father had said, "I hope that someday you can wed a man of his caliber."

Men had tried to court Siyaddah, men from good families, but her father hadn't approved of them. Siyaddah knew that her father was grooming her, hoping that she would meet Prince Urstone, and that perhaps they would fall in love.

What does she think of all this? Daylan wondered. Certainly she must look forward to this day with both some hope and apprehension.

But whatever she felt, she kept masked.

"I . . . am pleased to meet you," Siyaddah said to Kan-hazur with just the slightest bow. Her manner was courtly.

"You are not pleased to meet me," Kan-hazur growled with the bag hiding her face. "I am not pleasant, and therefore you cannot be pleased. Why must you humans lie?"

"It is called a pleasantry," Siyaddah said. "Among humans, we offer pleasantries when we meet a stranger. A pleasantry is not something that you, the stranger, have earned, it is a gift that I, the host, bestow."

"I want none of your pleasantries," Kan-hazur said.

"Too late," Siyaddah said. "I've already given it to you. Besides, it is indeed a pleasure to meet you. I've often wondered about your kind, and it is a rare treat to meet you under such hospitable circumstances, on such a beautiful day."

Kan-hazur pulled the bag away slightly and squinted at the burning sunlight, her eyes going red and puffy.

Daylan fought back a chuckle. Siyaddah had only just met the woman, but already sounded as if she had mastered the art of driving a wyrmling crazy.

Kan-hazur inhaled deeply, as if trying to think of an appropriate curse to hurl, but just growled.

"Don't snarl at me," Siyaddah warned in a more abrasive tone. "I won't tolerate it. I know how angry you must be. I too, am a princess, and have lost my home."

"Not lost," Kan-hazur said. "It was ripped from your warriors' dead hands. It was stolen because your people are weak and stupid."

Siyaddah gritted her teeth. It looked as if she were considering a dozen insults, trying to decide which first to hurl.

"Speak up," Kan-hazur challenged, "or are you so slow-witted that you can think of nothing to say?"

"I'll keep my thoughts to myself," Siyaddah said.

Kan-hazur's face contorted with rage, and she clenched her fists tightly, as if she so wanted to hear Siyaddah's taunts that she planned to beat them out of her.

Siyaddah smiled at the small victory. When it came to self-control, she was obviously the stronger of the two.

"There now," Daylan said, hoping to defuse the situation. "Look at you—the two of you have only just met, and already you're sparring like sisters."

Kan-hazur fought back her anger, apparently deciding that she wanted to beat Siyaddah at her own game. "Why . . . why do you treat me like this?"

"Daylan here teaches that we should show kindness to all living creatures," Siyaddah said gently, "including toads and wyrmlings."

"Then he is a fool," Kan-hazur growled dangerously.

"And yet, it may be that only his foolishness has kept you alive," Siyaddah countered. "When you were first captured, there were many who wanted your blood. But Daylan here argued against it. He argued that you should be set free."

"I owe him nothing," Kan-hazur objected. "If he argued for my freedom, he argued in vain—and he did it for his own . . . obscure purposes."

"He did it out of compassion," Siyaddah said. "He spoke of you as if you were a bear cub that had been lost in the woods. He said that you should have been returned to your own kind."

Where she would have been trained for war and given command of troops, Daylan thought. And having seen our defenses, she might well have led some devastating raids against us.

That is what King Urstone had argued, and though Daylan's stand was morally sound, there was much to be said for Urstone's more pragmatic approach: keep the princess as a prisoner, safe and unharmed—but more importantly, keep here where she could do no harm.

There came the sound of singing down the road, some bumpkin torturing an old folk tune.

Daylan threw the sacks back over Kan-hazur, looked to Siyaddah. "Will you come with me? We do not have to go far." He didn't want her to return to the castle, not now. He was afraid that she would have an attack of conscience, tell the guards what she knew. It would be better if she stayed close.

"You're going to make the exchange now?" Fear and excitement mingled in her voice. If the exchange took place as planned, it would be talked about for years. And Siyaddah would be the one that ears would lean toward as the story was told.

Daylan did not tell her precisely when or where, lest she warn others. But he nodded just a bit.

"Will there be wyrmlings?"

Daylan nodded again. She glanced down at his side, saw his long knife strapped to his boot. He was acquitted for battle, if need be, and Daylan's skill with weapons was legendary. And he had weapons at his disposal that she could not see, could not even begin to understand.

"All right," she said. "I will come."

AN EXCHANGE OF HOSTAGES

The enlightened man is incapable of plumbing the depths of a darkened mind, yet he places himself in danger if he does not try. —High King Urstone

In a more perfect world, Fallion thought, my father and mother are still alive.

He sat in the sun beneath the alder trees and dared to dream of this as he peered up. The sun beating down through layered sheets of leaves created a complex tapestry of shadow and light, all in shades of green. The day was only now beginning to really warm, and the air smelled sweet and fresh after a night locked in the stone box.

Fallion drew heat from around him and warmed himself and his friends, so that they quickly dispelled the bone-numbing chill.

They'd been so close to death, and now he felt that it was a miracle to be alive.

"Can you believe it, Jaz?" Fallion asked. "We've met the shadow of our grandfather, and we are going to see father again."

Beyond all hope, Fallion thought, beyond my wildest dreams.

Talon frowned. "We *might* see him," she warned. "The wyrmlings have been holding him captive." But Fallion could not think in those terms right now. Mights and maybes weren't enough.

No, I will see my father, he promised himself. I have come so far, been through so much, it is only fair that I should see him.

He held the hope in his heart, pure and clean and undefiled.

The soldiers were busy around the old fortress, taking the heads off of the enemy, preparing the dead. Some were taking lunch before heading back toward the garrison at Cantular.

But the king was preparing for a longer journey, hand-selecting the troops who would come.

Fallion peered up into the trees, noticed that the edges of the alder leaves were turning gold. Though it felt like high summer, as it had been at home, he realized that perhaps winter was coming on here, in this new world. Or maybe they were high enough into the mountains so that winter came early.

But no, at the edge of hearing, in a tree high above him, he could hear the peeping of birds in a nest. He watched a fluttering shadow until it disappeared in the crook of the tree, and the peeping became loud and insistent for a moment, and then fell silent. The birds were nesting.

No, it was early summer, Fallion decided. But the leaves were going already. There was a blight upon the land.

Fallion peered at Jaz, who merely sat with a bemused expression. He was off to dreaming, imagining what it would be like to see his father.

One of the big folk approached, a young man whose narrow face made him look almost childlike. He wore a blood-soaked rag around his head, and his brown hair was a riot, with a cow-lick in the back.

He muttered something, handed out their packs full of clothes, somehow managing to hand each of them the wrong pack. By the weight alone, Fallion knew that his forcibles were all gone, probably fallen into the hands of the enemy.

Fallion searched his pack, found that it was stuffed with some of Jaz's clothes and Talon's tunic. A bracelet fell out, one made of pale green stones and a single pearl upon a string. Fallion had never seen it before.

"That's mine," Rhianna said, snatching it before he could get a good look at it.

"Where did it come from?" Fallion asked.

"A suitor," she said.

"Who?" Fallion asked, amused to discover that he was jealous. Many young men had smiled at her back home, especially at the fairs and dances. But he hadn't realized that she had a suitor bringing her gifts, gifts that she kept hidden and treasured.

"No one," she said. Rhianna only hid the bracelet away in her pack.

"You should wear it," Talon told Rhianna. "It would look lovely with your hair."

"Do you think?" Rhianna asked, giggling like a younger girl. It sounded strange, Fallion thought, that she should sound so carefree after the events of the night. But somehow the woods were healing that way, like a balm to the heart. Or perhaps it was the news that his father lived again.

Or perhaps . . . he looked to the Wizard Sisel. Fallion had heard that Earth Wardens could affect people that way—calming their fears, making them feel whole and in touch with nature.

The Wizard Sisel was watching them with worry lining his brow.

Of course, Fallion realized. The wizard is having an effect upon us, healing our mood, filling us with renewed vigor.

Fallion felt grateful for this small favor.

They all exchanged packs, began dumping things out, each taking his or her clothing, folding it neatly. Fallion was relieved to find that he still had the silver locket with his mother's picture painted inside upon a piece of ivory, a picture from when she was young and lovely, with the endowments of glamour given to her at birth. In the picture she was forever young, forever beautiful. It was the only thing that he had of hers, and he had always treasured it.

But as he looked at it now, he wondered, Is there really some shadow world where she still lives? Is there perhaps some place even where she is young and beautiful?

If I could combine that world with ours, could I bring her back to life?

The thought made him tremble with excitement.

"Uh, Fallion," Rhianna said. She nodded toward the young man who had brought their packs. He was, with an air of tremendous dignity, holding out Fallion's long sword, presenting it to him, the blade un-sheathed. But the blade was covered with a thick patina of rust, and the ebony handle was cracked.

"No," Fallion said, suddenly afraid to take it. "It was touched by him—by the Knight Eternal. I can feel the curse upon it."

"Take it," the Wizard Sisel said, strolling close, "The curse is upon the steel. I doubt that it will make *you* rust. Besides, you may have need of it all too soon."

Fallion could see that he would hurt the young man's feelings if he did not take it. Obviously, the blade had been won in battle, and had been borne here at great price.

"Thank you," Fallion said, taking his sword.

"Alun," the wizard Sisel said. "His name is Alun."

"Thank you, Alun."

The boy smiled shyly.

Sisel bent near Fallion. "We found some forcibles in one of the packs," he said. "I had the king send them to Luciare already."

"You found them in only one bag?" Talon said.

"There were more?" Sisel asked.

"We each were carrying some," Fallion explained. "There were three hundred in all."

"I fear that most of them have fallen into the hands of the enemy," Sisel said. "Let us hope that they don't know how to use them."

Fallion sat for a moment, feeling disconcerted.

One by one, other warriors stepped forward and presented each of Fallion's companions with their weapons—Talon with her sword, Rhianna with her staff,

Jaz with his bow. Each of the weapons looked to have been cursed, all except for Rhianna's staff, which Fallion had found three years past.

It had once been his father's, the staff of an Earth King, and so was adorned in kingly fashion. It looked to be a branch hewn from some kind of oak, honey gold in color, and richly lacquered. It had a handle wrapped in leather, and beneath the leather were potent herbs that refreshed and invigorated any room where the staff was housed. Powerful gems encircled the staff both above and below that grip—jade to lend strength to the staff, opals to give light by night (should the bearer be a wizard with the power to release their inner fire), pearls to lighten the heart, cloudy quartz to hide the bearer from unwanted eyes. There were hundreds of runes etched into the staff, too, running up and down the length of it, runes of protection from various sorceries. Fallion suspected that even if the staff had been cursed, the Knights Eternal could not have succeeded. He knew for a fact that its wood could not be harmed by fire, and as a flameweaver, he could not handle the thing without feeling a strong sense of discomfort. Thus, he had given it to Rhianna, not because she had great talent with such a weapon, but because he suspected that there was great healing power in the staff, and given the torments that she had been put through in her short life, she needed healing more than anyone that he knew.

Not long after their belongings had been restored to them, a strapping warrior picked up the handles to the handcart and urged Fallion and the others to get on.

They sat back, using their packs as pillows, as the warrior began racing through the woods, pulling the cart faster than a horse would have. Fallion marveled at the warrior's size and strength, for he was every bit as tall as one of the wyrmlings, and his shoulders looked to be four feet across.

They rode then, with human warriors running behind the wagon and along its sides like an honor guard.

We're heading back to Cantular, Fallion realized, and then south to the human lands.

Fallion longed to see what the human lands would look like, with their enormous stone buildings, until Jaz laughed and broke out in a riding song. Jaz had a strong, clear voice, and often lately was asked to sing at the fairs among the minstrels. In a fairer world, Fallion imagined, that is what Jaz would have done to earn a coin.

Rhianna began to sing with him, and elbowed Fallion in the ribs until he and Talon joined in, and they sang:

> Ever the road does wind along,
> 'Tis fare to travel well,
> Riding in a fine carriage,
> While singing a song,
> Whether in sun or shadowed vale.
>
> Upon a road so far from home,
> 'Tis fare to travel well.
> Riding in a fine carriage,
> With a girl that I love,
> Whether in sun or shadowed vale.

The young man Alun was running beside them, doing his best to keep up with the larger warriors. Fallion saw him eying Talon, straining as he ran.

Fallion saw her catch his eye, glance away. "You have an admirer," Fallion teased. He did not need to say that the gawky young man looked to be the runt of the litter.

Alun said something to Talon in the guttural tongue of this land.

"He says we sing well," Talon said. "He thinks we sing like *wenglas* birds."

"Ah, is that some kind of vulture?" Fallion asked in a self-deprecating tone.

"No," Talon said. "They are birds of legend. They were women whose voices were so beautiful that they gave them flight, so that they rose up on pale white wings and flew through the heavens. From them all of the birds learned to sing."

"Oh," Fallion said. "So he's saying that I sing like a girl?"

"No," Talon chided. "He was just offering a compliment. He would like to hear more songs of our world."

But Fallion couldn't help but think that he must sound like a girl to these big folk. The men of the warrior clan were taller than the bears of the Dunnwood, and their voices were deeper than the bellow of a bull. Fallion could not help feel that he must look small and effeminate to them.

But Jaz burst out with a rowdy tavern song, all about "the glories of ale, whether drunken from an innkeeper's mug, or guzzled from your father's jug, or gulped from a fishmonger's pail."

So they sang as they rode, racing throughout the long afternoon. Fallion managed to fall into a deep sleep, and every hour or two he would wake up and look out over the land. The trees were taller than he remembered, and the land looked strange with its occasional pillar of wind-sculpted rock.

We are far from home, Fallion realized. Farther than I ever thought I would be.

He had not imagined how it would be. Nothing in his life could ever be the same as it had been. He could not unbind the worlds, re-make the old. He doubted that such a power even existed. He only hoped that the world that he made would be better than the one he had left behind.

The soldiers took turns pulling the cart and kept running through the heat of the day. Even Fallion's grandfather, a giant of a man, took his own turn at the handcart.

Every so often, Alun was given a chance to sit on the cart and gain a much-needed rest.

So it was that in the middle of the afternoon, they stopped in a huge meadow where they could see for half a mile around. The sun-bleached grass shone like ice in the blazing light of day.

Fallion's friends had all gone fast to sleep. But Fallion stretched his legs by walking for a bit.

He felt refreshed for the first time in days, as if he had finally gotten his energy back, and he wondered if it was because of some spell that Sisel had cast upon him.

The Wizard Sisel came and stood beside him silently for a moment, a huge and comforting presence, and together they just stared out over the silver fields, admiring a valley down below and the broad river twisting through it.

"It's beautiful here," Fallion said after a few moments of silence. "I did not know that it would be so beautiful."

"Yes," the wizard said. "This field is strong in life. The grass is good, the trees hardy. Let us hope that it stays that way."

"Can you keep them alive?" Fallion asked.

Sisel frowned. "Not for long, I fear. Can't you hear it—the voices of the stones, the cries in the brooks, the lament of the leaves? 'We are fading,' they say.

"All of the trees that you see now, these pleasant grasses, came from your world, not ours. They are like a dream to us, a welcome dream from our past, a dream that will soon fade to despair.

"The very stones beneath our feet ache. The earth is in pain."

The Wizard Binnesman had spoken those words to Fallion's father, and now they seemed an echo of the past. "What can you do?" Fallion asked.

"There are pockets of resistance, places where the earth's blood pools just beneath the surface. In these places, life is still abundant. The wyrmlings have little sway there. A week ago, I had little hope at all. But now . . . there is a wizard at the heart of the world."

"Averan."

Sisel frowned, bent his head like a fox that was listening for the rustling sounds of mice in the grass.

Averan should be alive, Fallion thought. With the worlds combined, it would have changed the great Seal of Earth there. She had healed the earth once, mended the seal. She could do it again. Fallion imagined Averan, the wizardess with her staff of black poisonwood, frantically at work.

But Sisel's worried expression spoke otherwise. "Yes," Sisel whispered, "my old apprentice Averan. Is she well? I wonder. Is she even alive? Or has our hope been spent in vain?"

Fallion bit his lip. He wanted to go find her, do his part to mend the world. But he wondered if it was even possible now.

Moments later, after a quick meal, they set out on the road.

In the late afternoon Fallion's wagon halted one last time, beneath the shadow of Mount Luciare. Its peaks were capped with snow even so late in the summer, and Fallion could see the city up on its slopes, enormous slabs of whitened stone along the castle wall providing overwhelming fortifications. There were tunnels carved into the mountain, their openings yawning with wide arches, so that they let in the light. Scrollwork had been cut around the arches and overlaid with gold so that they gleamed in the sunlight. Huge braziers lined the arches, too, and Fallion realized that these were not just for adornment. In case of a night attack, the braziers would cast a bright light, which would reflect from the white walls and gold foil, blinding any wyrmlings.

Even from a great distance, the castle was beautiful and inviting.

King Urstone left the handcart, and for several miles the small group made their way through a wooded fen. The king brought only Fallion, his friends, the young man Alun, and eight strong warriors to act as a guard. Dank trees huddled over brackish water where mosquitoes and midges swarmed.

For Fallion, negotiating the swamp was no great matter. The muddy trail was just dry enough to hold his weight. But those of the warrior clan found themselves slogging through mud that often reached their knees.

So it was late in the afternoon by the time that they reached a small tower in the marsh, a simple thing of sandstone, long ago fallen into ruin. The tower crowned a small hill, and to the east of it was a large dry meadow.

The Wizard Sisel walked around the tower, using his staff to trace a circle in the turf. Then he scratched runes upon it in six intervals. Fallion had never seen the like of it, and so he asked, "What is this that you are making?"

"A circle of life," Sisel said, after a little thought. "Here in this world, life is the power that I have studied—life magic, the power that can be found within all living things, within animals, and plants, water and stones."

"And what power do the Knights Eternal serve?" Fallion asked.

"They serve nothing," Sisel said. "They seek only to subjugate other powers, to twist them to their own use, and ultimately to destroy the very thing that they twist." Sisel fell silent for a moment. He pulled the stalk from a shaft of wheat, then began to chew the succulent end of it as he stared down over the valley. A pair of geese rose up from the river, honking, and flew along its shore.

"Life magic is different from the magic of your world. It is more . . . whole. On your world I served the Earth, and learned the arts of healing and protection. Healing is one of the arts I practice here, too. But there is so much more that one can do. . . ."

Fallion already knew that in his own world, the wizard had gone by the name of Binnesman, and was greatly renowned. "And so now that the worlds have combined, you are a master of both?"

Sisel shook his head. "Not a master. A servant. Those who serve greater powers should never lay claim to the title of master.

"Still, the circle will afford great protection in case the wyrmlings try to break the accord." Sisel glanced down the small hill. Though Fallion had heard nothing, Sisel said, "Ah, look, they're here."

Fallion glanced down the trail, saw the wyrmling princess first. Her pale skin looked like something dead in the bright sunlight, and she kept her arm raised to cover her eyes. She wore a sack draped over her head like a cowl, to give her a little more protection.

Behind her came a small man in a peasant's brown robe. His beard was graying, and Fallion saw nothing extraordinary about him.

But last of all came a young woman, her dark skin and hair contrasting sharply with a dress of white silk, adorned with a border of gray at the hems. She wore bangles of gold and a single black pearl in her nose ring, and she moved with extraordinary delicacy and grace.

Fallion found his attention riveted on her. His heart pounded and his breathing came ragged, and when the wyrmling blocked his view of her for an instant, he found himself stepping to the side, just to catch a glimpse of her again.

What is it about her? he wondered. She was not the most beautiful woman he had ever seen, but he found his body responding to her as if she was. Am I falling in love?

But such questions weren't warranted, he knew. He hadn't spoken to her, hadn't even been introduced. Yet he found himself drawn to her like no other.

This is the way it will feel, he thought, when you first meet the woman you will love. Whether this meeting turns out well or ill, this is how it will feel.

There was a shriek from Rhianna, who had been sitting on a rock at the door to the tower, and suddenly she leapt up. "Uncle Ael!" she cried, and went bounding downhill, where she met the wyrmling's escort, and threw her arms around him.

Fallion had to search his memory. He had heard the name of course. Ael was the mysterious uncle who had taught Rhianna swordsmanship as a child—in the netherworld. Of him, Rhianna had steadfastly refused to speak.

The Wizard Sisel smiled in greeting and called out in a relieved tone, "Daylan Hammer, well met!"

Fallion just stood for a moment, rooted to the ground. Uncle Ael was Daylan Hammer, the hero of legend?

Fallion nudged Talon. "The woman who is with them, the one with the dark hair, who is she?"

"You met her father," Talon said. "The Emir. He is a good friend and counselor to the king."

"Why is she so small? She looks like one of us."

"Her family is from Dalharristan. People are shorter there. And most of those that you've seen are of the warrior caste. They are larger and stronger than those of other castes. Her mother was not a warrior born, but was of a ruling clan, bred for intelligence, beauty, and strong character."

"Is she . . . spoken for?"

Talon gave him a knowing smile. "You're not interested in her. Trust me."

"Really?" Fallion asked. It was a challenge. Suddenly Fallion found his feet, and in Rhianna's wake he went trundling to meet Daylan Hammer.

After hugging Rhianna for a long minute, Daylan threw his hood back, and stood grinning in the sun. Fallion saw that his beard was not gray, merely begrimed with ash. "Little Rhianna!" he said. "Why, you grew up faster than a mushroom, but turned out as beautiful as a robin's egg!"

Daylan seemed genuinely pleased, and Fallion found that he envied their relationship.

"And your mother," Daylan asked. "Is she well? Is she here?"

"Dead," Rhianna said. "She's dead, these eight years back."

Daylan seemed crestfallen. "I am so sorry. She was a good woman, a great woman."

Fallion found himself wondering how many lives Daylan must have mourned. After so many, could he feel any real loss or pain anymore?

Yet Fallion could see it in the immortal's eyes. Yes, there was real loss there.

Fallion stood behind Rhianna, and she turned to introduce him, but Daylan stopped her with a wave of the hand.

"Hail, Torch-bearer," Daylan said with profound respect. He grabbed Fallion by the forearm, as was common among soldiers, shaking hands as if they were old friends or allies who had braved battles together. "I know you," Daylan said. "We have met many times."

Fallion knew that they had never met, not in this lifetime at least. And so Daylan could only be talking of past lives.

"This is your handiwork?" Daylan asked, cocking his head to one side, inclining it toward the valley that spread out below them, the trees and the grass, and the snow-covered mountain in the background.

"It is," Fallion said feeling a bit embarrassed. He had hoped to bind the worlds into a perfect whole, but this flawed thing was all he had been able to manage.

Tears flooded Daylan's eyes, and he grabbed Fallion and hugged him close, weeping freely. "You've done it, brother. You've finally done it."

Fallion could think of nothing to say. This stranger, this legend, had called him brother.

Then King Urstone clapped Daylan on the back, and the two began talking in Urstone's guttural tongue, and Fallion was excluded from the conversation.

Rhianna came and gave Fallion a sisterly hug while Daylan Hammer, the Wizard Sisel, the Emir's daughter, and the king's men huddled together making plans. The wyrmling princess retreated to the dark confines of the tower.

Sundown was less than an hour away, and the wyrmlings would be here soon for the exchange.

Rhianna nodded toward Daylan. "So, what do you think of Uncle Ael?"

"I don't know," Fallion said. He was still bewildered.

"He seems to like you," Rhianna said. "That's a good thing. He does not make friends easily."

"He seems to *know* me," Fallion corrected.

Sunset drew near all too soon for Fallion's liking. The sun descended in a crimson haze that smeared the heavens, for there was still much dust high in the atmosphere, and in the long shadows thrown by the mountain it seemed that night wrapped around the small band like a cloak.

Daylan Hammer assured the king that the proceedings had all been secured under oaths so profound that even a wyrmling dared not break them. He did not expect the wyrmlings to attack.

But time had taught King Urstone this one lesson: never trust the wyrmlings.

So his guards secreted themselves in the woods around the tower in case the wyrmlings tried an ambush.

Fallion waited with his hand upon his sheathed sword, now caked in rust, while the king, the Wizard Sisel, Alun, Siyaddah, and Fallion's friends all stood together in the tower's shadow. Daylan Hammer and the wyrmling princess climbed the tower and stood atop its ruined walls.

The first star appeared in the sky, and bats began their nightly acrobatics around the tower.

Fallion had begun to believe that the wyrmlings would not show when he suddenly heard a flapping.

A wyrmling rose up out of the shadowed woods, came circling the tower. Fallion was fascinated by her artificial wings, and peered hard to see them. Her wings were translucent and golden, like a linnet's wings, but there were darker bands through them, almost like bones, with webbing between the supports. They reminded him of the leathery wings of a graak.

There was no harness, no sign that the wings were any type of device. For all that Fallion could see the wings just sprouted from the woman's back.

She circled the tower, looking down upon the men, as if she were just another bat.

Then she let out a cry, strange and filled with pain, the howling of some evil beast.

In the far distance, several answering cries rose from the trees among the swamp.

King Urstone clutched his battle-ax and shouted a warning. Talon translated, "It's a trap!"

"No," Daylan Hammer warned, "Wait!"

At that moment, wyrmlings rose up out of the swamp. They came winging toward the hill rapidly, vastly faster than the first, and the Wizard Sisel whispered, "Ah, damn."

It wasn't until they drew nearer that Fallion recognized the source of his dismay: these wyrmlings wore red—crimson cowls over blood-red robes, with wings that looked to be made of darkest ruby.

There were three of them.

Each held a black sword in clasped hands, the handle clutched against his breast while the blade pointed back toward his feet.

"Knights Eternal," Talon intoned. "But I count three of them. We slew one yesterday, and another the night before. There should be only one left."

"Yes," Sisel said, "These Knights Eternal should not exist. Lady Despair has been hiding their numbers, and each of them is a hundred years in the making. It is only by luck that Lady Despair has revealed her secret. This is an evil omen. I wonder how many more there might be?"

Fallion let the energy in him build, drawing heat from the ground, preparing to unleash a fireball. The king's men drew weapons, and Jaz bent his bow.

"Hold," Daylan called down from the tower, lest one of the humans be first to break the truce.

The Knights Eternal flew toward them, crisscrossing and veering, as if to dodge archery fire.

And then a creature rose.

Something vast lifted out of the swamps, three miles

in the distance, lumbering above the trees upon leather wings.

It was like nothing that Fallion had ever seen. He had ridden upon sea graaks in Landesfallen. But the thing that came up out of the swamp could have swallowed one of those whole. It was black and sinister in color, and its wingspan had to stretch a hundred, perhaps a hundred and fifty feet. The length of its body was more than eighty feet long, and Fallion imagined that a small village full of people could have ridden on its back.

The shape of the body was serpentine, and the creature kept its head bent, as a heron will when it flies. But it had no heron's head. Instead, it was ugly and blunt, like the head of a blind snake, with a mouth filled with ungainly teeth. Its long body seemed to undulate through the air. A leathery tail fanned out in the back, almost like a rudder.

Upon its back, a small figure clutched at a chain, looking frightened and beleaguered.

Father! Fallion thought, his heart feeling as if it would break.

"What is that creature?" Jaz shouted.

Fallion looked to King Urstone, whose face was pale with fear, and then to the Wizard Sisel, who merely shook his head in bafflement.

"It is a graak," Daylan Hammer shouted from atop the battlements. "But only of a kind that has been spoken of in legend."

Fallion stood, heart hammering, in mounting fear.

Did I create that terror when I merged the worlds? he wondered. He had no answer.

There were too many of the Knights Eternal. The darkness was falling.

Suddenly, the wyrmling princess gave a great cry and leapt from the tower wall. She landed only feet from Fallion, and the ground trembled beneath her weight.

The huge beast, this graak of legend, landed in the field, two hundred yards away, and the lonely figure just clung to its neck. The graak reared up, its ugly neck stretching thirty feet in the air, and for a moment Fallion feared that it would lunge, take them in its teeth and kill them all.

Then it lay down as the wyrmling princess sprinted through the dry grass toward it.

"Areth?" the king cried out. "Areth?"

The lone figure raised up, peered in their direction, and let out a mournful cry, almost a sob.

He was a wreck of a man. His black hair had not been cut in years, and it fanned out from his head in disarray. His long beard reached nearly to his belly.

But even from a distance, Fallion recognized his father's blazing blue eyes.

Prince Urstone let go of the beast's neck, went sliding down its leathery hide, dropping twenty feet to the ground.

He got up on unsteady legs, as if he were not used to walking. He began staggering over the grass, calling out, sobbing.

He's a broken thing, Fallion thought, a wretch.

Fallion heard Talon sniff, looked over, saw tears of pity in her eyes.

Fallion, so focused on his father, almost did not see the wyrmling princess run and leap onto the monster's neck, quickly scrambling for purchase. The behemoth let out a strangled cry, then thundered up into the air.

For an instant, Fallion's father was there under blackest shadows, the wind beating down upon him, and then the stars reappeared.

At the edge of the glade, three Knights Eternal flew, wings flapping softly.

Fallion saw his father stumble, and King Urstone let out a shout, went rushing across the field, calling "Areth! Areth. Ya gish, ha!"

Fallion found himself running, too, legs pumping in an effort to keep up.

"Father!" he shouted. "Father, I'm here!" Fallion so wanted to see his father again, that for a moment he imagined that this "shadow father" might recognize him.

Then his father rose from the ground, and came stumbling toward them on unsteady legs.

King Urstone drew to a halt, took a step backward and shouted in his own tongue.

That's when Fallion saw it. There was something wrong with his father's eyes. Fallion had fancied that he'd seen blazing blue eyes a moment ago.

But now all that he saw were pits, empty pits.

They've blinded him, Fallion realized. They couldn't just set my father free. They had to blind him first.

And as the derelict came staggering forward, Fallion's dismay only grew. In the failing light, he realized that his father's skin looked papery and ragged. His hair was falling out in bunches. His face was shrunken and skeletal.

"Father?" Fallion cried out in horror.

"Fallion, get back!" the Wizard Sisel shouted a heartfelt warning. "There is no life in that accursed thing!"

King Urstone had fallen back, and now he drew his ax in his right hand and grabbed Fallion with his left, holding Fallion back.

The wretch drew closer, and with each step, the rotting horror of his features became clearer. Soon he was forty feet away, then twenty.

The shape of his face is wrong, Fallion decided. That's not my father at all.

Fallion felt bewildered, uncertain.

No, his features aren't becoming clearer. He is rotting before our eyes.

The thing came toward Fallion, staggering and bumbling, and fell. Almost, Fallion reached out to grab him, but he heeded Sisel's warning.

The derelict suddenly flicked his wrist, and a knife dropped from his sleeve, into his hand. Viciously, he took a swipe at Fallion.

Fallion raised his sword and slashed the creature's wrist, disarming it as the derelict fell to the ground and collapsed, its flesh turning to dust, leaving only a half-clothed skeleton with ragged patches of hair to lie at Fallion's feet.

Fallion stood there, his sword in hand, and peered down in dismay. He looked up at the Knights Eternal, but they were already winging away, over the dark swamps.

One of them threw back his head, and dimly Fallion realized, He's laughing. They're laughing at us!

There was no one to strike, no one to take vengeance upon.

The meadow was left empty and unbloodied. The wyrmlings had not violated the truce. Nor had they kept their word. They had their princess, and Fallion had . . . a corpse.

Sisel came up at their back, stood peering down in dismay. The others followed, the entire small group converging as one. King Urstone swore and raged at the sky.

"Was that my father?" Fallion asked, still uncertain.

"No," the Wizard Sisel said, "just some unfortunate soul who died long ago in prison. The Knights Eternal must have put some kind of glamour upon the corpse."

"But," Rhianna asked, "the dead walked?"

"Oh yes," Sisel intoned, "in the courts of Rugassa, the dead do more than walk."

"I . . . was a fool to hope," Fallion said, blinking back tears of rage and embarrassment.

"A fool, to hope?" Sisel said, "Never! They want you to believe that, because the moment you do, they have won. But remember—it is never foolish to hope, even when your hope has been misplaced."

High King Urstone knelt, his hands resting on the pommel of his ax, and just wept softly for a long moment. There was no one to comfort the king, no one who dared, until at last Alun came and put his hand upon the king's shoulder.

The king looked up at him, gratitude in his eyes.

"The wyrmlings lied," Jaz said bitterly.

"It is in their nature to lie," Sisel said. "The wyrms in

their souls find it hard to abide the truth. Daylan knew that they might try to deceive us. It was always a risk."

"A risk?" Daylan Hammer called out. "Yes, there was a chance that the wyrmlings would seek to cheat us. But if we had let things go as they were, the destruction of our souls was not a risk—it was a certainty. You know of what I am speaking, Sisel. You smelled the moral rot as well as I did."

Daylan Hammer came down from the tower now, and went striding up behind the group, peering down at the corpse.

"I smelled the moral rot," Sisel said. "It was like an infected tooth, that threatens the life of the whole body. Still, I suspect that we could have waited a little longer before pulling it."

"And I think that we have waited far too long," Daylan said. "The moral rot runs all through Luciare now." He sighed, studied the body. "I'm sorry Fallion, Jaz. I had hoped for a happier end than this."

"What will you do now?" Jaz asked. "Will you go to Rugassa and free my father?"

"We don't have the troops," the Wizard Sisel said. "We could throw ten thousand men against the castle walls there and still not be sure to breach their defenses."

"There must be something you can do—" Jaz said, "perhaps a better trade?"

But we've already offered a fair trade, Fallion thought. I know, he considered sarcastically, we could offer them me. It seems only right. Father saved my life once. Now I can save his.

Talon got a thoughtful look. "The wyrmlings have shown that they cannot be trusted. It was foolish to think otherwise. They will not barter for what they can easily steal."

Daylan Hammer argued. "Not all wyrmlings are so hopelessly evil. Some can hold to a bargain—even some that harbor loci."

"Ah," the Wizard Sisel objected, "but to do so, they

must fight the very wyrm that consumes their souls, and no wyrmling can resist for long—"

Daylan began to object, but Sisel cut him off, raising a hand, begging for silence.

He peered up into the air. In the deepening night, a great-horned owl flew up out of the field, swooping low over the ground, as if hunting for mice. Then it suddenly glided once around the old tower.

"Fallion, we can't go after your father," Sisel said. "We have more important concerns right now."

"What?" Fallion asked.

Sisel nodded toward the owl, and then cocked his head as if listening for some far-off cry. A pair of fireflies rose up from the grass and lit on the end of his staff, then sat there glowing, so that the wizard's worried frown could be seen in a pale green light. Fallion could hear nothing from the woods, could see nothing to justify the dismay in Sisel's voice. "Wyrmlings are coming. This is an ambush!"

❧ 30 ❧

THE BATTLE AT THE GATES

Luciare was never the greatest of castles. It was not the largest. Its walls were not the thickest. It was not the most heavily garrisoned or the most easily defended.

But of all of our castles, it was the most filled with life. It was not just the trees and flowers, the birds and the insects that gave it life. It was the spirits of our ancestors that guarded it.

How little we realize the debts we owe to those who have suffered for us, and sacrificed for us, and gone

before. How little do we realize how often they watch
over us, or what a vast role they play in our day-to-day
affairs.   *—the Wizard Sisel*

Daylan gave a shout in the king's tongue, and suddenly
the king drew steel while guards began sprinting out
from under the trees.

Sisel whirled his staff in the air once, and fireflies
began to rise up out of the grass, streaming toward the
king's group from hundreds of yards away.

The king began calling out to his warriors in dismay,
and they peered off toward Mount Luciare. With the setting of the sun, the mount was left half in shadow, but the
city suddenly blazed with light, and even in the distance,
Fallion could see its white walls and golden scrollwork
gleaming brighter than any fiery beacon.

Sisel translated, "The king is going to make for the
castle." The king's men pointed to the northeast, where a
fire suddenly sprouted on the horizon. Fallion had only
seen fireworks once before, as a child at a midsummer's
festival when traders from Indhopal had called upon his
mother's castle, but now he recognized fireworks soaring
up in the distance, two of bright red and one of blue, and
each mushroomed into flame.

"Wyrmlings," Talon said. "A large host of them.
They're advancing on Cantular!"

Then, to the northwest, another fire sprouted, and four
more fireworks soared into the air, three of red, and one
of yellow.

"And a larger host is coming for Luciare!" Sisel said,
his voice trembling. "They planned this. They planned to
attack as soon as the princess was gone!"

They will have the Knights Eternal with them, Fallion
realized. And that beast, the giant graak. And what other
horrors?

Sisel turned to Fallion. The king and his guards began
hastening away, striding across the field.

"Fallion," Sisel said. "The king is making for the city. He wants to be sure of its defenses. I should be there too. But there is a Circle of Life around the old tower. You can stay there for the night. It should be safe. Even the Knights Eternal could not find you, so long as you hide within that circle. But its powers will fade, eventually. You cannot stay there forever."

Fallion looked longingly toward the king.

"Stay," Daylan Hammer warned. "Unless you have runes of metabolism, you will only slow the war clan down."

"I'll not leave grandfather to fight alone," Fallion said. "Tell them to run ahead if they must. We will catch up to them when we can."

Daylan called out to the king, translated the words. The king responded. "He says that if you wish to stay, he and his men will draw off the enemy. But he can't guarantee your safety, even in Luciare."

Fallion drew his sword, peered at it grimly in the light thrown by Sisel's fireflies. The blade was caked with rust now. In a few hours, it would rust through and be good for nothing. Already, the king's guard was leading the way down through the trees.

"Let's go," he shouted to his friends, and they were off.

Fallion sprinted. He wanted to prove himself. He didn't have the breeding of a man of the Warrior Clans. He didn't have their size and stamina. Nor did he have endowments. But he learned long ago that a man can by will alone make himself more than a man. He can exercise until he is as strong as any three men. He can labor for long hours until it seems that he has taken endowments of stamina. And Fallion and his friends had been training from childhood.

So they raced under the trees into the marsh. Cool air was streaming down from the icy peaks of Mount Luciare, and as it hit the warmer water of the marsh, a layer of mist began to form, fog that hung in the air like spider's webs.

Overhead, the trees hung in a heavy canopy, their leaves blocking out the stars.

Under the heavy shade of the trees, the only light came from the fireflies that circled Sisel's staff, sometimes halting to rest on a bush, sometimes buzzing ahead as if to show the way.

The wizard slowed several times to strip the kernels of grain from off stalks of wheat. Each time he did, he would sprinkle the grain over the men, so that grass seeds clung to their hair and the folds of their clothes.

They traveled like this for miles, the king and his troops striding purposefully. Fallion and his folk struggled to keep up, and he found himself often dogging the steps of the slowest of the warriors—the Emir's daughter, Siyaddah.

He did not mind. He preferred the view of her shapely figure to that of one of the over-sized warriors. And as they marched, he found himself feeling protective of her, promising himself, *If we are attacked, I will fight at her side.*

For her part, Siyaddah could not help but notice the attention. Several times she glanced over her shoulder to catch Fallion's eye.

At last they slowed for a moment.

"Let no fear rule your heart," Sisel warned Fallion and the others. "We are encircled by life—the trees and seeds above us, the ferns and shrubs at our sides, the grasses and mushrooms beneath. The Knights Eternal will find it hard to spot us."

"What about your blasted light?" Jaz asked, for the fireflies were surprisingly bright. Hundreds of them circled now, perhaps thousands.

"My light comes from living creatures," Sisel proclaimed, "Thus it is almost impossible for the eyes of the dead to see. A torch on the other hand, is only fire consuming dead wood, and is easy for one of the dead to spot."

"The dead?" Jaz asked.

"Of course, the Knights Eternal are dead," Sisel said, "or mostly so. And so death attracts them. They know when you are close to your demise."

Fallion tried to make sense of this. "Do you mean they are drawn to us as we approach the moment of our deaths?"

"No, no," Sisel answered. "They don't know when you will die any more than a goat does. But every living creature has a measure of death in it. Bits of us die every moment—skin flakes off, hairs fall away, and even though we are alive, we slowly decay. You can smell it on the old. It is the decay that draws the Knights Eternal. It smells sweet to them. And if we are wounded, if the life within us ebbs, we draw their attention, and they gain greater power over us."

Fallion took mental stock of himself. He felt much stronger now than he had two nights ago, when the Knights Eternal had first begun hunting him. He had wondered even before the knights had begun stalking him if he was near death, for a great weariness had been on him.

On the trail behind them, perhaps five hundred yards back, an owl hooted once.

It was a common sound in the woods at night, but Sisel immediately tensed, and then whispered, "Shhh, they are upon us."

The king raised a hand, calling a halt.

Up in the air, the pounding of wings came heavily.

Fallion looked up to Sisel, for he was taller than men on Fallion's world, and saw the wizard standing with his eyes closed, leaning on his staff, mouthing some spell.

Fallion gripped his sword, found himself studying Siyaddah. If she felt any fear, she concealed it well. She peered up into the trees with seemingly as little concern as a housewife might show upon learning that it might rain on her clean laundry.

Rhianna, Talon, and Jaz only stood as still as a herd of deer, sensing for danger.

The Knight Eternal passed, flying ahead, and Fallion's group began their journey again.

They climbed up out of the marsh, into the foothills near Luciare; the mist drew back, and the trees thinned. Stars shone through bright swathes in the canopy. The hills became like a chessboard with dark blotches of forest skirting meadows where sun-bleached grasses shone ash gray under the stars.

Fallion felt exposed. The king called a halt at the edge of a clearing, and stood for a long moment. One of his guards pointed ahead. There were wyrmlings in the trees on the far side of the clearing, just beyond a gentle rise. Fallion could hear the tread of heavy feet, the clack of bone armor, a pair of grunts, followed by a snarl. There had to be a patrol of at least two dozen of them.

All of the fireflies suddenly winked out, and the king motioned for everyone to get down. Fallion soundlessly dropped to his knees, ducking behind a fallen log. He heard Jaz drawing heavy breaths to his left, saw his brother nock an arrow and then lie quietly, like a poacher waiting for a boar to come drink at a pond.

Talon and Rhianna were just beyond him.

To Fallion's right, Siyaddah lay with her face upturned, listening.

She caught Fallion staring at her, and she just lay there peering into his eyes.

There was a grunt on the far side of the clearing, the sound of a footsteps coming toward them.

Fallion clutched his sword, loosened it from his scabbard. He didn't fancy the notion of fighting wyrmlings in the dark.

He heard another gruff grunt, and the wyrmlings suddenly halted. One of them began to sniff the air, like a stag checking the trail ahead.

They've caught wind of us, Fallion realized. He saw his own warriors tensing nearby, gripping battle-axes, preparing to leap up.

The Wizard Sisel was only ten feet away, just beyond Siyaddah.

He raised a hand, pointed his pinky finger downhill. Fallion spotted the glint of a golden ring.

Something ominous sprung from the ground. It was a boiling mist, numinous and fog-like; the air suddenly chilled, as if they were in the presence of a wight.

The hair stood up on Fallion's neck; goose bumps rose along his arms as the mist went hurtling through the brush like an arrow shot from a bow.

It glided almost soundlessly away, making only the faintest rustle through the grass and bushes, like a small wind; its effects were chilling. A hundred yards away, a grouse suddenly erupted from a bush, squawking in terror. A moment later, in the field beyond, a hare thumped its feet in warning, while its fellows hopped in every direction. Farther on, in the oaks beyond the clearing, a hart bounded three times, its rack snagging in a branch.

For all the world, it sounded as if someone were fleeing in fear.

With a growl the wyrmlings went charging south, racing after their invisible prey.

Moments later, once the wyrmlings had departed, the king headed north, and Fallion had to sprint to keep up.

They reached a narrow ravine that headed up the skirts of the mountain. A small brook ran through the ravine, its waters burbling over rocks and moss. The trees overhead grew thick and dark, and had it not been for the return of fireflies to give their light to the wizard, the troops could not have negotiated the thick brush.

Three times they had to cross the broad road that wound down from Caer Luciare. Each time, the king sent his scouts to watch for long moments before they made their crossing.

It was not until they neared the castle, perhaps three hundred yards from the gates, that they met resistance.

The king and his men climbed up out of the ravine, beneath the shadows of the oaks, and reached the last stretch of road. It was paved with thick stones, each four-foot square and fitted so closely together that a knife blade could not have been inserted between them.

Ahead the city blazed. Blue-white lights played beneath the arches on the mount, flickering and twisting, like some ethereal bonfire, and these lights reflected from the golden scrollwork and the freshly limed walls.

To Fallion, it looked beautiful, as if the walls of the city were made from enchanted crystal, and the Glories themselves stood guard beneath the arches.

Little did he know that it was not far from the truth.

As they waited, a deep growl came softly from the trees off to their left.

Four wyrmlings stepped from the brush.

"Watch out!" Rhianna cried, leaping forward with her staff. The king's guard seemed startled, and many a weapon was drawn.

One of the wyrmlings held up his hand, three fingers extended in the air.

Jaz let an arrow fly, but Sisel bumped him just as he did, and the shot went wide.

"Scouts," Sisel whispered. The wyrmlings began to talk softly and urgently to the king, their voices deep and guttural.

"Scouts?" Fallion whispered.

"Not all of the wyrmlings are evil," Daylan Hammer whispered. "Not all of them have wyrms inside them, and though they are taught that they should desire one, they resist the teachings. They long for peace, just as we do. These few here are friends."

Fallion looked to Talon, who seemed shocked. "Did you know about this?"

She shook here head. "I did not know that the king employed such creatures."

As the wyrmlings spoke, Talon began to translate. "They say that the road ahead is dangerous, and they were afraid to try to reach the castle. They say that a horde of wyrmlings is approaching Luciare, a horde so vast that the city cannot withstand it. Another horde is already upon Cantular."

Fallion nodded. Taking Cantular had been a vain gesture, it seemed. The men of Luciare had taken it in the morning, and the wyrmlings would have it again by midnight.

The wyrmling scouts finished relaying their message, and the king gave a nod, waved his men forward with his battle-ax.

So the men came out of the trees and bracken, and they could not hide any longer. The king's men began to sprint, and the little road filled with light as Sisel's fireflies streamed along beside them, a cloud of green fire.

Suddenly there was a strangled cry from Rhianna behind, and Fallion whirled to see something huge and dark spread its wings. It had been sitting in the crook of an oak, and now the branch went bobbing and waving as if in a strong wind.

Down the mountain, other cries arose, strange and vile, like the cries of peasants as they die, and suddenly the Knights Eternal were winging toward them.

Now it was just a race, the king's men sprinting up the even road, calling for help in their strange tongue, as three Knights Eternal winged toward them like a murder of crows.

Siyaddah was running just ahead of Fallion. Suddenly she stumbled over something in the road. She fell in a tangle, and Fallion saw that it was a dead man, a scout who had not made it to the castle in time.

"Fallion," Jaz shouted, "give me some light!"

Fallion stood above Siyaddah and reached inside himself, tempted to hurl a killing blaze, but instead cast a far weaker spell. He sent a nimbus into the air, a shimmering ball of heated gases that did not blind so much as it revealed.

A Knight Eternal in blood-red robes was swooping toward the fleeing form of King Urstone, the knight's slender black blade aimed at the king's back.

Jaz slid to one knee, drew an arrow to the full, and sent it blurring. It took the knight in the belly, six inches beneath the sternum.

The Knight Eternal howled in grief like a wounded bear, then veered slightly and crashed to the ground, mere feet ahead of Siyaddah.

A cheer rose from the castle walls, from defenders hidden up in the shadows behind the merlons, and Fallion felt a small thrill of hope to realize that they were so close to safety.

He and his friends ran with renewed vigor.

But howls of rage erupted from the other Knights Eternal, and they redoubled their speed.

Fallion felt a spell wash over him, an invisible hand. It reached inside him grabbed the heat that he had stored there, and began to pull.

A flameweaver is here, Fallion realized.

Fallion did not fight the creature.

He let the heat go, even though it would mean that Jaz would not have light to see by. The Knight Eternal absorbed the heat, imagining that his own powers were superior to Fallion's.

They were only two hundred yards from the wall, then a hundred and fifty. Fallion heard the thud of heavy wings behind him.

He spun, reached out with his mind, and pulled the energy back from the Knight Eternal. Fire came whirling from the sky in twisting threads, and before the knight could react, Fallion sent it hurtling toward the creature in a bright ball of flame.

Jaz pivoted, dropped to one knee, and fired another arrow. The knight shrieked like the damned and veered away.

The arrow sped upward and went ripping beneath the knight's wing, mere inches from the shoulder.

Fallion waited to hear the creature's death scream, but it only went lumbering toward the trees.

A miss, Fallion realized, his heart sinking.

The arrows that Myrrima had blessed were few in number, and with the curse laid upon them, their wood was rotting away. In another day, they would be good for nothing.

"Give me more light!" Jaz cried.

Fallion could not help, but Sisel whirled and aimed his staff. Fireflies went streaking up into the night sky like green embers, filling the air.

But the last two Knights Eternal wheeled back, soaring like a pair of hawks above the trees.

Jaz and Fallion waited a long moment, acting as a rearguard for the king and his troops, even as the castle gate opened, and a mighty host spilled out.

Jaz shouted a taunt to the Knights Eternal, "Come on, will you? We're not *that* dangerous. Give it your best try."

But the Knights Eternal were gone, soaring away down over the valley.

Wearily, Fallion turned and trudged into Castle Luciare.

❧ 31 ❧

A BATTLE JOINED

Until one has found himself in a pitched battle, where every moment brings the threat of death, he cannot truly value peace. —the Wizard Sisel

In Cantular, Warlord Madoc stood upon a tower wall and peered to the north with nothing to give him light but the stars and a slender crescent moon that clung tenaciously to the horizon.

Wyrmling troops sprinted en-masse in the distance, starlight glinting off helms of bone and off of flesh that was paler still. Among them, something monstrous crawled, a creature huge and humped, like a living hill. Hundreds of wyrmling lords rode upon its back. Madoc could see a head, vaguely adder-like and triangular, larger than a house, low to the ground. Kezziards stumped along too, like giant lizards among the wyrmlings, their warty skin as gray as a toad's. They towered above the normal troops, like oxen among toddlers. The wyrmlings roared as they came, beating hammers against their shields. The sound snaked over the miles and reverberated among the hills like a groan, as if the very earth cursed at the folly it was forced to bear.

Above the dark throng, three huge black graaks wallowed through the air. This was not a battle that Madoc could win. He knew it. His men knew it.

But neither could they run. The people of Luciare needed their sacrifice this day. The preparations had all been made, the conclusion foregone.

The wyrmlings were still two miles away, rushing forward, their battle cries becoming a dull roar. Warlord Madoc took one last moment to utter defiance against the oncoming horde.

"Men," he shouted, "let us be called brothers henceforth. For here in our hour of darkness our deeds shall make us brothers, and the bonds we form this day on the battlefield shall make us stronger than brothers.

"This is the twilight of our race. And if this be our final hour, let it also be our finest hour!"

His men cheered and for a moment their battle cries rose above the din of wyrmling troops, the incessant clash of arms.

"Back home our sons and daughters can huddle in fear, wrapped in the arms of our wives and sisters. They can hope that our stout hearts and sturdy arms will be enough to turn back the deadly flow of wyrmlings. Let their hopes not be in vain!"

His men cheered wildly, but the sound of enemy troops nearly drowned them out. Madoc peered across the fields. The wyrmlings were running faster now, sprinting into battle. The pounding of their feet made the earth shudder. They'd soon be at the fortress walls, breaking against them like the sea in a winter storm breaking over rocks.

"I will tell you the truth," Madoc cried. "We are marked for death this night. Perhaps none of us will escape." At his back, his son Drewish made a frightened little moan, as if he'd never thought of that. "But I will tell you a greater truth: Dying is easy. Anyone can do it. A babe can die in his cradle in his sleep, seemingly from nothing at all. Dying is easy. All of us will do it.

"But living is hard! Staying alive tonight—that will be a battle royal. So I challenge you, dole out death tonight. Let the wyrmlings take the easy path. Let them die. Make them pay for every moment while you yet live!"

There was a thunderous roar as his men cheered, but Warlord Madoc could see that the cheering would be short. The wyrmlings were charging, less than a mile away now. He could make out individual troops in the starlight, their bone helms gilt with silver, painted with evil symbols.

There was a flaring of light as archers put their arrows to the pitch pots, then let loose a hail. The arrows soared out over the battlefield, landed in the dry grass. It would give his men some light to fight by and dismay the wyrmlings.

Madoc stood tall on the battle tower, then turned and looked down at his sons. He could not bear to watch them die.

"As soon as the wyrmlings break through the wall," he said softly enough so that others could not hear, "I want you out of here. Get to the south end of the river, and then head through the woods. Those giant graaks will kill any man who dares the roads."

Connor licked his lips and said, "Yes, father."

Madoc glanced toward the coming wyrmlings, then back down to his sons. "You cannot rule if you do not live out this night. Go and warn that fool Urstone what has happened here. Tell him how his men died gloriously, but in vain. Make sure that when you reach him, you have respectable wounds."

Drewish nodded cunningly. "And what of you, father?"

"I'll direct the battle for as long as I can," Warlord Madoc said. "And then I will try to join you."

Madoc turned back. The grass was afire now a hundred yards out. The wyrmlings reached the wall of fire, with flames leaping thirty feet in the air, but did not stop. They roared in defiance and hurdled through the flames, while humans made targets of them, hurling war darts.

Clouds of smoke were rising over the battlefield, filling the air with ash, reflecting the firelight back down to the ground.

Wyrmlings took poisoned darts to the chest, bellowed in rage, and continued rushing on. Here and there, one would stagger and drop, but most kept coming. The poison would be slow to work.

Many wyrmlings rode upon the backs of kezziards, great lizards some fifty feet in length. The monsters were fierce in battle, fighting with tooth and claw, lashing with their tails. The kezziards' claws could easily get a purchase on the walls of the fortress, and then the monsters would scurry in, carrying attackers. Madoc began crying out, ordering his dart-throwers to target the kezziard riders.

The walls of the fortress were high, but at only thirty-two feet, they wouldn't be high enough. The kezziards would reach his men easily.

Suddenly the battlefield was white with skull helms as the wyrmling troops filled it. Poisoned war darts began whistling up from them through the smoke.

Some of Madoc's men cried out while others merely

fell back and died without a sound, heavy iron darts sticking from their throats and faces.

The troops were roaring now, his men singing a death hymn while the wyrmlings hurled back curses.

Madoc spared a glance toward his sons, to see if they had stayed or if they had already fled.

He saw them scuffling in the shadows. Drewish had a knife that flashed in the reflected firelight, and he lunged with it. Connor staggered away, blood flowing black from the back of his tunic. He grunted softly, fearfully, as he dodged his brother's blade.

Madoc did not think. He leapt from the tower into the midst of the fray, used his round war shield to club Drewish across the face.

"Damn you, you brat, what are you thinking?"

"I will inherit!" Drewish said. "I'm most fit to rule! First I'll kill him, then I'll take down the king!"

"Not if I get you first, you damned coward!" Connor roared, finally gathering enough wits to clear his warhammer from its scabbard.

He tried to leap past Madoc to get at his younger brother, but Madoc stopped him with an elbow to the face. Connor staggered under the impact of the blow.

Drewish took the opportunity to lunge, his knife lashing at his brother's throat, until Madoc punched him in the ear.

Both boys fell to the ground, beaten.

Warlord Madoc put one foot on Drewish's shoulder, holding him down, while he grabbed Connor by the throat and wrestled him around to get a look at his wound.

Blood stained Connor's back just above the kidney, but the wound did not look deep. Already the flow was clotting.

"Not too bad," Madoc judged. "The armor foiled it, just by a bit."

"I nearly had him," Drewish spat, trying to struggle up to his feet. "But he ran away."

Madoc glowered. It was bad enough that Drewish tried

to murder his brother. It was made worse by the fact that he had bungled it.

"Here's the deal," Madoc growled. "You will both live to reach Luciare. If either of you dies—either at his brother's hand or at the hand of a wyrmling—I'll kill the survivor. And, believe me—I'll take my pleasure doing it. Understand?"

"Yes, father," Connor sniveled, fighting back tears of rage.

Madoc stomped on Drewish's shoulder. "Got it?" Madoc demanded. He swore to himself that if this one didn't understand, he'd slash the boy's throat with his own blade for being too slow-witted.

"Got it," Drewish finally agreed.

"Good," Madoc said. "When I get home, we'll have a council, figure out how both of you can have a kingdom." He thought fast. "There are these small folk that will need someone to rule them with an iron hand. They'll need big folk to be their masters. It will require great work to subjugate them, to properly harvest their endowments. I need both of you alive. Understand?"

Both boys nodded. "Yes, sir."

"Good," Madoc said. He heard screams along the castle wall, one of his men shouting, "Get them! Get them. They're coming over the wall!"

"Now, drag your asses back home," Madoc growled. "I've got a battle to fight."

He turned and studied the castle wall, searching for the source of the commotion, even as a huge shadow fell over him, blocking out the starlight. An enormous graak soared over the fortress. And there he saw it, a kezziard's head rising over the north wall, its face covered in a barding made of iron chains, its silver eyes reflecting the fires.

Warlord Madoc listened to his sons scuttle away even as his mind turned to war.

Now comes the hard part, he thought: staying alive.

32

LUCIARE

So often we celebrate life's small victories, only to discover how life is about to overwhelm us.
                                                    —*Daylan Hammer*

"Why are they cheering so?" Jaz asked, for as they marched through the city gates, the warriors beat axes against shields and roared. Nor did the applause die, but kept growing stronger.

Talon leaned down and said softly, "Because you slew a Knight Eternal. They saw it, and even now there are tales circulating of how you slew another at Cantular. No hero of legend has ever slain *two* of them. The warriors of Luciare have often driven them back from the castle, and sometimes escaped their hunts. But never do they slay the Lords of Wyrm."

As they entered the city, the warriors cheered Jaz and gathered around, then lifted him onto their shoulders and paraded him through the streets.

Fallion gazed up at the city in wonder. The streets wound up through the market district here, and higher on the hill he could see a stouter wall. Above them, the lights played across the whitened walls of the mountain, flickering and ever-changing in hue, like an aurora borealis.

Soldiers patted Fallion on the shoulder and would have borne him away, but Fallion shook his head and drew back. In his mind, the words echoed, "though the world may applaud your slaughter, you will come to know that each of your victories is mine."

Fallion felt a wearying sadness. Once again, men applauded him for his capacity to kill, and he could not help but worry that somehow he was furthering the enemy's plans.

Fallion looked around; people were smiling at him, but they were strange people, oddly proportioned. He saw a boy that could not have been more than ten, but he was almost a full head taller than Fallion.

Shrinking back, Fallion felt very small indeed. He was a stranger in this land of giants.

Talon had said that men of the Warrior Clans had grown large over the ages due to selective breeding. But even the commoners here seemed massive.

The warriors' seed has spread throughout the population, Fallion realized.

The king was marching up through the throng, the crowd parting for him like waters before the prow of a ship. He suddenly turned and called out, peering at Fallion.

Talon, who had been separated from Fallion in the crowd, called out the translation, from several yards away, leaping up to catch a glimpse of Fallion. "He thanks you for your help, and regrets that he must now go prepare for battle. He says that the wyrmlings will attack before dawn." There was a question implied in that last bit. He needed help, Fallion realized, and wondered if Fallion would give it.

Fallion drew his sword, dismayed at the rust building upon it, and put its tip to the ground. He walked forward, and the crowd parted until he stood before the High King. Fallion knelt upon one knee, bowed his head, and said, "Your Highness, my sword and my life are yours to command."

The king answered, and Talon translated, "Your sword and your life are yours to keep. I will not command your service, but I welcome your friendship—and that of your people."

"That you shall have," Fallion said.

The king smiled then, warmly, and a wistful look crossed his face. He whispered into the ear of the Wizard

Sisel, then turned and strode up to the castle, his cape fluttering behind him.

Fallion retreated from the throng, tried to find a place in the shadows, away from the crowd, but the Wizard Sisel sought him out. "The king will be taking counsel with his troops. He has battle plans that must be seen to. But there are matters of great import to both of you that must be discussed. He wonders if you and your friends would like to refresh yourselves, perhaps wash up, and then meet him in his council chambers for a meal."

"Tell him that I would be honored," Fallion said.

Sisel headed through the throng. Reluctantly, Fallion and the others followed him up the winding streets, through the merchants' quarter. The air was perfumed with the honeyed scent of flowers, for beneath every window was a flower box where blossoms of pink or yellow or white grew in a riot, streaming down from the second-story windows like waterfalls. Flowering vines sprang in curtains from mossy pots that hung from the lintels. Great bushes struggled up from pots beside the doors, and small forests rose up just behind the houses, while ivy climbed every wall. Lush grass and colorful poppies rioted at the margins of the road.

Life. Everywhere was life. Fallion had never felt so . . . overwhelmed by plants. It was almost oppressive. Even in the steaming forests of Landesfallen, flying among the trees upon his graak, he'd never felt so dwarfed.

And as he passed through the gate to the upper levels of the city, light was added to the foliage. Three vast tunnels opened as portals into the mountain. The mountain walls were paneled with huge stones, all limed a brilliant white, while runes of protection were embossed in gold there upon the walls outside of each tunnel.

Beneath each portal squatted a golden brazier, perhaps eight feet across, where pure blue-white lights flickered and played like lightning, sometimes changing hues to soft pink or fiery red.

They were fires, but they had no source. Fallion reached out with his senses, tested them. There was no heat there, only a piercing cold.

"What are those lights?" he asked Talon.

She hesitated, as if he had asked her something crude. "The soul-fires of those who died guarding this city. They come each night, and guard it still."

Fallion veered to get a closer look as they passed under the arch, but Talon grabbed his sleeve and pulled him away, giving him a silent warning.

"I want a glance," he said.

"Peering into the light is considered to be both disrespectful, and dangerous—" Talon said, "disrespectful because you would only witness the refuse of their souls, and dangerous because . . . seeing their beauty, you would long to become one of them. Leave those sad creatures to their duties."

Light and life, Fallion realized. Sisel had said that he protected the city with light and life.

Then they were under the arches, into the tunnels, which grew dark and gloomy. The tunnels were lit by tiny lanterns that hung from hooks along the wall. Each lantern was blown from amber-colored glass and held a pool of oil beneath it. The oil traveled up a wick to a tiny chamber, where a candle-sized flame burned. Fallion had seen similar lanterns from Inkarra. There they were called "thumb lights," for each lantern was no longer than a thumb.

The throng broke up, warriors retreating to their own private halls, and Talon led Fallion's group down a long passage. The ceiling lowered and the hallway became almost cramped.

The mountain was a warren, a dangerous warren, for portcullises and dangerous bends were strewn all along the way. If it came to fighting, Fallion could see where an army could fight and then fall back, always defending from a well-fortified position. The wyrmlings with their great height would be at a disadvantage in such tight quarters.

We should be safe here, he thought.

33

THE REPORT

One has not failed, until one has quit trying.
—*Vulgnash*

"You failed?" Lady Despair asked.

Vulgnash knelt upon the parapet beneath Fortress Rugassa, the smell of sulfur clotting the air in the chamber as the unbearable heat rose up from the magma. The great wyrm had risen beneath him, its maw working as it spoke.

He wore a new corpse. It was two hours past sundown. It had taken time to find a new body, to prepare the spells that invigorated it.

Never in five millennia had he failed his master. His voice was thick with shame. "I captured the wizard, as you asked, and was bringing him here. But we were set upon by a great war party of humans. A king led them, a king upon whose shoulders rested the hope of his people. He bore a blessed sword. There was no fear in him that I could use, no hatred."

The great wyrm did not hesitate. "Go back," she said. "A war party will attack Luciare this night. The battle itself shall provide a distraction. Join the battle. Kill the king who bears the hopes of his people, and when he is dead, bring the wizard to me."

"I will need new wings," Vulgnash said humbly, "if I am to make it before dawn."

"You shall have more than wings. . . ." Lady Despair said.

"The branding irons from the otherworld?" Vulgnash asked, excitement rising in him. He had not had time to play with them, to test them.

"They are called *forcibles*," Lady Despair said. "There are slaves who will endow you with strength tonight. You will find them in the dungeon."

Vulgnash's mind raced as he considered the implications. For centuries now, Dread Lords like the emperor had been Lady Despair's favorites, for they were wise in the ways of death magic. But they had rejected their own flesh, and thus could not benefit from this new magic, from these forcibles.

Vulgnash could. He could heap strength upon himself, and speed. He could become as beautiful as the moon and as fearsome as the sun. With enough forcibles, he could win back the trust and respect of his master. Indeed, Vulgnash imagined the day when *he* would become the new emperor.

"Thank you, master," he said. "Thy will be done."

❧ 34 ❧

THE KING'S COUNCIL

Even the wisest of men cannot foresee all ends.
                                        —*Hearthmaster Waggit*

King Urstone sat in his dinner chair, shoulders slumped as if in defeat, elbows resting on the table. A feast was spread before him—a shank of roast boar, calf's tongue, boiled baby carrots with onions, and bowls and baskets filled with breads and other things—some of which Fallion could not name. But King Urstone had not touched them.

The king's long white hair hung down over his shoulders, and his face was lined with creases of worry. Yet there was still strength there, and Fallion could see the handsome man that he had once been.

As Fallion entered the room, Urstone's blue eyes shone with an inner fire.

No, he is not defeated yet, Fallion realized. Jaz had come to the dinner, along with Rhianna and Talon. Daylan Hammer and the Wizard Sisel had also come.

There were various warlords at the king's table. Like the king, they wore armor carved from bone, capes of forest green or burgundy, and cape pins with intricate designs. Fallion suspected that the pins denoted rank, but he could only guess which of the warriors were most senior.

At the table sat another man, smaller than the warriors, with a narrow face, finely groomed beard, and chains of gold. He looked like a wealthy merchant. He smiled like a fox as Fallion entered, his dark eyes tracking him across the room. Fallion studied his face, long and oval, the smile predatory. He felt sure that he knew the man from somewhere, but could not place him.

Fallion felt most surprised to see Siyaddah sitting at the king's table, a pace to the king's right. She had changed into a fresh dress of white silk, but painted with bright flowers this time, with a dark purple border.

She looked at him, and Fallion glanced away, not wanting to catch her eye.

The king's voice was weary as he began to speak, as if he could not muster the energy for passion. He spoke in a deep monotone. Sisel translated, "Master Thull-turock, do you recognize these young men?"

The merchant pointed a finger adorned with three rings at Fallion, and began to speak. "This one is the son of the Earth King Gaborn Val Orden, Fallion Sylvarresta Orden by name. I knew him when he was but a child, living at Castle Coorm. He had all the makings of a great warrior, even in his youth. He was strong and tenacious in battle, fair to those who served him, honest and humble. The young man next to him is his younger brother,

Jaz. He too was a child of sound character, but he was always more interested in bugs and mice than in preparing to become a prince."

King Urstone smiled at that, and nodded. "As a child, I was much fascinated by fish. I used to go out to the brook and stand in the shadows of the willows for hours, spearing trout. All of that practice greatly improved my aim with the spear. Do you also like to fish, Jaz?"

Fallion grinned. For Jaz, it bordered on an obsession.

"I do indeed, Your Highness," Jaz said, "but I prefer to use a hook and line."

King Urstone looked around his table, baffled. Sisel explained something to him. "Then," King Urstone said with a smile, "perhaps when this is over, you could teach me how to fish with a hook and line."

"Gladly, Your Highness," Jaz said.

King Urstone sighed, and said wearily, "In the blink of an eye, the world changes. My scouts have been pouring in for two days, bringing reports. To the west, upon the plains of the hoary elephants, mountains have burst up out of the ground. Rivers had to turn their course and flow east. To the north, a great rift has appeared, a canyon so deep that the eye cannot see to the bottom. To the east, castles seemed to rise from the dust, and perhaps a million people now live among the ruins where none could have lived before.

"They are small folk, humble folk, living in houses made of mud and sticks, covered with roofs of grass. Having seen them, I fear for them. We cannot protect them from what will surely come.

"There are urgent reports from Cantular. A large host is rushing down from the north. Warlord Madoc will try to hold the bridge, but there are *things* he must battle, creatures that no one has seen before. Some are like the great graak that we saw, others he says look like hills that move upon many legs. . . .

"Another such horde is marching upon this city from the northeast."

King Urstone peered down at his hands. His brow furrowed in consternation.

"We tried to exchange hostages with the wyrmlings, and in doing so, I may have called doom down upon my people. Already there are those who whisper that I sold my kingdom for a foolish dream, and if we live out this night, they will revolt—as they should.

"Some say we need a miracle to save us.

"Fallion Sylvarresta Orden," the king said. "Is this the miracle that we need?"

He nodded toward some guards in a corner, and they lugged an enormous wooden box out into the center of the dining hall, then spilled its contents out upon the floor.

Thousands of metal rods rolled onto the tile. Fallion knew what they were by sound alone. There was a soft clanking, almost as if the rods were made of bamboo instead of some metal.

Fallion rose to his feet, electrified. They were not forcibles, not yet anyway, for there were no runes cast upon their heads. But they could be turned into forcibles in short order.

"Your Highness," Fallion said warily, "those could be the miracle that you are seeking. Where did you find so much blood metal?"

The king smiled. "We call it corpuscite. There is a hill of it, not two miles from here."

Fallion left his seat, went to inspect the metal. He tasted it, found that it tasted salty sweet and of copper, much like blood. Pure blood metal.

"A hill?" Fallion asked.

"A large hill," the king corrected. "Large enough to make . . . millions of these."

Fallion saw what he was proposing immediately. There were only thirty-eight thousand of Urstone's people left in the world, but there were millions of Fallion's. They needed to become allies.

"If you called upon your people," King Urstone asked, "would they unite with us?"

"I . . . don't know," Fallion admitted. He hesitated to even think about it. His enemies had hunted him to the ends of the earth, yet his foster father, Sir Borenson, had longed for the day when Fallion seized control of the world, allowing poor nations to throw off the tyrants' yokes.

"Some would," Fallion admitted. "But there are many lords who fear that they will lose their place if we were to unite under one banner. These lords have long sought to take my life."

"And failed," the king pointed out.

The merchant Thull-turock spoke up. "Fallion, my lad, you can buy a lot of friends with this much blood metal."

It was then that Fallion recognized him. He had changed. He had merged with his shadow self, but Fallion recognized him by mannerisms. No one had ever called Fallion "my lad" but one man—his mother's facilitator, Sir Greaves. He was the one making the forcibles, and there would be no one better.

But Fallion worried. An army was coming, a vast army. How would King Urstone's people mine the blood metal if they were put under siege? Even worse, what if the enemy simply overwhelmed them, slaughtered them all?

"Sir Greaves," Fallion begged, "how soon will we have working forcibles?"

"I have a dozen smiths pouring them into molds now. We'll have brawn, metabolism, stamina, and grace blanked out within the hour. After that, it will be down to file work. I won't have many, perhaps two dozen forcibles before dawn. But we should be able to make fifty a day this week, once we get into full production. And once I train my jewelers properly, in a month or two, we can get a thousand a day."

"I have seventy-five good forcibles in my pack," Fallion said. "They should be of some help in protecting the city. Do you have champions that we can give them to?"

The king nodded toward the two guards who stood at his back. "The Cormar twins. There are none better in battle, and they are used to fighting as a pair, anticipating each other's moves."

Fallion bit his lip, considered.

I came to save my people, he thought, not put them to the forcible.

And what will happen if I do? What kind of masters would King Urstone's people be?

Certainly, they would make better masters than the wyrmlings.

He wondered. Would the Warrior Clans even try to subjugate his people? He doubted it. There were too many of the small folk. Besides, Fallion's people could create champions as well as the big folk. No, it wouldn't be a master-servant relationship. At least, it could not stay that way for long.

"You need allies," Fallion said. "You need my people to give their lives as Dedicates. For generations my people have given themselves in service this way. But will you protect them in return?"

"My warriors will crush the wyrmlings, once and for all," King Urstone said. "We will bleed and die for you."

Fallion wondered. "Will it even work? You have an army at your gates. They'll attack by dawn."

"We will hold them off," the king said. "And the morning sun will drive them back."

He sounded so sure.

"And what if they aren't coming to attack the fortress at all?" Fallion wondered aloud. "What if they're coming to take the blood-metal mine?"

A black look crossed the king's face, and Fallion's friends gasped.

"Of course!" Daylan said loudly, rising from his chair. All eyes turned to him, and he hastened to explain. "It is not by chance that these two worlds were brought together. It is not by chance that our greatest hope, Areth Sul Urstone, languishes in prison. Think back, the wyrmlings won him only at great cost. Lady Despair could not let a potential Earth King roam free. Fallion melded the worlds together, but it was not his plan. It was laid by Lady Despair. He was only an unwitting tool in her hands. I believe that she has planned this for years."

King Urstone peered up, thoughtfully, "Yes," he said. "I remember. The wyrmlings did seize my son at great cost."

"So that his two halves could not meld together," Daylan said. "I didn't see. For years now, I was blind to it. The wyrmlings have been summoning aid, bringing dark creatures to their lairs, things like the giant graak, and worse. I thought they were preparing for one final assault."

Fallion thought back. On his own world, Shadoath and Asgaroth had also hunted him nearly to extinction.

Fallion had always felt sure that he'd won his own life. But in bringing these two worlds together, hadn't he been playing into the hands of his enemies? Perhaps he hadn't won his life after all. Perhaps they'd only loaned it to him.

Daylan spoke, his eyes resting on Fallion, "Lady Despair would not have brought these two worlds together unless it gave her great advantage. What has she won? The strength of her armies vastly outnumbers yours. Those who might have granted you aid have all been destroyed. But more importantly, the lore of your world, Fallion, combines with the resources of another. Blood metal is what she is after."

"If it was just blood metal that she wanted, didn't she already have it?" Fallion asked.

Daylan shook his head. "The lore that you used on your world would not have worked on this. Both worlds are but shadows of the One True World, broken pieces of a greater whole. Now, you have combined two pieces of the puzzle, and the magic that worked in your world can be used with the blood metal that can be found here."

The Wizard Sisel peered up at the king, bright eyes

flashing. "How fast can we move a hill? How much ore can we move before the wyrmlings come?"

"A great deal of it is already inside the fortress," Greaves said. "I've had workmen at it since yesterday. We have tons now, much of the richest vein."

But everyone knew that there was far more to get.

"And what makes you think that the wyrmlings will leave us alive to use it?" Jaz asked. "What do we matter to them?"

Daylan Hammer's eyes riveted on Fallion. "There is only one person here that Lady Despair really needs alive. The rest of us are just . . . inconveniences."

Sisel grunted, a noise that made it sound as if he'd just woken from an inadvertent nap. "You're right, old friend. Daylan, you know her mind—perhaps too well." His tone suddenly became soft, dangerous. "And I wonder how? You are a puzzle, Daylan Hammer. I have known you long on this world, and yet my shadow self recognizes you from that shadow world. For years on end, it seems, you have traveled between our worlds. Yet Rhianna here calls you Ael, and met you elsewhere on a third world."

Daylan sat back down in his chair, gave Sisel an appraising look, and seemed to consider each word before it was spoken.

"I am but one man," he said, "and it is true that I sometimes travel between worlds. I am here as . . . an observer, mostly. For ages now, I have traveled between four worlds. I come to see the workings of the evil ones in your lands, and to report to . . . higher powers."

"You were born a Bright One of the netherworld," Fallion said. "Weren't you?"

"Yes," Daylan said. "My name, you could not pronounce." He began to sing, his voice low and musical, "Delaun ater lovaur e seetaunra . . ."

Fallion had no idea how old Daylan might be. "So the stories, the tales that said that you had taken so many endowments that you had become immortal. . . ."

"Are fables," Daylan said. "There have been men of your world who discovered the truth, but I outlived them, and my stories replaced theirs."

"Can you help us?" King Urstone asked.

"In war? No," Daylan said. "I am . . . a lawman, of sorts, and our laws forbid it. I am Ael."

He looked to Fallion, as if Fallion should know what that meant. Fallion reached up to his cape pin, stroked the silver owl there. He knew the name. If he clutched that owl, he would be carried away in vision, and he'd see an enormous gray owl flying over a great forest of hoary oaks. In the vision, the owl called the name Ael.

"This pin is yours, then," Fallion said. "I took it off a fallen enemy."

"No," Daylan said. "It was once yours, in another time, another life. You were Ael, too."

"How can aiding us in battle be against your laws?" King Urstone demanded. "There is no law in any land that prevents one from preserving his own life."

"In my land, my life is my own," Daylan said. "It cannot be taken from me. To try to preserve it is needless. But there are other ways to die. The death of a spirit is to be mourned more than the death of the flesh. And so, that my spirit may be renewed, there are higher laws that I must obey."

Fallion remembered something from his childhood, a half-memory that haunted him still. His father's mysterious dying words. "Learn to love the greedy as well as the generous, the poor as much as the rich, the evil as well as the good. Return a blessing for every blow. . . ."

Daylan nodded his head, just a bit.

"What good is that?" King Urstone demanded. "You would have us empower our enemies, submit to them?"

But Fallion suspected that Daylan sought to do something more than empower his enemies. He was resisting them, subverting their influence. He was fighting evil without seeking to destroy those who were under its sway.

Daylan looked to Fallion and asked gently, "Do you remember?"

"Being one of the Ael?" Fallion asked. "No."

"Perhaps then," Daylan said, "you should waken from this dream—before it is too late."

"How?"

Daylan fell silent a moment, thinking. "The past is not held there in your mind. Only your spirit recalls. You must waken your spirit, and that is not easily done."

"And if he wakens," King Urstone asked, "will he be able to destroy the armies that march upon us?"

Daylan shook his head no.

"Then what good are his powers?" King Urstone demanded.

The young woman, Siyaddah, dared speak. "My lords," she said. "Lady Despair has had time to plot our demise, but surely she cannot see all ends?"

"You're right," Daylan said. "She may have considered ways to defeat us, but there are things that she doesn't know, things that she could not know. She is blind to goodness, to love, to hope. . . ."

"Fine," King Urstone grumbled. "We can smite her over the head with goodness, and stab her through the heart with hope."

But the Wizard Sisel merely sat, scratching his beard, pondering. "When Fallion combined the worlds, he fused two lives into one. I feel stronger than ever before, more . . . hearty and wholesome. I do not think that the evil one could have foreseen that."

"Nor, do I think," Talon offered, "that she knew the day and hour of our coming. If she had known *when* Fallion would combine the worlds, she would have had her troops there to greet us."

"Which means that the army she sent isn't coming for the blood metal," the Wizard Sisel decided. "It would have taken a good week for the troops to make their way from Rugassa. And so they came . . ."

"Because they knew that their princess would no

longer be our hostage," King Urstone finished. "I wish that Warlord Madoc were here. He claimed that the emperor was incapable of loving his own child."

"One does not have to love a thing to value it," Daylan cautioned. "The emperor may have hated her, yet needed her alive. She was the last of his flesh."

"She is a thoroughbred," King Urstone admitted. "A ghastly thoroughbred, but a thoroughbred still."

"I have heard it whispered," the Wizard Sisel said, "that there are spells, abominable spells, that can only be cast using the blood of one's offspring. The emperor has cast off his flesh and chosen to become a wight. He may need his daughter more than we knew."

"Perhaps I can thwart Lady Despair's plans," Fallion suggested. "I could resume my trip to the underworld, find the Seal of the Inferno, and bind the worlds into one."

"Can you even find it?" Daylan asked.

"I have my father's map," Fallion said, reaching into his vest and pulling out the old leather tome that his father had written.

"Much has changed," Sisel warned. "Mountains have risen, seas are running dry. Is there even a path for you to follow anymore? I think it is gone, the tunnels broken up. Your map will be useless."

"Still," Fallion said, "I mean to try."

"Please, don't try it yet," Daylan said. "For millennia we upon the netherworld have wondered what would happen if someone could manage to bind the worlds. Would the good that was done be greater than the harm? We couldn't know for sure. The Wizard Sisel here had his shadow selves bound into a more perfect whole, but I have heard of many of the elderly and sick who merely expired. If we look across the lands, I suspect that tens of thousands have died. So, now we know. We cannot create one world without . . . destroying others. There is a moral question we must answer: do we, does anyone, have that right?"

"If I had to choose," Jaz suggested, "having seen the alternative, I would choose to die so that others might live in a more perfect world."

"As would I," Rhianna put in.

"And I," Fallion said knowing full well that in binding the worlds he might well be dooming himself.

"Eck!" a voice cried off to Fallion's left, *No!* It was the young Master of the Hounds, Alun.

A warrior grumbled, and Daylan offered the translation, "And any man who would choose not to die for the good of others is no warrior at all, but a coward!"

The king smiled gently at Alun, spoke in his own tongue. Talon translated, "Let no man call him a coward. Alun has proven himself otherwise, slaying wyrmlings in combat. And there is many a tenderhearted mother who would choose that her child should live, even in a broken and imperfect world like ours, than to die. To love life and embrace it is not cowardice."

"Is life," Siyaddah asked, "lived as wyrmlings, life at all? What if the wyrmlings conquered us, as seems so likely to happen? What if they sought to make wyrmlings of our children? I would rather die and kill my child too, than see my child raised as such."

King Urstone looked pointedly at Fallion, "As some of our mothers have chosen to do. Destroying another, taking a life, may also be an act of love."

Siyaddah peered hard at Fallion, as if to bore some message into his soul. He didn't need Talon's translation to know that she was saying, Kill us both if you must.

Fallion felt grateful for Siyaddah's support, and found himself longing to thank her.

"Eck," Alun said forcefully, rising to his feet. Talon translated, "I would rather watch my sons and daughter live in a broken world than to die. I would raise them to be strong, so that in their own time and in their own way, they could rise against the wyrmlings."

"Have any of you considered," the Wizard Sisel said softly in Fallion's tongue, "that evil, too, might have been perfected in this change? There were evil men on your world, Fallion, who were infected by loci. Have they combined with wyrmling counterparts here? If so, we well may be facing an enemy stronger than any of us knows."

A hush fell over the room, and Fallion considered. He had met creatures like Asgaroth and Shadoath in his own world, sorcerers who held vast powers. Had he inadvertently empowered their kind?

He could not help but believe that he had.

"In my own world," he said slowly for the benefit of those who had not known his world, letting Talon be his voice, "there was a race of men called Inkarrans, a race of people bred to the darkness. I think that your wyrmlings are their counterparts on this world. If that is so, some of the Inkarrans will have merged with their shadow selves, and they may have endowments. What wickedness this portends, I cannot say.

"On my world, the loci attacked my father in the form of reavers, and then sent strengi-saats among us, led by corrupted Bright Ones.

"I do not doubt that a great evil is brewing, greater than any that we can foretell. Vile bonds are being forged. Will your wyrmlings command reavers in battle? I do not doubt that they can. Will they send strengi-saats by night to steal your women? I do not doubt that they will. And it may be that Lady Despair has even more arrows in her quarrel. Any horror that we have faced before will pale in comparison to what Lady Despair prepares for us now."

There was a profound silence after Fallion spoke these words. Fallion had hated to speak thus. Sir Borenson had once told him, "A great leader will engender hope in his men, even in the face of oblivion. Never speak or act in a way that diminishes hope."

But Fallion needed these people to understand that they were facing an enemy that had never attacked in the same way twice. These people needed to expect, and if possible prepare for, the unexpected.

High King Urstone smiled gently. "Fallion, our enemy has all the tools that she needs to crush us. She will not have to search for greater weapons."

"Yet she will worry that we might find aid unlooked for," Fallion said. "For I do not believe that even she can foresee all ends, when shadows combine."

"Aid unlooked for," Sisel said. "Yes, I wonder. . . ." he said, peering off at nothing. "There is still a great blight upon the land. Our forests are dying. You may not see it yet, but the rot is spreading, growing stronger. The wizardess Averan should be able to stop it, but why hasn't she?"

No one could hazard an answer.

"What of your people?" Fallion asked, turning to Daylan. "Is there no way that they can help? The enemy has brought creatures from the netherworld. Surely you could do the same."

"The great graak that you saw is not from my world," Daylan said. "It came from a shadow world. Which one of the millions it was, I do not know. I have traveled to only a few. Many such places are desolate, empty of life, or nearly so. There are whole worlds where nothing lives but an occasional colony of mold, and blue slime molds make endless war with the yellow, struggling for no greater prize than a cozy shadow beneath a wet rock.

"Other worlds are more like this, filled with higher life-forms. On some of those worlds dark creatures dwell, vile and ravenous, incapable of human comprehension. Our enemy is plundering such worlds, I fear, enslaving such creatures. By bringing them here, they endanger this world, planting these horrors upon fertile ground. Such enemies are not easily rooted out. My people will not risk doing the same, for to do so could ensure your eventual destruction."

"Surely though," King Urstone insisted, "some of your people will fight in our behalf."

This was the great hope, of course. Daylan was a Bright One from the One True World. The magical powers of his people were legend.

Fallion peered hard at Daylan, hazarded a guess. "Are there even any left to fight?"

"A few," Daylan demurred. "As you have deduced, your problems are but a shadow of our own. The worlds have a way of mirroring one another. My people are hunted, bereft. They live in hiding in the vast forests, a family here, and another there. We have no great warbands that can come to your rescue."

By now, the conversation had taken on its own rhythm. Whenever one person spoke, Talon or Sisel would offer up a translation.

"Then we are left to our own resources," King Urstone said. "We are left to the blood metal, and to our own counsel, and to the small folk of the world."

"And to my father," Fallion said. "Do not forget him. There is hope there."

"Yes," Sisel agreed. "There is your father indeed—if we can get him out of the prison in Rugassa!"

"I don't have the troops," King Urstone said. "Besides, he would be slain if we try."

"Then let us not send an army to batter down the door," Sisel suggested, his eyes seeking out Fallion. "One warrior, or a handful of them, could be enough—if they were endowed with both the attributes and the hopes of our people. . . ."

Fallion peered up at Siyaddah. Worry was plain on her face, worry for him. She held his gaze.

He could not speak her language, but he vowed to himself to learn.

"I will agree to such a plan," King Urstone said. "Indeed, I would hope to be one among that handful—if we live out this night. But I fear that all hope for us is vain.

Perhaps the best that we can seek is to die valiantly in the defense of our people."

Jaz peered up at King Urstone, and a sad smile crossed his face. "You died for your people once before, grandfather," Jaz said. "I don't wish to see you make a habit of it."

❧ 35 ❧

HEROICS

He who would be a hero must first conquer himself: his fear, his uncertainty, his own weakness and despair.

    And sometimes, we must conquer our own sense of decency.
                        —Warlord Madoc

At Cantular, Warlord Madoc fought for his life, swinging his battle-ax, cleaving a wyrmling's head even though he had to strike through the creature's helm. As the wyrmling fell, Madoc peered back across the bridge.

The fortress on the north end of the bridge was lost, and for nearly a mile along the bridge's length the wyrmling troops were backed up, pressing to reach the fortress on the southern banks.

Madoc and his men were fighting their way into the south fortress, trying to fend off the wyrmlings on their tail. They hadn't been able to get the drawbridge up in time, and only managed to close the portcullis gates. And so his men fought the wyrmlings as they tried to climb the gates and walls.

The floodwaters roared through the river, which was white with foam. Apparently it had rained in the mountains, and trees and brush raced past, swirling in the moil.

There had to be ten thousand wyrmlings on the bridge, while enormous graaks glided overhead, snaking down to strike at Madoc's troops on the fortress wall.

The battle was lost. Fewer than a hundred men held the south fort, and they could not hold out for long.

But Madoc had one last trick for the wyrmlings: It was there, under the bridge—a trap, cunningly wrought. It had been there for a hundred years.

A single rope woven from cords of steel held the bridge aloft. The rope connected to a series of supports, and if it was pulled hard enough, the supports would tumble, and the bridge would collapse. Even now, the Emir and a dozen men were under the bridge, turning the great screw that would pull the cable while Madoc and his men fought.

Madoc screamed "Beware above!" as a giant graak swooped. His men hurled a dozen war darts, most of which went hurtling into the monster's open maw, burying themselves in the roof of its mouth or in its gums. Their poison seemed to have no effect. But one dart went hurtling into the beast's eye and disappeared in the soft tissue of its eyelid. The creature blinked furiously, snapped its head.

Madoc leapt away as the giant graak's lower jaw hit the tower wall, knocking over stones, sweeping them away.

Then the monster was past, and wyrmling warriors leapt into the breach, howling in glee.

"Despair take you!" a great wyrmling lord shouted, leaping toward Madoc with two axes in his hand.

Madoc ducked beneath his swing, even as a battle dart whizzed past Madoc's shoulder.

"Not today," Madoc spat as he split the lord's skull and then instantly kicked the wyrmling, sent him tumbling thirty feet to land on his fellows. A pale hand grasped onto the wall, and with a quick stroke, Warlord Madoc severed it from its owner.

There was a sudden grinding sound and a series of

snaps beneath the bridge as the steel rope pulled its first support free. "Beware!" the Emir shouted. "Everyone out of the way!"

Then the bridge collapsed.

The first break appeared forty yards out from the fortress. Huge blocks of stone went crashing into the wine-dark waters. Wyrmlings screamed in surprise—a fearful shout, deliciously cut all too short as they were swallowed by the river.

Then the whole bridge suddenly snapped for a mile in the distance, seeming to shatter one section after another, and great portions of it sank beneath the waves.

Dust and debris rose in the air, and the water churned, sending white plumes high, creating a silver streak across the river where the black bridge had spanned.

Only on the bulwarks, every two hundred yards, did portions of the bridge remain standing, and even those began to tilt inexorably into the river as wyrmlings screamed and tried to hold on.

Perhaps five thousand wyrmlings were suddenly gone, while here and there a few dozens or hundreds clung to portions of the bridge, now stuck out on small islands in the roaring flood.

Madoc's men screamed and cheered and went leaping over the gates onto what little of the bridge remained intact, driving the wyrmlings toward the water.

The wyrmlings that were closest drew back a pace, tried to find the room to fight. But their fellows behind were pushed, and some of them went screaming into the waves.

Madoc turned away, left his men to finish the job. He had more urgent concerns back at Caer Luciare.

With mounting excitement he realized what a victory he had won here this night. He would be hailed as a hero at Caer Luciare. And when Urstone was dead, the people would beg him to be their new king.

All he had to do now was race back to Luciare and save what he could of the city.

SMALL GIFTS

I have always felt a peculiar longing, a sense that I am incomplete. I'd hoped that when Fallion joined the worlds that the sensation would have lessened. But Fallion has left me forever incomplete. —Rhianna

After the council and dinner, King Urstone suggested that any warrior who could sleep should do so.

Rhianna wasn't tired. She'd slept most of the day in the cart during the ride south.

Siyaddah came to Rhianna's table and spoke softly in her strange tongue. Talon listened and said to Fallion, "All of that ogling that you have been doing must have paid off. Siyaddah has invited us to her father's apartments to rest."

"I didn't make eyes at her," Fallion objected.

Rhianna and Talon looked at each other, then both just shook their heads, as if to disabuse Fallion of the idea that they were fools.

"But tell her that we would be grateful for a bed," Fallion said.

I'll bet you'd be grateful, Rhianna thought—especially if she was in it.

Rhianna could not help but be jealous. She had fought beside Fallion, stood beside him for years. She had openly declared her love for Fallion only two days ago, and he had said that he loved her too. But she could see how attracted he was to this stranger.

Why doesn't he look at me like that? she wondered.

Fallion earned a smile from Siyaddah with the news, and moments later Fallion, Jaz, Talon, and Rhianna were following Siyaddah's shapely form through the tunnels, until at last she stopped at a door beneath some thumb-lanterns. Words were painted in yellow beneath the lights, and Rhianna tried to remember their shapes as they entered a plush apartment.

The room was decorated in a style that somehow felt familiar to Rhianna. The walls were draped in rich, colored silks in palest blue, as if to mimic a tent. The floor was carpeted in lamb hides, their thick hair as inviting as a bed. And all around the sitting room, pillows lay for the guests to recline on. It was much like the great tents that the horse-sisters of Fleeds lived in.

"Make yourselves comfortable," Siyaddah said. She nodded, and a servant went through the room, blowing out most of the lights so that they could sleep. Rhianna went and lay down upon a huge pillow, and just rested there, thinking.

Talon apologized to Siyaddah and told Fallion, "I lived in this city until three days ago," Talon said, "or at least my shadow self did. My father disappeared in the melding. You and I both know where he went. His two halves joined, and now he is across the Carroll Sea, on the far side of the world. But I have a mother here—not Myrrima, but the woman my father married on this world, Gatunyea. I need to go see her, to let her know that I am well, and to explain where I think father is. Will you excuse me?"

Rhianna did not envy her that sticky task.

"Go," Fallion said, "and may luck follow on your heel."

Talon asked permission of Rhianna and Jaz, too, for she would be leaving them without a translator.

"Would you like me to come with you," Rhianna asked, "for moral support?"

Talon thought for a moment. "No. I think . . . I think that I should tell her alone. I don't know how she will take it."

"All right," Rhianna said. She got up and hugged Talon, then sent her out the door.

Without a translator, Siyaddah could not speak to them, but she did her best to be a good hostess. She showed them the water closet, an affair much nicer than any that Rhianna had ever seen. In it, a waterway was cut in stone and then covered, so that any waste would just wash away.

After showing them this room, Siyaddah waved at them, urging them to find a cushion to sleep on.

They each found a pillow, and Siyaddah showed them that they could pull a lambskin over them if they got cold.

Rhianna lay down, and wondered how long Talon would be gone.

All night, she thought. Her mother here in Luciare would be sick with grief, Rhianna imagined, and she would need Talon to comfort her.

Rhianna wondered about her own mother. Common sense said that her mother was dead. On her own world, Rhianna's father had killed her. Rhianna had been blindfolded at the time, and had not seen it. But she'd heard the blow land, a blow to the head that hit with a loud crack, and she'd heard her mother's body fall.

But what about on this world? Rhianna wondered. Fallion and Jaz had a father here, or at least his shadow-half. Could I have my mother's shadow self here?

She suddenly found herself growing misty-eyed at the prospect, and she fought back a sniffle. It was too much to hope for, but she dared imagine that she had a mother here.

Would I even know her if I saw her? Rhianna wondered.

Rhianna tried to recall her mother's face. Sometimes she still saw it in dreams, but the memory had faded: red hair tied in a single braid, hanging down her back, an oval face generously dotted with freckles, fierce hazel eyes that were almost green, a small nose just a tad too thin.

Her body had always been well toned and muscled,

and she had walked with the deadly gait of a trained fighter.

There was so much fight in that woman, Rhianna thought, I cannot believe that she was bested in battle.

But she remembered the sound of her mother's skull cracking open, and a knot in Rhianna's belly tightened.

At that moment, there was a call at the door, and Daylan Hammer entered.

He spoke softly to their hostess for a moment, and then turned to Rhianna.

His smile was broad, but sad.

"My little one," he said as he came to sit beside her. He took her hand, leaned his shoulder against her, but he sat facing Fallion.

"It has been many years," he said softly to Fallion, "many years since you last appeared. Do you remember anything of your past life, of why you have spent so many centuries hiding, healing?"

Fallion shook his head.

"You should," Daylan told him. "Your spirit has mended sufficiently. It, like your body, needs time to rest and heal when it is injured. I think it is healed, but now it is time for it to awaken."

Daylan unclasped Rhianna's hand, reached out to Fallion, and touched him with one finger, on the sternum. He said nothing that the human ear might hear, but Daylan was an expert at speaking as lords did on the netherworld, from spirit to spirit. Rhianna distinctly heard the words within her mind, "Waken, Light-bringer. The world has need of you and the hour is late."

Fallion's eyes widened just a little in surprise, then Daylan spoke in words for all to hear.

"Once there was One True World, where mankind thrived, beneath the shelter of a great tree. We lived in peace, and there was great prosperity, for men did not seek their own gain, but sought to enrich each other as much as themselves. The True Tree spread above us, hiding us from the eyes of our enemies, and whispering words of peace.

"We had enemies, but we also had each other. There were Darkling Glories that hunted us, creatures of great power that carried darkness with them wherever they went. And there were heroes among us who hunted the Darkling Glories in return, men called the Ael.

"You were one of the Ael," Daylan told Fallion. "You were a champion who swore to serve his people, and for this the people gave you their support.

"So you were gifted with runes of power, much like the runelords on the world where you were born. But in those days, the taking and giving of endowments was not such a horrid thing. Dedicates did not die in the exchange. People chose their champions wisely, offering up endowments only to the most deserving, and as one of the Ael you would draw upon those runes only in moments of great extremity.

"To give an endowment, the best part of yourself, was not a sacrifice; it was an act of pure love."

Rhianna had heard these stories before. She had learned them on Daylan's knee as a child, in her brief stay in the netherworld. Now, she realized, Daylan was telling them to Fallion in an effort to waken the memories.

"Let me tell you how it will be," Daylan said. "Tonight, Fallion, when next you sleep, you will recall your time beneath the great tree. You will remember the great hurt you suffered, and your valiant struggle to fight the Queen of the Loci. And when you wake, you will know what you must do. . . ."

Daylan was not a large man. He did not tower over the group, and Rhianna imagined that if you spotted him in a market, you would not have thought him special. He did not look wiser than other men, or stronger.

But at this moment, she looked into his eyes and it seemed that he grew old. There was great sadness there, and infinite wisdom. He looked scarred and aged, like the majestic sandstone mountains in Landesfallen that have been battered and sculpted by the wind over the ages until their sides have worn away, creating faces as smooth as bone, revealing the inner majesty of the mountain.

For a moment, Daylan did not look like a man, but a force of nature.

Fallion smiled weakly and looked down at his hands, as if unsure whether to believe Daylan.

"Fallion," Daylan said. "Have you ever tried clutching your cape pin when you go to sleep?"

Rhianna smiled. As Fallion had discovered when he first touched it, if you held the pin long enough, it would show you visions of the One True World. A huge owl would fly to you and carry you away on a dizzying journey. It was more of a thrill than a comfort. No one could hold onto that pin for more than a few moments. As teens, Rhianna and Fallion had once made a game of it, trying to see who could hold it the longest.

"No," Fallion said.

"Try it when next you sleep," Daylan said. "It will show you the One True World as it once was, and help you to remember."

Fallion nodded. "Okay," he said.

Daylan climbed to his feet, and said, "I should let you get whatever rest you can. There will likely be fighting before morning."

Fallion smiled at him, then glanced at Siyaddah. There were questions in her eyes, and she spoke softly to Daylan for a moment.

Daylan smiled at a question and began to translate. "She asks, why are you so brown? She says 'You have the hair of the raven.' "

"Tell her that in my world," Fallion said, "my grandmother was from Indhopal, a land far to the east. Her skin was dark and beautiful, like Siyaddah's. My lineage connects with men and women of Indhopal many times over the past thousand years."

Daylan translated, then relayed another question. "Oh," Siyaddah said. "So you are of mixed breed, east and west?"

"Yes," Fallion answered. "And I even have ancestors among the white skins, the Inkarrans to the south."

Siyaddah asked a question. Daylan said, "She says that your eyes follow her, and that she has caught you looking at her many times. She wants to know, 'Do you think she is beautiful?' "

Rhianna found her heart beating hard at the question, and she held her breath.

"Yes," Fallion admitted, as Rhianna feared he would.

Daylan spoke a single word, and Siyaddah repeated Fallion's answer in his own tongue, "Yes."

Siyaddah smiled at him, began to speak. Her gaze was penetrating, frank. "She says that you are beautiful, too. She is not attracted to most of the men in Luciare. The warriors are too huge, too pale. If she were to mate with one of them, the chances are good that the child would be over-large, and she would die in childbirth. She wants to know if it is true that on your world, you were the son of Prince Urstone."

Daylan smiled at this. Rhianna knew that Daylan knew the answers, but he seemed to enjoy watching Fallion squirm.

"On our world, Urstone was not a mere prince. He was the king, the High King of many realms, and his name will be forever revered. I am proud to be his son, and heir."

Siyaddah smiled nervously at that news. She bit her lip, and spoke softly and rapidly. Daylan offered in a humble tone, "She thinks it would be good if all people were to be united, the small folk of your world with the true men of her world. She wants to know, 'Do you agree?' "

"Yes," Fallion said.

Daylan smiled secretively, as if he had just sprung a trap. "This is not just a question of principle with her," Daylan corrected. "She is asking if you think, as leaders, you should unite. She is asking if you think that it would be in your . . . political interests to marry."

Rhianna felt all of the air go out of her lungs. She hadn't expected the questions to take this turn, at least so soon. Siyaddah was talking marriage. This was no declaration of love. It couldn't be. Fallion and Siyaddah didn't really even know each other. But in many lands, on Rhianna's own world, political marriages had nothing to do with love. Siyaddah was frankly acknowledging that she felt attracted to him, and that Fallion, with potentially millions of followers, could be a powerful ally. Indeed, Siyaddah had to recognize that if the human alliance managed to overthrow the wyrmlings, in time Fallion could become the single most powerful lord alive.

She was right to consider such an alliance.

From his pillow, Jaz clapped and said, "Do it! Go ahead. I've never seen you this silly over a woman."

Fallion froze, as if unsure what to say. He blushed and looked to Rhianna, as if seeking her advice.

Don't ask me, you fool, she thought. *Don't beg my permission.* Rhianna had proven her love for him. She'd offered up her life to Shadoath, hoping to rescue him. Rhianna had tendered her soul when she tried to kill Shadoath's Dedicates, knowing that Fallion could never murder a child.

But Fallion begged Rhianna's permission to marry another. He didn't ask with his voice, but with his eyes.

And as Rhianna's heart seemed to break, she realized that she could not deny him.

Right now, Rhianna could think of no greater way to prove her love than to give him the one thing that he wanted most.

"Jaz is right," Rhianna said. "It could be a good match." From the expression of disbelief in Fallion's eyes, she knew that he wasn't convinced of her sincerity, so she added more forcefully, "I'm telling you as a sister, one who loves you and wants you to be happy, consider the offer well."

Fallion looked evenly at Siyaddah. "Yes," he said, "I think that *politically* it could be good for us to marry.

And it may be that when we know each other better, we would find more personal reasons to do so."

Siyaddah smiled, joy spreading across her face slowly, as pretty as an apple blossom opening. Rhianna could not help but admire her dark hair, her sparkling eyes, and her infectious smile.

She was not evil. She wasn't trying to hurt Rhianna, and Rhianna could not hate her for being smitten by Fallion.

Then Siyaddah's smile fell, and she looked to the floor and spoke.

"She will suggest this to her father," Daylan interpreted, "but she fears that he would not approve. For many years, here upon this world, your father and hers were the best of friends, comrades in arms, until Prince Urstone was captured. Her father longs for his return, and he has been saving her, for Prince Urstone's return. Her father hopes to marry her to Prince Urstone."

How long could he have been saving her? Rhianna wondered. Siyaddah did not look to be old. Rhianna would have guessed that she was eighteen, certainly no more than twenty at the most. But Rhianna also knew that in many cultures women married young, and in royal families matches might well be made at birth.

What was Siyaddah really saying? Rhianna wondered. Was she so weak that she thought of herself only as a pawn to be used to make the strongest political alliance? Was she that calculating?

Or maybe she didn't want to marry Prince Urstone. After all, he would be much older than her, and would be terribly scarred after years of torture among the wyrmlings. And if he was a large man, she had to fear the consequences of bearing his child.

But Rhianna suspected that she understood something about the woman. In Indhopal, a woman had always been expected to be perfectly subservient. There was no greater compliment to a princess than to say that she was a "dutiful daughter."

As much as Rhianna might hate such attitudes, that is

what Siyaddah was, dutiful. Whatever mate her father chose for her, Siyaddah would smile and accept her fate.

"I see," Fallion said, looking as if he had been slapped.

Daylan must have sensed the rising tension in the room. He looked from Fallion to Siyaddah to Rhianna, then abruptly excused himself.

Rhianna took his hand and walked with him to the door. Once outside, Daylan whispered, "You love Fallion, don't you?"

Rhianna nodded.

"You may have to fight her to win his affection. You should fight her, you know. If you don't, my robin's egg, you will always regret it."

"I know," Rhianna said.

Daylan smiled. "If she were a woman of the horse clans, it would be a simple matter. You'd get on your horses and joust, the winner taking the spoils."

"I'd win," Rhianna said. "She's weak."

"I dare say that you would. But don't make the mistake of believing that Siyaddah is weak. There are many kinds of strength, and you will never find a more worthy opponent. Dare I suggest an alternative?"

"What?" Rhianna asked.

"In Dalharristan, it is quite common for a king to take several wives."

Rhianna gritted her teeth. "I will not share a husband. To do so would be to marry half a man."

"I only suggest it," Daylan said, "because once Siyaddah recognizes your love for Fallion, she will see it as a perfect solution to your problem. I thought that you should be forewarned."

Rhianna found that the conversation was becoming uncomfortable. She sought to change the subject. "Uncle," she said, "of all the millions of worlds, how is it that you keep watch upon these two that Fallion combined?"

"It's not by accident," Daylan admitted. "The two worlds *fit* together, locking like joints from hand to arm. Both worlds retain something unique from the One True

World, a memory of how the world should be. That is what drew Fallion's spirit to his world."

Rhianna thought for a moment, bit her lip. "You know the people of Luciare. Is it possible that I have a mother here?"

"Ah," Daylan said. "You know that not everyone on your world had a shadow self."

Rhianna nodded.

"And even those who do," Daylan said, "may not be much like the people that they were on your world. . . ."

She did have a mother here, Rhianna realized. She could see it in his eyes.

"Rather," Daylan said, "they are like dreams of what they might have been, if they were born in another time, another place."

Rhianna had the distinct impression that he was trying to prepare her for bad news. She tried to imagine the worst. "Is my mother's shadow self a criminal, or mad?"

Daylan considered how to answer. "I don't know who your mother is, or if she is even alive. Some people, if they saw their shadow selves, would not be recognizable even to themselves."

"So you don't know if my mother lives?"

"No," Daylan said gently. "I have no idea."

"Then who are you thinking of? Who would not recognize themselves?"

Daylan smiled as if she'd caught him. She knew the oaths that Daylan lived by. He felt compelled to speak the truth, always. He also felt free to hold his silence. So if he spoke, he'd speak the truth.

"Siyaddah's father, the Emir," he said at last. "In this world, he is one of the greatest of heroes of all time, a staunch ally to the High King. A dozen times, his strategems have saved this kingdom. Yet in your world, his shadow self became mankind's greatest enemy. How do you think Fallion will feel when he realizes that Siyaddah is the daughter of Raj Ahten?"

Rhianna stood for a moment, heart beating madly.

Should I warn Fallion? she wondered. Any feelings that Fallion might be developing for the girl would quickly fade.

But Rhianna fought back the urge.

The Emir was not Raj Ahten. That was what Daylan was trying to tell her. The Emir would not even recognize his shadow self.

Rhianna could see what Daylan was doing. Daylan wasn't the type of man to pry into another's personal affairs, but Rhianna had known him when she was a child, and so he counseled her now as if she were a favored niece.

Daylan was testing her.

For Rhianna to ruin Fallion's and Siyaddah's chance for love, that was a small and selfish act. To destroy another person's chance for happiness in any way violated Daylan's mind-numbingly strict code of ethics.

No, Rhianna promised herself, if Fallion ever learns the truth, he will not hear it from me.

She smiled and hugged Daylan goodnight.

In the morning I will go hunt for my mother, Rhianna thought. All I have to do—and that we have to do—is survive the coming battle.

❧ 37 ❧

THE ENDOWMENT

Men can be turned into tools if we but learn how to manipulate them. —Vulgnash

Areth Sul Urstone lay near death in the crystal cage, while a child tortured him, creating a symphony of pain. He did not mind. He was too near death to care. He had grown numb to his surroundings, accustomed to pains that would have made another man's knees buckle.

The cage itself was made of quartz and shaped like a sarcophagus, one which conformed nicely to his body and forced him to lie prone, with legs splayed and his hands stretched painfully above his face. Drilled into the sarcophagus were hundreds of small holes. Through these, the wyrmlings had shoved crystalline rods, which pierced his body and pricked certain nerves—the ganglia in his wrists and elbows; the nerves in his sinuses, ears, and eyes; the pain sensors in his stomach, kidneys, groin, toes, and hundreds of other areas.

Some of the rods were as thin as eyelashes, others as thick as nails. By simply tapping them with a willow wand, the child could create indescribable pain.

Tap. A touch to the small rod made it vibrate, and suddenly Areth's eye felt as if it were melting in his socket.

A brush over his lips made Areth's teeth feel as if they had exploded.

Yet the pain could not touch Areth anymore. Free of all hope and desires, he had discovered a reservoir of inner calm. Yet with each tap, he groaned, in order to satisfy the young wyrmling girl who seemed to think that torture was play. She smiled, tapping the rods in a rhythm as if to some mad melody, creating her symphony of pain.

"You're lucky," the apprentice torturer told him as she played. "By dawn you'll be the last human alive."

Suddenly, all of the pain receded. "Wha?"

"Our armies are marching on Luciare," the girl said. "Didn't anyone tell you?"

Of course no one had told him. The girl tapped a rod, and Areth's stomach convulsed as if he suffered from food poisoning.

"Lie," Areth groaned. "You lie." They had told him so many lies before.

"Have it your way," the girl said, brushing her wand over dozens of crystals at once. Suddenly the world went away in a white-hot tornado of pain.

When he resurfaced to consciousness, Areth heard the clank of locks and the squeak of a wooden door that announced a visitor, followed by the tread of feet.

It could not be someone bringing a meal.

Too soon, he thought. Too soon since the last one.

He had learned to gauge the time by the knot that formed in his stomach.

Locked in his crystal cage, skewered in so many places, Areth could not turn his eyes to see the stranger. Even if he had, he would have seen little. The wyrmlings seldom used lights. Their skin was faintly bioluminescent, so faintly that a human could hardly see it. Yet it sufficed for the wyrmlings.

Blessedly, the girl shrieked in fear and the torture stopped. "Welcome, Great Executioner," she said.

That was a title reserved only for Knights Eternal.

"Open the cage," a soft voice hissed.

"Immediately," the girl answered.

Suddenly the cage's lid flipped open, and Areth cried out as hundreds of crystalline rods were ripped from his flesh. For a moment he lay gasping in relief to feel the rods gone. He had been in the cage for more than a day.

Strong hands grabbed Areth and pulled him from the cage. He did not fight. He no longer had the strength for it. His head lolled and he fought to hold onto consciousness as he was dragged down a hall. He lost the fight.

When next he woke, it was to the sniveling of some wyrmling child. Two wyrmling warriors held Areth upright, while his knees rested on the cold stone floor. The chamber was dim, for it was full night outside, and the only light came from a single thumb-lantern that hung from the ceiling. Beneath the light, a gawky boy of perhaps eleven huddled in a fetal position, jaws clenched, as if fighting back tremendous pain.

Areth peered around the room at several dignitaries. Some were wyrmling warlords, dressed in fine mail. Several others, shadow creatures with wisps of black silk as their only covering, hovered at the head of the room in a place of honor. These were wights, Death Lords. One of them, the tallest, wore silks with diamonds sewn into them, so that they shimmered in the wan light.

Emperor Zul-torac, Areth realized in sudden awe. I've been brought before the emperor.

But why? he wondered. To be put to death for the emperor's amusement?

That seemed likely. But Areth wondered if it had to do with the alleged attack on Luciare. Perhaps the city really had fallen at long last, and the emperor wanted nothing more than to watch Areth be put to death.

Areth waited for some explanation as to why he was here, but the wyrmling lords said nothing. Instead, they merely watched.

A Knight Eternal held up a metal rod and inspected it, his eyes straining in the gloom. The rod was red, like rusted iron perhaps mingled with copper. At one end was a glyph. He scrutinized the glyph under the light of a thumb-lantern, and pronounced it "Exquisite."

Then he held the glyph-end of the rod overhead and began to sing. His song came out as a deep bass. The sounds were soothing, and after several long moments, the metal rod began to glow like a branding iron, turning white at the tip, as if it were being heated in a forge.

What magic is this? Areth wondered.

The whimpering child looked at the glowing iron, eyes widening in fear, for it appeared to be scalding hot. He licked his lips and sweat streamed down his forehead.

But the Knight Eternal began to whisper soothing words.

"Have no fear," the Knight Eternal was saying. "You are in great pain now. But that pain can leave you. All that you have to do is give it away—to him."

The Knight Eternal held the glowing rod, peered over his shoulder at Areth.

"There will be pain," the Knight Eternal promised, "but it will only last for a small moment, while your honor and glory will remain for all eternity. Will you give your pain away?"

The child was in such fear and agony that he could not speak, but he managed a small nod of the head.

"Good," the Knight Eternal said.

He pressed the glowing rod to the child, and began to sing. The rod brightened, and the smell of singed skin and burning hair filled the chamber. The child did not wince or cringe away from the heat. But as soon as the metal rod flared and gave off a flicker of flame, the Knight Eternal pulled it away.

The lad grunted in pain, like a boar that has been struck with a lance.

The rod left a white trail of light, which lengthened as the Knight Eternal pulled back. Around the chamber, wyrmlings growled or oohed and aaahed, for the trail of light was far brighter than the illumination thrown by the small lantern. The Knight's singing became faster, more insistent. There were no words to his song, only calls like a lark and harking sounds.

He waved the branding iron—for Areth had decided that it was some sort of branding iron—in the air, and then studied the trail of light that remained.

He nodded, as if the light passed his inspection, then whirled toward Areth, and approached, leaving a trail of light as he came.

"What is this?" Areth demanded. He was weak, so weak. His muscles had wasted away in prison. But it was more than that. He felt a sickness deep inside him. The crystal rods had pierced him deeply, in his gut, in his liver and groin. He had been fighting infections for years, and losing. It was only the spells of the Death Lords that kept him alive, feeding him life from those around him.

"It is called a forcible," the Knight Eternal said, his blood red robes flaring as he approached. He spread his wings out, flapped them in excitement. "It is used to grant endowments, to pass attributes from one person to another. Those who give endowments are called Dedicates. This boy will be your Dedicate."

Areth knew that this couldn't be good. Wyrmlings

were notorious for not giving information. This one would only be explaining himself if the news was going to be bad.

"This child has taken endowments of *touch* from four other Dedicates, four who are at this very moment being placed in crystal cages.

"And now we will give his endowment of touch to you."

"Why?" Areth asked.

"This is an experiment," the Knight Eternal said as he ripped off the stinking rag that served as Areth's only scrap of clothing, "an experiment in pain. So far, we have been very gratified at the results. For years you have endured our tortures. Now you will learn what it feels like to endure others' pain."

The Knight Eternal plunged the forcible into Areth's chest. The skin sizzled and puckered as his hair burned.

The white snake of light raced from the boy's arm, blanking out, until it reached Areth's chest and entered with a hissing sound.

From across the room, the young boy cried out in unimaginable anguish, then wept for joy at his release.

Areth drew back in surprise, for the first kiss of the forcible gave him great pleasure, surprising in intensity, and just as suddenly it turned to agony.

The pain that smote him drove him to his knees, left his head whirling. He vomited at the distress as his stomach suddenly cramped. Unseen tortures assailed him from every side. His ear drums felt as if they would burst, and his sinuses flared. His groin ached as if he'd been kicked by a war horse, and it seemed that every bone in his feet had suddenly been cracked into gravel.

Wordlessly, Areth collapsed, gasping for breath. No scream could have expressed his torment.

"Is that it?" Emperor Zul-torac demanded, speaking for the crowd of nobles that stood in attendance. "Did it work?"

Areth Sul Urstone could not speak. Through tears of

affliction he peered at the gawky boy beneath the thumb-light, who now stared at his hands clenching and unclenching them as if mystified by his own lack of feeling.

"The transfer is complete," the Knight Eternal confirmed.

Emperor Zul-torac nodded, and the guards dragged Areth away.

He gasped for breath as they did, drowning in pain, until they threw him in his cell, where he lay naked and quivering and overwhelmed.

❧ 38 ❧

THE SWALLOWS

The transition from infancy to adulthood is hard in people, but it is much harder for animals. Consider the minnow, which oft hatches from its egg only to swim into the gaping jaws of a bass—or the swallow, that so often leaps from its nest only a day too early, and thus falls to its death. How much better it is to be a man, even when the going is at its hardest.

—the Wizard Sisel

Fallion and Jaz had not even laid down to rest when the Wizard Sisel came and whistled outside the chamber door.

Siyaddah opened the door, and the wizard strode into the room and addressed Fallion. "The High King requests the company of you and Jaz . . . in his war room."

Without a sound, Jaz followed Sisel out the hallway.

Fallion stopped at the doorway, peered into Siyaddah's eyes, and spoke the old farewell of his court, "Sworn to defend," then hurried after his brother and the wizard.

"So, how do you like the nursery?" Sisel asked.

"What do you mean?" Fallion asked.

"The upper portions of the fortress are where we keep the children," Sisel said. "They are our greatest treasure. The wyrmlings will have to fight through every man among us to reach them."

Fallion had not been aware of many children in the rooms around them, but then, he had come to the citadel late at night, and most likely they were all abed.

Still, he made a mental note. Siyaddah's apartments were on the seventh floor above the streets. The names of the occupants were painted in yellow beside the doors.

The wizard took them down four levels, into a huge map room.

There on the floor was a map of the world, painstakingly sculpted from mud and painted. It bore little resemblance to Fallion's world.

At the center, it seemed, was Luciare. Crude lines had been scratched in the mud with a stick, superimposing the boundaries of Rofehavan and Indhopal and Inkarra, lands that Fallion knew. Red dots indicated major cities and fortresses.

Jaz peered at the map and let out a gasp, then sank to his knees with a moan.

And as Fallion stared at the map, it filled him with fear. The borders were all wrong. The lands of Toom and Haversind and many of the northern isles had not existed in King Urstone's world. The continent of Landesfallen had not existed. What happened to them in the change? Fallion wondered. Did all of the people living in those lands suddenly find themselves falling into the sea?

Fallion was horror-struck. He and Jaz had left family and friends in Landesfallen. Myrrima, Borenson, Draken, Erin. He imagined them flailing in the depths, no land in sight—not for hundreds and hundreds of miles.

"Sisel," Fallion said, staring at the map. "What have I done?"

"We . . . are not yet certain," Sisel said. "It will take months, perhaps even years, to learn the extent of the change. But the Earth Spirit whispers peace to my soul."

"We have family in Landesfallen!" Jaz said.

"My heart tells me that they live and love you still," Sisel replied softly. "Many changes have taken place, but haven't you noticed—no one, to my knowledge, found themselves in a river or pond. I believe that there is a good reason for that. It was inherent in the spell you used to bind the worlds together."

Fallion hoped that Sisel was right.

Still, he was not completely at ease.

High King Urstone approached slowly, put a hand upon Jaz's shoulder, and whispered words of comfort. Sisel translated. "If we live through this night, an expedition will be sent out to map our new world, to find survivors, and to claim them as allies and friends."

"Thank you," Jaz said, trying to hold back a sob.

"You are welcome," Sisel translated. "And now, the King has a question for you. His champions are taking endowments even as we speak, and he thanks you for the use of the forcibles. But he wonders if you would like to take endowments this night, too?"

"Tell him no," Fallion said. "We thank him for the offer, but he will be better off having one champion with forty endowments than eight champions with five."

"The king agrees with you," Sisel said after listening to the king, "and is also foregoing the kiss of the forcible. He wants you and Jaz to follow him."

The king left the war room and its maps and retainers, took Fallion and Jaz through a rich red curtain, back through a short hall.

A second audience room opened. On the floor were three sets of enormous wings, like those of a bat. Each set was splayed wide. A thin red membrane connected the struts. To Fallion, they looked like living flesh, cut from a body.

"These are yours," Sisel told Fallion and Jaz. "You two slew their previous owners, and the king has proclaimed them yours, as spoils of war."

"Great," Jaz said, trying to lighten the mood. "So, how do we cook them?"

"They are not to eat," Sisel said. "They are to wear. He wishes for you to put them on before the battle. It may well be that you are forced to escape, and these would be a great aid. You can travel faster than a horse, and few could catch you. The Knights Eternal might, but they will not fly in the full sunlight. Remember that.

"Such wings are exceedingly rare. We do not believe that the enemy has more than a dozen pair, all told.

"Most of all," Sisel continued, "these will aid you in your travels. You need to go to the Courts of Tide and begin to enlist the help of your people. With these, you could be there by noon tomorrow."

"How do they work?" Jaz asked, excitement rising in his tone.

"Work?" Sisel asked. "Just put them on. It will take a few minutes for your body to learn how to respond, and it will be weeks or months before you become proficient with them. But in time they work like your legs do, without any thought on your part."

Jaz hurried to the nearest set of wings, picked them up. Each wing met at the back and joined. When he lifted them, the wings began to fold, leaving their tips upon the floor. Where the wings joined was a pair of spikes, as white as bone, each about ten inches long. The spikes were wet, as if they had just been cleaned, but Fallion could see blood on them. Their purpose was obvious. Fallion could see that if he pulled the wings up onto his shoulder at the apex, the spikes would have to be inserted through his flesh.

"Are you afraid?" King Urstone asked.

"I," Jaz began. "They look too big for me."

"They are fine for someone your size," Sisel said. "Besides, it is better if they are a little large. All the better to get the wind beneath you. Your glide will last longer, and your flights will be farther. Did you not notice that the Knights Eternal choose bodies that are smaller than those of most wyrmlings? This is the reason."

"Does it hurt?" Jaz asked.

Sisel admitted, "More than you'd like."

"I'll go first," Fallion offered.

He went to a set of wings, picked them up, and grabbed onto the bone-like prongs. He set the prongs up on his shoulder, in front of the clavicle. The design suggested that they should fit that way, but he wondered if the prongs would pierce a lung or some other vital organ. Perhaps it was meant to go behind the clavicle. "Like this?" he asked the wizard.

"Take off your tunic," Sisel suggested. "You don't want to get blood on it."

Fallion removed the tunic and his cape, leaving only his black leather trousers.

Sisel adjusted the wings, so that the apex met at the center of his back and the prongs set just in the flesh of his shoulder in front of each clavicle. He said, "About there, I would think."

Without further warning, Sisel shoved the wings on. The spikes pierced Fallion like lances, and he felt white-hot fire in them. He staggered forward a step, suddenly growing faint, and fell to one knee.

He could feel the spikes twisting, seeming to bend back, fusing with his scapula.

For a moment, the wings were just dead weight on his back. Blood oozed from the wounds, running in rivulets down his back, and he imagined that he would die.

And then, an instant later, the wings came to life. He could feel the skin between the webbing as if it were his own skin, could feel blood coursing from wingtip to wingtip.

Without a thought the wings began to flap on their own, clumsily at first, but he could feel the lift in them, as if they were sails catching a strong wind.

Then he flapped them consciously, stretching out, grasping at air, pulling down eagerly so that his feet suddenly lifted off the floor.

The pain eased quickly, and Fallion said in wonder, "It's, it's like getting . . . new hands. You can feel everything."

"And it hurts?" Jaz asked.

It hurt. Fallion could still feel the pain. The spikes in his shoulder still burned, but the sensation was swallowed up in joy and wonder.

"A bit," Fallion admitted.

"I think maybe I'd still rather eat them than wear them," Jaz said.

"The pain will dull in a few minutes," Sisel offered. "In a week, the wings will feel as if they were born to you."

King Urstone fitted his own wings upon him, and Sisel gave them a shove. He did not stumble as Fallion had, but only stood for a moment, wincing, until the pain began to subside.

He spoke, and Sisel translated. "Come. Let us take our maiden flight!"

Sisel drew Jaz's wings to his shoulder and let them pierce him, and eagerly Fallion followed the king down a short corridor and into an alcove that had been gouged into the cliff.

Here, the folk of the city could come for a breath of fresh air when they tired of the tunnels, or could stand and peer out over the countryside. Only a low rock wall stood between them and death.

They were high above the ground, hundreds of feet up the mountainside. Fallion had known that he was traveling up as he walked through the twisting hallways, but he hadn't realized how far they had climbed. The wind was boisterous, gusting this way and that. A layer of clouds had begun to rush in from the east, blotting out the stars. The brightest light came from down below, from the spirits of Luciare's guardians. Blue-white, the light reflected from the city walls onto the grounds below.

"What do we do now?" Jaz asked nervously.

High King Urstone climbed up on the rock wall and stood for a moment, his legs shaking nervously.

"You've seen young birds leave the nest?" the Wizard Sisel asked. "Do what they do!"

"Most of the young birds I've seen," Jaz said, "wind up dead at the bottom of some tree." The king stood for several moments, flapping his wings experimentally. "Isn't it kind of windy?"

Then Urstone jumped, and went plummeting.

Fallion raced to the edge of the balcony, stood peering down. He could see the king flapping frantically, his wings catching for a moment, then seeming to lose purchase.

The king screamed, and Fallion thought that he was dead, that he would crash onto the rocks below, but suddenly the wind caught beneath his wings, and he went soaring for a few dozen yards, then flapped frantically, canted to the left, and soared again. The king screamed again, and Fallion realized that he was not screaming in fear, he was shouting in exultation.

"I'm next," Fallion said, and before he could change his mind, he took a running leap and jumped over the cliff.

He forced the wings to beat rapidly, found his heart pumping hard from exertion. He rose as he did.

It was not effortless, not like the childhood dreams he'd had of floating across the sky like a wind-blown leaf. He found that he had to concentrate. He had to pull the wings in and up on the up-stroke, stretch them wide on the down. He had to pull them forward vigorously to gain speed, let them relax when he soared.

It was not easy. In fact, it was hard, like running a race. And it was pure ecstasy.

Fallion fluttered about the tower, and found that he had a better knack for it than the king did.

Perhaps it's the weight, Fallion thought. The wings were all roughly the same size, but the king, with his Warrior Clan blood, outweighed Fallion by at least a hundred pounds, probably closer to a hundred and fifty.

In moments, Jaz came winging up beside him, and shouted, "Let's go over that hill!"

He pointed to a hill at least four miles away, a dark hump rising out of the night, stately evergreens at its peak, all weathered and blasted by lightning over the years.

And so they raced, laughing, as they had done when they were children, their wings beating rhythmically. Fallion thrilled to the wind coursing beneath his wings, and fought back tears. In a choked voice he said, "When last I rode a graak, I thought I would never fly again."

"I think," Jaz shouted, "we could give those graaks a good race, now."

And it was true.

They reached the hill in less than four minutes, but the quick flight left Fallion with sweat streaming down his cheek, sweat that would quickly dry in the cool night air. They circled the trees, looked out above the valley in the distance—and saw the wyrmling horde.

It was miles away. A few stars still shone over the valley, and by their pale light Fallion could see wyrmlings in the distance, starlight glinting on their bone helms. They looked like cockroaches thick upon a floor, for they covered the land.

There were larger things among them, a trio of moving hills and enormous lizard-like kezziards, while giant graaks winged sluggishly above, casting vast shadows. And fluttering around them were tinier figures, like midges, the Knights Eternal.

"Come on," Fallion said in rising concern. He glanced back toward their mountain fortress, its peak gleaming white in the distance. "Let's go."

39

THE GATHERING OF THE HORDE

A lord must have armies to daunt and destroy his ene-
mies. To lead his armies, he must elevate the most
intimidating of his troops. Therefore, if you would be a
great leader, it is imperative that you learn the finer
points to the art of intimidation.
        —*Emperor Zul-torac, advice to his daughter*

The night filled with snarls and roars as new troops
joined the wyrmling horde camped on the plains below
Luciare.

Soldiers had been gathering from the east and the
north. The great giant graaks had come just after midnight, with the Knights Eternal in their wake. And there
was word that a wyrmling host had slaughtered a human
army at Cantular. Each new addition had been a cause
for celebration, until now.

The troops that joined the camp now wore black robes
with the symbol of the great wyrm emblazoned in red—
a circle with a world wyrm rising from it. But they also
wore black helms and had their cape pins adorned with
the skulls of wolves, covered in silver foil. These were
the emperor's elite troops, the fang guard.

Their skin had gone gray, and their faces had the ema-
ciated look of those who are more dead than alive.

They growled and shoved as they made their way
through the throng, clubbing or kicking lesser warriors
who were too slow to move out of the way. Their eyes
had gone red with rage, and the air felt stifling with
menace.

The Death Lord watched as the fang guard leader
approached, his face distorted by wrath. He glared up at

the Death Lord, who had been standing upon a pinnacle of rock, peering out over his wondrous army.

"Fourteen fang guards reporting for duty," the captain said.

The Death Lord did not like the looks of him.

"Grovel," the Death Lord commanded. It was only right that such creatures debase themselves before him.

The captain lowered his neck slowly, as if it were made of steel and he could bend it only with great difficulty. His eyes blazed.

There is something wrong with these troops, the Death Lord realized. The whole world seemed to have turned upside down. There were forests where there should be none. Some of his troops had vanished during the great change, and others now claimed to recall other lives lived upon another world. Two of the men had even shown marvelous powers, gained from wondrous runes.

What had become of the fang guard? Obviously, he thought, the emperor has placed some spell upon them, to make them more feral. Perhaps it was an experiment, with some new type of harvester spike. Still, he thought, I cannot allow them to show insubordination.

The Death Lord leapt thirty feet to the ground so that he could stand before the captain, his black robes fluttering as he landed.

He reached out to the captain, his hand but a shadow that escaped from his robe, and raked the captain lightly between the eyes with a single fingernail.

The captain's gray skin flayed wide, and blood oozed from the wound.

The captain struggled to retain control, but his wrath would not let him. He trembled and shook from head to foot, as if straining to keep from lashing out.

He should have showed no emotion at all.

What a waste, the Death Lord thought, realizing that he would have to kill the soldier. Then the Death Lord uttered a small curse.

With a sound of shredding, the captain's flesh began to rip from his body. Skin peeled away like parchment. His robes and armor were rent as if by some great beast.

There in the pale light, the Death Lord suddenly glimpsed runes upon the creature's pale skin—runes of strength, speed, stamina, and bloodlust.

Ah, the Death Lord realized, our master is experimenting with some new magic. He must have sent these reinforcements only hours ago!

That seemed almost impossible. They would have had to run hundreds of leagues in a single night. But the Death Lord could not deny the evidence.

And I, he thought, have killed one of her special tools. I will have to hide the deed, for it is too late to stop.

Again and again the tearing came. The captain roared and fell to his knees, naked, while skin continued to flay, exposing fat and muscle. In a moment he pitched forward and lay silently twitching as the peeling continued.

The Death Lord peered upward. A layer of clouds sealed the heavens, blocking even the starlight. Upon the mount, just four miles away, Luciare shone with intense brightness, lit by lesser spirits.

The Death Lord had far more than he needed in the way of armaments, men, and spells to take the castle. There would never be a better time for a bloodbath.

40

A MEETING OF THE MINDS

A mastiff is bred for battle. The spinner dog is bred to turn a wheel. The beagle is bred to hunt rabbits and foxes. But what was I bred for?

Reason tells me that I have no purpose in life—that I am only the byproduct of my father's lust and my mother's want for affection.

But my heart whispers that I am free to choose my own purpose and to create my own destiny. —Alun

Horns blared throughout Luciare, clear horns as piercing as the cold of a mid-winter's night, horns that told a tale of wyrmlings toiling up the slopes of the mountain.

Alun raced down the hallways to the lower levels. As he did, he heard shouts. "Warlord Madoc has returned! He stopped the wyrmlings at Cantular!"

Alun could hardly believe the good news.

The city was shut. Huge slabs of rock had been brought to seal every portico, every window. Through the hard work of thousands, the city's defenses had been repaired in only a day. From outside, the stones fit so cleanly that it would be hard even to tell where the openings had been.

Inside the castle, light and life were everywhere. Children had been put to work lighting extra thumb-lanterns and placing them in the lower corridors where the wyrmlings would first enter. The stark white walls reflected the light, making the halls almost as light as day.

Flowers were strewn upon the floor, fresh leaves of rose and lavender and pennyroyal, so that a sweet scent filled the city. With each step, Alun perfumed the halls, and seeds were strewn beside the flowers—poppy and bean, wheat and rye.

It made the footing all that more treacherous.

Alun gained the lowest levels and had to fight his way past warriors in order to reach the portal.

Outside Warlord Madoc and his sons could be seen marching up the city streets now, capes flapping behind them, faces grim, only moments ahead of the wyrmling hordes. Crowds of warriors cheered them as triumphant heroes. Alun could see the wyrmlings racing up the mountain road, just moments behind, but Madoc was safely within the city walls.

Last of all among the returning heroes, came the Emir of Dalharristan, head lowered in humility. There were so few troops returning, Alun saw, that this could not really be celebrated as a victory.

"Ten thousand wyrmlings they slew!" someone shouted. "They died on the bridge of Cantular."

Madoc trudged up to the main gate and made to pass Alun. "Milord," Alun begged, "if I may have a moment?"

Madoc glared. "Is it important?"

"I have news that you should hear," Alun suggested, "before you see the king."

Madoc considered a moment, as if nothing that Alun could say would be more urgent than his own report to the king. Then he grabbed Alun by the sleeve and ushered him from the hall into the first living chamber that they reached. It had been a stately room for some merchant who did not want to travel far to get into the city. It was spacious and elegantly appointed. Now it was empty, the valuables hastily removed, the merchant having fled to higher—and presumably safer—quarters.

"What is so important?" Madoc demanded as he closed the door.

"High King Urstone tried to exchange Princess Kanhazur for his son, and the wyrmlings cheated him. They took the princess, and gave nothing in return."

"The king was a fool," Madoc said. "Still, we can take

comfort in one thing—the princess will not live out the week."

"What do you mean?"

Madoc smiled. "My men have been poisoning her food with shavings of red-wort root for years. It will not harm her until she stops eating it."

Alun considered. He wasn't sure that his people could survive the night. But if they did, what would happen once Emperor Zul-torac discovered this act of treachery?

He'll hunt us down to the very last woman and child, Alun thought. Between Urstone's folly and Madoc's treachery, we are doomed.

What had Daylan said? Hadn't he said that there was but a hair's difference between the wyrmlings and mankind? Madoc seemed little better than Zul-torac at that moment.

So much evil in the world comes upon us from poor leaders, Alun thought. Why was it my fate to be caught between these two?

We suffer them, he realized. We, the people, suffer them. We forgive their stupidity and their small-mindedness. We follow them into battles that should not be. We accept their flattery and petty bribes—when we would be better off to sweep them away, like flies from our dinner table.

"So," Madoc said. "What do the people think of this debacle?"

Alun tried to think fast. He wasn't sure that he wanted to support Warlord Madoc anymore. But Alun had the habit of telling the truth, and it came easiest to his lips. "There are many who blame him for this attack, saying that he sold his kingdom for a dream. There are those who believe he should be removed from the throne!"

The words of treason came to his tongue, yet his heart was not in it. He almost felt as if he stood outside himself, listening to someone else speak.

"Are any of his own warriors saying it?" Madoc asked.

"Some," Alun admitted. "Still, the king has strong

supporters, and there are those that love him. It would be foolish to come out openly against him.

"There is something more," Alun said. "The king has shown favor to Fallion Orden, the wizard who merged our two worlds. He plans to do it again, binding many worlds into one. If he does, many people, folks like me who had no shadow self upon the other world, will simply die."

Madoc seemed to consider this for a long moment.

"Our young wizard must also be stopped," Madoc said. Madoc looked thoughtful. Alun could see plans of murder circling in his skull. He looked hopefully at Alun, as if wondering if Alun could be trusted to do the wizard, but then thought better of it. He smiled at Alun, a reassuring smile, the smile of a killer who meant to do his business.

"You have done well, my friend. When my kingdom comes, you will have a high place among my counselors."

At the sudden blare of trumpets, Madoc whirled and left the room.

Alun felt sure that he didn't want to see Madoc reign. The people needed someone of greater wisdom and compassion. But Alun could use the man. He could make Madoc a tool, use him to get rid of Fallion Orden.

But it wasn't Fallion that Alun was worried about at the moment. It wasn't even Warlord Madoc or King Urstone. No, there was a far more pressing danger. Outside, distant cries and the crashing of weapons against shields announced the advance of the wyrmling horde.

THE BATTLE FOR
THE OUTER WALL

*A warrior's life depends upon his ability to read the
enemy, to know what he will do before he even tries.*

—Sir Borenson

Fallion suspected that it was only two hours before dawn
as he and Jaz winged back to Caer Luciare. The air felt
chill and heavy, as it does in the hours before dawn.

Fallion studied the castle's defenses from the air.

Luciare climbed the mountain in steps, houses built on
terraces that bordered a winding road. Two walls protected the city—a lower wall that surrounded the market,
and an upper wall to defend the warrens. Both walls had
moats filled with water that cascaded down from the
mountain's heights.

The lower walls were well defended. It looked as if
every able-bodied man and woman in the city had turned
out.

Fallion spotted Rhianna above the upper wall, standing on the broad terrace, looking about as if unsure what
to do.

Fallion swooped and landed beside her, found himself
hitting ground so fast he tripped and fell headlong.

Jaz whooped with laughter and touched down beside
him, managing to be only slightly less graceless.

Rhianna studied the wings, tried to hide a twinge of
jealousy. Then turned and peered down over the hills.
The wyrmlings were coming through the trees, banging
weapons and singing.

"Have you seen Talon?" Fallion asked.

Rhianna shook her head no. "She's been gone all

night. I think she might be down on the lower wall. Where do you want to fight?"

"The closer we get, the better the view," Fallion said. "But with an unfamiliar enemy, that might be dangerous."

"You've been training with weapons all of your life," Rhianna said. "I doubt they have any tricks they can teach you."

"Yes," Jaz teased. "He's been training all of his *short* life."

Fallion felt nervous. He could feel the electric thrill in the air that comes before battle. Yes, he'd trained all of his life, but not to fight against giants that outweighed him by three hundred pounds. "All right, I'd like a front-row seat, if it's okay with you."

"I've always wanted to get front-row seats to something," Rhianna teased uneasily. "I'm just not sure if this is the best time start demanding them."

Jaz asked, "So, how long do you think it will take before the wyrmlings bow to our superior skills?"

"Oh," Fallion said, "they look like slow learners. I bet it will take them hours."

"Good," Jaz said. "We should all have quite a pile of dead at our feet before they catch on."

"Let us hope," Rhianna said, as they strode down the winding road to the lower levels.

Thousands of human warriors crowded atop the lower wall as the wyrmlings marched on the castle. But breaching the wall would not be easy. Luciare was no minor fortress. The lower wall rose eighty feet. Moreover, it was carved from living rock and thus had no seams, save the cracks made by frozen water over the eons. Even a kezziard could not climb it.

Fallion raced down the city streets to the outer wall, and stood upon the precipice, peering down. Clouds had wandered in overnight, sealing the skies, releasing a cool rain in some places, a slight mist that had abated only moments ago. A wayward breeze blew down the mountainside, mussing Fallion's hair, buffeting his wings.

Out in the darkness, under the cover of trees, he could make out wyrmlings stirring in the shadows. But none dared the road, and he could not see what they were up to.

Young boys stood upon the walls, torch-bearers.

Fallion drew light from the nearest torches, sent it snaking down the hill under the woods, where it lingered among the fallen leaves beneath the trees.

Suddenly the outlines of the wyrmlings appeared.

The wyrmlings had brought enormous drums unlike anything that Fallion had ever seen—black drums, made from hollowed baobab trees. Each drum was at least forty feet long and was lugged by dozens of wyrmlings. One end of each log was covered in some dark hide, while the other end opened with a narrow hole.

The wyrmlings stayed afar off, about a quarter of a mile, and wrestled the drums, aiming the holes toward the city wall.

Upon the wall, the human defenders hunched low and braced themselves. There were cries of awe, and Fallion saw defenders counting in their own crude tongue. He estimated fifty drums in the woods, and the defenders seemed dismayed.

What are our people so afraid of? Fallion wondered.

Then huge wyrmlings with enormous clubs began to pound.

The first drum snarled and boomed, as if to hurl a curse. The drum exuded a percussive force like a physical blow that lifted Fallion from his feet, and set his very bones to aching.

"Ah!" Jaz cried. Fallion looked up to see him wiping blood from his nose.

The wall beneath them cracked. Stone shattered and rained down from the ledge.

"What makes them so powerful?" Fallion wondered aloud, for he had never seen such terrors. His very skin seemed to ache with the roll of the thunder drum.

"Spells," Rhianna guessed. "Some type of rune of the air?"

Fallion wished that Talon were here so that he could ask her of the lore, but he had not seen her all night.

A second drum called out in a tone higher than the first, and did far less damage. The wyrmlings struggled with it, loosening the lid of the drum, and then a third called out, slightly deeper than the first.

"They're looking for just the right pitch," Rhianna guessed, "to break this stone."

"Or my bones," Jaz proclaimed.

Four or five more drums rang out experimentally, until the wyrmlings found the pitch they wanted.

Suddenly dozens of drums opened up. A wall of sound hit, blasting and thrumming, causing the mountain to shake as if it would collapse. Fallion had heard terrible thunderstorms in the summers back in Landesfallen, the thunder echoing from mountain to mountain. But this was fifty time worse. The air filled with snarls and booms, and the mountain shook mercilessly.

The wall beneath them cracked. Rubble began falling as the lip of the wall crumbled away. With each blast, the wyrmlings shifted their drums, taking aim at an unblemished portion of the wall.

Fallion had thought that the wyrmlings would take hours to breach this wall, but suddenly he realized that the lip was dropping at a rate of inches every moment. He could not have imagined the damage done with each blast. It was like striking soft stone with a mallet. The outer wall was crumbling, and with each crack, each indentation, it left an invitation for the kezziards' claws.

In mere moments, the walls eroded as if a millennium's worth of wind and ice had wrought upon them.

Fallion had imagined that it would be a long siege and that the humans might hold the outer wall all night. But the wall looked as if it might be breached in moments.

In dismay he realized that it had never been Luciare's

strong walls that had protected the city. Nor was it the power of its fighting men. Only a single hostage had stood between mankind and destruction.

The emperor must prize her more than we ever guessed, Fallion thought.

Fallion felt for sources of heat, wondering if he might set the woods ablaze. There were torches at his back all along the wall. But a light rain had fallen earlier, little more than a mist.

At this distance, it was enough to foil even his strongest spells.

A few men upon the walls fired huge bows or hurled the massive iron war darts that seemed to be favored here. They did little damage. The wyrmlings in the wood were shielded by leaf and limb.

Fallion drew heat from the torches into himself, savoring it. He exhaled, and smoke issued from his nostrils. He knew that if anyone looked at him, his eyes would be shining. He felt powerful, dangerous, even as the fortress walls shattered beneath him.

Then a huge shout erupted from the woods, and trees began to tremble as kezziards rumbled past them. The ground beneath the woods suddenly filled with white— the white of helms and armor whittled from bone, the white of the wyrmlings' pale skin, and the white of their eyes shining like crystals.

Suddenly something huge lumbered up over the woods, giant graaks on heavy wings. A dozen of them came at once, wingtip to wingtip, forming a living wall. Scores of wyrmlings rode their backs.

Shouts of warning erupted as human warriors recognized the danger. The wyrmlings wouldn't need kezziards to breach the walls. They could drop troops from the sky.

Upon the stone archway above the great gate to the city, the Wizard Sisel stood. Flowers and vines hung from the arch like a living curtain, and he stood there surrounded by greenery, as if in a forest. Down below, the wyrmling troops rushed forward, roaring, and the giant graaks came winging well above the trees, the rush of wind from their wings rising like a storm.

The human defenders braced themselves, terror plain upon their faces, and Sisel raised his staff.

And there, from the grass along the castle wall, a million fireflies suddenly rose, arcing into the air like bright green sparks, filling the fields with light.

"Now," King Urstone called at the wizard's back. "By life and light, now is the time to strike!"

The humans charged to the crumbling lip of the wall, risking their lives to hurl war darts.

Wyrmlings cried in despair, as if to greet the Dark Lady herself in death.

The kezziards clambered forward, crushing wounded and fallen wyrmlings in their path, terrifying in their masks of woven chain. The lizards themselves were the color of fire, with enormous eyes that shone silver. Their tongues snapped and flickered as they scented the battlefield, yet despite the dying all around them, they trudged stupidly on.

Fallion saw dozens of kezziard riders die, iron darts splitting their faces.

Giant graaks neared the city.

Fallion stood, his wings nervously adjusting, preparing for flight.

High up on Mount Luciare, where clouds collided with stone, a pair of Knights Eternal clung to the wall, gripping it with dead fingers and the tiny claws at the joints of their wings.

There at the edge of the coming battle, in the sputtering light of the torches, they spotted the nervous unfolding wings.

The knights looked at each other.

"Fools," one of them whispered. "They almost beg for death."

The two winged human warriors hadn't had time to

adapt to a life of flight, and so they squatted along with
the rest of their kind. Their attention was riveted on the
enemy in front of them, when they should have been
scanning the sky above.

With a kick, the Knights Eternal soundlessly broke
away from the mountain wall, unfolded their wings, and
swooped into a dive.

Like hawks they stooped, using all of their strength to
focus on the wingtips, keeping them rigid against the driving wind, gently tilting, making corrections, as they
guided themselves toward their targets.

They gained speed as they fell, and soon were rushing
toward ground. With just a tilt of the wingtips, they
began to break, and went shooting just feet above the
crowd.

Thunder drums continued to boom, cracking walls and
shattering stone. The wyrmlings wailed and snarled in
death as the humans hurled their iron darts, and everywhere men were shouting battle cries. Fallion's nerves
jangled, and for a moment it seemed that all went silent
as he tried to block out the sound.

From the castle wall above Fallion, he heard a roar of
warning and imagined that from their higher vantage
point the lookouts must have spotted some new threat.

Jaz leapt forward, taking aim with his great bow and
loosing a black arrow into the throat of a wyrmling
kezziard rider. He grabbed a second arrow in a blur, and
took aim at a kezziard's eye.

A war dart came hurtling up from a wyrmling below,
and Jaz dodged aside even as he let his arrow fly.

A tall warrior stepped in front of Fallion, blocking his
view; quickly Fallion ducked to his left to get a glimpse
of the battlefield.

He heard a heavy *chunk, crack, chunk.*

The warrior that had blocked Fallion's view suddenly
grunted. Fallion glanced at him, and saw that a black dart
now sprouted from his back.

The warrior staggered forward a pace and moaned as he toppled over the wall.

That dart barely missed me! Fallion realized. He wondered where it had come from. Obviously, there was an enemy behind him.

At that instant Jaz cried out, falling to his knees.

Fallion heard the muffled flapping of wings, a sound an owl might make as it takes a mouse. A Knight Eternal, he realized.

He ducked. At the same instant something enormous swooped above his head.

Then Fallion spotted a huge black iron war dart protruding from Jaz's back.

For an instant, time froze. Fallion saw the panic in Rhianna's eyes, saw her swing her staff wildly as a pair of Knights Eternal blurred above her. But as quickly as they had come, the enemy was gone, winging off into the shadows.

Fallion thought to follow, but knew that it would be too dangerous. He could no longer see them, and their flying skills far outmatched his own.

Jaz knelt on his hands and knees, gasping for breath. He coughed, and gobs of blood spattered to the ground.

He began to laugh just a bit as Fallion drew near.

"What?" Rhianna asked, grabbing for his shoulder, trying to pull him up. Jaz shook his head no, refusing her help.

Jaz looked up at Fallion, smiling broadly, while blood poured freely from his mouth. Tears glistened in his eyes.

"Do you hurt?" Rhianna asked, trying to comfort him.

"The poison . . . is cold."

Jaz collapsed, his face banging onto the stone.

"Jaz!" Fallion cried, and reached down to grab him. He listened for Jaz to breathe, but only heard the air escape his brother's throat.

Rhianna's face was blank with shock.

All of the roaring, all of the snarl and bass of the thunder drums, all seemed but a small and distant noise.

In that instant, Fallion knelt with his brother, utterly alone.

Then Rhianna was on him, trying to pull him back from the wall. "We've got to get away! They're coming!"

Even as she spoke, a great sky serpent flapped overhead, and they were washed in the wind from its wings. Something wet splattered from the sky, and there was a crackling sound as it splashed to the stone walls.

Oil? Fallion wondered. Some vile poison?

But drops of red hit his face, and he wiped it away with the back of his hand. Blood, he realized. Putrid blood, that smelled as if it had been days rotting in a barrel.

The very stench of it made him want to retch, and, oddly, the touch of it began to burn his skin. He heard a hissing sound around him as foul liquid landed on vines and trees and set them steaming.

Death, come to conquer life. It was more than mere blood. There was a spell upon it.

It was an omen.

Suddenly, Fallion felt disoriented. All of the rules of combat he had learned as a child meant nothing here. The wyrmlings fought a different kind of war.

Rhianna grabbed Jaz's scabbard and bow, then pulled on Fallion's shoulder, trying to lift him up.

Fallion staggered to his feet, went tottering behind her. He stared back, his eyes on Jaz, hoping that his brother might show some sign of life.

A huge human warrior reached down, grabbed Jaz by the wings, and began trying to lift him.

"He's dead," Fallion called back uselessly.

At that instant there was a tearing sound, and Jaz's wings ripped free. His corpse sloughed away, slapping to the cold stone battlements.

Ah, Fallion realized. He wasn't helping Jaz, just taking a prize of war.

Rhianna led Fallion away in a daze, racing up the cold stone streets. He couldn't feel his feet. His body had gone numb. There were shouts everywhere. Giant graaks flapped high over the city while wyrmlings spattered their bloody elixir onto trees and gardens, set the trees and grass sizzling, then found a place to land.

Behind Fallion, there was a shout as kezziards hit the outer wall. Fallion did not understand the war clan's language, but he knew what they were crying. "Pull back, pull back! The wyrmlings are over the wall."

Fallion peered back toward Jaz one last time, but could not see him. The human warriors behind Fallion were in full retreat, blocking Fallion's view, and a kezziard was climbing over the spot where Jaz's body lay, the wyrmling riders looking fearsome in their thick armor.

In a more perfect world, Fallion thought, my brother is still alive.

He ached to take wing, to fly to the Mouth of the World and dare the tunnels down, seeking out the Seal of the Inferno.

Soon, he promised himself.

But there was a battle to fight first.

❧ 42 ❧

A VISION

Every man is a prisoner of his own making. The size of our jail is defined by the limits of our vision.
                                        —Daylan Hammer

Time had no meaning in Areth's cell. Seconds seemed to draw out into hours, hours into centuries. As his unseen Dedicates endured unimaginable tortures, only Areth felt their pain.

Several times he lost consciousness, then rose again to

the surface, like a drowning man. From time to time, voices came to him, hallucinations caused by the extremity of his torture.

Other times, he heard groaning deep in the earth, as if rocks were colliding and rubbing together, struggling to form new hills. It was almost as if the earth had a voice, and if he listened hard enough, he could hear it.

"Pain. I am in pain," the earth said. That is all that he could discern in the noise, that and a sound like groaning.

Areth whispered, "I would help if I could."

Areth heard his wife's voice.

"Areth, awake," she said softly.

He looked up and saw that he was in a meadow.

I am dreaming, he realized, but only stared at his wife. She had been dead for sixteen years. Areth knew that she could not be here, and he peered into her face not because he loved it, but because he had not been able to recall what she had looked like now for nearly a decade.

A dream such as this, it was rare and precious, and he hoped to recall it when he woke.

Her skin was dark, beautiful, as it had been in life. Her eyes sparkled like stars reflected in a pool at midnight.

But there was something wrong. Her face was mottled and of different colors. He peered hard. White sand, pebbles, twigs, leaves and mud all seemed to be pressed together, forming her face.

A vague worry took him. Areth feared that he was mad. He knew that this was a dream, but the meadow somehow seemed too real, too lush. He could smell the sweet scent of rye and the bitter tang of the dandelions in the grass. Bluebells rose up at the roots of the aspen trees at the edge of the glade. There was too much detail in the grass. He could see old blades lying on the ground, the new grass rising up from them. He could smell worms upon the ground.

He listened to the bickering of wrens and calls of cicadas deeper in the woods, and he felt sure that it was not a dream.

"Who are you?" Areth asked the woman, for he suddenly realized that she could not be his wife. She was a stranger.

"I am the Spirit of the Earth," the woman whispered, smiling down at him. "I have come to beg your help. The world is a wasteland, and soon will succumb. The very rocks and stones cry out in agony. Soon, mankind will pass away, like a dream."

Sooner than you know, Areth thought. He could not say why, but he believed the wyrmling torturers this time. They were attacking Luciare and would slaughter the last vestiges of mankind. Perhaps a few might escape, but only a few, and they would be hunted.

"I can grant you the power to save them," the Earth Spirit whispered. "If you will accept the gift, you can save the seeds of mankind. But it comes with a great price—all that you are, all that you ever will be. All of your hopes and dreams must be relinquished, and you must serve me above all."

Areth felt as if his knuckles had grown thick with arthritis. Pain blossomed in them, as if they had been crushed. He laughed in pain.

If this is a dream, then I must not be sleeping very soundly, he thought. The torturers are still at me.

"Do you accept?" the woman asked.

"Why not? Sure, I accept."

The woman faded without another word.

Areth opened his eyes, found himself lying upon the greasy floor of his cell. There were no lights nearby to let him see. The stone floor was covered with his sweat and stank of rotting skin. A corner in the back was reserved for his waste, and bore an appropriate odor.

He was wracked in pain. It felt as if one of his lungs had collapsed, and his right arm had been pulled from his shoulder joint.

But as he peered into the darkness, groaning in pain, he could not help but remember for the first time in years the scent of sweet rye grass bursting from ground swollen by spring rain.

43

BATTLE FOR THE UPPER GATE

In a fight between flameweavers, everyone gets burned.
          —*a saying of Fleeds*

Thunder drums kept snarling as the Warrior Clans beat a hasty retreat from the lower wall. There were cries of pain, shouted battle orders. Amidst the bedlam, Rhianna raced over the paved streets of the market, hanging on to Fallion with her left hand while she struggled to hold her own staff and Jaz's weapons in her right.

The enormous graaks flew over her head and landed on the upper wall. Wyrmling troops slid down their scaly backs, then raced to take the upper gate, leaving a host of slaughtered defenders in their wake. The wyrmling troops moved too fast to be commoners.

They've taken endowments of metabolism, Rhianna realized.

There were cries of despair from the defenders on the upper wall, and all around Rhianna in the market streets below, human warriors began sprinting to meet the threat, jostling her, nearly knocking her down.

Fallion staggered beside Rhianna in a daze, trying to peer back at his lost brother.

With a sudden rattle of chains, a huge iron door slammed down on the upper wall, and there were groans of shock and despair from the defenders nearby.

The defenders had just been locked out of the upper levels of the city. Rhianna whirled and glanced behind. Wyrmling troops were swarming over the lower walls by the tens of thousands.

We're trapped! she realized. With wyrmling runelords manning the wall above them and a host charging up from behind, the human warriors were caught between a hammer and an anvil.

It was going to be a slaughter.

And she could see no way to beat the wyrmling runelords. There couldn't be more than four hundred men at the mouth of the warrens. If they charged out, they *might* be able to take the gate—but in doing so they'd leave the warrens undefended.

The Warrior Clans weren't prepared for the wyrmling tactics. They had planned to make an orderly retreat, exacting a heavy toll from the wyrmlings for every step that they took.

But now, once the defenders in the city had been handled, the wyrmlings would be able to stroll through the warrens, wiping out the women, the children, the elderly and the babes.

"Fell-ion!" a deep voice cried above the tumult. "Fell-ion!"

Rhianna whirled, saw King Urstone not a hundred feet away. He pointed toward the upper gate, gave a silent nod, then leapt into the air, flying rapidly.

Fallion just stood, his face a blank. He was still in shock.

"Fallion," Rhianna cried, "we have to win back the gate! Carry me up there!"

Rhianna pointed up. It was a short flight, but a steep climb. The guards from the outposts along the upper wall were all racing to the gate, but these weren't the city's grandest fighters. Most of them were mere boys, and they would be fighting runelords.

Fallion seemed to snap out of his daze. He grasped Rhianna around the lower belly and leapt into the air, flapping his wings for all that he was worth.

Rhianna peered down. Beneath them, the wyrmlings had breached the lower wall in twenty places; kezziards were climbing over it. The gate to the lower levels had come down, and the wyrmling hordes were rushing through. There seemed to be no end of them. A few human hosts, realizing the danger, had turned to meet them, but there wouldn't be enough of them.

Up ahead of her, the monstrous graaks leapt into the air and dove back toward the markets.

They're going to pick up reinforcements for the gate, Rhianna realized.

One monster winged straight toward them, as if it would attack. Rhianna let out a little cry of despair, and adjusted her sweaty grip on her staff and bow.

Fallion strained, flapping hard, and then went into a dive, veering beneath the oncoming monster. He struggled to pull out of the dive, then suddenly went swooping up like an owl.

Fallion didn't have a wyrmling's bulk, and his wings were made to fit the giants. Rhianna figured that together they weighed about as much as a single wyrmling. The wings could carry them, but sweat was streaming from Fallion's brow by the time they reached the upper wall.

As soon as he landed, he stopped and knelt, gasping for breath. Below them the thunder drums were deafening, and the cries of the warriors were like the roar of the sea.

"Fallion," Rhianna cried. "We have to clear the gates!"

There were at least a hundred wyrmling troops at the gate to their east, fierce creatures in black capes, with huge strange swords and battle-axes that glinted like molten metal in the torchlight.

King Urstone had landed on the far side of the gate, and now he gathered some young warriors around him, shouting battle orders. But there were not a hundred humans manning the entire upper wall.

Down in the lower markets, the human warriors were charging the gate to the upper portion of the city. The Wizard Sisel led the charge, striding boldly forward, his staff held high. Thousands of warriors marched at his back. A great cloud of fireflies swarmed among the human hosts, lighting the way.

Rhianna did not doubt that the wizard was preparing some spell to bring down the gate.

Fallion glanced up into the sky, as if afraid that one of the Knights Eternal would swoop down on him, but for the moment the skies were clear.

He reached out with his left hand, as if endlessly straining to grasp something in the valley below, something almost beyond his reach. Fires burned in the valley, hundreds of torches in their sconces, dozens of small brushfires.

Suddenly, nearly every torch and burning bush winked out.

Their energy came whirling toward Fallion in a fiery tornado, ropes of burning red flames that twisted in the air and then landed in his hand, forming a white ball that blazed like the sun.

He hurled the energy down among the wyrmling troops that bristled just inside the gates. A fiery ball whooshed into their midst and burst, incinerating a dozen wyrmlings, searing and setting fire to perhaps fifty more.

King Urstone shouted, and his young warriors leapt into battle. Some of them simply hurled themselves over the wall, down to the gate, leaping sixty feet to land atop wyrmling warriors.

It was suicide, but Rhianna saw big wyrmling runelords devastated by the assault, bones crushed by the weight of their attackers.

Fallion reached out again toward the few fires that had flickered back to life. The fires blacked out, and coils of burning energy shot toward his outstretched palm.

Just as suddenly, the coils arced up into the sky, like a fiery tornado that was upside down.

A Knight Eternal grabbed the energy, and came swooping toward them at astonishing speed, holding a glowing ball of molten fire.

"Watch out!" Fallion shouted, stepping in front of Rhianna, using his body as a shield.

Rhianna cowered, afraid that the fireball would take her.

But the Knight Eternal hurled the ball away at the last instant, sent it roiling into the castle's defenders. Young soldiers let out a wail of pain as they died.

The knight stooped from the sky and dove straight at Fallion, who only now drew his sword.

The knight's own black blade was in his hand. He winged toward Fallion at a falcon's blinding speed, his blade held forward.

Rhianna had wondered why Talon had called these creatures "knights." Now she saw: it was racing toward them like a lancer, but instead of a warhorse, it rode upon the wind.

"Damn you!" Fallion roared, "this is for my brother!" He leapt toward the knight, twisting his blade as they met.

There was a spark and a clang as metal struck metal, then the unmistakable snick of a breaking sword.

The knight blurred past Fallion in a thunder of wings—just as Rhianna leapt up and smashed the creature with her staff.

She'd expected the jolt to rip off her arms. Instead the Knight Eternal seemed to explode, as if she'd just hit a sack filled with dust. Bits of desiccated flesh and dry bones rained down all around her, messing her hair and getting grit in her eyes.

The remains of the creature landed in a heap not ten yards away, then went rolling and rolling until its corpse lay leaning with one wing dangling over the wall.

Fallion was on the ground. He moaned a bit, then rolled over. Rhianna saw fresh blood smearing his robes.

"Sword broke," he said, his face white with shock. He was patting his robe, as if to find the source of the blood. The blade of his own rusty sword was lodged just below his rib cage, somewhere between his right kidney and a lung. The point stuck out from him, as if he'd been run through. Rhianna realized that the blade must have been driven back and struck him when the sword shattered. He pulled it free. The last three inches of blade was bloody.

Not a deep cut, but it was three inches wide, and given its proximity to vital targets, it could be a deadly wound.

"Fallion," Rhianna cried, then knelt over him. She held her hand over the wound, fingers clasped tightly, trying to staunch the flow. Warm blood boiled out. She cast her eyes around, looking for someone to help, but the young soldiers on the wall had all run down into the fray, where they engaged the wyrmling troops.

Rhianna saw something flash past her—a second Knight Eternal diving into battle.

It swooped over the oncoming troops, diving through the cloud of fireflies that shone like a million dancing stars.

There its blade found the head of the Wizard Sisel, and nearly set it free.

One moment, the wizard was striding toward the city gates leading the charge, and the next instant he tried to duck beneath the Knight Eternal's blow. The sword glanced off Sisel's leather helm, and he slumped onto the cobblestones.

Cries of grief and despair rose from the human hosts as the Knight Eternal climbed back into the sky. A few black war darts followed in his wake, then fell pitifully in a deadly rain among the crowd.

Warriors swarmed around the wounded wizard, creating a shield wall. Sisel struggled to his feet, took a step, and fell in a swoon.

Rhianna stared blankly at the devastation. That steel gate was meant to hold off wyrmling attackers. The men below had no siege towers, no way to breach the city's defenses. Without Sisel to save them, they were trapped.

King Urstone's young warriors had thrown themselves into battle, and just as quickly they were dying beneath the swords and axes of the enemy.

Down at the lower gates, the giant graaks were lifting off, ferrying more troops to hold the upper wall. Kezziards were racing into battle with troops upon their backs, and the whole wyrmling horde now charged through the streets, wading into the human defenders.

Farther back, walking hills moved through the forest, crushing trees. Thousands of wyrmling troops rode upon their backs, and Rhianna could not guess what horrors these creatures held in store.

Fallion gave a wan chuckle. He was looking toward the dead knight, trying to keep his eyes from rolling back in his head. "You killed him? You killed a Knight Eternal?" Rhianna nodded silently. "Then, you've won your own pair of wings."

Fallion passed out. The blood was still pumping from him, and Rhianna could not stop the flow. She reached under her tunic and ripped off a strip of cotton undershirt, then lay down atop Fallion, feigning death, and hoped that she could staunch the flow of blood.

She saw High King Urstone leap into the air, angrily brandishing an ax, hot on the tail of the Knight Eternal that had struck down Sisel. Urstone's flying skills were no match for those of his immortal enemy. He flapped clumsily, straining to catch up.

Seeing that the race was lost, King Urstone suddenly swooped and dove back among the troops in the market. He grasped the fallen wizard and flapped his wings in a frenzy, lugging Sisel into the air, well above the crowd, making for an open door high up on the mountain.

The defenders that had stood over the fallen wizard raised a cheer as he was carried to safety. But the cheer turned to cries of dismay as the wyrmlings charged into their midst.

In astonishment, Rhianna gaped at the battle raging below, a few thousand human warriors pitted against the might of the wyrmling horde. The wyrmlings were led by harvesters, boosted with extracts from the glands of fallen enemies. They raced through Warrior Clan's troops, chopping men down as if they were saplings.

In moments the battle would be over.

Rhianna realized, We are all as good as dead.

44

AT THE BRINK OF RUIN

It is when a man is confronted with eminent ruin that despair grows within him. And when overwhelmed by despair, he becomes pliant, and can be made a tool to fit your hand.   *—Emperor Zul-torac*

Through the streets of Luciare, the Death Lord rode atop a walking hill, surrounded by his wyrmling captains. The great hill was the product of some strange world that he had never seen. Its back was armored with chitin, like a giant snail. It had thousands of strange tendrils hanging from its front, each like an elephant's trunk, and with these it harvested anything in its path—grass, trees, or wyrmlings, and shoved them up into one of its maws as it continued to trundle forward upon thousands of marching feet.

The walking hills were supposed to act as archers' towers, to help the wyrmlings breach the castle walls, but the walking hills would not be needed on this trip.

Up ahead, the wyrmling troops were slaughtering the last of the human defenders, who had found themselves trapped between the upper and lower walls.

Streets that once had been teeming with life now were filled with the dying and the dead.

The Death Lord reached out his hand and pulled the life from those human defenders who still gripped it so tenaciously, and then sent it to his own troops, lending them greater vigor, making them drunk on bloodlust.

"Take off their heads!" the Death Lord cried. "There are still wounded among our enemy, and some feign death. Turn their lies into truth. Leave their glands for the harvesters!"

His troops raced through the small shops and houses,

engaging any defenders that tried to hide. There were occasional shouts as a human was found alive and offered a last desperate battle.

His walking hill climbed the streets to the upper gate, but there could go no farther. The upper wall was too steep for the creature to climb.

The last of the human warriors were being slaughtered as his hill came to a halt, and now the guards began to raise the upper gate.

The Death Lord took a great leap, and went fluttering from the hill to the wall, a jump of some twenty yards. It was no great feat for the Death Lord. He was mostly spirit now, and only the weight of his robes dragged him earthward.

Here in the courtyard he halted at the gates to the warrens. A few pitiful humans guarded the warrens still. They had closed the huge iron battle doors in one last attempt to fend off death.

But I have come for them anyway, the Death Lord thought. I will take them this night, ridding the world of the warrior clans.

The lights of Luciare still burned blindingly bright to the Death Lord, there in the braziers to each side of the iron doors. The spirits were dancing, flickering emerald and blinding white, then dying down to dazzling blue.

The Death Lord could not kill such creatures, for their lives had been taken. But even spirits had enemies.

The Death Lord stretched forth his mind, sent it into the shadows, and summoned an army of wyrms.

The dark creatures came by the hundreds, flying as if in a mad and tangled flock, descending upon the lights of Luciare.

In an instant, the lights were snuffed out.

The wyrmlings cheered as they raced up from the lower quarters to take the warrens.

In the sudden darkness, Rhianna crept on hands and knees to the fallen knight, hoping to pull his wings free.

There were no lights from Luciare, none from fires or torches below. She knew that the night vision of the wyrmlings was legendary, but she had to hope that for a few moments, at least, that the wyrmling horde would be distracted. And she had to hope, for a few moments, that Fallion's blood-flow had been staunched.

If I can only reach those wings, Rhianna thought, I can grab Fallion and carry him to safety.

"Dying is easy," Warlord Madoc shouted to his troops inside the warren. "Anyone can do it."

He grinned. He wasn't accustomed to giving speeches and did not account himself a fancy talker. Now he was getting the use of the same speech twice in one night. The troops crowded the tunnel. Archers with great bows would form the front ranks, taking out the first wyrmlings who managed to batter down the door. Daylan Hammer would be the champion guarding this corridor. In a strange twist of fate, the man who Warlord Madoc had hoped to kill was now entrusted with saving them all. The Cormar twins were in charge of championing the other two entrances.

"A child can die in the night from nothing at all," Warlord Madoc said. "Dying is easy. It is staying alive on a night like this that will be hard."

There were grunts of "Well put!" and "Death to all wyrmlings!" But there were no cheers, no wild applause. The troops were too thoughtful, too scared, and too subdued.

His men huddled behind the great iron war doors that were the last major defense for Caer Luciare. Up near the top of the door were cleverly constructed spy holes. Lookouts there watched the wyrmlings, reported each little defeat as it came—the fall of the Wizard Sisel, the wounding of Fallion. Sobering news all.

"The fate of all our people rests in our hands," Warlord Madoc said. "It is but an hour till dawn, an hour and a half at the best. We must hold the gates until then. If we can hold them through the night, the wyrmlings will be forced to retreat."

What would happen next, he could not guess. He imagined that he would gather all that he could and flee into the mountains or head for the settlements of the small folk to the north or west. But it was a daunting task, and he did not believe that they would make it.

"Warlord Madoc," a woman's voice called. "King Urstone is still trapped outside."

It was the Emir's daughter, Siyaddah. She stood in a shirt of bright ring mail beneath a thumb-lantern. She bore a crescent shield that the folk of Indhara used as a slashing weapon, along with a fine sword.

Damn King Urstone, Madoc wanted to say. Look what he has brought down upon us. I should have killed him years ago.

"I wish that his strong arm was here to fight beside us," Warlord Madoc said in mock sorrow. "But he has gone to fight other battles, and we must wish him well."

Suddenly a great boom sounded, blasting from the hollow throat of a thunder drum, and the ground shook beneath their feet.

Madoc heard rock crack, and great slabs of wall that had been hastily repaired only a day ago suddenly broke free, their mortar never having had time to set. Rock came tumbling down outside, crashing from above.

The warrens will be exposed, Madoc knew, tunnels showing up like the burrows of woodworms through a rotting tree. The Knights Eternal will have easy access to the apartments above.

Damn, he swore, all hope draining from him.

The final battle for Caer Luciare had begun.

45

AN UNHOLY PROPOSITION

Anyone can be convinced to sell their souls, if offered the right coin. Most will gladly part with it for nothing at all.
　　　　　　　　　　　　　　　　　—Vulgnash

Vomiting from pain, Areth Sul Urstone was dragged up an endless flight of stairs to the uppermost chamber of the dark tower at Rugassa.

There, he was thrown to the floor, where he lay on cold marble tiles that had been swept by the wind. The top of the tower was an observatory with a domed roof. Around it, pillars of black marble carved to look like tree trunks and vines held the roof aloft. Between the pillars was nothing, only open air, sweet and cold at this height.

From here, Areth could see the dark forests in the distance, crowded with hoary pines. Closer by, the bulk of the great bastion of Rugassa stretched—mile upon mile of stone walls and fortifications, manned by hundreds of thousands of wyrmling troops.

I could throw myself over the edge of the tower, Areth thought. *I could put an end to my pain.*

But a pair of guards hunkered over him, and Areth's muscles were so cramped that he could hardly move. He'd never make it to the tower's edge.

From before one of the dark pillars a shadow separated, a phantom in black robes that floated above the floor. It was the Emperor Zul-torac.

"Do you wonder why I have brought you here?" he said, his voice a whisper so soft, it seemed almost to echo in one's head, like a thought. "There is a battle raging at Luciare, a battle that is already lost."

The light was faint. Only starlight from the skies above filtered into the observatory. But Areth had spent long years in the darkness, and he had become well accustomed to it. He spotted a glint, saw the emperor raise a golden tube and aim it into the distance—an ocular. The emperor hissed the name of the glyph upon the instrument, and an image leapt into the room.

Areth could see Luciare there under the starlight, its image unnaturally bright. Thousands of warriors lay in ruin before the upper gate. Their heads were heaped into ghastly piles.

The ancient spirit lights of the city had gone black, and now a wyrmling army stood before Luciare itself. Thunder drums pounded, blasting at the city walls. Sheets of stone tumbled free, revealing the sacred halls of Luciare.

Even as Areth watched, a fast-flying Knight Eternal went winging into the upper levels where the women and children would be hiding.

He goes like a jay, to pluck the chicks from the nest of his enemies, Areth thought.

The ocular carried some sounds from the distant battle, the snarl and boom of the thunder drums. Suddenly, the frightened screams of babes was added to the mix.

Areth turned away, unable to look any longer.

Haven't they tormented me enough? Areth wondered. How much more do they think I can stand?

"You can save them," Emperor Zul-torac whispered. "You can save the last seeds of mankind."

Areth's mind seemed to do a little flip. The emperor had nearly echoed the words from his dream only an hour before. And now he heard the Earth Spirit begging him once again to save the seeds of mankind.

Had it been a sending? Had he truly been given such a charge?

In all of the history of the world, Areth had never

heard of such a thing. He had no reason to believe that the dream was anything but madness.

Suddenly his feet cramped, and he felt as if they'd been placed in a fire. Were they burning one of his Dedicates? Areth could not be sure.

"What?" Areth begged. "What do I have to do?"

"Nothing much," the emperor said softly. "Lady Despair desires you. You have only to open yourself, allow a wyrm to feed upon your soul."

My soul, Areth wondered, to save a city?

How often he had dreamed of freeing himself, of slaughtering the emperor and returning to Luciare as a hero. How often he had imagined the cheers and the adulation.

Now, in a twisted way, those dreams could come true.

One soul. One tormented soul was all that it would take.

"You have taken an endowment of touch from a single boy," Zul-torac said. "I will take a knife, hold him down. When I cut his throat, you will be freed from the source of your pain, and then the wyrm will enter you, and the city will be spared."

A wave of pain and nausea washed through Prince Areth Urstone, and he peered at the image of Luciare through eyes misted by tears.

46

DARKNESS FALLS

*In darkness men breed and dream. The poets write the
songs that fill their hearts with longing.*

*For this, Lady Despair shall give men eternal dark-
ness.*   —Emperor Zul-torac

Dogs can talk, Alun knew. And right now, his hounds
told a tale of wyrmlings in the warrens above him.

Alun stood beneath a thumb-lantern in the yellow
light, holding the leash to Wanderlust in one hand and
the leash to Brute in another. He was supposed to be on
lookout, a mere rearguard.

The wyrmlings had not yet even attacked the front
gate. Instead, for five minutes now they had been pounding the thunder drums, crumbling the façade that hid
some of the tunnels of the warrens, making a dozen
entries. Tremendous booms and snarls snaked through
the tunnels, accompanied by the sounds of cracking
rock. Motes of stone dust floated in the air, and Alun had
worried that the whole mountain would collapse.

But now Wanderlust was barking in alarm and peering
up the empty tunnel. Her ears were drawn back flush
with her leather mask. Her rear legs quivered in anticipation, and her tail was still.

"We've got problems," Alun called to the troops in the
cavern. "There are wyrmlings above us!" He strained his
senses.

Warlord Madoc was in charge. He glared at Alun.
"You certain, lad?"

Distantly, Alun heard a woman's scream echoing as if
out of some nightmare. "Yeah."

Madoc looked at his troops, shook his head in dismay.

He obviously didn't want to split his forces, for that is precisely what the wyrmlings were after.

"Hold the gate!" he shouted to his men. "Let me see what we're up against." He came rushing toward Alun. His sons, Connor and Drewish stared at him in terror, as if afraid that he'd ask them to follow, but he just shook his head no.

Madoc alone would brave the tunnels above, it seemed.

But at the last instant, Siyaddah peeled away and rushed to join him, followed by a pair from the warrior clan, a young man that Alun did not know, and the girl Talon, that he had helped rescue from the Knights Eternal.

"Let's go," Alun told the dogs. Wanderlust gave a strong jerk on her leash and went racing up the tunnel into the warrens, barking.

"Quiet!" Madoc shouted at the dogs. "Quiet now."

Both dogs went silent, for they were well trained. Still, they strained at their leashes, leading the way.

These won't be common troops up here, Alun realized as he tried to hold the dogs back. No common troops could have climbed the sheer walls of the mountain.

With a pounding heart, he realized that there would be Knights Eternal ahead.

In the darkness, Rhianna reached the corpse of the dead knight and grabbed at his wings. The creature's skin had gone gray with age and his flesh felt dry and mummified. As she pulled at his wings, his whole body followed. It could not have weighed fifty pounds. Even his bones must have rotted and dried up.

Rhianna's blow had taken the creature square in the skull, bursting it like an overripe melon. All that was left of its head was a single mandible hanging by a scrap of skin.

Rhianna was afraid to move, afraid to draw attention. She could not see much in the darkness, but wyrmlings were filling the courtyard in front of the warrens, and the snarl and bang of thunder drums filled the night. Stone slabs were sliding down from the mountainside, revealing its secret passageways, and for the moment, that seemed to hold the wyrmlings' attention. But at any instant, the wyrmlings could come for her.

Grasping the wings with both hands, Rhianna gave the knight's remains a swift kick, and the wings came free with surprising ease.

She studied the fearful prongs in the powdery starlight, wondering how to insert them, afraid that the obvious answer was the only one.

There was a rush of wings behind her, and Rhianna whirled, afraid that a Knight Eternal had found her.

High King Urstone landed with a grunt.

"Gesht," the high king whispered, casting a worried look into the sky. The word might have meant *hurry,* or *follow me.* Rhianna could not be certain, so she tried to do both.

She grasped the wings, held them over her head.

The high king leapt forward, shoved the metal prongs into her back, hard.

The pain that lanced through her drove a gasp from Rhianna's lungs.

But the king spared her no sympathy. He raced to Fallion, took one look at him, and picked him up.

"Gesht! Gesht!" he hissed, and King Urstone leapt into the air, his wings flapping madly, trying to lug Fallion up along with his own bulk.

Wait for me, Rhianna thought forlornly. Her wings felt like dead weight on her shoulders, and she had to wipe away tears of pain.

She heard a shout off to her left, saw a trio of wyrmlings charging out of the darkness. Her own staff was at her feet, so she grabbed it and went sprinting along the wall, fleeing the wyrmlings. In a hundred yards, the wall ended.

Rhianna ran, swiped the tears of pain from her face, and tried furiously to flap the wings.

She had only gone fifty yards when she felt a tingling sensation as the wings came alive.

The heavy footfalls of wyrmling warriors closed in behind her, accompanied by the sounds of bone mail clanking.

Rhianna raced, fearing that at any moment a poison war dart would strike her square in the back, the way that one had with Jaz.

She peered upward, saw King Urstone flying high up the mountain toward a parapet.

A wyrmling roared at her back, came racing up with a burst of speed. Rhianna knew that she couldn't outrun the monster, so she whirled to her right and leapt over the wall.

A wyrmling leapt after her and grabbed her right wing. She pulled free. The wyrmling plummeted with a scream.

Her wings were barely awake. She could feel blood surging through them, and she flapped frantically as she went into an uncontrolled spin.

She hit the ground with a thud some eighty feet below, her fall softened both by the flapping of her wings and a pile of dead bodies.

There were shouts off to the east. She heard a clang as an iron war dart bounced off the ground beside her.

Rhianna took off, running and flapping her wings feverishly, and then it seemed that some power outside herself took control of the wings, began forcing them to stretch forward and grasp the air in ways that she had not imagined, then pull downward and back, propelling her into the air. The wings had awakened.

Rhianna pumped furiously, aware that it was her own blood that sang through the veins of the wings, that it was her own energy that drove them.

It took great effort to get off of the ground. It was as

hard as any race that she had ever run. Her heart hammered in her chest and blood throbbed through her veins as she took flight, but with a final leap she was in the air, her feet miraculously rising up from the ground.

She was boxed-in ahead. A two-story market rose up on one side, a sheer cliff face on the right. She flew to the market wall, batting her wings, and raised herself high enough so that she could grab onto the roof. With a burst of renewed fear, she clambered over the wall and rose into the air, flapping about clumsily like a new fledgling, grateful only to be alive and flying.

She wheeled about, heading upward, her heart pounding so hard that she grew light-headed. She had only one desire: to reach Fallion's side.

Thunder drums roared and a deafening concussion blasted through the tunnels. Daylan Hammer, with his endowments of hearing, drew back from the door.

"King Urstone is flying up, bearing the wizard Fallion to safety," the lookout called. "The wyrmlings have got battering rams."

The thunder drums snarled, and from pedestals inside the iron door, archers shot arrows out through small kill holes.

There was a tremendous boom. Rocks cracked overhead; a split ran along the tunnel wall creating a seam, and pebbles and dust dribbled down. There were strange rumblings, the protests of stones stressed beyond the breaking point.

"Run!" Daylan warned. "The roof is going to collapse!" He whirled away from the great iron door, heard rocks sliding and tumbling outside, banging against the iron, sealing them in.

The warriors of the clan just stood, peering up at the widening rent. Time seemed to freeze.

Daylan could outpace them all, and right now he realized that he needed to do so. There would be no saving them if the roof came down.

"Flee," he warned, hoping to save at least a few men, and then he darted between them, shoving men aside as lightly as possible, hoping not to throw them off balance.

A cave-in, he thought. This passage will be sealed, leaving only two entrances to defend.

By the time that most of the men had begun to react, he was thirty yards from the door and gaining speed. His ears warned when the rocks began to come down behind him.

He yearned to go back and dig out what men he could, but his duty was clear. Fallion Orden was of greater import than all the men in this cavern.

Vulgnash dropped from the wispy clouds, bits of ice stinging his face, and for a moment he just soared, floating almost in place as he studied the battle below. He was hidden up here, a shadow against the clouds.

Starlight shone upon Mount Luciare, turning the stone to dim shades of gray, almost luminous.

Distantly, he could hear the triumphant battle-cries of wyrmling troops, the rumble of thunder drums.

The city was in ruins. Mounds of dead men littered the streets between the lower gates and upper gates, and now the wyrmling troops had brought up battering rams and were attacking the great iron doors that sealed off the warrens.

Rents had opened up in the mountainside where great stone slabs had slid off, exposing some of the tunnels that had been dug into the mountain.

And there above the battle, a tiny set of wings fluttered clumsily.

It was no Knight Eternal flying there, he knew instantly. The wing-beats were ineffectual, and the body was too small to be one of his own kind. It was one of the small folk, a fledgling, new to wings!

Vulgnash knew that it was the custom among humans to claim wings won in battle.

If that small fledgling is not the wizard I seek, Vulgnash thought, it is one of his kin.

He studied its trajectory, saw where it flew—there, a parapet where another winged human lay wounded.

With a slight folding of the wings, Vulgnash went into a dive.

On the fifth level of the warrens, Alun raced up the gently sloping tunnel. Tiny thumb-lights, hanging from their pegs, lit the way like fallen stars.

But suddenly, the path ahead went black, and the smell of fresh air impinged on his consciousness. He'd found a rent. Part of the rock face had collapsed to his left, leaving the tunnel exposed.

And up ahead, the lights were all out.

He heard a distant wail, the death cry of an old man.

Alun raced past the rent, which was no more than twenty feet wide, and peered down. A hundred and fifty feet below, the wyrmling army crowded in the courtyard. A Death Lord stood at their head, a chilling specter whose form was so dark, it seemed that he sucked in all of the light nearby. There was a boom and the ground shivered beneath his feet, but there was no snarling as was found in the report of a thunder drum.

The wyrmlings had taken battering rams to the iron gates, the city's last defenses.

"Hurry," Warlord Madoc urged, racing past Alun.

Alun chased after Madoc, feeling naked, exposed to the sight of the troops below. The wyrmlings could not help but see them sprinting along the open cliff. But soon they were back in the darkened tunnels.

Madoc halted to light a thumb-lantern, and then they hurried ahead.

The knight's trail would not be hard to follow. He left darkness in his wake.

He can't be far ahead, Alun realized. It takes time to kill people, even women and babes.

They passed an apartment that had its door bashed in.

Warlord Madoc stopped to survey the damage. The apartment looked like a slaughterhouse, with blood-splashed walls. Alun did not dally to gaze upon the faces of the murdered mother and her boys, the youngest just a toddler. Yet he could not help but notice with a glance that upon each of the dead, there was a red thumb-print between the eyes, as if the Knight Eternal had anointed them with blood. Alun knew the family, of course. The dead woman was Madoc's wife.

Warlord Madoc roared like a bear when he saw her body, and went charging back out into the corridors, brandishing his war ax.

King Urstone is a dead man, Alun thought. If there was ever a chance that Warlord Madoc would forgive him for this debacle, the chance has passed.

No, Urstone had tried to save his son, and the imprudent attempt would bring ruin upon them all.

For that, it was only right that King Urstone should die.

Yet a part of Alun rebelled at the thought. It was not fair that Urstone had lost his son. It was not fair that he should die for loving too well. This was all a tragic mistake, and Alun worried that he was supporting a monster, that Warlord Madoc, despite his bravery and his prowess in battle, was the kind of man who would bring them all to ruin.

Let him die first, Alun silently prayed to whatever powers might be. Let Madoc die at the hands of a Knight Eternal.

They passed apartment after apartment, each much the same, each smelling of blood attar, each dark and bereft of life.

There were cries up ahead, a woman's scream, and Warlord Madoc went bounding up the hallway.

Talon gave a cry and raced up at his back.

Alun felt strangely disconnected from his body. His heart pounded in fear. He couldn't bear the thought of fighting a Knight Eternal in the darkness like this. It was madness. They'd all be killed.

Yet he sprinted to keep up, realizing that at the very least he would not die alone.

"Here!" Warlord Madoc shouted as he rounded a corner. Up ahead, thumb-lanterns still burned merrily. The Warlord raced to an open door and peered in.

"Welcome," a voice hissed from within, "to your demise."

"If I die," Madoc growled, "then you will lead the way." He raised his ax and charged.

Timing is everything in battle, Alun knew. Even a Knight Eternal might be struck down with a lucky blow. But it required perfect timing, and perhaps the element of surprise.

"Kill!" Alun growled, as he released his dogs.

Wanderlust and Brute bent double as they dug their paws into the floor and bounded down the corridor.

The dogs swarmed past Warlord Madoc as he raced into the room. Talon and Siyaddah charged in at his back, while Alun drew up the rear.

He heard a smack and a yelp, Brute's cry. The dog went flying, thumped against a wall.

Madoc roared like a wounded animal, and as Alun rounded the corner, everything was in chaos.

The room was as cold as a tomb. Dead children littered the floor.

Wanderlust had hold of the Knight Eternal's left wing and was dragging it backward and thrashing her head.

Madoc himself had taken a mighty swing with his ax, nearly lopping off the knight's right arm.

The knight growled like a beast and lunged past Madoc. It grabbed Talon by the throat and hurled her to the floor, just as Siyaddah leapt in with crescent shield, slashing at the knight's wrist.

Talon's own small sword clanged to the floor and came spinning near Alun, just as the Knight Eternal caught his balance and leapt in the air, kicking with both feet, sending Warlord Madoc flying over a chair.

Alun looked at the small sword, its blade covered with

rust, and knew that it might be the only weapon in this room that had the power to unbind the knight, to drain the stolen life from its organs.

The Knight Eternal threw off Wanderlust and then leapt upon Warlord Madoc, grabbing him by the throat. He slammed Madoc's head back against the wall, smashing the warlord's helm and leaving a smear of blood, then howled in victory and gaped his teeth, ready to tear out Madoc's throat.

Alun grabbed Talon's sword and lunged at the Knight Eternal, aiming for its face.

The creature whirled and caught the blade in its hand, almost absently.

Too late it realized its mistake.

The blade struck, and the Knight Eternal gripped it like a vise. Alun struggled to pull it free, like a sword from an ancient scabbard, and the blade sliced into the creature's palm.

It had been focused on Warlord Madoc, but now the Knight Eternal whirled and peered at its hand as if a serpent had just bit it.

"How?" it cried, raising its palm.

Black blood came boiling from the wound. The Knight Eternal studied this phenomenon, then looked up to Alun in consternation.

Already the creature had begun to change. Its dry flesh was turning papery, and it suddenly weaved, unable to keep to its feet.

"Death take thee," Alun said thrusting the sword into its throat. The Knight Eternal fell back and collapsed.

Wanderlust leapt on it, wrestled free a leg, and then stood growling and shaking it.

Siyaddah stood in a fighting stance in the corner, as if afraid that the creature would get up and attack. Talon was crawling on her knees, shaking her head clear.

Warlord Madoc lay against the wall, blinking and breathing heavily for a moment. Alun had expected him to be dead, but suddenly he regained his feet.

The only fatality in the fight was Brute, who lay against the wall, lips drawn back in a permanent snarl.

Siyaddah raced to the Knight Eternal, grabbed it from behind, and pulled off the valuable wings. She could not leave such a prize for the enemy.

Alun stood above his dead dog, mourning.

"These are yours," Siyaddah said, shoving the wings toward him. But Alun only stood. He peered up at her for a moment, and shook his head.

"I don't want them."

"Then bring them," Warlord Madoc said. "I'll wear them proudly. Come on. We've got a war to finish." He whirled and raced through the tunnels, outdistancing his companions as he searched for a target for his wrath.

In Emperor Zul-torac's observatory, Areth Sul Urstone lay in a fetal position, groaning in pain, watching the destruction of his city.

Suddenly the snarl and boom of thunder drums went silent. All of creation seemed to pause on the brink of ruin as the Death Lord raised a spidery hand, then turned his cowled head toward Rugassa, as if seeking permission to put an end to mankind.

"Will you concede?" the Emperor hissed. "Your soul, the life of your spirit, in exchange for the city?"

Areth knew that the Death Lord only awaited the Emperor's command. Such wights, being less than half alive, could communicate across the leagues, whisper thoughts to the spirits of one another. It was for this reason that Lady Despair had elevated them in position, giving them charge of her armies.

They are waiting only for me, for my word, Areth knew. It is in my power to save my people, or to let them die. He let out a whimper of pain and despair.

Rhianna landed upon a parapet above the city, where High King Urstone knelt above the body of the wounded Fallion, examining the splotch of blood smeared over

Fallion's ribs. The thumb-lanterns here had blown out, apparently when the great stone doors that concealed this place had fallen. Now the parapet was open to the cool night air. Stars rained down light, sprinkling it liberally over the gray stone. Flowers, overflowing from gray pots, gleamed like starfish in the darkness, perfuming the night air. Pennyroyal petals and seeds had been strewn upon the floor, giving a heavenly scent.

This would be a pleasant place to die, she thought.

Rhianna gasped, sweat streaming from her face after the short flight, and peered down at Fallion, her heart burdened with worry.

Down below, the thunder drums had fallen silent. Rhianna had seen the huge battering rams that the wyrmlings carried through the city, entire trees felled just for this purpose, bound with iron rings, fitted with brass heads shaped like snarling lions. With a single thrust of each battering ram, sparks and fire had flown out, and the great iron doors had shattered, torn from their hinges.

There was nothing to stop the wyrmlings from taking the city now. It had no defenses left. The warriors that held the tunnels were too few in number. They might slow the wyrmlings for an hour, but that was it.

Dawn was still an hour away. The eastern skies were brightening on the edge of the horizon, washing out the stars.

King Urstone spoke. Rhianna did not understand his words, but she understood the tone. He pointed to the east.

"Take him and go," King Urstone said, "if you can carry him. Save yourselves. There is nothing more that we can do. The city is lost, and I wish to die with my people. The wyrmlings will be inside within an hour, and nothing can save us."

Rhianna nodded. "Give me a little while more." She knelt and gently touched Fallion's wound. He had already fainted from loss of blood, and it was just beginning to clot. To try to move him would only cause the wound to break open. She didn't dare risk it.

With a heavy heart, High King Urstone nodded, then took a fighting stance above Fallion's body and just stood above him, battle-ax gripped in both hands, on guard. "I will watch with you as long as I can."

Vulgnash studied the three as he plunged from the clouds, and his heart filled with glee. They were unaware of him until the instant that he landed in a rush of wings, standing upon a stone railing above them.

High King Urstone roared and whirled, his battle-ax swinging at Vulgnash's legs. The movement seemed painfully slow. With five endowments of metabolism, Vulgnash easily leapt above the blow and still had time to cast a spell that drained Fallion of precious heat, chilling his body to near death.

The air on the parapet suddenly turned to ice, and fogged from the mouths of Vulgnash's enemies. The flowers in their pots began to rime with frost.

Rhianna shouted and batted at Vulgnash with her staff.

He knew that weapon. It was a deadly thing. He had tried to curse it into oblivion, and he had imagined that it would be rotted by now, full of wood worms, but the staff still glittered in the starlight, hale and deadly.

The relic was a curiosity. He was amazed that it held such power, and at some future time, he hoped to study it further.

Vulgnash stepped aside, and Rhianna's blow connected only with stone.

"Be gone, foul beast!" King Urstone roared, twisting his battle-ax to come in for another blow.

Vulgnash smiled. With his endowments of brawn and metabolism, he felt stronger and swifter than ever before. He had just made a flight that should have taken all night in less than two hours.

Soon, he thought, I will be Lady Despair's most trusted servant.

Already he had begun to figure out new ways to twist

forcibles. In Rugassa, torture was considered both a science and an art. And tonight, Vulgnash had advanced the science to new heights. He had created special forcibles for Areth Sul Urstone. By binding a rune of touch to a rune of empathy, he'd created forcibles that not only let a lord feel more strongly, but feel the tortures that the runelord's Dedicates endured.

In the days to come, Vulgnash felt certain that he could raise the art of the runelords to heights that had never been dreamt of on Fallion's world.

Now Vulgnash was eager to test his new-found strength in battle.

"Come with me," Vulgnash said softly to those who stood between him and his prey, "and I will lead you to the land of shadows."

The High King swung his ax, and Vulgnash leapt out and swiftly kicked the elbow of the king's left arm. The ax went flying from his hand, over the parapet and into the darkness.

Rhianna shouted a war cry and swung her staff at Vulgnash's waist. To Vulgnash the blow seemed laughably slow.

He reached down with a foot and kicked the High King, whose brows were still arced in surprise, shoving him into the path of Rhianna's blow.

The great staff slammed against Urstone's head with a snapping sound, as if it had hit stone. The king's helmet shattered and a fine mist of blood sprayed out from the back of his head. Urstone fell. His body slumped over the railing.

Rhianna only stopped, heart pounding in horror at what she'd done.

Vulgnash leapt from the railing, his movements so fast that his speed was blinding.

He's a runelord, Rhianna realized.

She swung her staff. The Knight Eternal dodged, and the staff struck the ledge with a jolt. He kicked her arm, and the staff tumbled over the parapet.

He smiled down at her, and Rhianna stood gasping. She had no weapon that could touch him. He knew it. Her only hope was to go after the staff.

But in doing so, she would leave Fallion alone, unprotected.

Fallion. All that the Knight Eternal wanted was Fallion.

Rhianna swiftly pulled a dagger, then put it to Fallion's carotid artery.

"Leave," she demanded. "Or so help me, I'll kill him."

This is what Fallion would want me to do, she thought. Fallion feared that his powers would be turned to evil. He knew what Lady Despair wanted. She wanted Fallion to bind the worlds into one, all under her control.

Vulgnash hesitated, studied her, and Rhianna dug the blade into Fallion's flesh.

The Knight Eternal spoke, his thoughts whispering into her mind. "You love him more than your own life, yet you would kill him?"

"It's what he would want."

"It would please me to see you take his life," Vulgnash said.

She studied his eyes, and knew that he meant it. Yes, he wanted Fallion, but he also wanted to see Rhianna commit this one foul deed.

He's testing me, Rhianna realized. My pain amuses him.

Vulgnash did not move forward, and for a long moment he stood waiting. There were shouts from the tunnel behind Rhianna, accompanied by the frenzied yap of a dog.

She dared not turn away from the Knight Eternal.

"Rhianna," Warlord Madoc cried. "Hold it. Stop."

Warlord Madoc raced up at her back, keeping his distance from Vulgnash. For a moment he studied the scene, the Knight Eternal held at bay by a woman willing to sacrifice the man that she loved, King Urstone slumped over a railing, the back of his head smeared with blood.

"Get back from him, girl," Warlord Madoc said. "Let me handle this." He spoke to Rhianna in her own language.

Then he spoke to Vulgnash in the wyrmling tongue. "You need us," he told the Knight Eternal. "Your harvesters need humans to prey upon. Leave us in peace, and we will be your vassals."

"The land is filled with humans now," Vulgnash said. "Great will be our joy as we hunt them and harvest them. We need *you* no more."

"Still," Madoc said. "I propose a truce: a thousand years. Give me a thousand years, and I will prepare these people to be your servants. We will join you, and Lady Despair whom you serve. If not, we'll take the life of the Wizard Fallion, and you can go back to her empty-handed."

Vulgnash knew the will of his master. For decades she had been plotting this, and right now the future balanced upon a precipice. Sometimes he could hear his master's thoughts, like whispers in his mind.

He glanced off to the north, straining to hear the will of Lady Despair in this matter. At last, he felt her touch.

Tell him what he most wants to hear, she said. Vulgnash smiled.

"Lady Despair agrees to the trade."

Warlord Madoc took the news hard, felt the breath knocked out of him. It was almost more than he could have hoped. Yet, now that the wyrmlings had agreed, he wasn't sure that he liked the truce. He wasn't sure that he could trust the wyrmlings. They might take Fallion and simply raze the city.

And even if the wyrmlings kept to the bargain, what then? Mankind would survive, but they would fall under the shadow of Rugassa, and his children's children would serve his enemies.

Still, he hoped, in a thousand years, our children might multiply and become strong. The wyrmlings were notoriously hard on their spawn, and the mortality rate for wyrmling children was high. Madoc could only hope that his own descendants might someday outnumber the wyrmlings and win back their freedom.

Rhianna had her back to him, and she was peering up at the Knight Eternal resolutely, ready to slit Fallion's throat at a moment's notice. Warlord Madoc gave her a light kick to the back of the skull, and she went tumbling forward.

Madoc could hear the sounds of running feet and that damned dog barking in the tunnel behind him. His companions were drawing near, but came forward only slowly, unsure what to do.

"Take him," Madoc told Vulgnash.

"No!" Talon cried at his back, and came lunging out of the tunnel.

The Knight Eternal moved with blinding speed, dropped, and seized Fallion's sleeping form, like a cat pouncing upon a bird. In an instant he rose up, reeled and dove over the parapet.

Wings flapping madly, Vulgnash carried his prey into the sky.

Warlord Madoc whirled to meet Talon. The girl charged him with her small sword. She did not strike fear into him. She was, after all, only a child, and Madoc had decades of practice to his credit.

She lunged with a well-aimed blow, but he slapped it aside with the flat of his ax, then punched her in the face. He outweighed the girl by nearly a hundred pounds, and Talon flew back and crumpled from the blow.

Siyaddah and Alun were right behind her. Siyaddah dropped the wings that she'd been dragging, and pulled a weapon as she stalked toward him. "Wait!" Madoc cried. "I can explain. I'm buying our lives here, saving the city."

And it was true. The wyrmling armies had halted outside the city gates. The wyrmlings waited as if in anticipation.

"We heard," Siyaddah said. "We heard the bargain that you made. But I'd rather die than honor it."

They leave me no choice, Madoc realized. He could not leave witnesses to his unholy trade.

Madoc glared at her. "Stupid girl. If you'd rather die, then you shall."

Behind him, he heard a groan and some small movement.

Siyaddah stepped forward to duel, her gleaming shield held clumsily at her side. She wasn't a tenth the warrior that Talon had been.

Alun only held still at her back, the gawking lad who had been willing to sell his people out for nothing more than a title. Madoc wasn't worried about him.

But suddenly the boy hissed a command, "Kill," and unleashed his war dog. The beast leapt at Madoc in a snarling ball of fury, going for Madoc's throat.

Madoc brought his ax up, hoping to fend the dog off, and stepped backward, just as something sharp rammed into his back.

He peered down and saw a dagger there just below his kidney. Rhianna's small, pale hand gripped it. With a grunt she twisted the blade and brought it up in an expert maneuver, slicing his kidney in half. White-hot pain blinded Madoc.

He did not have time to cry out before Siyaddah slammed into his chest and sent him tumbling over the parapet.

Rhianna dropped and knelt in shock.

She crawled to the end of the balcony, her arms shaking, her legs and knees feeling frail. She climbed the balcony wall and peered over the parapet, into the starlight, and far in the distance, she saw leathery wings flapping madly. The morning air was beginning to brighten, dulling the stars. The Knight Eternal was carrying Fallion away in a frenzied blur, like some great bat.

He has endowments of strength and speed, Rhianna

realized. He's flying faster than I ever can. Her arms trembled as they tried to bear her weight. Her stomach was turning, and she felt ill, on the verge of collapse.

How fast is he going? she wondered. A hundred miles per hour, two? How far will he get before dawn? Will he reach Rugassa?

She'd barely been able to manage the flight to the parapet a few minutes ago. And in her current condition, she couldn't manage even that. Even if she had been able catch up with Fallion's captor, she was no match for him.

He's gone, she realized. Fallion's gone. Maybe forever.

Rhianna looked down, her heart breaking. She saw Madoc's form sprawled on the pavement hundreds of feet below, broken, ringed by wyrmlings who hacked and stabbed at the corpse, making sure of it.

She turned back to her friends. The parapet was a grisly mess. Talon was out cold. Rhianna could see that she was breathing steadily, but though Rhianna crawled to her side and called her name, Talon would not wake.

Siyaddah went to High King Urstone and stood over him for a long moment, seeking signs of life. She studied his face, then leaned over his back, trying to hear his heartbeat through his armor. At last she put her silver buckler to his face to see if he was breathing.

After a moment, she let out a sad cry and tears rolled down her cheek.

"He's dead," she moaned in dismay. "He's dead."

Rhianna could not speak to Siyaddah or Alun, for she did not know their language.

Down below, the wyrmling hordes still filled the courtyard. The army did not surge forward into the tunnels, nor did they fall back. Instead, they merely waited, as if for some further command.

Rhianna reached up and felt the knot at the base of her skull, smeared with blood. She could hardly think.

Footsteps came echoing up from the tunnel, and Daylan Hammer appeared around a bend, bearing a thumb-lantern.

He rushed up, spoke softly to Alun and Siyaddah for a moment.

"So is it true that they have Fallion?" Daylan asked Rhianna.

"Yes," she said, looking back. Vulgnash was gone, far from her sight.

Daylan peered into the sky for a long moment, as if he could see what Rhianna could not. He was a Bright One of the netherworld, and as such, his powers of sight were legendary.

"Yes," Daylan said at last. "He is gone . . . far beyond our reach—for now."

He peered down at the armies massed before the gate, and said, "I wonder what they're waiting for. The sun is coming. Surely they must be eager to take the city before dawn?"

He studied the army for a moment longer, then shouted, "Quickly, we must get down into the tunnels. There is one great battle left to fight!"

"When next you sleep . . ." Daylan Hammer had said. The words rolled over and over in Fallion's mind, "When next you sleep . . ."

What had Daylan commanded?

That I dream, Fallion recalled dimly.

He was lying in the arms of a giant, flying through air both thin and cold. He could hear wings flapping, but he was so far under, he could not even open his eyes to look.

In a stupor, he reached up and grasped his cape pin, and immediately was thrust into another world. Here the skies were bluer than the darkest sapphire, and oak trees rose up like mountains among the hills, as if to bear heaven upon their limbs. Fallion was standing in a field of wheat that rose up to his chest, and an enormous owl came to him with broad wings and spoke an ancient name, Ael.

For the first time, Fallion realized that it was a question.

Yes, Fallion answered, *I am Ael.*

Fallion climbed its back, and as the great owl flew through a world that was now only a remembered dream, soaring over crystal lakes, swooping up to climb tall mountains whose skirts were covered with evergreens and whose mantles were draped in snow, finally to make his way at the end of the day toward a vast tree whose branches were filled with lights, Fallion began to recall.

I know that tree, Fallion thought. Its limbs and trunk were golden. Its broad leaves were dark green on the top, almost black in the failing light, but brighter underneath. He could hear the voices of women and children singing beneath the One True Tree, singing in a strange tongue that even his spirit had almost forgotten.

And the memories came. He had lived beneath the boughs of that tree once, had lived there for ages, in a city dug beneath its roots. And in its shade he had helped to maintain the great runes.

He remembered standing there, tending the runes hour after hour. His was the Seal of Light, a great circle of golden fire that bound the Seal of Heaven to the Seals of Earth and Water.

He knew its every texture and nuance, for over countless ages he had not only nurtured it, but with the help of the tree had formed it.

Now in his memory he stood above it, tending the multitude of tiny flames within it.

"Careful," a still voice whispered in his mind. "The passions in that one are too strong. She must be mellowed." It was the voice of the One True Tree, his companion and mentor, his helper in this great endeavor.

Fallion had turned his attention to the flame in question. It represented a young woman, one whose passions often rose high.

"Light-bringer," a woman's voice called. "What are you doing?"

Fallion turned and saw a beautiful young woman with raven hair and sparkling eyes. It was Yaleen, the woman whose passions he needed to soothe.

She strode toward him like a panther, like a huntress, her movements liquid and powerful. . . .

And as Fallion's body slumbered, and Vulgnash bore him to Rugassa, Fallion's spirit began to wake.

❧ 47 ❧

A BARGAIN MADE TO BE BROKEN

Every man is but half a creature, longing to be whole. It is not until a wyrm fills your soul that you become complete.   —*from the Wyrmling Catechism*

Inside Mount Luciare, the humans huddled, awaiting the final onslaught. The hand of doom seemed to cover them like a roof. The thunder drums had gone silent. Everything was hushed.

Rhianna and the others came upon the Wizard Sisel down in the lowest depths of the tunnels. His head was wrapped in a bloody bandage. Thumb-lights lit the way, burning like the brightest stars, and the floors were strewn with herbs and seeds, so that the tunnel smelled like a garden. A roof had collapsed, and beyond a knot of warriors, rocks barred the way. The scent of stone and soil only helped to heighten the illusion that this was somehow a garden.

"What is happening?" Daylan Hammer called out.

"The enemy has withdrawn," the wizard said in exasperation. "I do not know why. They are waiting . . . for something. My heart tells me that this bodes ill."

"A Death Lord leads the wyrmling horde," Daylan said. "He cannot risk the touch of sunlight, yet dawn is not half an hour away. He *must* enter the city before then."

"I thought at first that the collapse of the tunnel had slowed them," Sisel wondered aloud. "But that cannot be it."

Suddenly, it seemed that his eyes caught the light of one of the thumb-lanterns, and they went wide.

"The wyrmlings will come, they must come. But when they do, we must hold them off until dawn. Unless . . . Quickly—gather the people. Get them to the eastern end of the city!"

The soldiers all stood for a moment, unsure what to do. Sisel was no warrior lord, with the right to command. No one seemed to be in command.

"Quickly," Daylan shouted, for he seemed to divine the wizard's plan, "do as he says!"

Areth Sul Urstone had never been inside a wyrmling temple, where those who hoped to receive wyrms committed foul deeds in order to prepare themselves for immortality. He had never wanted to be in one. He had only heard of the bloody rites performed there in whispered legend.

Areth was too weak from hunger and pain to stand. But he heard the red-robed priests shout in triumph. They stood with their backs to him, on a dais near the front of the temple. They suddenly backed away from an altar. One of the priests gripped a sacrificial knife.

Upon the altar, the wyrmling boy that had given Areth his endowment jerked, his legs pumping uselessly, as if in a dream he ran one final race with death.

Then the boy stopped, his muscles eased, and he lay still, blood dribbling from the open wound at his throat. His eyes stared uselessly toward the heavens.

With that, a bond was broken. Most of the ache and fatigue that Areth had felt eased away, dissipating slowly, as if it had all been an evil dream.

"Well done," the emperor whispered. A wyrmling priest stuck his thumb into the blood at the boy's throat, then pressed the bloody thumb between the child's eyes, anointing him.

He stepped down from the dais, crossed the stone floor, and pressed his bloody thumb between Areth's eyes, anointing him with the child's blood.

Around Areth, on the stone benches beneath the altar, a crowd of wyrmling supplicants made a low moaning noise, a groan of ecstasy.

Areth closed his eyes and waited for the wyrm to take him. He thought that it would be a violent act, that he'd know when it came. He thought that he would feel a sense of entrapment, like a creature being forced into a cage.

Instead he felt a rush of euphoria.

The child's endowment had been stripped from him, and Areth Sul Urstone, who had endured greater tortures than any man had ever known, was suddenly free of pain.

Over the past fourteen years his body had become so accustomed to torture that the sudden absence was like a balm, sweet and soothing beyond measure.

But it was more than just physical pain that he found himself freed from. There was something more, something that only the presence of a great wyrm could explain. He suddenly felt released of all responsibility, of all guilt.

All of his life, his well-exercised sense of morality had guided his every deed.

Suddenly it was stripped away, and he perceived that he had been living his life in shackles. For the first time he was truly free—free to take whatever he wanted; free to kill or steal or maim.

Areth leaned his head back and laughed at the folly of the world.

"It is done," the emperor cried, and wyrmling priest's eyes went wide. It seemed that he could not drop to his knees and prostrate himself fast enough. "The Lady Despair walks among us in the flesh—" the emperor shouted, "let all obey her will."

In the temple, the crowd let loose with cries of rapture. As one the wyrmlings fell down upon their faces, so that Areth was ringed by a throng of worshipers.

Areth felt surprised at first, but recognized the truth. Yes, Lady Despair was with him, the Queen of the Loci who had lived from the beginning.

In his mind's eye, he imagined her just-discarded form, a world wyrm that now lay dead, floating in a pool of molten lava, a deserted husk.

Yaleen moved Areth's hand, stared at it as if it were some foreign object. How long has it been since I have worn a human form? she wondered.

"You shall call me by a new name," the Lady announced to her followers. "My name is Yaleen, as it was in the beginning; and you shall call me by a new title: I am your Lord Despair."

Yaleen closed his eyes, and images flashed in his mind, the view of the world as seen from the eyes of a thousand evil creatures and men. A great war was brewing. Wyrmling troops had begun to destroy the newly discovered human settlements, harvesting the small ones, but now the small ones were arming themselves with bows of steel, mounting knights in armor with great lances. They would fight tooth and nail for their lives.

In the underworld, Yaleen's great servants, the reavers stood ready to enforce his will.

Upon the One True World, the last remnants of the Bright Ones fled from his Darkling Glories.

But most imposing upon his vision was the city of Luciare. Yaleen's Death Lord now held the city in his grip. Its troops had been slaughtered, and its doors were broken. Vulgnash had carried Fallion down from the mount and was flying rapidly to the courts of Rugassa.

The Death Lord waited now only for Yaleen's final command.

Areth Sul Urstone had given his soul to save this city. Now, some small corner of his mind that still functioned peered at the miserable wreckage. He could not remember why he had paid such a price.

Yaleen sent his thoughts out, like a dark and grasping hand, and probed for the mind of his servant.

Leagues away at the ruins of Mount Luciare, the Death Lord now felt a familiar touch to his mind, and whispered, "Master, reveal thy will. What shall I do with this city?"

There was a moment of hesitation. Areth Sul Urstone felt almost as if Yaleen waited to consult him, to let him make the choice.

I gave my soul for my people, Areth reminded Yaleen.

Yet what did they give you in return? Yaleen asked. They left you in prison to die in torment. They never mounted an expedition to rescue you, never offered a coin to buy your freedom. You gave your all for them. And they offered you nothing in return. For many years now, they have laughed and loved in your absence. They have thrown their feasts and spawned their children. They have forgotten you.

The words felt like truth. How many times had Areth lain in his cell, wondering if anyone worried for him, or even remembered his name?

Areth felt empty inside, numb and lifeless. He no longer hoped for rescue. He needed none. Now he felt hurt. He only wanted to strike back at these petty creatures who had left him to his fate.

The choice was made.

"Go into the city, and make of it a tomb," Yaleen whispered to the Death Lord.

The Death Lord shouted a command, and with a roar his troops raced through the ruptured gates.

Yaleen opened his eyes and gazed down now upon the wyrmlings in the temple, all lying prostrate before him.

For countless millennia, Yaleen had longed for this moment—when the great wyrm could claim the soul of an Earth King.

Now, in triumph, Yaleen raised his left hand and peered down upon the wyrmling hosts that prostrated themselves. "I choose you," he shouted, his commanding voice echoing through the stone chambers. "I choose you for the twisted Earth."

He felt a connection establish between himself and his acolytes, like an invisible thread that bound him to each and every soul in the room. He would know where they were at all times. He would sense when they were in danger and he would utter the warnings that would spare their lives.

Thus, his armies would sweep across the worlds, destroying everyone who opposed him.

In Caer Luciare, thousands of women and children gathered at the eastern edge of the city, filling every room and every tunnel. They stood silently, straining to hear. The terror in the tunnels was palpable, and lay thick in their throats. Some of the children whimpered.

With a roar, the wyrmling troops flooded into the warrens, their Death Lord leading the way.

Inside the city, dark as a tomb, the floors rumbled beneath iron-shod feet, and wyrmling cries shattered the stillness.

"They are coming!" guards shouted down the corridors, each man gripping his weapon, falling back behind the Wizard Sisel. The warrior clans stood ready to oppose the enemy for as long as possible.

Siyaddah looked toward her father. At her side, her father placed a comforting hand on her shoulder.

The city's long war with the wyrmlings was over, and the men of Luciare had lost.

The wizard glanced down the halls one last time. He waited for long and long, until the wyrmlings could be seen down the corridor, the lights winking out before them. A dark, nebulous form floated ahead—the Death Lord, eager to feed.

The guards backed off, leaving Sisel alone to bar the way. The Earth Warden raised his staff protectively, singing an incantation so softly that Siyaddah could not hear his words.

At Sisel's back, the people huddled.

"Fear not," Siyaddah's father called out. "The Death Lord feeds on fear." His command was fruitless. The women and the children still sobbed. But it gave them some comfort to hear from a warlord, particularly one of her father's stature. With Madoc and High King Urstone both dead, the warriors were confused as to whom to follow. Had one of Madoc's foolish sons had the wits, he would have stepped into the breach and taken command. But Siyaddah's father was filling that void.

Lights winked out in the darkened corridor as the Death Lord drew near.

The Wizard Sisel raised his staff, as if welcoming the creature to battle. "So, my old friend," Sisel said, "you come to me at last."

"We were never friends," the Death Lord whispered.

"You were my master," Sisel said. "I loved you as a friend. My respect for you never languished. My faithfulness never faltered. It was you who faltered. . . ."

"Do you expect a reward?" the Death Lord demanded. "I have little to offer."

Siyaddah breathed, and the breath steamed from her throat. The walls of the cavern had suddenly grown icy, rimed with frost. Already, the Death Lord was leeching the life from the seeds and herbs here.

"Come then," the Wizard Sisel said, "and give me what you can."

With a cry like wind screaming among the rocky crags of some mountain cavern, the Death Lord came, rushing toward Sisel.

Wyrmlings by the dozens followed in its wake.

The wizard stood calmly as if waiting, and as the Death Lord neared, he swung his staff.

But he swung too early. The Death Lord was still at least a pace away.

The dark specter halted for half an instant as the wizard's swing went wide.

He missed! Siyaddah realized, fear rising up in her throat.

Then the staff struck the wall. Rocks and dirt exploded outward by the ton, and a crude opening gaped wide.

Beyond the fissure, dawn light was beginning to fill the skies. The rising sun rimmed the horizon in shades of pink, as was befitting a perfect summer morn.

At the touch of the sunlight, the Death Lord shrieked, and for an instant it seemed that the shadow gained more substance, becoming a creature of flesh. She could see a man, like her, not a wyrmling. His face was lined with countless crags, as if he had aged and aged for a thousand years. His eyes were a sickly yellow, and his silver hair hung as limp as cobwebs.

He held up his hands, as if seeing them for the first time in centuries, and shrieked in terror.

His hand looked like ragged paper, torn and aged. But it was thin and insubstantial, a ragged leathery covering wrapped over a hollow spirit.

At that instant, the Wizard Sisel swung his staff again, catching the Death Lord with a backswing, and its dusky form exploded into a cloud of dust.

Confronted by the sunlight, stunned by the loss of their master, the wyrmlings shrieked in pain and horror as the warriors of Luciare plunged into their ranks.

"Hold them back!" Siyaddah's father shouted at the guards, racing into the fray. "Hold them back."

"Go, now!" Sisel cried to the people. "Run while you can!"

Suddenly, hundreds of soldiers began shouting, "Flee, this way! Run!"

Already there were crowds shoving at the wizard's back, trying to make their way into the light. Siyaddah found herself being pushed forward. She longed to stay with her father, fight at his side, but she was like a leaf carried by a stream, out through the tunnel.

In a moment she found herself at the lip of a precipice. The sides of the hill fell away steeply below, but not so steeply that one could not climb down with care.

She did not go with care. Someone shoved her from behind, so that she went sliding and tumbling in the scree. She managed to grasp onto a small tree and pull herself upright.

People were falling behind her, rolling down the hill, like an avalanche of flesh. Siyaddah got her footing and darted from their path, angling down and away from the steady stream of humanity.

The sun crested a tree, and its light struck Siyaddah full in the face.

I made it, she thought in wonder. I'm alive!

Far away, Vulgnash raced through the sky, winging just above the treetops of a great pine forest, racing from the rising sun. He used his flameweaver's skills to draw the light into him, so that he was but a shadow in the pre-dawn. But it wasn't enough.

The light blinded him and pained him. He roared in frustration as he dove beneath the trees, seeking the shadows of the forest, and perhaps some cave to hide in from the coming day.

In a daze, Fallion heard the roars and for a long moment struggled to regain consciousness. His eyes opened, and he strained to peer upward, saw the monster that held him as if he were a slumbering child.

The Knight Eternal.

He's taking me away, Fallion realized. He's taking me to Rugassa, where he hopes to break me.

But Fallion knew something that his captor could not. He remembered now, his life from before.

I am eternal, he realized. They can kill me, and I will come back. They can beat me, and I will heal.

But I will not break. How can I, knowing how much the world depends on me?

The sleeper had awoken.

Fallion felt the heat all around him. He reached out stealthily with his mind, sought to grasp it.

Instantly, Vulgnash felt the touch, and drew heat from Fallion, slamming him back into unconsciousness.

But Vulgnash looked down at the small one, this young wizard, and felt alarmed.

In his pain and fatigue, Vulgnash had nearly missed Fallion's probe. In another hundredth of a second, the boy could have sucked the heat from the air and made his attack.

Lady Despair was watching. Vulgnash felt the touch of his master. "Careful, my pet," Lady Despair whispered. "I need the boy. I need him, though he can destroy us. You must be ever vigilant."

"Fear not," Vulgnash whispered as he stepped into the deep shadows thrown by the pines. "I will serve you perfectly, as always."

Far away on the slopes of Mount Luciare, the folk of the city fled through fields, the golden sunlight all around. Wildflowers grew in abundance in the fields, huge white daisies rising up from the golden wheat, while flowering thistles dotted the hill with purple.

Few of the folk had been injured in the mad stampede to escape the city. By rough estimate, some forty thousand inhabitants still lived.

But Rhianna knew that they were in trouble.

She now glided above the people on leathery wings, riding the morning thermals. She used her height to keep watch both ahead of the group and behind. The wyrmlings did not give chase. They were hidden now within Caer Luciare.

But there was panic on the peoples' faces. They could run, but how far, and for how long? Women and children would not be able to outrace wyrmling troops. Moreover, they only had one direction that they could go to escape— toward Cantular. The lands elsewhere were all flooded, and if the Wizard Sisel was right, Luciare was quickly becoming an island in an endless sea.

A hundred miles they would need to run in a day.

Rhianna wondered, And even if they make it, where will they find refuge?

After the better part of an hour, the Emir of Dalharristan called the people to a halt. Not all of the people were warriors, bred to battle, and many of them were already gasping for breath. Some of the wounded had to be carried. Among that number was Talon, who still lay in a swoon.

Rhianna looked around and realized that she could see no way to save them.

During the brief halt, Rhianna dropped to the ground, giving her wings a rest.

The Wizard Sisel, the Emir, and Daylan Hammer held a brief counsel, speaking rapidly. Rhianna could not understand what they said, and no one bothered to translate.

Daylan Hammer explained to Rhianna, "We are trapped. The women and children will not be able to outrun the wyrmling hordes. But there is still a chance that we can save them—a small chance."

"What chance?" Rhianna asked.

"I will open a door through fire and air. . . ."

Instantly, she knew what he was planning. And she knew the dangers. "Into the netherworld? You can't! These poor folk, they won't know what they are getting into."

Rhianna had been there as a child, for a few months. Daylan had managed to keep them hidden, but the magics in that land were strong and strange. To Rhianna's mind, she'd rather face the wyrmlings.

"I must risk it—an uncertain future over certain death."

"Your own people will not accept them," Rhianna argued. "The White Council—"

"Is broken. My people are destroyed. Those who survive are hunted and helpless. If any of them find us, perhaps they will rejoice to discover allies."

Rhianna bit her lip, in doubt. Daylan's people would not rejoice, she knew. People from her world were scorned. "Shadow men" they were called.

"I will help you all that I can," Rhianna said.

But Daylan shook his head. "This task is not for you. Your people need you. They need to be warned. They need to prepare for the wyrmling attacks that will surely come. And now that you wear wings, there is no one better than you to warn them."

Rhianna stood for a moment, torn. She had thought of Daylan as her uncle when she was a child, and she loved him still. But she knew that he was right. Millions of people were depending upon her.

Fallion was depending upon her.

"The Emir will help," Daylan said. "He and his men have brought blood metal, to make forcibles. They plan to strike out ahead, with the hopes of attacking Rugassa and freeing its prisoners. But they will need to take endowments if they are to win through. You will need to find Dedicates for them, and convince them to aid in the quest."

Rhianna looked to the Emir. He stood beside his daughter Siyaddah, holding her close, comforting her. He was a tall man, with a gladiator's build and a hawkish face. With his over-sized canines and the bony plate in his forehead, he looked like some evil beast. In another life, on another world, he had been her enemy. Even now, she did not know if she could trust him.

How will I persuade people to give their endowments to this monster? she wondered.

Tell them that they are doing it to save the Earth King, she realized. And Fallion, whom I love. Tell them the truth.

Rhianna flew high and the morning sun touched her wings, so that they sparkled like rubies in the sky.

Turn the page for a preview of

THE WYRMLING HORDE

 DAVID FARLAND

Available in September 2008

TOR°
fantasy

A TOR HARDCOVER

ISBN-13: 978-0-7653-1666-0   ISBN-10: 0-7653-1666-8

In all of his dreams, Fallion had never dreamt with such intense clarity. He dreamed that he was soaring above the Courts of Tide. He was not riding a graak, nor did he wear a magical wing. In his dream Fallion's arms stretched wide, holding him aloft, like some seagull that hangs motionless in the sky, its wingtips trembling as the wind sweeps beneath them.

Nothing below obstructed his view.

And so he glided over houses where the sweet gray smoke of cooking fires floated lazily above thatched roofs, and Fallion darted above a palace wall, veering between two tall white towers where a guard with his pike and black scale mail gaped up at Fallion in astonishment. Fallion could see each graying hair of the guard's arched eyebrow, and how the man's brass pin hung loose on his forest-green cape, and he could even smell the man's ripening sweat.

Fallion swooped low over the cobbled city streets, where fishermen in their white tunics and brown woolen caps trudged to their dank homes after a hard day working the nets; the young scholars who attended the House of Understanding stood on street corners arguing jovially while sipping tankards of ale, and a boy playing with a pet rat in the street gaped up at Fallion and pointed, his mouth an O of surprise.

"The king has come!" the child cried, and suddenly the people looked up in awe and rejoiced to see Fallion. "The king! Look!" they cried, tears leaping to their eyes.

I must be dreaming, Fallion thought, for never have I seen the world so clearly.

There is a legendary stream in the land of Mystarria.

Its icy waters tumble down from the snowfields of Mount Rimmon, beneath pines that guard the slopes, along moss-covered floors where huge marble statues of dead kings lie fallen. The stream's clean flow spills into forest pools so transparent that even at a depth of forty feet every water weed and sparkling red crayfish can be seen. The enormous trout that live there "seemingly slide through the air just by slapping their tails," and all of them grow fat and to a ripe old age, for no fisherman or otter can hope to venture near in waters so clear.

So the stream is called the Daystar, for it is as clear and sparkling as the morning star.

That is how preternaturally clear the dream came to Fallion, as clear as the waters of Daystar.

He longed to continue dreaming forever, but for one thing: the air was so cold. He could feel frost beginning to rime his fingernails, and he shivered violently.

This frost will kill me, he thought. It will pierce my heart like an arrow.

And so he struggled to wake, and found himself . . . flying.

The wind rushed under him, cold and moist, and Fallion huddled in pain sharp and bitter.

He could feel a shard of steel lodged below his ribcage like a dagger of ice. Drying blood matted his shirt.

He struggled to wake, and when his eye opened to a slit, it was bright below. The wan silvery light of early morning filled the sky. He could see the tops of pines below, limbs so close that if he had reached out he could almost have touched them.

Where am I? I'm flying above a forest.

In the distance he could descry a mountain—no, he decided, a strange castle as vast as a mountain. It was built into the sides of a black volcano whose inner fires limned the cone at its top and spewed smoke and ash air.

All beneath, along the skirts of the volcano, a formidable fortress sprawled, with murderously high walls and thousands of dark holes that might have been windows or tunnels into the mountain.

There was no fresh lime upon the walls to make the castle gleam like silver in the dawn. Instead, the castle was black and foreboding. A few pale creatures bustled along the walls and upon the dark roads below, racing to flee the dawn, looking like an army of angry ants. Even a mile away, Fallion could tell that they were not entirely human.

Wyrmlings, he realized.

Fallion shivered violently, so cold and numb that he feared he would die. His thoughts clouded by pain, he struggled to figure out what was happening.

He was not flying under his own power. He was being borne by some great creature. Huge arms clutched him tightly. If a stone gargoyle had come to life, Fallion imagine that it would grip him so. He could hear powerful wings flapping: the wind from each downstroke assailed him.

Fallion could not see his captor, but he could smell the arm that clutched him. It smelled like . . . rotten meat, like something long dead.

Fear coursed through him.

I'm in the arms of a Knight Eternal, Fallion realized, one of the dead lords of the wyrmlings. And he began to remember . . .

The battle at Caer Luciare. The wyrmling warriors with their sickly pale skin and bone armor had attacked the mountain fortress, a fortress so different from the one he was going to. The limestone walls of the fortress had been glistening white, as clean as snow, and in the market flowers and fruit trees grew in a riot along the street, while leafy vines hung from the windows.

The wyrmlings had come with the night. The pounding of their thunder drums had cracked the castle walls. Poisoned war darts had pelted down in a black rain. Everywhere there had been cries of dismay as the brave warriors of Caer Luciare saw their plight.

Jaz! Fallion thought, almost crying aloud, as he recalled his brother falling. A black dart had been sprouting from Jaz's back as he knelt on hands and knees, blood running from his mouth.

After that, everything became confused. Fallion remembered running with Rhianna at his side, retreating up the city streets in a daze, people shouting while Fallion wondered, Is there anything I could have done to save him?

He recalled the Knights Eternal sweeping out of dark skies. Fallion held his sword at guard position, eager to engage one, heart hammering as the monster swept toward him like a falcon, its enormous black long sword stretched out before it—a knight charging toward him on a steed of wind.

Fallion twisted away from the attack at the last instant, his blade swiping back against the tip of the Knight Eternal's sword. Fallion had meant to let his blade cut cleanly into flesh, but the Knight Eternal must have veered at the last instant, and Fallion's blade struck the thick metal—and snapped.

As his tortured blade broke, Fallion had felt pain lance just below the ribcage. A remnant of his shattered blade lodged in his flesh. He fell to his knees, blood gushing hot over his tunic as he struggled to keep from swooning.

Rhianna had called out "Fallion! Fallion!" and all around him the noise of battle had sought to drown out her voice, so that it seemed to come from far away.

Struggling to remain awake, Fallion had knelt for a moment, dazed, while the world whirled viciously.

Everything went black.

And now I wake, Fallion thought.

He closed his eyes, tried to take stock of his situation.

His artificial wings were folded against his back. He did not know how to use them well, yet. He'd worn the magical things for less than a day. He could feel a sharp pain where they were bound tightly, lest he try to escape.

I dare not let the monster know that I am awake, Fallion realized.

Fallion's sword was gone, his scabbard empty, but he still had a dagger hidden in his boot.

If I could reach it, he thought, I could plunge it into the monster's neck.

Fallion was so cold, his teeth were chattering. He tried to still them, afraid to make any noise, afraid to alert the creature.

But if I attack, what then? The monster will fall, and I will fall with it—to my death.

His mind reeled away from the unpleasant prospect.

Moments later the Knight Eternal groaned and cursed, as if in pain. They had been flying in the shadow of a hill, and suddenly they were in open sunlight. Fallion's captor dropped lower, so that he was flying beneath the trees, well in their shadow.

There was a nimbus around them, a thick haze. It gathered a bit.

Of course, Fallion realized, the Knight Eternal is racing against the coming of day. He's gathering the light around him, trying to create a shadow.

He's struggling to get me back to the castle before dawn!

They had dropped lower now, and Fallion judged that he was not more than twenty feet above ground. On impulse, Fallion reached for his boot dagger, and by straining managed to reach it, grasping it with two fingers. He tried to pull it free.

Just as suddenly, his captor tightened his grip, pulling Fallion's arms mercilessly. The boot knife fell, spinning away to land on the ground.

The Knight Eternal was crushing Fallion against his chest. It apparently had not even noticed what Fallion was doing. But the creature's grip was so fearsome that now Fallion had to struggle for a breath.

Fallion despaired. He had no other weapons.

Fallion wondered about Rhianna. If she was alive, she would have protected him to the last. He knew that about her at least. No woman was more faithful, more devoted to him, than she.

Which meant that like Jaz, she must be dead.

The very thought tore at Fallion's sanity.

My fault, he told himself. It is my fault that they're dead. I am the one who brought them here. I'm the one who bound the worlds together.

And as quickly as Fallion had fallen into despair, rage and determination welled up. Fallion was a wizard of unguessable power. In ages past, there had been one sun and one true world, bright and perfect, and all mankind had lived in harmony beneath the shade of the One True Tree. But the great Seal of Creation that governed that world had been broken, and as it broke, the world shattered, splintering into a million parts, creating millions upon millions of shadow worlds, each a dull imitation of that one true world, each less virtuous, each spinning around its own sun so that now the heavens were filled with a sea of stars.

Now Fallion had demonstrated the skill necessary to bind those shadow worlds back into one. He had bound two worlds together. He had yet to bring to pass the realization of his dream: binding all worlds into one world, flawless and perfect.

But his enemies had feared what he could do, and had set a trap. Fallion had bound his own world with another, as an experiment, and everything had gone terribly wrong.

Now Fallion's people had been thrust into a land of giants, where the cruel wyrmlings ruled, a ruthless people thoroughly enthralled by an evil so monstrous that it was beyond Fallion's power to imagine, much less comprehend.

I hoped to make a better world, to re-create the one true world of legend, and instead I brought my people to the brink of ruin.

The Knight Eternal that carried him suddenly rose

toward a gate in the castle. Fallion could hear barks and snarls of alarm as wyrmling warriors announced their approach.

Where is the Knight Eternal taking me? Fallion wondered.

The knight swept through an enormous archway and landed with a jar, and then crept into a lightless corridor, carrying Fallion as easily as if he were a child.

Fallion's toes and fingers were numb. He felt so cold that he feared he had frostbite. He still could not think well. Every thought was a skirmish. Every memory was won only after a long battle.

He needed warmth, heat. There was none to be found. There had been no sunlight shining upon the castle. There were no torches sitting in sconces to brighten the way. Instead the Knight Eternal bore him down endless tunnels into a labyrinth where the only illumination came from worms that glittered along the wall and ceiling.

Sometimes he passed other wyrmlings, and whether they were mere servants or hardened warriors, they all backed away from his captor in terror.

Fallion could have used his powers to leach a little heat from a wyrmling, if one had come closer.

Maybe the stone is warm, Fallion thought. Maybe it still recalls the sunlight that caressed it yesterday.

Fallion could have reached out to quest for the sunlight. But there was a great danger. Fallion was a flameweaver, a wizard of fire. Yet he knew that at least one Knight Eternal had mastered such skills better than he: Vulgnash.

In earlier battles, each time that Fallion had tried to tap into some source of heat, Vulgnash had siphoned the energy away.

Of course, Fallion realized. That is why I am so cold now. The creature has drained me. I am in Vuglnash's arms.

I must not let him know that I am awake.

Vulgnash had no body heat that Fallion could use. Though the Knight Eternal mimicked life, the monster was dead, and it had no more heat in it than did a serpent.

So Fallion held still, struggled to slow his breathing, to feign sleep, as the Knight Eternal bore him down, down an endless winding stair.